EBURY PRESS

THE DEADLY DOZEN

Anirban Bhattacharyya is the co-creator, producer and writer of *Savdhaan India*, one of the most popular crime shows in India, as well as the producer of *Crime Patrol*, the longest-running true crime show on Indian television. Previously, he has been head of content at Channel [V]. An alumnus of St Xavier's College, Kolkata, where he earned a bachelor's degree in English literature, Bhattacharyya also holds a master's degree in mass communication from Jamia Millia Islamia, New Delhi. He conducts motivational speaking tours and is a stand-up comedian and actor when he isn't deep-diving into true crime stories.

PRAISE FOR THE BOOK

'Appearing straight-faced when talking about the gruesomeness of crime and criminals comes naturally to someone who has engaged with the subject for a while'—*Mid-day*

'In this bone-chilling collection of stories, Anirban Bhattacharyya explores what made India's most devious murderers kill and why'—*Reader's Digest*

'Delve into true stories of some of India's most heinous serial killers'—*New Indian Express*

'With profiles of 12 of the most famous serial killers of India, this book sets out to debunk the notion that serial killers are a Western phenomenon . . . The author has tried to get into the heads of the murderers to explore what made them kill'—*Pune Mirror*

'As I have always said, reality is stranger than fiction; these true accounts are gut-wrenching and make us question our surroundings' —Anurag Kashyap, film director

THE

India's Most

DEADLY

Notorious

DOZEN

Serial Killers

ANIRBAN BHATTACHARYYA

EBURY
PRESS

An imprint of Penguin Random House

EBURY PRESS

USA | Canada | UK | Ireland | Australia
New Zealand | India | South Africa | China | Singapore

Ebury Press is part of the Penguin Random House group of companies
whose addresses can be found at global.penguinrandomhouse.com

Published by Penguin Random House India Pvt. Ltd
4th Floor, Capital Tower 1, MG Road,
Gurugram 122 002, Haryana, India

First published in Ebury Press by Penguin Random House India 2019

ISBN 9780143445722

Typeset in Sabon by Manipal Digital Systems, Manipal
Printed at Repro India Limited

www.penguin.co.in

To the memories of the hundreds of victims who died needlessly at the hands of these killers and to the brave investigators and officers who brought these murderers to justice

CONTENTS

INTRODUCTION

What is it that attracts us to the stories of and the heinous crimes committed by a serial killer? What is it that draws us to read about the exploits of these depraved people?

Is it because of a vicarious pleasure that we derive from the macabre methods of these killings? Or do the sheer number of their killings gobsmack us into fearing them?

Perhaps, it is the brazenness of the killers who believe that the law will never catch up with them.

Or maybe it is their unique modus operandi.

Or are we curious about what happens inside their sick, twisted heads?

Or maybe something that appeals to our basic, primal instincts.

Perhaps, we all have a latent serial killer in us . . . waiting for that push to the dark side.

We have heard of the famous serial killers who have tormented the West: Jack the Ripper, Ted Bundy a.k.a. 'the Crazy Necrophile', Charles Edmund Cullen a.k.a. 'the Angel of Death', Pedro Alonso Lopez a.k.a. 'the Monster of the Andes', among others. But if you thought they exist only in the West, then think again. Crime and depravity are not contained by borders or endemic to a particular culture. They can flourish anywhere and everywhere.

India has seen some crazy, cold-blooded and dastardly murderers who have gone on insane killing sprees. And these have been both women and men.

What you are about to read will shock you, make you disbelieve and even scare you.

The world is not a nice place, after all . . . look after your children, guard your family and take care of yourself. Because you never know when and where who is watching you.

GOWRI SHANKAR

A.K.A. AUTO SHANKAR

'You will not be punished for your anger,
you will be punished by your anger.'

—Buddha

'*Niruttu!*' The cops at the roadblock signalled the three-wheeler to stop. It was 2 a.m. The streets of Madras (now Chennai) had long emptied out. The only life visible was the dogs, the homeless and the cops.

The passenger in the three-wheeler was on edge. There were three jute sacks at his feet. They were too large to hide and it was too late to dispose them of. The enemy was at the gates, at this roadblock.

'*Anna, ippodu enna nadakkum* [Big brother, what will happen now?],' the passenger asked.

The driver, a dark, thin man with a drooping moustache, watched as the officer on duty approached the vehicle.

'*Ōy viduda! En peyar Gowri Shankar* [Relax! My name is Gowri Shankar].' The passenger, bathed in sweat, could not believe the driver's composure.

'*Nan pidipada virumpavillai* [I don't want to get caught],' he whispered in a voice that quivered with nervousness.

Shankar chuckled as the light from the cop's torch fell on his face, making him squint momentarily.

The officer smiled.

1

'*Ada, Shankar! Ni eppadi irukkai?* [Hey, Shankar! How are you?]' The officer shook Shankar's hand, as if they were two old friends meeting after a hiatus.

'*Nan nalla irukken, sir!* [I am fine, sir!]' Shankar replied, emphasizing the word 'sir'. Shankar knew where his place in the ecosystem was. And he had no qualms about it, as long as he made money.

The officer shone the torch on the passenger's face. Mohan shielded his eyes. The officer laughed loudly.

'I think your passenger has shat his pants, I can smell it from here,' he said, pretending to hold his nose before guffawing.

Shankar laughed. Mohan wasn't amused.

'Sir, meet my younger brother, Mohan; Mohan say hello to sir,' Shankar instructed his brother. Mohan, sweating profusely, muttered a barely audible hello. He could not get his head around how his brother, the arrack smuggler, was on such friendly terms with a police officer.

The officer pointed his torch on the sacks at Mohan's feet.

Mohan could taste the bile at the back of his throat. He knew if they were caught, the jailhouse would become their home for a long time. Mohan waited for the officer to ask him to open the sacks. Instead, the officer switched off his torch.

'Let the auto pass,' the officer yelled at the constables manning the roadblock. Shankar and the officer shook hands again, this time holding on for just a little bit longer. Mohan noticed a few currency notes being passed through the handshake.

According to the autobiography that Shankar would go on to write for *Nakkheeran*, a Madras-based weekly, he was initiated into bootlegging by none other than the police, who also allegedly persuaded him to become a pimp.[1] This was obviously an effort on the part of Shankar to whitewash his life of crime and debauchery. But more on that later.

Shankar cranked the auto to life and the contraband was smuggled into the city of Madras effortlessly.

This was Gowri Shankar, the smooth operator who knew how to grease palms, make friends in the right places, fuck like a dog in heat and kill like a man possessed. A man who would transform the streets of Madras into his killing fields. This is his story.

* * *

It is said that you become your name. In this case, a little boy born in 1955 in Kangeyanallur, Vellore, was named Gowri Shankar, which is another name for Lord Shiva—the god of destruction. Was it sheer coincidence that his father chose this name? Or was it destiny that made Shankar a man who, unable to control his temper, ended up destroying the lives of others as well as his own?

Shankar loved the movies. He would unflinchingly steal money from the little steel box that his mother kept hidden in the kitchen, and go to the movies. In front of the screen, he would sit transfixed, as the heroes danced, wept, fought and loved like there was no tomorrow. And then he would re-enact the scenes with his friends. When Shankar was a child, his family could never have predicted that the distance between their home and their son's doom would just be 140 km—Madras. And this is where Shankar's obsession with the movies took him—to the heartland of Tamil Cinema.

With no proper education, Shankar became a daily wage painter. But his hunger for money was evident since he had discovered the magic of movies. He craved the good life, the good times, and the women whom he had seen his screen idols enjoy. From a painter he became an autorickshaw driver, hoping to make ends meet.

* * *

There were a number of small fishing villages, with coconut and palm plantations, along the coastline from Thiruvanmiyur to Mahabalipuram in those days, a perfect location to brew arrack. Palm, which is the main source for the spirit, was found in abundance in that area.

The fishermen would return at the end of the day to sit, sing and drink arrack, which was cheap and readily available. But it turned into a precious commodity after the implementation of prohibition in Tamil Nadu during the 1970s and the 1980s. The villages barely had roads, the law-keepers were few and the demand for the local brew boomed, creating an ideal situation for bootleggers. It became the no. 1 contraband cash cow.

Three things worked for Shankar. Firstly, he had a nose for business; he could smell out an opportunity like a dog could smell out a bitch in heat. Secondly, he had a vehicle—his trusted three-wheeler autorickshaw. And, thirdly, he knew the source and where to get arrack at the cheapest possible rates. He started smuggling the local brew from these seaside hamlets into Madras. Life couldn't get better for Shankar. Suddenly, the struggling and poor Shankar found himself with money. And this quick money introduced him to the next stage of life—good clothes; cash; and marriage to Jagadeswari, who saw in him a man that oozed confidence and charisma. But she didn't spot the Machiavellian nature behind this jovial facade. And she would pay for it dearly in time to come.

Then, prohibition was removed and arrack was no longer in demand. But Shankar the entrepreneur had already come up with his next business plan. He loved to ride his baby in the night. No, not Jagadeswari, but his three-wheeler auto. Mohan often asked him, 'Don't you feel like sleeping? How can you stay up the whole night?'

'*Namakku orē oru vālkkai irukkiratu! Ēntūkkaga thooni nasam paananum?* [We have only one life! Why sleep and waste it?]' Shankar would reply.

As an auto driver, Shankar often transported beautiful women and their pimps late at night, dropping them off to clients' homes, hotels or shacks. The dog in Shankar sniffed around. Here, he saw two things that gave him his next idea: whores and money.

They say never mix business with pleasure, but Shankar only knew how to live life mixing both. With the help of Mohan, his brother-in-law Eldin, and his accomplices, Shivaji, Jayavelu, Rajaraman, Ravi, Palani and Paramasivam, Shankar became a name to be reckoned with.[2]

He first rented out and then bought a line of huts in the slums of Periyar Nagar in Madras. Business flourished. His stellar line-up of ladies included Banu, Kundu, Vijaya, Asthina, Begum and Viji. Shankar's clout grew as he started supplying girls to political leaders and senior police officials.[3] Once again, Shankar knew which strings to pull and at what cost.

'*Yar anta pen?* [Who is that girl?]' Shankar asked Eldin one day, as his eyes scanned a pretty young girl wearing a red sari. It was her first day and she was nervous and angry. Her cousin had sold her off to a pimp instead of getting her a job in the city as he had promised. She had been crying for the past two days, but now realized that crying was not going to get her out of the whorehouse.

'Her name is Sumathi. She was brought here from Maduravoyal,' Eldin said, as Shankar walked towards Sumathi, who mistook him for a customer and told him to not choose her. Shankar laughed loudly. 'I am not a customer; I am the owner of this place. Come with me.' The other girls looked at her with jealousy, as Shankar took her inside one of the rooms.

'You don't like it here, I presume?' Shankar asked Sumathi. Bursting into tears, Sumathi narrated her story about how her cousin had sold her off. Shankar was smitten. His soft heart made his dick hard.

He gently pulled her towards him, saying, 'You don't have to sleep with any customers if you don't want.' She felt a sense of comfort. 'I'll marry you.' In the blink of an eye, Shankar went from a one-woman man to a polygamous one. And this became a pattern. Every pretty girl who would come to his brothel, Shankar would keep her for himself. He married Sumathi, Durga, Vijaya, Madhu, Sundari and Lalita. And his first wife, Jagadeswari, obviously did not take too kindly to his philandering ways. She attacked him, screaming and tried to hit him. Shankar pushed her against the wall and held her by her throat. The lack of air almost caused her to black out.

'Don't you ever fuck my head over this again! You are my wife and I will look after you. But you have no right to tell me what I can or cannot do. If I hear you complain one more time, I will feed you to the dogs!' Shankar threatened, letting go off her throat. Jagadeswari coughed as her body fought to stay alive. She would have to learn to accept Shankar's ways without any complaints.

* * *

Two things fuelled Shankar's existence—rage and sex. Mixed together, it was a deadly cocktail that would take him down the road to hell. His carnal desires were always streaked with violence, which was symptomatic of his depraved mind.

Vijaya, Shankar's third wife, knew about his other wives but was glad to be a part of his harem. She looked at him as her saviour. One day while having sex, as she threw her head back in a spasm of ecstasy, Shankar bit her neck like a rabid dog. She screamed in pain. He held her tightly and ripped the blouse off, exposing her breasts. 'What has happened to you?' she asked, completely baffled by his behaviour. He kissed her back passionately. He pulled her up and made her mount him. He took a drag of his cigarette and blew the smoke on her face slowly as she inhaled it. She held him in a tight embrace, her breasts flattened against his chest. Vijaya knew that life could not get any better than this. And everything seemed normal. Till she felt a searing hot pain on her back and screamed. Shankar continued to burn her back with a lit cigarette while clamping down on her mouth with his lips to mute her screaming. By the time the night was over, Vijaya had cigarette burns on her back, buttocks and breasts. She winced and screamed each time Shankar's cigarette made contact with her ebony skin. And Shankar's eyes lit up in depraved pleasure. This became routine, till Vijaya had had enough. She escaped from her golden cage and was never seen or heard from again.

It is often said that good girls are attracted to bad boys. And Shankar was bad to the core.

On 14 March 1987, Shankar took his third wife, Madhu, to a tattoo parlour. 'It will hurt!' Madhu said and tried to pull her arm away. 'It will hurt a little, but can't you endure a little pain for me? See, I have tattooed your name on my arm,' said Shankar, as he showed her the tattoo on his forearm that read 'Madhu'. She put her hand forward and the tattoo artist dipped his needle in black ink and began. As she screamed, Shankar laughed. On her forearm was tattooed the barcode that would make her his property: 'Gowri Shankar'.

Shankar had two sides to him. One was a loving, charming Casanova; the other, a debauched, violent pervert. Vijaya's escape from the coop did not teach Shankar a lesson. And he would do the same with another one of his wives, Sundari. Sundari would self-immolate, unable to bear the torture at the hands of Shankar.

Then came Lalita, or wife no. 6. She was beautiful, with a curvaceous body and bewitching eyes. Shankar loved her like a fool possessed and then tortured her like a kinky pervert.

Lalita knew that turning her back on Shankar would mean returning to the streets and to poverty. So she latched on to Sudalai, a gang member of Shankar's. With his help, she escaped. Till this point, Shankar had not shown any signs of being a murderer. But something inside him flipped when Lalita escaped. His ego took a double whammy. Firstly, her escape meant that she had rejected him; and, secondly, she had rejected him for a lowly accomplice. This was not easy for him to digest.

Over the years, Shankar had made many friends in important places. And now, he pulled strings, asking favours from police officers. He went on a hunt to locate Lalita. Finally, inspector Hari of Pallavaram police station located Lalita and Sudalai.[4]

While Hari kept Sudalai in custody, Shankar took Lalita.[5]

'You better not do anything to her!' Sudalai screamed from his cell. Shankar turned to look at Sudalai and gave him a wry smirk as a reply. He caught Lalita's wrist firmly and dragged her out of the police station.

Shankar brought Lalita home and cracked open a bottle of rum. Lalita needed a drink badly, and Shankar played his charming self as he made her a drink, one after another. He chugged down a few pegs himself. When their heads were buzzing with the alcohol, Shankar pulled Lalita into his arms and asked, 'Why did you betray me? I gave you the world and you ran away with Sudalai the idiot?' Lalita tried to wriggle out of Shankar's grasp. But even a drunk Shankar was too strong for her to overpower. Shankar flung her on to the bed and raped her.

She screamed with every thrust of his, while Shankar kept looking at her and smiling.

'Does Sudalai fuck you as well as I do? Does he fill you up like me?' All that Shankar could do now was to forcefully take her, even though her heart belonged to someone else. He knew that power could get him anything.

After he had had his fill, she replied to his question, 'I ran away because I love Sudalai!'

Shankar felt like a tinderbox whose fuse had been lit by this statement. He slapped her and she retaliated. At that moment, hearing the commotion, Mohan and Eldin entered the room. Shankar, whose vest was torn in the scuffle, ordered the two to beat up Lalita. Mohan pulled her by her hair, while Eldin caught her hands and pinned them back. Shankar lunged at her and throttled her. They held each other's gaze till Lalita's eyes became glassy, as life was squeezed out of her. The three men let go of her and her lifeless body crumpled to the floor. Adrenaline was rushing through their veins.

'What do we do with the body?' Shankar asked in his alcohol-laced haze.

Mohan answered, 'Let us bury her in the garden near my liquor shop. That way no one will ever find her.' Mohan was catching on fast under the tutelage of Shankar. Shankar nodded and yanked off Lalita's gold earrings and the gold chain that she was wearing.

Then they lifted the body into the auto and headed towards Kuttumadu, where Mohan's arrack joint, which had become a decent-sized liquor godown, was located. They buried her body and her clothes. Just before her face disappeared forever under the mud, Shankar hocked a mouthful of saliva and spat on her corpse, calling her, '*Paccha theyvidiya!* [Bitch!]'

Shankar's rage and ego fueled him to commit this murder. But it was not his last. Life resumed and Shankar put this behind him. Except, Sudalai was hell-bent on taking revenge. He started his own whorehouse and began poaching Shankar's customers. When the news reached Shankar, he was livid. He drove around the city with Babu, a gang member, hunting for Sudalai. They spotted him outside the Taj Hotel.

'You bring him to my house. He is mine to finish!' Shankar ordered Babu. His eyes were bloodshot and his hands were shaking with anger. Shankar drove off, leaving Babu to deal with Sudalai.

Babu found Sudalai busy talking to a foreigner, trying to entice him with 'fun time with hot, sexy Indian beauty, bang-bang lot times'. The moment Sudalai spotted Babu, he tried to bolt. But Babu caught hold of him.

'Why are you running? I just wanted to meet you and have a drink!' Babu said. 'Let's go to Mohan's liquor shop.' And off they went, where Eldin and Shivaji joined them.

'Is Shankar angry at me?' Sudalai asked, as he took a swig of brandy. The gang members exchanged looks.

'Why will he be mad at you?' Mohan asked. 'In fact, he was saying that he hasn't met you for a long time. Why don't we all go and meet him?'

'Yes, and if there is any misunderstanding, we will help you sort it out with Anna,' Shivaji piped in.

'Where is Lalita? What has he done to her?' Sudalai asked hesitantly.

Eldin dispelled his doubts, '*Arre*, she was a whore . . . She played both of you and ran away. Why spoil an old friendship for the sake of a whore?'

'She ran away?' Sudalai was surprised. 'Then why didn't she get in touch with me?'

'Because she found a new man!' Shivaji kept lying.

Having swallowed the freshly cooked story, Sudalai heaved a sigh of relief. 'Let us go and meet Shankar. If he is angry, I will ask for his forgiveness,' Sudalai said, now confident that Shankar was not angry with him.

When they reached Shankar's house, Sudalai was met with a warm embrace. 'Where have you been all these days? Come, let's celebrate!' Shankar ordered food and opened up a bottle of brandy. After having dinner and drinks, the men started talking about their good old days. Sudalai lay on the floor, supporting his head with his left hand as he blew out smoke rings and held the cigarette in his right hand. All his fears had dissipated.

It was about nine in the night when Shankar broached the topic of Lalita.

'You turned out to be quite a Romeo, eh? Where all did you take Lalita?'

Shankar's first question appeared to be shrouded in brotherhood and machismo. Sudalai rattled off the names of the places where he had taken her while they were on the run from Shankar. What Sudalai didn't notice was the increased pace in Shankar's drinking. Suddenly, Shankar leapt up and hit Sudalai. He was taken completely by surprise.

'*Thevadiya mavan* [Son of a bitch], not only did you steal my girl, but you also tried to steal my business!' Shankar thundered. He pinned Sudalai to the ground with his knee on his chest. Before Sudalai could react, Eldin got hold of his feet and Shivaji of his hands. Babu wrung a towel around Sudalai's neck and pulled hard. While Sudalai was gasping for breath, Shankar repeatedly kicked him on his vital parts (as mentioned in the court papers). He screamed: 'This is what you used to take Lalita away; this is what you think makes you a man?'

Life was refusing to ebb out of Sudalai so Mohan clamped down on his nose and mouth with his hand. After Sudalai stopped struggling, it was decided that his body would be burnt.

Eldin and Mohan were sent off on a rickety TVS 50 moped to get petrol. Meanwhile, Shankar, Shivaji and Babu carried Sudalai to the ground floor. Shankar removed the gold chain and a ring from Sudalai's body, poured 6 litres of petrol and lit a cigarette. He took a long, satiated drag and then exhaled. He was at peace. He then threw the lit matchstick in slow motion, like he had seen his screen idols do, on to Sudalai's corpse, which burst into flames. The gang closed all the doors and windows and stepped out of the house to wait. A muffled explosion was heard as the stomach burst. They went in after the fire had consumed Sudalai. At about 2.30 a.m., the unburnt portion of the body was packed into a bed sheet, loaded into the boot of Eldin's car and driven to the Muttukadu Boat Yard, where it was dumped into the backwaters.

Now that his rage was ebbing, Shankar looked at his ground-floor room. It was covered in black soot and the ground where the body had been burnt was completely damaged.

'Mohan, get Thoppai *mistry* [repairman] and painter Manusamy immediately,' Shankar ordered, wanting to erase all evidence as soon as possible.

'Anna, it is 5.30 in the morning,' Mohan said, as he looked at his watch.

'WAKE THEM UP AND GET THEM HERE!' was all it took for Mohan to rush out. When the repairman and the painter came, the condition of the room was enough to jolt them awake.

'The bed caught fire,' Shankar said quickly. He assumed that his cock-and-bull story would mislead the duo. In less than a year, Thoppai and Manusamy would take the stand in Shankar's trial as prosecution witnesses.

Two days later, Shankar and Mohan received a visit from Ravi, who used to work for Shankar but had defected to Sudalai.

'Where is Sudalai? People are saying they saw him last with your men.' Ravi's bravado seemed to have increased manifold since he had shifted his allegiance.

Shankar looked up to see his former gang member standing there, demanding answers. He laughed and asked, 'Ravi, you've come to meet me after so many months and no *vanakkam* or how am I doing?'

Ravi's stance did not change. 'Shankar Anna, please tell me where he is. I don't have time to exchange pleasantries.'

'Do you have time for a drink at least?' Shankar tempted Ravi. Free liquor, free women and free money, no man with zero moral scruples can resist. Shankar gave him a hundred-rupee note and asked him to get some whisky. In his absence, the plot was hatched.

Ravi returned with the booze. Eldin, Mohan, Shankar and Ravi started drinking. It's said that alcohol makes for loose tongues. And that is what happened. Under the influence of alcohol, Ravi started accusing Shankar of having killed Lalita and Sudalai.

'Do you know what your fate will be if I inform the inspector of Thiruvanmiyur?' Ravi threatened. Shankar and his men watched him quietly. And then Ravi's greed took him over the edge.

'If you buy me an autorickshaw, I will not open my mouth to the police,' Ravi said, not knowing that he was blackmailing the wrong person.

Immediately, Eldin, Mohan and Shankar pounced on him. Using the same towel that had been used to kill Sudalai, they throttled Ravi. They buried him in a pit near Mohan's liquor shop. Eldin asked, 'What happens if somebody else comes looking for Ravi? We can't keep killing them all, can we?'

There was a tinge of nervousness in his voice, as he wasn't sure what Shankar's reply would be. Mohan smiled and said, 'I have an idea!'

When Ravi's mother came asking about her son, Shankar told her that he had left for Bombay. And lo and behold, two days later, she received an inland letter from Ravi asking her to not worry as he was apparently in Bombay looking for a job! The letter was Mohan's masterstroke.

Shankar was now on a killing spree. What made him different from other serial killers was his motive. He wasn't killing for pleasure or because he was mentally disturbed. His killings had stories attached to them. He knew the victims and in his head, their deaths were justified.

Three down, three more to go!

In the meantime, Shankar's prostitution business was at an all-time peak. He kept the law at bay with girls being sent to the right people. He wrote an autobiography from jail in which he claimed to have supplied girls to Tamil movie stars and ministers, even hinting at their names.

It was 29 May 1988. Anita had been working for Shankar for the past six months. She was walking by when three men attacked her and tried to abduct her. These three men— Sampath, Mohan and Govindaraj—had no clue who they had just fucked with.

Eldin tried to intervene but the three men thrashed him. When Shankar heard about the incident, he stuffed his car with his men and picked up the trio. He and his men first thrashed the three with casuarina sticks, and then brought them back to Shankar's house.

Shankar stood in front of the inquisitive crowd that had gathered at the entrance of his house. His shirt was soaked with the blood of the three goons.

'You see this?' he said, pointing to the blood on his shirt. 'I will have no problem dispatching you to your maker if any one of you snitch about me to the police.' Scared to incur the wrath of Shankar, the crowd immediately dispersed.

The three of them were locked up and beaten. Two of them died during the thrashing, while Govindaraj was throttled. Their bodies were buried in the basement of an under-construction building. Shankar's anger had now claimed six victims. And the tide was bound to turn . . .

While all this was happening, there were reports that nine girls had disappeared from the area. The reports suggested that they had been abducted. To infuse fresh meat into his flesh trade, it was Shankar and his men who had abducted these girls, ensuring that they were never heard of again.

When the families of the missing girls tried to lodge complaints, the Thiruvanmiyur police feigned ignorance, as Shankar was the uncrowned king of all nefarious activities in the area. No action was taken.[6] But the families that were fed up with the inaction now approached Governor P.C. Alexander.

He immediately swung into action, and a new team of cops was formed. Within that team, coincidentally, was a constable called Aari, who knew Shankar very well.[7] Led by Jaffer Ali (deputy inspector general, Madras) the team roped in two honest inspectors, Thangamani and Ranganathan.

* * *

A few days before the Christmas of 1988, Shanti was walking in the Tondiarpet area of Madras. She hated walking there at night because of the wine shop. But she had had no other choice that evening. She had to collect a few clothes from the local tailor, who, of course, had not done his work. So, she waited for him to complete the work. A few men were hanging out at the wine shop, waiting to buy their daily fix. Out of nowhere, a three-wheeler drove up next to Shanti. Screeching to a halt, a man with his face covered jumped out of the passenger seat and tried to pull her into the auto. She screamed and resisted. The customers from the wine shop ran to help her. The abductors knew that they were outnumbered. They pushed Shanti to the roadside and drove off.

Thangamani and Ranganathan (they almost sound like an auditing or a legal firm) had a hunch that this incident had something to do with the missing people. And so they went undercover to local wine shops, hanging out with drunks and the staff. It was there that they first heard about a cold-blooded and ruthless man who drove an auto and supposedly abducted girls. Mind you, at this point, the police had no clue about the six murders that Shankar had already committed. They were only investigating a series of missing people/supposed abductions.

In the backrooms of the wine shops, Shankar was being spoken about in the language usually reserved for mythological villains. The people described him as a fearless man who liked to burn his victims and dispose of them in the sea.

Meanwhile, Shankar had no clue what was going on behind his back. So when he opened the door one morning, he was shocked to see a posse of policemen at the threshold of his Periyar Nagar house.

Upon searching his house, his nexus with the police was discovered. Shankar had maintained a diary in which he had written details about all his marriages. It also contained photos of him posing with policemen of different ranks. This really stirred the hornet's nest, creating a furore. Two policemen were suspended immediately, while a third was sent on a long leave and then axed. The news of Shankar's arrest reached his gang members, who immediately absconded.

Aari now used his past knowledge of Shankar's hideouts and safe houses to help the cops round up the absconding members.

But Shankar continued to be his arrogant self. He thought he would only need to pull the right strings to walk out free. Eldin quickly confessed and turned an approver.

But all of Shankar's efforts to reach out to his old 'friends' came to naught. Everyone turned their backs on him. He had no other choice but to confess to his crimes.

'I am not responsible for the crimes. It was the movies that influenced me,' was Shankar's justification in court. When he realized he was cornered, he gave a series of interviews to Tamil journalists and claimed that he had kidnapped the girls to service politicians. Once they had had their fill, Shankar had to kill them and get rid of the bodies. Shankar hoped that his interviews would expose the supposed ringleaders who had created the demand for such girls. But predictably so, no inquiries were made into the allegations and no politician was ever pulled up in court.

What now shocked the police was the revelation that Shankar and his accomplices had murdered six people. These were crimes that the police had had no knowledge of. As they say—'It ain't over till the fat lady sings.' In this case, it was Eldin who brought down the curtain on Shankar as he began to squeal and sing to reveal where the bodies were buried. Five bodies were recovered. Shankar could not believe that the glamorous life he had envisioned and then created for himself was now crumbling right in front of his eyes. What he did achieve was the moniker 'Auto Shankar'. The press gave him this name as it was his modus operandi—picking up girls in an auto and abducting them. The irony was that he was never tried for the abduction and supposed murders of the girls. What took him to the noose were the anger- and jealousy-fuelled murders that he had committed.

* * *

The Madras Central Prison, constructed in 1837, is a grand, colonial campus spread across 13 acres. It has a great history associated with it. The prison served as a pit stop for prisoners being sent to 'Kala Paani', the dreaded cellular jail in the Andaman and Nicobar Islands. It was here that Veer Savarkar was imprisoned before he was shipped off to the Andamans. And it was here, within the historical edifices, that Shankar and his accomplices were housed.

The walls of the prison may have confined Shankar and his men, but they did not manage to change his lifestyle. Shankar could get anything he wanted within his cell. And so whisky and chicken were aplenty and cigarettes were always available. The party, it seemed, continued. But there was a dampener in the offing.

Shankar, Eldin and Shivaji, the three main accused in the murders of six people, lost the case and were sentenced to hang.

A quiet descended upon the three men. The prison rule stated that people accused in the same case could not be housed together in the same cell. So the three of them could only meet during the brief recesses throughout the day. One day as they were sitting in the sun after their lunch of watery dal, bland vegetable and boiled rice, Eldin, the most scared amongst the three, suddenly said in a quivering voice: 'I don't want to die.'

'You won't die. *En peyar Gowri Shankar*! [My name is Gowri Shankar!]' If there was anyone who appeared calm while the barrel of a gun was pointed at him, it was Shankar.

Shankar knew that his supposed clients/friends had turned their backs on him. But he had a few friends in prison. He worked his charm, trying to win them over with loin-inspiring bribes outside the jail. When that didn't work, he resorted to blackmail. He threatened to reveal the names of the police officers and politicians who were his clients and who had helped him run his brothel under the radar.[8] And miraculously, he found the door of his cell open on 20 August 1990. Eldin, Shankar and Shivaji vanished into thin air. They managed to escape the gargantuan Madras Central Prison.

The next morning the authorities found the cell door open, an iron rod bent in the common hall and several footprints on both sides of the compound wall. Shit had officially hit the fan! There was a hue and cry, and twelve junior-level officials and warders were suspended. Three were arrested for abetting the escape. The government also suspended central jail superintendent K. Chelladurai for dereliction of duty.[9] The citizens of Madras were now divided in their opinion about Auto Shankar. Some were petrified that a serial killer was on the loose, while others looked at him as a legendary criminal akin to Charles Sobhraj, who had managed to evade the authorities and escape from prison. The mythology about Shankar was growing.

After all, Shankar and his men were the first inmates to escape from this prison post Independence. Shankar had planned the escape with a trump card up his sleeve. It was the close proximity of the prison to the railway station, the bus depot and the port. He could choose any of the three transport options, depending on where he intended to make his safe house. And three escape options meant that the police force would have to send out three times the amount of personnel to search for him.

'I want the bastards to sweat their balls off!' Shankar hissed, a night before D-Day.

'Do you think it will happen?' Eldin asked.

'Do you think the fuckers would prefer me to reveal their names?' Shankar could smell the air of freedom already.

The police now started a manhunt, the magnitude of which had never been seen before. Chief Minister M. Karunanidhi himself initiated a judicial probe. The officers knew a few heads would roll again if Shankar and his men were not caught.

As a clichéd Bollywood line goes, '*Kanoon ke haath bahut lambe hote hain!* [You can't escape the long arms of the law!]' And so the law caught up with Shankar and his men who were hiding in Rourkela, Orissa. They were brought back to Madras.

If you thought that Shankar would give up now and get ready to face his maker, you are wrong. He had one more trick up his sleeve. It was his final attempt to paint himself as an innocent man.

Shankar granted exclusive rights to *Nakkheeran* to serialize his autobiography. The issues were sold out every week. In them, Shankar claimed that it was the police who had initiated him into bootlegging and persuaded him to become a pimp! In his last attempt to pull some strings, he started naming people in his book. He indirectly named politicians, police officers and film stars of the Tamil film industry.

Nakkheeran's editor, Rajagopal, had no problem with the attention that his weekly was getting: 'We have altered things in such a way that those who are sharp will be able to understand who is being referred to.'[10]

He mentioned a top cop as 'Mr Milk', whose wife's friendship Shankar claimed to have enjoyed. He named a political leader to whom he had supposedly supplied women. The man is described as an ageing leader using the Tamil term, which not only means 'age' but is also a synonym for the politician's name!

Feathers were not only ruffled, but also literally plucked off, so to speak. The infuriated director general of police, S. Sripal, issued a statement, saying, 'Shankar is a third-rate character from a third-rate slum. Neither he nor *Nakkheeran* should be taken seriously. Whatever action was taken against him, was taken by the police. What connivance is he talking about?'[11]

Nakkheeran was warned not to publish the autobiography, as the case was sub judice and could influence the verdict. But *Nakkheeran* knew this was too good an opportunity to pass. And as expected, the readership increased by thousands.

And as if the drama in Shankar's life was not enough, the circus now moved to the courts. There were desperate attempts to clamp down on Shankar to prevent him from revealing alleged names and his shady connections.

After the first part, 'Shadowed Truth' or 'Auto Shankar's Dying Declaration', was published, *Nakkheeran* received a mail from the prison authorities that questioned the authorship of the article, which said that Shankar did not write it. It also warned *Nakkheeran* that writing in the name of a prisoner was against prison rules, and threatened legal action.

Rajagopal immediately filed a petition in the high court against Tamil Nadu, the inspector general of prisons (Madras) and the superintendent of prisons (Tamil Nadu) to stop them from interfering in the publication of the subsequent episodes of Shankar's story in the weekly. The high court would have none of it and squashed the writ.

Rajagopal knew that he had the goose that laid the golden eggs. And he wasn't going to let go so easily. He moved the Supreme Court, seeking relief under Article 32 of the Constitution, which seeks 'remedies for the enforcements of rights'.

On 7 October 1994, the Supreme Court ruled in favour of Rajagopal. However, Justice B.P. Jeevan Reddy cautioned *Nakkheeran*, saying it could publish the alleged life story of Shankar without his permission and only insofar as it was in the public domain. But it could not go beyond that and publish his 'official' life story without his permission, as that would be invading his right to privacy.

Again, predictably, no action was taken against the supposed names mentioned by Shankar. And Eldin, Shivaji and Shankar were sentenced to hang. Shankar's final trick is what sealed his fate. It seemed that the people in power thought it best to shut him up forever rather than have him reveal more.

On 27 April 1995, the saga of Gowri 'Auto' Shankar finally came to an end. Shankar, Eldin and Shivaji were hanged till death.

Auto Shankar has now gone down in the pages of Indian criminals as one of the deadliest serial killers. For someone who dreamt of becoming a Tamil movie star, and rich and famous, this was an ignominious end.

BEER MAN

BEERLY A SERIAL KILLER

'If I had to murder someone, why would I kill some homeless fellows? Why wouldn't I kill a gangster in jail and come out as a don instead?'[1]

—Ravindra Kantrole a.k.a. Abdul Rahim

If there was one crime in the last decade that glued every Mumbaikar to the TV channels and newspapers—this was it. It also glued people to their homes—most streets between Churchgate and Marine Lines got deserted by 10 p.m.—lest they be stripped of their pants, buggered and killed. Or at least that's how a few of the victims turned up. And if there ever were a case where the media was flummoxed, it was this one. Rumours became official stories, where each newspaper printed their own sordid version to grab eyeballs.

Let's go back to 2006.

Some of the *Times of India* headlines on 5 October 2006 were on these lines:

1. NGO's Bribe Payer Index 2006, an audit body, declared India as the World leader in greasing palms[2]
2. Shiv Sena wanted to break away from the BJP[3]
3. US Miss World finalist and India-born Kanshka Mehta found herself on a hijacked plane belonging to Turkish Airlines[4]
4. Madhuri Dixit announced that she will be coming back to Bollywood[5]

The mention of a dead body that was found on a foot overbridge near Marine Lines train station was probably buried in the inside pages and carried in less than 150 words. Because it was just another body, turning up in a city of 15 million people. And, of course, nobody knew that the killer was just getting started.

The police first thought the victim was a homeless man who was beaten to death. But investigations revealed that he was a taxi driver named Vijay Gaud. The case was soon lost amongst the many dusty files of Mumbai Police.

Exactly four days later, another body turned up near Mumbai Hockey Association on Marine Drive. And another turned up on 16 November near the Al-Saba building on NS Road. The police, who had ignored these murders as everyday unconnected occurrences, suddenly found itself walking on glass when bodies began turning up regularly.

On 14 December 2006, a homeless man's body was found near Churchgate station, beaten to death. The only clue: an empty Kingfisher beer can that was found beside the body. Between November 2006 and January 2007, seven more bodies turned up. They were all found between Marine Lines and Churchgate stations—a radius of a few kilometres. The victims were all either clubbed or stabbed to death and were naked below the waist, which suggested sexual assault. But what fascinated the press were the beer cans found next to the bodies of the victims. And it went to town and gave the serial killer the moniker 'Beer Man'.

But the truth is, beer cans were found beside only two bodies. Anyhow, the circus started. This was just an indication of how the press was reporting, and twisting, the story to sell it, portraying a serial killer who left beer cans in his wake, to the readers. And if the police or the press had looked around, they would have seen that many homeless people use empty beer cans for storing and drinking water!

But that headline wouldn't exactly have sold the newspapers, would it?

Apart from the first victim, Vijay Gaud, none of the others could be identified, as they were all homeless migrants with no IDs. Forensic examination of the victims revealed signs of sexual intercourse, which led the police to believe that the murderer was homosexual.

Mumbai was abuzz with Beer-Man conversations. The afternoon dailies had gory pictures of the victims, sordid details and, of course, their own version of the investigation.

If speculation had been a scrip in the Bombay Stock Exchange—millions could have been made by the newspaper companies. And in this media tizzy and obsession with Beer Man, a few observations and questions arose . . . some logical and some downright funny.

—The number of victims varied between seven and eight, depending on the newspaper that you were reading. And some even attributed *all* deaths on the streets to this alleged gay serial killer, who apparently loved his lager as much as he liked to bugger and kill.

—When some conscientious newspapers corrected the fact that there were only two beer cans found, the public/other newspapers dissed them by saying: 'Oh! He is no longer leaving behind beer cans! And, therefore, it isn't his signature move to stamp his crime—so maybe he was just a casual beer drinker!' *Do you see where this circus was headed?*

—According to all the reports, the victims were all killed either by being stabbed in the chest or by being hit on the head with a stone. *Okay, so this at least was true!*

—Though all the victims who were killed were homeless migrants, the conclusion was that the killer himself was not poor because . . . (*hold your breath*) he drank beer. The press just could not control the temptation of reporting and exploiting the 'beer' angle repeatedly.

—And there was this report (*the obvious inspiration being the rich-aristocrat-turned-killer phenomenon in England like that of Jack the Ripper*) that said he owned a car and was well off because . . . (*okay, you know where this is headed*) he drank beer.

—The assumption was that he was young—aged between thirty and thirty-five—and well built, as he was able to overpower his victims.

—The newspapers claimed that the killer chose his spots well—they were secluded and, therefore, the killer was well versed with the south Mumbai area. This made the real-estate market of south Mumbai shaky. But it probably made the people of Andheri and Thane very happy, knowing that the killer wouldn't be showing up in their part of the world any time soon.

—Based on forensic reports (*some of which were still awaited*), the killer was only targeting homosexuals. And the killer himself was believed to be gay as he had had sex with five of the men whom he'd killed. Suddenly, the rape and sodomy story went out of the window as the press now labelled the victims as homosexuals as well, which (*as per this ridiculous assumption/theory*) meant that Beer Man first asked the victims their sexual preferences before buggering and murdering them. Or else how would he know whom to target? Or was it that Beer Man first spied on these victims making out in some dark alleyway, and then decided to use his dipstick as well?

Every day would bring forward some new revelation, claim or conclusion that was a 'fact!' And the police were not exactly helping the case. They just didn't know where to start. They had not faced such an epidemic of murdered people who turned up at such frequent intervals like spam mail from real-estate companies in one's inbox.

And then the plot thickened. Things began to get hairy when the police recovered a handwritten note next to one of the victims. 'The note we have recovered is full of seemingly senseless, disconnected sentences that may reflect his [the killer's] state of mind,' said a senior policeman investigating the case.[6] But amidst the nonsense, one sentence stood out. It read: 'Welcome to the clan.'[7]

This for some reason strengthened the police's belief that the killer was homosexual. When journalists asked for details of the rest of the note, the police refused to reveal them. And rightfully so, seeing the circus that the press had made of the reportage so far. 'It is the only evidence we have. I cannot divulge details of the note,' said additional police commissioner (south region), D. Kanakaratnam.[8]

It seemed the police were having a hard time trying to fathom this brewing mystery. 'The serial killer is smart and never leaves any clues behind. We have not recovered the knife used by the killer. And he also collects the victims' belongings,' admitted Arup Patnaik, joint commissioner of police (law and order).[9]

They rounded up fifty-eight people for questioning and a ninety-member task force was put on the case.

* * *

In 2006, *Dhoom 2* was one of the biggest blockbuster movies of the year. In the film, the two cops, Ali and Jai, are on the trail of a professional thief, 'Mr A'. One of the scenes in the film shows them trying to predict where Mr A will strike next.

Partly inspired by studying profiles of psychopaths and partly by *Dhoom 2*, Mumbai Police now tried to map out where Beer Man's next attack could be.

And BOOM! A pattern emerged.

A senior cop, on the condition of anonymity, said, 'Beer Man has been striking thrice in each area. The first set of murders were committed on a sea-facing stretch, the next batch was around Wankhede Stadium and the Mumbai Hockey

Association and the following three killings were on MK Road on the other side of the railway line at Churchgate. Now, with the latest murder being unearthed at Grant Road overbridge and before that at the Metro overbridge, we feel that he might be striking again in the vicinity.'[10]

Another pattern emerged: eight out of the ten murders had been committed on Thursday nights.[11]

Police put out requests cautioning people against loitering alone around the Grant Road and Charni Road overbridges late at night. He was the boogeyman of Mumbai. And just when all seemed bleak, the police had a breakthrough.

In a public toilet, near the Marine Lines railway station, where the last victim was found, a police sniffer-dog retrieved an ironed grey shirt.

Pavement-dwellers said it belonged to a member of the Dashrath Rane gang, Ravindra Kantrole.

On 22 January 2007, the sniffer dogs traced the owner of the shirt and the police nabbed Abdul Rahim, the name Kantrole had adopted after his conversion to Islam. The city breathed a sigh of relief.

Rahim's grainy photograph appeared on the front pages of newspapers. He looked menacing, with a long beard, a *taqiyah* (skullcap) on his head and shoulder-length hair. His eyes burned through the cover pages. If one were to judge the book by its cover, Rahim (thirty-five) had already been tried, convicted and sentenced to hang by the media and the public. He looked every bit like Beer Man or what Beer Man should look like. He fit the casting.

Fireworks were set off in celebration. The nightlife in south Mumbai resumed. People were no longer confined to their homes. But if you thought this was the end, you were mistaken.

So who was Ravindra Kantrole?

Kantrole was born in Cama and Albless Hospital to a family of a washerman. He lived with them in an illegal tenement in

Dhobitalao. He studied till Class V at the Our Lady of Dolours School at Marine Lines.

His first-ever visit to a police station was when he was sixteen years old. He had been called to the Azad Maidan police station to bail out his father, who had been charged with stealing gold ornaments from the statue of Our Lady in the Church.

'Someone else stole them, but my father was blamed,' he claimed.[12]

When the tenement that they stayed in was razed to the ground, his father moved into his mother's house at Mahalakshmi, and Kantrole was shipped off to Pune to stay with his father's relatives.

Kantrole was a boy of the streets and found life in Pune too sedentary for his liking. To top it off, his uncle constantly taunted him about his gambler father. He would say, 'If he was half a man, he would do something useful and not send his son to live with his relatives!' And so, Ravindra returned to Mumbai, preferring to be on the streets or in his friends' homes.

'[I'd] rather be the raja of the street than a *ghulam* [slave] in someone else's house,'[13] he had told a journalist at the time of his arrest. Still in his teens, he joined the Dashrath Rane gang, where his job was to extort money from hawkers and illegal establishments that were selling country liquor. The underworld introduced him to drugs, which he soon got hooked on to. He was often picked up by the police.

The cell at the Azad Maidan police station became a home for him. And when he wasn't in there, he visited whorehouses, showing the girls there who 'Mumbai *ka* Raja' was. And it was during one of these encounters that he met a girl, Anjali, and fell madly in love. As if straight out of the Salman Khan–starrer *Baaghi*, after a year of wooing her, Kantrole raised Rs 25,000 to pay the brothel and got her released. He married Anjali and they rented a small house. Soon, their daughter, Deepa, was born.

If you are thinking that this does not fit the profile of a serial killer, you are right. But then you have to read on to find out.

Notwithstanding his marriage and the birth of his daughter, his visits to the prison continued. During one of his stints in Arthur Road Jail, he met a devout Muslim man who greatly influenced him, so much so that when Kantrole came out of prison, he headed straight to the Garib Nawaz Dargah in Ajmer and converted to Islam. He chose Abdul Rahim as his Islamic name and was determined to lead a clean life. He quit the gang and started running a street-side vada-pav stall. From the life of a criminal, he did a complete volte-face and became a police informant. The police promised him rewards for every piece of information he gave them. He was a very able informer. Having lived off the streets, Rahim had his ear to the ground. His information led to many successful arrests, raids and recoveries of contraband. But post his arrest, he claimed that the police had not given him the promised rewards.

More on that later. Let us return to the story.

Rahim was surprised to be arrested on charges of theft. One report said that he was arrested from the Dhobitalao area, wearing a blood-soaked shirt and holding a chopper/dagger at the time of his arrest.

Now read the previous line again. Firstly, he was in the laundry area where thousands of clothes are washed every day. What would it take for him to get rid of a blood-soaked shirt and steal a clean one? Nothing! Secondly, the murders were committed at night and he was arrested during the day. Which means if he was wearing the blood-soaked shirt throughout the day, isn't it strange that no one noticed or reported it? And you would expect Rahim to get rid of the shirt that would connect him to the murder, no?

Sitting for an interview years after his arrest, he said, '*Mujhe hamesha meri daadhi, baal aur mazhab ke vajah se pakda gaya hai* [I have always been targeted for my long hair, beard and religion].'

'*Sab chod badalne ki koshish karoon toh bhi mujhe nahin chodte hain* [Even if I try to leave it all and mend my ways, they don't let me],' he added.[14]

When the police had taken him for interrogation, Rahim had pleaded with them, saying, 'Sir, *maine ganda kaam karna chodh diya hai. Mujhe yeh sab murder-wurder ke bare mein kuch nahi paata!* [I have left doing illegal stuff. I have no clue about the murders!]'

'*Meri ab biwi hai, bachhi hai—hum sab Marine Lines ke kholi mein rehte hai! Allah kasam, inspector saab, main dharm badalne ke baad ekdum clean ho gaya le!* [I have a wife, a daughter—we live in a shanty on Marine Lines! I swear on Allah, inspector saab, that after converting to Islam I have given up all illegal work!]'

The police had seen hundreds of criminals come in and plead innocence, taking the emotional route of swearing on their non-existent mothers, fathers and finally on gods and holy saints! The criminals thought it was a great way to convince the cops of their innocence.

But Mumbai Police was sharp and agile, and having none of it!

'*Maa ka kasam nahi khayega?* [You won't swear by your mother?]' the interrogating officer joked.

As much as Rahim denied his involvement, the police had one clinching piece of evidence that could connect him to the murders. The handwritten note. So he was told to write.

'*Abdul ya Ravindra—kya bulayoon tujhe? Full confusion hai!* [What should we call you: Ravindra or Abdul? It's fully confusing],' the constable taunted him, as he pushed a pen into Rahim's hands and gave him a writing pad.

'*Ab likh! Mumbai mein Christian log ko apun kya naam diya hai?* [Write! What is the local expression by which Christians are colloquially known?]'[15]

Abdul scribbled down: *maka pav.*

Time for a lesson in Mumbai slang. One theory states that the term 'maka pav' traces its roots (*which are unsubstantiated*) to the Goans of Portuguese origin who were among the early settlers of Mumbai. Most of them ran bakeries that made bread or pav (as it is known in Konkani) and, therefore, were called Maka Pav (pronounced as Maa-ka Pow).

The other more credible story is that the sobriquet originated from the staple breakfast of the working-class Goan, bread and coffee. So when the Goan would go to the bakery in the morning, he would say: '*Maka pav de,*' which means: 'Give me bread,' that was shortened to 'maka pav'.

The police compared the two notes and found that the handwriting matched. They also pointed out that at the time of his arrest they had found a chopper/knife on Rahim, which, of course, didn't prove anything. Of the seven known murders by Beer Man, stones were used in two cases, but a chopper was not used in any of them.

It seemed that police had faced flak due to the delay in finding the serial killer and were now in a hurry to confirm and shut the case. Rahim was whisked off to Bangalore for a narco-analysis test. As per the report, the police came out triumphant, claiming that Rahim had confirmed that he had killed fifteen people and was involved in twenty-one criminal cases.

The police also claimed that the 'beer' angle was confirmed in the narco test as Rahim supposedly verified that he made the victims drink beer to inebriate them before killing them. But he denied sexually assaulting them, saying he was against homosexuality because of his religious beliefs and practices.

So if you are with me till this point—read the previous line again.

This meant that although Mumbai Police might have caught Beer Man, it should rather have been hunting down a serial necrophiliac! If the narco test was to be believed, the police should have been looking for a man who followed Rahim, waited for him to kill these men and then had sex with the bodies every time. This would only be possible if this imaginary gay rapist was following Rahim's every movement!

The desperation to prove and close the case was tremendous. Answers and results were being demanded from higher authorities. The police started to fit their stories to match the narrative. This was a conspiracy akin to the JFK assassination and the single-bullet theory.[16]

Even though, as per law, DDT or Deceptive Detection Tests such as narco analysis, polygraph and brain-mapping are not admissible as evidence in court, the police wanted to close all loopholes and continued to do the tests. And all the results supposedly pointed to Rahim being Beer Man!

The official narrative was being written impromptu by people who had read too many pulp-fiction books, as can be seen from a statement given by a police officer after he came out of the narco test room: 'Said he loves seeing blood.'[17] There was an effort to sensationalize the case, to keep milking it as much as newsprint and TV channel TRPs could exploit!

These kinds of statements in afternoon dailies ensured that they were sold out. And so the newspapers and TV channels were extremely happy when sound bites like these were given. Contrary to this, a Bangalore source said that at no time during the narco-analysis test did Rahim say that he loved blood or violence.[18]

But the media wasn't giving up that easily. As they say, the excitement of falling in love is in the chase. The chase to catch the killer was over and before things could become mundane, the newspapers continued the circus. Now they went on to contradict their previous theories!

—He wasn't a homosexual, as previously thought. He hated homosexuals and apparently believed that it was against his new religion to perform such a sinful act. And, therefore, targeted gay people! Abdul had apparently taken it upon himself to eliminate such *na-paak* (impure) people! It seemed no one was asking the more important question: if he did not sexually assault his victims, then who did? Did he hire a gay assaulter to do the task? And assuming he was the assaulter, why would he do it if he was against homosexuality or hire someone to do it?

—One report said that he had killed at least forty-five people and flung most of their bodies into the sea.

—The pièce de résistance of speculation was that Rahim had killed them not because of their sexual orientation but so that he could take their blood to a cemetery near Marine Lines where a tantric could use it for black magic.[19] The journalists, in all probability, were angling for scriptwriter jobs for horror shows on television!

And then, within the first four days of March 2007, two bodies were found in the same area that Beer Man was supposed to attack, as predicted. But Rahim was in jail. This was a twist that the police had not anticipated. If he didn't do it, there were three other possibilities:

1. Rahim was *not* Beer Man
2. These were *copycat crimes*
3. Rahim was part of a gang that carried out these signature killings—so while he was in jail, the associates continued making merry

But the press was desperate not to lose their golden goose. And the police were desperate not to lose their prestige and the hard work they had done so far to maintain the narrative. And so a fourth option was offered.

A leading news channel concluded that Rahim had an accomplice who carried out the killings in the absence of his boss.

* * *

Anjali walked into Arthur Road Jail to meet her husband. As she waited, there were catcalls and whistles. She looked over her shoulder, clearly uncomfortable at the gazes she was receiving from the men around her. She could not make out whether the catcalls came from the constables on duty or the prisoners. She tried to stay calm.

Rahim walked up to her, accompanied by two constables. He looked haggard, tired and kept scratching himself. His forearm had red splotches. He smelt putrid. Anjali looked at the man who had rescued her from hell. Here he was, in hell himself.

'What are they saying?' she asked him.

'They are hell-bent on pinning this on me,' Rahim answered.

'I'll speak to the lawyer; there has to be a way out.' Anjali broke down.

'The only way they will allow me to go out of here is when they hang me,' Rahim said slowly. He was despondent; the weight of the false accusations was getting heavier by the day for him to bear.

He asked Anjali to take their infant daughter and leave Mumbai. 'The media will make your life hell. I don't want anything to happen to both of you. Deepa is too young to experience this insanity,' he told her. And so, Anjali took their daughter and headed to her village in Madhya Pradesh, where she still stays.

Rahim recalls, 'Initially when my wife would come to meet me, policemen would pass crude remarks. Then there were journalists who wanted to talk to them. My daughter was too young to even understand what was happening [she's thirteen now]. I was afraid that they would be harmed by all this, so I sent them away.'[20]

And so Rahim went on trial for the murders.

* * *

Sushan Kunjuraman was a short, dark, bespectacled man with a bushy salt-and-pepper moustache. He stood up and addressed the court. He was the defence lawyer fighting on behalf of Rahim. Kunjuraman maintained his client's innocence, saying he was nowhere near the murder sites and was being made a scapegoat.

However, the court was having none of his histrionics. According to it, the handwritings matched. His past record was suspect. He was a drug addict. And the alibis about his whereabouts were weak. The police had filed charges against him in three murders. They knew that they had their man with his back against the wall. It wouldn't be long before he was in the can.

In January 2007, a sessions court found Rahim guilty on one count of murder and sentenced him to life imprisonment. The other two cases were dismissed as the evidence was not good enough. Following this, Rahim went to prison. He gave up hope of ever being free. Once again, Mumbai breathed a sigh of relief. Finally, Beer Man was behind bars.

* * *

Kunjuraman was not an intimidating presence. But what he lacked in size, he made up in spirit. He was convinced that his client was innocent. Not one to give up easily, he was determined not to let an innocent man hang. His efforts moved the trial to the high court.

The state produced witnesses, evidence, and even quoted the questionable narco-test results. The ridiculous 'fact' of him being in collusion with a tantric was brought up in court. Rahim quashed it by saying that he had been set up by another informer.

In September 2009, the Bombay High Court overruled the sessions court, acquitting Rahim of all charges. The 'facts' that the media and the police had shared as true could not be verified. Rahim walked out free, but was condemned for life because of what the police and the media had done to him.

He remembers some policemen telling him, '*Adalat ne tujhe bari kar diya . . . hamaari nazar mein toh tu hi gunehgar hai* [In the eyes of the court you're innocent, but in our eyes you're still guilty].'[21]

Rahim has a sad smile on his face as he asks, 'Now, isn't that outright contempt of court?' A legally valid point.

But if Rahim thought he was finally free, he was wrong! The tag of Beer Man had been permanently inked on his forehead, so much so that wherever he went, people talked in hushed whispers, before moving away from him.

'I knew they were talking about me. No one seemed to be bothered that I had been found innocent,' he recounted to a journalist.[22]

And so he cut his hair and shaved the beard that had appeared in the front pages of all the newspapers, thereby giving himself a new look, hoping for a new life.

Rahim was desperate to put the past behind him. He rented a shanty on Marine Lines; he started a small stall along with a friend. But the past was not ready to part ways with him. Every time there was a crime in the area, be it theft or murder, he was picked up and hauled to the Azad Maidan police station.

In an interview to *Open* in July 2012, Rahim recalled: 'Even though the court had acquitted me. For [the police], I am the serial killer who got away.'[23]

And it really did seem that the police had not forgotten how he had managed to slip through their grip, and their humiliation at being unable to sew up the Beer Man case. In May 2012, when the bodies of three girls turned up, they picked him up again.

The victims had been raped. Two of them were bashed with a stone and the third was strangulated and thrown into the sea.

And the headlines once again screamed: 'Beer Man Is Suspect in Cuffe Parade Rape–Murders!'

Journalist Gajanan Khergamker writing for the website Fountain Ink said:

> On grounds of suspicion, the police may arrest a person and then, with permission from a magistrate, get him to take a blood test to investigate his complicity in a crime but in this case, the police have picked him up on 'suspicion' and made him undergo a DNA test after getting him to 'sign my consent' he wasn't even aware of doing.[24]

The DNA results came out negative. But the damage had been done. The media found another *masale-wale chutkula* (spicy nugget) to report. Every newspaper flashed the headline: 'Beer Man Was Subjected to a DNA Test for Cuffe Parade Rape–Murders', suggesting his complicity in the crime.

Kunjuraman, who still looks out for Rahim, was aghast. 'Simply picking him up and forcing him to take a DNA test was excessive,' he said. 'It is a human rights violation that warrants a judicial rap from the court.'[25]

Rahim was once again cleared of all charges.

It has been almost thirteen years since the first murder by Beer Man came into the limelight.

Kunjuraman has written a movie script based on Beer Man and how he was the advocate who heroically saved him from the gallows. But there doesn't seem to be any taker to produce the film. Rahim smiles, as he says, 'Someday, the film will be complete and people will know my real story. A hero will play my role.'[26]

The murders remain unsolved to this date. In the end, it is about a serial killer who got away, while an innocent man was made to pay the price. Or Rahim was *beerly* (I just couldn't resist the pun!) the serial killer he was being made out to be. Or was he a killer who slipped away?

K.D. KEMPAMMA

CYANIDE MALLIKA

'For the female of the species is more deadly than the male.'[1]

—Rudyard Kipling, 'The Female of the Species' (1911)

Hoskote is a small taluk and one of the thirty districts in Bangalore Rural. Home to more than twenty prominent temples, Hoskote is a well-known pilgrimage site. One of these is the Jalageramma temple.

On 19 October 1999, thirty-year-old Mamatha Rajan removed her sandals at the entrance of the Jalageramma temple. She had been moody and irritable since that morning and knew that if she spent another second at home, then she would probably have a nervous breakdown. The only one who could understand her was god. And so she bathed, tucked fresh flowers in her braid, wore her best sari and jewellery, prepared a thali of offerings and walked to the temple. She had bottled up a lot inside her and wanted to have a conversation with god.

She entered the temple's outer courtyard, which was relatively empty. She stood in the queue to enter the sanctum sanctorum. An older woman joined the line and stood behind her. Mamatha turned to look at her and the woman flashed a big smile. Vulnerable Mamatha suddenly felt a surge of warmth while looking into the eyes of this older woman, who was dressed in a simple sari. She gently touched Mamatha's hand and nodded at her to move forward. Mamatha made her offerings, said her prayers and instantly felt lighter.

'*Ninna hesarēnu?* [What is your name?]' the woman asked Mamatha.

'Mamatha Rajan. And yours?'

An unnoticeable beat. And then the woman replied, 'Lakshmi. Come, let us sit here.'

They sat in one of the silent corners of the temple complex—a shaded area, which was cool and comforting.

'Sister, whatever seems to be bothering you, you must leave it to god. He challenges us in many ways. He puts obstacles in our path to test our faith. You must never lose hope and faith,' Lakshmi said calmly. Her words were like a balm to Mamatha's agitation.

'How do you know something is troubling me?' Mamatha asked.

'I know many things, child.' Lakshmi raised Mamatha's chin and continued, 'Your eyes are sad. And in your heart you carry a great burden. You find it difficult to sleep at night.'

Mamatha could not believe how easily this woman had read her. What she did not realize was that Lakshmi was a master observer. She knew that people came to temples when they were either extremely happy or in misery. When devotees are overjoyed, they are raucous. When they are sad, they cry and the kohl under their eyes get smudged. Sleepless nights also manifest themselves as dark circles around eyes. And you just need to add a comforting line of what a great burden they seem to be carrying, and it's a sixer.

'Are you a saintly woman?' Mamatha asked.

Lakshmi said: 'Not at all. But I do have a connection with god. He listens to my prayers. Would you like me to help you?'

Mamatha held Lakshmi's hands in hers and pleaded: 'Yes, please! You must help me. You must let god know my prayers.'

Lakshmi made it seem like a once-in-a-lifetime offer: 'I don't usually do it for everybody. However, I know you need it and you seem like a lovely person.'

'Thank you! Thank you!' Mamatha could not believe that this was happening.

'I perform a special mandala puja that will help your prayers reach the gods faster and more efficiently. The puja has the power to make your wishes come true,' Lakshmi said.

Mandala puja is considered to be the ultimate prescription in Hinduism to transform one's life for the better. It is usually done to please the favourite deity of the person, whichever god it might be, and thereby be blessed with boons and good tidings.

'When can we do it?' Mamatha asked eagerly.

'On 29 October,' Lakshmi said with authority. 'I will come to your house at night and perform it. But you must send everyone away from your house for at least a couple of days. Remember, no one must know about it or else the prayer will not work.'

During those ten days, Lakshmi procured cyanide from a jewellery store where she used to work.

And so, on the said date, she arrived at Mamatha's house armed with fruits, flowers and some utensils to be used for the faux ceremony. She started reciting the prayers, or what was gibberish but said in a cadence that made it sound as if she was invoking the gods.

Lakshmi asked Mamatha to close her eyes and pray. Mamatha closed her eyes, her heart exploding with joy and gratitude. Then she heard Lakshmi say: 'When I give you the holy water, you must swallow it at once or else the prayer will not be complete. Understood?'

Mamatha nodded. Lakshmi pulled back Mamatha's braid and poured the liquid into her mouth. Then she clamped down on her nose and mouth to prevent her from breathing. As soon as Mamatha gulped down the holy water, which was cyanide, she started gasping for air. She opened her eyes to see Lakshmi's kind face now contorted into a vicious sneer. Mamatha struggled to free herself from Lakshmi's death grip, but Lakshmi only tightened her hold. Within moments, life ebbed away from Mamatha.

Lakshmi looked around. There was nobody in sight. She removed Mamatha's gold earrings, toe-ring, the gold ring on her finger and the gold chain around her neck. She lay down Mamatha's body on its side such that it faced the wall.

K.D. Kempamma a.k.a. Mallika a.k.a. Jayamma a.k.a. Shivamogga a.k.a. Lakshmi stuffed the jewellery into her handbag and walked out of the house, fearless and unrepentant.

God had heard someone's prayers. Unfortunately, it was not Mamatha's.

This is the story of India's first convicted woman serial killer—K.D. Kempamma, who earned the moniker of 'Cyanide Mallika' for her modus operandi.

Rudyard Kipling in his poem 'The Female of the Species' had written: 'For the female of the species is more deadly than the male.' He was, of course, referring to a female Himalayan bear who tore up a peasant into bits when accosted. But here, Kempamma seems to embody this quote and more.

Kempamma would go on to use various aliases; but for the sake of clarity, we will stick to Mallika.

* * *

Kaggalipura is a village in Uttarahalli in suburban Bengaluru. It is named after the kaggali (khair/acacia) trees that grow in abundance in the area. The tree is the source of khair or kaththa, which is used in betel leaf, or paan, to give it its red colour and flavour.

Mallika was born in Kaggalipura, located just 23 km away from Bengaluru. She studied till Class V, as her parents could not afford to pay for her education after that.

'Tell your mother that I am no longer giving her things on credit!' the grocer told a ten-year-old Mallika. 'If she cannot afford to buy rice, she should cook with sawdust!' The crowd gathered at the shop laughed at her loudly.

Mallika ran as fast as she could, tears streaming down her face, the laughter echoing in her head. She hated her life and she hated poverty. She wanted to be rich. She wanted to be able to afford anything she desired. And that thought stuck inside her head. But daydreams don't fill an empty stomach. As she grew up, she worked as a maid to make ends meet. But somehow she knew that she would one day wear the best of saris and deck up in gold jewellery just like her mistresses.

Soon, Mallika was married off to Devraj, who worked as a tailor at the National Institute of Mental Health and Neurosciences (NIMHANS), Bengaluru. It seemed Mallika went from the frying pan of poverty at home into the fire of 'barely making ends meet' at her husband's home. She was ambitious and her craving for a better life started gnawing at her. Greed made her steal things from the houses that she worked in as a maid.

Mallika used to travel to neighbouring suburbs and towns to work in various houses. Bidadi was one of them. It is well known for thatte-idli, the bigger and flatter version of the rice cake. But, it was here that Mallika committed her first crime.

* * *

The Bidadi police barged into the house from where they had received a phone call. The inspector found a woman sitting on the floor, her hands tied with a nylon rope, and the rest of the household's members gathered around her.

'What has she done?' the inspector asked.

'We caught her trying to steal some jewellery from the cupboard,' the owner of the house replied.

Mallika was arrested and sentenced to six months in prison.

It is said that prison straightens out the wicked and scares the innocent to never again get tempted by crime. But Mallika was not an ordinary woman. She spent the next six months plotting.

When she was released, she was even more impatient to get rich than before. She launched a chit fund. However, luck was not in Mallika's favour. Her chit fund was busted and she lost money. Devraj, who was a respectable and honest man, had had enough of his wife and her waywardness. He asked her to leave. It seemed like fate was pushing Mallika towards her destiny. And for Devraj, a man of modest, honest means, the severing of ties with the dormant volcano came at the right time.

She left home in 1998 and did odd jobs here and there. Mallika was street-smart enough to not give up and beg on the roads. One of her jobs was assisting a goldsmith. And it was there that she found the inspiration to launch her new career.

* * *

'One drop can kill a person?' Mallika asked the goldsmith in awe.

'Yes. In a matter of seconds,' the goldsmith replied, as he cleaned some gold ornaments with potassium cyanide.

And that is when the wheels inside Mallika's devious head began to whirr into motion. She realized that in her hand she held the *Brahmasthra* that could lead her to a world of riches and out of her poverty-stricken misery.

She bought some of the potassium cyanide powder from the goldsmith. Though the amount was small, it was enough to kill a village full of people.

'What do you need it for?' the goldsmith asked suspiciously.

'I need to clean some of my own jewellery at home,' Mallika lied confidently.

The goldsmith looked at her for a moment and handed over the powder.

However, Mallika knew that having the weapon was not enough. She roamed around, scouting for targets and realized that there would always be eyewitnesses and people would not interact with her willingly.

She decided to target only women. She knew many women always wore gold; they were softer targets than men (whom she would not be able to overpower). Mallika knew that she needed to target emotionally fragile women who would easily trust her. She thought about it for a while—where could she find women at their most vulnerable? A temple! Everybody who visits a temple drops their guard as it is considered to be a holy place, where god protects them. And this is the same belief that Mallika would use to her advantage. Her targets would be vulnerable women, who appeared distressed and were visiting the temples seeking divine intervention to solve their personal woes or marital problems.

Mallika recced a nearby temple. She sat and watched the women come and go, dressed in their finery. Her eyes were trained on the ones who looked sad.

And that is how her first victim, Mamatha Rajan, was netted on 19 October 1999.

Sympathy + role play + cyanide = death + jewellery

But after Mamatha, Mallika continued doing odd jobs, probably spooked and scared like a first-time murderer. Soon, eight years passed by. She woke up from her slumber in 2007.

* * *

Elizabeth (fifty-two) was from Banaswadi. Her granddaughter had gone missing a few weeks ago. Endless searches had proved to be futile. She had visited churches and prayed earnestly, begging God for a miracle. But nothing happened. That is when somebody told her about the famous Kabbalamma temple in Kabbal village in Ramanagara district.

The white Kabbalamma temple is set against the backdrop of a huge stone hill. If you see pictures of it, then you will realize that the hill looks very familiar. It is the same kind of terrain in which *Sholay* was filmed, in this very district of Ramanagara.

At this temple, goddess Shakti is worshipped as goddess Kabbalamma. The story goes that the cliff behind the temple was used by British soldiers to throw off native convicts as punishment and also to set an example for the others to never go against the Crown. All the people who were thrown off died gruesome and painful deaths. But one of the men prayed to goddess Kabbalamma, promising her that if he survived, then he would present her with a golden tiara. Miraculously, he did survive. The man gifted the goddess with the most magnificent tiara.

Over the years, the temple became famous, a go-to place for people in distress and looking for solutions.

Mallika could not have asked for a better venue.

Elizabeth arrived at the temple with hope in her heart and a prayer on her lips. She could not bear the thought of her beautiful granddaughter being lost, lonely or . . . No, she didn't want to think that she was dead. Elizabeth was willing to walk till the end of the earth to find her.

In a cruel twist of fate, Elizabeth's woes would be rewarded not with deliverance, but with death. Mallika had been watching her for a while. As Elizabeth finished her prayers and wiped away her tears, Mallika walked up to her and asked: 'Are you okay?'

Elizabeth looked at her and smiled sadly. 'Yes, I am fine.'

Mallika immediately said, 'If you were fine, then you would not be here, crying like this. Tell me, I might be able to help you out.'

Elizabeth narrated her story. Mallika latched on to her immediately. She said, 'I know a very special puja that will help you get back your granddaughter. It is called mandala puja.'

Elizabeth could not believe what she was hearing. 'Really? You are indeed a godsend. I hadn't believed a word when people had told me about this temple and the miracles goddess Kabbalamma performs. But I prayed, and see, Kabbalamma sent you to me.' Tears flooded down Elizabeth's cheeks.

'But you must follow everything I say. Are you willing to do that?' Mallika asked.

'I am willing to do anything to get my child back,' Elizabeth replied.

The game was afoot.

'We will meet here tomorrow at dusk. I have the power to conduct the special puja, which will tide you over,' Mallika was laying it on thick and fast. Seeing that she had Elizabeth's attention, she continued, 'And this has been taught to me by a special priest. As it is a religious ritual, you must wear your finest clothes and jewellery or else the goddess will get upset. And you must not tell anyone about this secret ritual or else the puja will not work.'

The next afternoon, Mallika went and bought a box of Mysore pak, a sweetmeat, and laced one of the sweets in the box with potassium cyanide. She then broke off one corner of the sweet to mark it. At dusk, when she arrived at the temple, the crowds had already begun thinning. She spotted Elizabeth standing nearby in a beautiful sari. Mallika escorted her to a deserted corner of the huge temple complex.

'You are looking beautiful,' Mallika complimented, 'but is that all the jewellery you have?'

Mallika's sharp eyes had already scanned the goods on display and she was disappointed. Elizabeth had two gold bangles, a pair of flimsy gold earrings and a thin gold chain around her neck.

'I have most of my jewellery back home. I have been travelling for the past one week, visiting temples and shrines and, therefore, did not carry anything valuable with me.'

Elizabeth looked crestfallen. She continued, 'Maybe this puja will not work. Maybe the goddess will not grant my wish as I am not dressed properly.' Saying this, she started getting up.

Mallika panicked. It was as if she had the prey in the crosshairs of her gun, but it was moving away. She reoriented her gun, so to speak, and aimed again.

'Not at all, the goddess is pleased with you. She says that we should begin the puja immediately.' Saying this, Mallika pulled out some small brass utensils from her handbag, along with sandalwood paste and red kumkum powder.

Mallika murmured some made-up mantras and incantations and smeared the powder and sandalwood paste on Elizabeth's forehead. With each passing minute of the puja, Elizabeth's heart soared. From the depths of despair, hope arose, slowly floating up to the surface to breathe again.

'The puja is over,' Mallika suddenly declared. 'It is time to have the prasad now.' Saying this, she opened the box of Mysore pak and froze. She distinctly remembered chipping off the corner of one of the sweets; however, now there were two sweets with broken corners. She was in a dilemma. With the help of a spoon, she scooped out one of the sweets and offered it to Elizabeth, who took it in her hand, touched it to her forehead, and bit into it.

Every passing second was filled with anticipation and agony for Mallika. Elizabeth watched Mallika staring at her. It was the wrong one.

'Is anything wrong?' Elizabeth asked.

Regaining her composure, Mallika replied, 'No, nothing. Err . . . you must have one more sweet.' Saying this, Mallika scooped up the second sweet with the broken corner and offered it to her prey. Elizabeth had barely managed to finish the first one.

'I cannot have any more. I have sugar. The doctor has told me not to eat too many sweet things,' Elizabeth said, as she got up to leave. Mallika could not believe what was happening.

'You have to eat it!' Mallika said sternly. Elizabeth was taken aback at the change of tone in her benefactor's voice. Something clicked inside Mallika's head. She got up, saying she had to leave urgently. Seeing this, Elizabeth got worried—had she offended this kind woman who had promised to help her find her granddaughter?

'I'll eat the sweet,' Elizabeth said. Mallika turned around. And within seconds, Elizabeth's body was racked in spasms as it fought for oxygen. Mallika watched Elizabeth choke to death.

She removed all the jewellery from Elizabeth's body and melted into the night.

* * *

Exactly a month later, in December 2007, Mallika was loitering outside a government hospital in Yelahanka. A hospital is one of the most depressing places to visit, second only to a morgue. No one comes out of a hospital with a smile. The joys of recovery are obliterated by the memories of the bill paid.

Sixty-year-old Yashodhamma was a chronic asthma patient. She had hocked, wheezed and coughed for most of her life. At this age, her lungs were gasping like a runner who was nearing the end of a marathon. Savings were constantly being pumped in to keep her retired husband and her healthy and fed. As she stepped out of the hospital after her check-up, she wheezed in the polluted air. The nebulizer at the hospital had managed to give her temporary relief. She slowly walked to the bus stand and waited.

A woman sat beside her.

'I saw you coming out of the hospital. I hope everything is fine,' the stranger asked gently.

Yashodhamma replied, 'I have not been well. Asthma is killing me.'

Mallika thought for a bit as she cooked a story in her head. 'I had an uncle who suffered from asthma. But he was lucky. He got fully cured and lived up to the ripe old age of seventy-eight.' She paused to see the effect her story was having on Yashodhamma.

'Fully cured, you say? But how? I have had this for more than thirty years and I am unable to get rid of it.'

Mallika smiled. '*Ajji* [grandmother], he wasn't cured by all these nonsense modern tablets and capsules. He had experienced a miracle!' She was slowly reeling in the catch.

'Miracle? What nonsense! What was it?' Yashodhamma was a believer in doctors and modern medicine, even though both had failed to cure her ailment. However, she was curious.

'If you are not going to believe it, then why should I waste my breath telling you all about it.' Mallika pretended to be hurt and sulking.

'Don't be offended by an old woman's rant. Come. Tell me the details.' Yashodhamma was suddenly all ears.

'Have you heard about the famous Siddaganga *Mutt* [temple/ashram] in Tumkur?' Mallika asked.

'Yes, of course. What about the Mutt?' Yashodhamma had been impaled on the line.

'It is said that the holy water that is in the temple has the power to heal illnesses. My uncle went there, drank the water and got cured.'[2]

'I can take you there, if you want,' said Mallika, tempting Yashodhamma. 'We can stay there overnight and do a special puja. You can drink the water and we can come back the next day.'

'Why would you want to help an old woman like me?' Yashodhamma asked suspiciously.

'Because I don't want you to miss out on this miracle cure. I am like your granddaughter. Can't a granddaughter think about the welfare of her ajji?' Mallika was on a roll.

And so the duo made the one-and-a-half-hour journey to the Mutt in Tumkur. There, Mallika rented a room in a guest house for Rs 20. She waited for the darkness of the night to envelop the Mutt before uncovering her evil intentions.

'It is time to get dressed for the ceremony,' Mallika informed Yashodhamma. 'Wear all the jewellery that you have brought with you. It is an auspicious occasion.'

Yashodhamma's breathing seemed to have got better; the wheezing was nearly gone. 'I am feeling better already!' she declared.

Mallika smiled. 'I told you, Ajji! It is your faith. Faith can move mountains, and you merely have asthma!'

Poor Yashodhamma dressed up and wore all the jewellery that she had carried from her home. Mallika went out and returned with a plastic bottle of water. 'Are you ready to be cured?' Yashodhamma nodded. 'I will conduct a prayer and then I will make you drink this holy water. You will feel the change immediately. You will be free from your breathing problems.' Little did Yashodhamma know that far from holy water, it was just tap water spiked with the harbinger of death—potassium cyanide.

Yashodhamma and Mallika sat on the floor, facing each other with their hands folded in prayer. Mallika went about her usual charade of mumbling gibberish, swaying now and then for effect, and asked Yashodhamma to close her eyes. As soon as she closed her eyes, Mallika slowly opened the bottle. While uttering gibberish under her breath, she came close to Yashodhamma. She gathered a fistful of Yashodhamma's loose hair, like a jockey grips the rein of a horse, and with a sudden, swift movement, yanked it back. Yashodhamma's eyes flew open in shock and her mouth opened to scream. Mallika immediately poured the water down her throat.[3] Thinking it was the holy water, Yashodhamma gulped it down in gratitude. Within seconds, the poison started taking effect. As her body fought to absorb oxygen, Yashodhamma thought it was the miracle transforming her body. She didn't fight it for the first few seconds. But that was all the time the poison needed to possess her. Her body thrashed. Her vision became blurry as she choked.

Mallika kept her promise and Yashodhamma was finally cured of asthma.

Five days later, Mallika set sixty-year-old Muniyamma's soul free. Muniyamma lived in Chikka Bommasandra in Yelahanka. A god-fearing woman, she wished to sing devotional songs. Mallika seized the opportunity and told her that she knew the very difficult mandala puja, which would please the gods and fulfil Muniyamma's wish.

On 15 December, Mallika took her prey to the Yediyur Siddheshwara Swamy temple, located 95 km away at Yediyur. The temple has rooms for devotees to stay in. Mallika paid for a room, signed in the hotel register under the alias 'Lakshmi' and was allotted room no. 28 in the Parvathi block of the temple.[4]

At 12.30 in the afternoon, Mallika stuffed the cyanide into Muniyamma's mouth while she was praying with her eyes closed. Mallika removed the gold chain, the ring from her finger, her gold earrings and stole her mobile phone. Then she left the room after locking it from outside.

This was a master stroke in Mallika's modus operandi. She always lured the victim far away from her home, so they could not be identified in a short time, which would give her enough time to sell off the jewellery and lay low for a while.

Madhava, the secretary of Siddheshwara Swamy temple, was rudely awakened on 18 December 2007 by Renukaprasad, an engineer who worked in Yediyur, and was visiting the temple.

'Sir, there is a foul smell coming from one of the rooms in Parvathy Block,' Renukaprasad said.

Upon asking Venkatesh, who was in charge of signing in the guests before handing them their room keys, Madhava found out that room no. 28 was occupied by a woman called Lakshmi from Pandavapura for the past three days.

'Where is the room key?' Madhava demanded.

'Sir, it is with the guest. The room is locked from outside,' Venkatesh replied.

The moment Madhava went in front of the room, a putrid smell hit him, making him almost gag.

When the police arrived and the room was opened with the duplicate key, they saw Muniyamma lying on the floor. Beside her were a coconut, a lemon, a pair of spectacles and a box of sandalwood.

'I want to meet all the people connected to this *choultry*,'[5] the inspector said.

'In whose name is the room booked?' the inspector asked Venkatesh.

'Sir, three days ago, two women, one old and the other young, had arrived here. They claimed to be mother and daughter and told me that they had come here for a day to do a puja,' said Y.R. Kumar, a clerk at the temple, who was quaking in his chappals in front of the cop.

'What did you do?' the inspector asked.

'As per procedure, I issued them a receipt for room no. 28 and told them to go meet Venkatesh and pay the rent and collect their room key.' Never in his life had Kumar thought that he would be embroiled in a murder case.

Venkatesh continued the story. 'At 11.30 a.m., the two women came to meet me. The younger woman had the room receipt from the office. I made them sign the ledger.' He showed it to the inspector.

'Lakshmi? Hmm . . .' the inspector trailed his finger over the signature.

'Sir, she said they were from Pandavapura. She gave me an advance rent of Rs 200, even though our daily rent is only Rs 80. I gave them the key and accompanied them to their allotted room,' Venkatesh continued.

The inspector thought for a minute, scratching the faint stubble on his chin. 'Isn't it strange that the woman told Kumar that they had planned to stay only for the night? And yet she paid three days' rent to Venkatesh?' Along with the fetid odour of the decaying corpse, the inspector smelt a plot brewing.

Meanwhile, Muniyamma's son Anjanappa was worried. It had been three days since his mother had left the house on a pilgrimage. He called up his sister, Anjanamma.

'Are you sure she didn't go alone?' It was news to Anjanappa that a woman had accompanied his mother.

Anjanappa rushed to Amruthur police station.

The police took down the details and asked for a photograph of his mother. 'She is a devoted person. She visits temples regularly. But never before has she not come home for so long,' cried Anjanappa.

A few days later, someone knocked on Anjanappa's door. The Amruthpur police station inspector was at the door. He looked solemn and serious. Anjanappa felt bile rise up to the back of his throat. He felt nauseated.

'Please sit down. I have something to show you,' saying this, the inspector took out a few photos and handed them to Anjanappa.

With a quivering hand, the poor boy held the photographs briefly. His face contorted and he screamed, as the photos fell from his hand.

The inspector looked at the accompanying constable and nodded his head—the identification of the corpse had been done. It was Muniyamma.

Anjanappa picked up the photographs from the floor and looked at them again. This time, his expression changed.

'Sir, my mother was wearing jewellery when she went to the temple. She was wearing a mangalya chain, gold earrings and a large ring. Everything is missing!' Anjanappa said.

'Son, your mother was accompanied by a woman named Lakshmi to the Siddheshwara Swamy temple at Yediyur. There, the woman poisoned her with cyanide. Now the motive is clear: robbery.'

Mallika, of course, had no clue that the law had become aware of her devious modus operandi.

The year wasn't yet over and she was ready for her next hunt.

She met Pilamma, a sixty-year-old priest at the Kempamma temple, who had devoted her life to god and social work.

Mallika befriended her and realized that the only route to Pilamma and her jewellery was through god and service. It had been Pilamma's dream to build a new arch on the temple. Mallika stepped in to support Pilamma's reverential ambition as a kind-hearted, god-fearing benefactor.

'I will sponsor the new arch for the temple,' Mallika said, as she held Pilamma's weathered hands in hers. She assured Pilamma, 'I will perform a special mandala puja that will appease the gods. But for that, we need to go somewhere else.'

This kind-faced, benevolent, soft-spoken woman, who called herself Lakshmi, swept Pilamma off her feet. 'I have always prayed to the gods to help me fulfil my dream, and here you are, a total stranger and yet so kind, who is willing to give so selflessly.' As she said this, tears of gratitude flowed down Pilamma's cheeks. Her heart was filled with happiness.

'But why can't this mandala puja happen here?' Pilamma asked the most logical question. The arch was to be built on this temple, so why not perform the holy rites there itself?

'I need to conduct the puja at the Vaidyanatheshwara temple near Maddur,' Mallika told Pilamma.

The Vaidyanatheshwara temple is located on the banks of the Shimsha river, a tributary of the Kaveri. The ruling deity, Srivaidyanatheshwara, is an incarnation of Shiva, and is in the form of a serpent. It is said that the deity has cured many illnesses and fulfilled many wishes of the devotees.

'He will grant your wish too,' Mallika assured the devout Pilamma.

Mallika took Pilamma to this temple, rented a room in the choultry and helped her meet her maker. She then walked into the night with the jewellery seized from Pilamma.

To recap, between 1999 and 2007, five murders had been reported from six districts of Karnataka: Bangalore City, Tumkur, Bangalore Rural, Kolar, Mysore and Mandya. Of these, two had been registered as murders and three as unnatural deaths.

Mallika had no clue that the police had started joining the dots and were closing in. She prepared for her next kill: Nagaveni.

Thirty-year-old Nagaveni from Hebbal had been married for a while. But her domestic bliss was always fraught because of her inability to bear children. People in her locality constantly whispered behind her back, often calling her *banjaru* (barren). She was desperate to have a child.

Mallika called herself Savithramma and befriended Nagaveni.

'Mandala puja? Is there a guarantee that I will be able to bear a child?' Nagaveni asked. She could see a glimmer of hope finally appearing on the horizon of despair.

'Guaranteed! I have performed this special puja many times and it has always been successful,' Mallika assured her.

'Shall we do this puja at my home?' Nagaveni asked eagerly.

'No. We shall go to the Ghati Subramanya temple in Doddaballapur to perform it.'

The Ghati Subramanya temple is over 600 years old and houses the deities Karthikeya and Narsimha. The temple is renowned for hosting cattle fairs. But what attracts thousands of devotees from across the region is the deities' blessings to fulfil the wishes of childless couples.

And so Mallika took Nagaveni to the temple in the early hours of the morning. In the darkness of the breaking dawn, Mallika killed her by making her drink cyanide-laced water. She kept her promise to Nagaveni. She could no longer hear anyone call her barren.

When Nagaveni's body was discovered in Doddaballapura on 18 December 2007, it was inspector S.K. Umesh from the Kalasipalyam police station who realized that the temple murders were connected.

K.V. Sharath Chandra, then deputy commissioner of police (DCP) in 2007, was interviewed by Ashwaq Masoodi of *Mint* regarding these murders on 14 October 2016. Chandra, now the additional commissioner of police (crime), Bengaluru City, recalled how the police had started joining the dots.

'First, we analysed the murders. All were happening in temples. We found out the days of the week when the murders happened, the profile of those visiting the temple, the rooms taken for rent, the neighbours.'[6] He recalled how the teams began retracing the last footsteps and the movements of the victims.

'We contacted the families of all the victims to find out whom did the women befriend in the period they had come to the temple [. . .] who accompanied the women to the temple.'[7]

Previously, the police had been expecting the murderer to be a burly man with a criminal background. But once they joined the dots, what shocked them was the fact that all the victims had met a woman before being found dead. It was not easy for the police to comprehend and digest the fact that they might be dealing with India's first female serial killer.[8]

The police started searching and trawling through the cellphone records of all the victims. But nothing concrete emerged. New Year was around the corner and the police were eager to end this gruesome saga. With the murders on the news, strict warnings were issued to jewellers to alert the police if somebody tried to sell them stolen goods. Mallika was in a fix. She had the goods but couldn't get rid of them. The police had cut off her income.

In the next twenty-five days, the police team spread their dragnet and there were multiple near misses. They were so close to catching her and yet . . .

On 30 December, the Kalasipalyam police received a tip-off. A woman had been sighted at a bus stand, trying to sell used cell phones.

When they reached the bus stand, Umesh and his team found a woman, around forty-five years old, trying to sell two mobile phones to bystanders. The police team compared her to the sketch that they had drawn up from eyewitness accounts. The faces matched. It was now time for a takedown.

As soon as Mallika saw the police swooping down on her, she realized that her game was over. She tried to run but was cornered. A crowd gathered at the scene of the arrest.

'We need to get her out of here before the mob realizes who she is,' Umesh whispered to his team. They quickly spun into action and in no time had left the clueless mob behind.

When the police took her into custody, they found a cross, two cell phones, a keychain belonging to room no. 28 of the Siddheshwara Swamy temple, a receipt belonging to a pawnshop, one Godrej key and two SIM cards. During interrogation, Mallika narrated her journey from being a poor girl to the cyanide killer. The police gave her the moniker 'Cyanide Mallika'. For the world, the name K.D. Kempamma disappeared forever.

The police could not believe that a woman could so ruthlessly and cold-bloodedly murder six innocent women. Soon afterwards, Mallika's trial began. The charge sheet was filed for the murder of Muniyamma. The police finally got a definitive glimpse into Mallika's mind and her modus operandi in detail.

As many as thirty-nine witnesses were examined during the trial and each person helped to hammer the nails into Mallika's coffin.

One of the first people who took the stand was Anjanappa. Mallika did not know that Muniyamma had told him about her and the puja.

He said that his mother had befriended a woman called Lakshmi and had gone with her. The police, of course, had known her to be either Mallika or Lakshmi. But Mallika's lawyer argued that Lakshmi and Kempamma were two different people and that his client was innocent as her real name was Kempamma!

The ledger from the hotel was produced in which Mallika had signed. The signature did not match Mallika's real signature. The lawyer argued again about how his client was not present at the hotel and that she had not signed in the book.

The lawyer further pointed out that there was a discrepancy in the number of items found in the possession of his client when she was arrested at the Kalasipalyam bus stand. He also claimed that the police had 'created' the documents and articles in order to suit the purpose of the prosecution.

It seemed Mallika had hired a brilliant lawyer. However, the state public prosecutor pointed out that when Mallika was arrested on 30 December 2007, amongst the articles found in her possession was the keychain of room no. 28 of the Parvathi block of the Siddheshwara Swamy temple. The police had also recovered a receipt issued by Mangalram Bankers, which mentioned the jewellery items that she had pawned.

Mallika had hoped that some pieces of the puzzle that she had created would go missing and save her neck. But that wasn't to be.

Bheram Chowdhary, who ran a pawn-broking shop called Mangalram Bankers, in the Kengeri Satellite Town area was called in to testify. He identified the receipt and said that on 15 December 2007, the woman standing in the dock had come to his shop and pawned one pair of earrings, which weighed 6 gm, for Rs 3000.

When the jewellery items were recovered, Muniyamma's son, Anjanappa identified them to be his mother's—the same ones that he had found missing in the photographs of his mother's body.

During the trial, Kumar and Venkatesh also testified and identified her.

But the drama wasn't yet over. Mallika had been arrested for the alleged murder of six women. That's what the police had unearthed so far. But then, a seventh victim emerged.

Seeing the reports on TV and hearing about her arrest, other police stations started comparing notes and that is when the story of Renuka emerged.

In December 2006, Mallika was working as a cook in the same house where Mani, a maid, worked. They became friends and Mallika started visiting Mani's house, where she met her sister, Renuka. She had been pining to have a son—a male child, the patriarchal, misogynistic cynosure of all Indian families. Mallika seized the opportunity and told Renuka about the mandala puja and how it would help her give birth to a male heir. And so on 7 December, she took Renuka to a temple in Kolar district to perform the puja. They checked into the temple dormitory. And predictably, Renuka fell for the scheme and soon found herself to be rather still and very much dead.

The Chintamani police registered a case when they found a woman's body at the Kaiwara Yogi Narayan Ashram guest house in Kolar. But the case was closed, as they could not find any leads.

Meanwhile, Renuka's husband, Shankar, returned from Dubai and found his wife missing and promptly reported it to the Mico Layout police station on 29 December 2006. Just when it seemed Renuka would never get justice, Mallika's arrest made headlines, and the tide turned. Her face was flashed continuously by news channels, and that is when the guest house authorities recognized Mallika and reported back to the police. Mallika had used the name of Jayamma in the guest house register. She had been the one who had checked into the Kaiwara Yogi Narayan Ashram guest house with Renuka.

And then, five more cases of missing persons were associated with Mallika. Two of the five bodies were found and subsequently linked to her. It seemed that the closet was hell-bent on spitting out all the skeletons to nail India's first woman serial killer.

Under Section 302[9] of the Indian Penal Code (IPC), Mallika alias K.D. Kempamma alias Lakshmi alias Shivamoga alias Jayamma was awarded the death sentence.[10] On 31 March 2012, the first additional rural court in Bangalore awarded the death sentence in the case of Nagaveni.[11] In August 2012, the death sentence was commuted to life.[12]

But wait, there is still some masala left in this story.

In 2014, when Jayalalitha was arrested and lodged in Bengaluru's Parappana Agraharaa Central Jail, Mallika, who is a self-confessed fan and was lodged in the same jail, had requested for a meeting with her idol. But that didn't happen.

In 2017 when Sasikala was arrested and housed in the same prison, Mallika was overjoyed to find that she was her next-cell neighbour. This created massive headlines and unconfirmed news reports mentioned that in one instance, Mallika even stood in line for food and brought it to Sasikala, as she did not want her to stand in queue like an ordinary criminal.[13]

Soon afterwards, Mallika was secretly and swiftly transferred to Hindalga prison in Belagavi, reportedly for posing a threat to the politician's life.

There, you have it. The story of an everyday, ordinary woman who will forever be known all over the world as India's first woman serial killer.

THUG BEHRAM

THE WORLD'S MOST DANGEROUS SERIAL KILLER

'The cunningest robbers in the world are in that country.
They use a certain slip with a running-noose, which they
can cast with so much slight about a man's neck, when they
are within reach of him, that they never fail; so that they
strangle him in a trice.'[1]

—Jean de Thévenot

The caravan moved silently through the night. The clanging of the bells around the necks of the bullocks pulling the canopied carts was the only sound that could be heard. Around fifteen men and women were travelling to a nearby village to attend a wedding. Fatigue was clawing at their bodies. They had been on the road for the past eight hours. But the men in the group knew that they had to be alert. They had planned to leave their village at dawn so they could travel by daylight. Unfortunately, the village headman's wife had fallen down the steps of the ghat leading down to the river. There had been much hullabaloo. The vaid (doctor) had come and administered a *laip* (ointment) of some sorts and bandaged her injured hands and legs.

'Should we not go for Bhushan's wedding?' one of the villagers had asked the headman.

'No, it will look bad if none of us go to represent our village at the wedding,' the headman had replied. 'You people go ahead. I'll stay behind to look after Sushma. Do apologize for my absence to Bhushan and his family,' he had added.

That is how the wedding party ended up leaving their village much later than they had planned to. They soon lost the comfort and solace of daylight, only to be enveloped by the swallowing darkness around them.

'How much farther do we need to travel to reach the village?' one of the men asked. He was on the driver's seat of the second bullock cart.

'*Aur dus kos*,'[2] replied an old man, the senior-most person in the group. Beside each cart, men walked with fire torches. The light cast ghostly shadows on the forest.

The cry of a jackal sliced through the night. The animal was nearby. The men grew alert, lifting their torches to see if they could spot the wild animal.

Suddenly, the leader of the caravan halted his cart and put up his hand, signalling the others to do the same.

'Men, arm yourselves!' he yelled.

Two of the seven men in the party pulled out daggers from their cummerbunds. They were carrying these to protect themselves, having heard about a dangerous group of dacoits prowling in the area.

But what they saw instead was one of the victims.

In the middle of the road lay a man who was groaning in pain. The caravans halted as the men approached the man.

'They left me for dead. They robbed me of everything. Water! Please give me some water!' The man looked injured and his forehead was bloody.

The men helped him lean against the wheel of one of the carts. After drinking his fill, he narrated his story.

His name was Sukhram and he had been travelling with his wife. They were headed to a nearby village. He was poor and hence travelling by foot. A gang of dacoits pounced on him, looting everything, including his wife. At this point, he broke down. The travellers were shocked.

One of the them gathered his courage and asked, 'Was it him?'

Sukhram looked up and whispered, as if he were too afraid to even say the name out loud, 'Yes, it was him. Thug Behram!' At the mention of the name, a shudder ran through the crowd. The women inside the caravan who had been eavesdropping began crying.

Behram was notorious for running a large band of bloodthirsty dacoits. Fear and Behram went hand in hand, piercing the heart of every man and woman who lived in the area.

'How did you manage to live? He kills everyone!' a young man asked.

Sukhram got up slowly and said, 'How can Behram kill his own self?'

He let out the scream of a jackal as he said this, and out of the dark forest, some fierce-looking men appeared. They were bearded and red-eyed, wearing turbans. With a blood-curdling cry, they lunged at the travellers, who were no match for the dacoits. Within minutes, a hush fell upon the caravans. Men, women and children, no one was spared. But there was not a single drop of blood spilt. All the travellers were garroted to death.

The gang dug graves and dumped the bodies after robbing them. Two dacoits held each body by its arms and legs and swung it into the pit. The bodies landed unceremoniously on top of each other. With their arms and legs splayed in different angles, they formed a macabre tableau of dancers frozen mid-pose. Their eyes wide open; their faces embodying their last efforts to gasp for air.

This was Thug Behram, the most dreaded serial killer in the world. A man who would go on to acquire 931 kills under his belt. And this is his story.

* * *

What do modern-day memes, '90s American hip-hop, the British Raj and a ruthless gang of dacoits who killed a million people in fourteenth-century India, have in common?

The word 'thug'.

Let's rewind. Time for a lesson.

Present day: Memes of 'thug life' are common these days on social media. They describe someone who is defiant or describe a person undertaking a deed that's extraordinarily brave.

Rewind.

Early '90s: This phenomenon was an extension to the term 'thug life' coined by none other than Tupac Shakur in America in the early '90s. It was used to describe people who had nothing but overcame all obstacles to reach their goals. Don't believe me? You can watch this clip here of Tupac saying it: https://bit.ly/2QCR3w0.

Rewind.

Early '30s: Americans started using the word thug because of its appearance in Hollywood movies to describe a criminal or an unruly person. And Hollywood borrowed it from—

Rewind.

Eighteenth century: The Oxford dictionary absorbed the word from Hindi, amongst the many words that travelled back to England during the British Raj and became a part of the British English lexicon. Words like pucca, veranda, dinghy, pyjama, chit, dekko, to name a few. Thug was originally taken from—

Rewind.

Sixteenth century: The Sanskrit word '*thag*' or '*sthaga*' meant a sly, fraudulent person, and the word 'thugee' was used to describe a bloodthirsty gang of dacoits who killed a million people across two centuries in ancient India.

And thag or Thug Behram was their undisputed king.

So there you have it, memes meet American hip-hop meets Hollywood meets British swiping words from India (*along with the Kohinoor and vast amounts of riches*) meets eighteenth-century band of dacoits meets ancient Sanskrit!

How old are the thuggees?

According to author and editor Vincent A. Smith, the earliest historical mention of thuggees appear to be in the royal court documents of Firoz Shah Tughlak (1351–88). During his reign, about a thousand thugs were arrested in Delhi on the denunciation of an informer. The sultan, with misplaced clemency, refused to sanction the execution of any of the prisoners, whom he shipped off to Lakhnauti or Gaur in Bengal, where they were let loose. That absurd proceeding may well have been the origin of the band of thuggees who only operated along the rivers of Bengal.[3]

The thuggees continued to terrorize people during Akbar's reign. And in the year 1666, towards the end of Shah Jahan's rule, the traveller Jean de Thévenot noted that the road between Delhi and Agra was infested by thugs. He said, 'The cunningest robbers in the world are in that country. They use a certain slip with a running-noose, which they can cast with so much slight about a man's neck, when they are within reach of him, that they never fail; so that they strangle him in a trice.'[4]

* * *

It was 1765 and Behram came into the world like all of us—innocent, wide-eyed and crying.

The village where he was born was a few miles from modern-day Jabalpur in Madhya Pradesh. Little did his proud parents know that their son would one day be a murderer, claiming over nine hundred lives.

Some accounts describe Behram as a quiet, contemplative child, seemingly normal. But things were about to change. At the age of twenty-two, Behram bumped into a fair, good-looking boy in the village.

'*Tor naam ka hai?* [What is your name?]' he asked Behram.

'Behram. *Aur tohar?* [And yours?]' he asked.

'Firangee.' And that's how Behram met Syed Amir Ali alias Firangee. Their friendship lasted over fifty years, only to break when one betrayed the other.

It was Firangee who introduced Behram to the powerful men feared by the villagers. There are no known accounts of whether Firangee himself was part of the thuggee cult before he met Behram. But he went on to become Behram's lieutenant.

It was around 1780. In the dead of night, a group of forty burly, dangerous-looking men formed a circle in the middle of a forest. They were standing in front of an ancient idol of goddess Kali. She looked down on them with wrath in her eyes. In the centre of the circle stood Behram. He was about twenty-five years old.

The ustad or sardar placed his hand on Behram's head and said, 'They [the British imperialists] call us thugs. But we are far from that. We kill only for her.' He bowed his head in obeisance to the goddess. 'She thirsts for blood and we are her children. Should a son not fulfil the thirst of his mother? We were born of her sweat when she battled demon Raktabij. And if we don't give her blood, she will destroy mankind!' There was pin-drop silence in the group.

'Before we accept you, there is a test you must pass. Are you ready?'

Behram nodded, a little unsure. The ustad signalled to one of his men who ran off into the darkness. Seconds later, Behram heard a man screaming. Out of the dark forest, the thug dragged out a young man whose hands were tied. He was pushed on to the ground at Behram's feet, who noticed that the man was about the same age as him.

Sensing what was about to happen to him, the young man made an attempt to run. The ustad caught him and screamed, 'Sit! You have been chosen as the special one who will sacrifice his life for Ma!' His deafening growl made the man whimper. The ustad now took out a new yellow *rumaal* (handkerchief) and handed it to Behram.

Behram's hands shook. The ustad held them and steadied them.

'Do it for Ma. She craves blood. And we are her children!' he encouraged Behram, trying to dispel any doubts that he might have about the morality of what he was being commanded to do.

Behram stepped forward, holding the rumaal in his hands. He moved behind the cowering man, who was pleading for his life, crying, 'What have I done? Please, please, don't kill me! I beg you!'

Behram tied the rumaal around the man's throat and slowly tightened it, cutting off the air entering his windpipe. Two other thugs held the struggling man's feet. The group started chanting the name of the goddess. As the rhythmic chanting grew louder, Behram felt himself entering into a trance-like state. The world around him melted into the darkness. It was him, the offering and the mother goddess. A door in Behram's mind was unlocked that would never shut again. The grip tightened. The man thrashed, his voice a gurgle, his eyes bulging. His soul craved release while his body begged for air. The thrashing grew wilder. And then there was silence. Behram had garroted his first victim. There was an uproar as sweat dribbled off his forehead. He stood up. His hands were not shaking any more. They were rock steady. As Behram pulled the rumaal away, the man's limp body collapsed.

The ustad came forward and hugged Behram, 'The first one is always the most difficult. Now Ma will give you the strength to carry on.'

With this, the ustad pulled out a dagger and ran the sharp blade over his right thumb. Immediately, a crimson line of blood trickled down the side of his palm. With the blood of his thumb, he drew a tilak on Behram's forehead. 'Give me your right hand,' he commanded. Behram held out his right hand. With the same, sharp dagger, the ustad drew a line across Behram's palm, as if drawing the new lifeline that he was to follow. With his bloody hand, Behram bent down before the goddess and touched her feet. He asked for her blessing as he swore to become her follower, foot soldier and faithful son. Thereby, the Seeker of Blood blessed the Messenger of Death. Thug Behram was born.

There was a roar of approval from the gang. Behram was now their brother.

Before every skirmish, the thuggees always performed a puja for Kali. They would place their tools of destruction— the noose, knives, and pickaxe—before the goddess, along with offerings of flowers, fruits and alcohol. Then a sheep would be sacrificed. It would be presented to the goddess with a burning lamp on its head and its right forefoot in its mouth.[5, 6]

The thuggees were a superstitious lot, who held pagan beliefs and often relied on nature for omens to determine whether their skirmish would be successful or not. The favourable signs included: the clicking of a lizard, a crow cawing on the left side of a tree and the appearance of a tiger. The noise of a partridge on the right side of the road that they were travelling on would mean they would grab a good booty on that very spot. Unfavourable signs included a hare or a snake crossing the road before them, or even a crow cawing on a rock or a dead tree. Or an owl screeching. Or even a single jackal howling. If a dog managed to carry away the head of the sacrificial sheep, it would be considered a bad omen and would signal that they would get no booty for many years to come.[7]

The thuggees became an organized, professional gang of robbers and murderers. Their origins have been traced to seven breakaway Muslim tribes. But they soon expanded to include Hindus as well. Their common love for goddess Kali brought them together. It was a secret cult. Membership often passed on from one generation to the next. For 600 years, this band of highway dacoits made India quake in its shoes. More importantly, they kept the British imperialists in check and at bay. The Indians supported the thuggees, as they often took down British officers and soldiers. It was this group of repeatedly humiliated Britishers that coined the word 'thug' to denounce these bandits as criminals. They were also referred to as '*phansigar*s' or stranglers in central India. In the southern states, they were called '*Ari Tulucar*' or Muslim stranglers in Tamil Nadu and '*Warlu Wahndlu*' or '*Warlu Vayshay Wahndlu*' (people who use the noose) in Telugu.[8]

According to colonial sources, the thugs themselves believed that they played a positive role in saving human lives. They believed that without their 'sacred service', the goddess would destroy all mankind.

Behram had proven to be a worthy son of goddess Kali. He soon became he who must not be named. His only problem was, 'We take too much time and effort to kill. And what if the person is stronger than one of us?'

Firangee asked, 'What do you mean too much time and effort?'

Behram looked at his lieutenant and said, 'What if I told you I can kill a person in less than ten seconds?'

'Impossible! It takes at least a minute to kill and three of us to hold the person down,' Firangee replied.

That is when Behram showed him something that would make him go down in the record books as the 'world's most dangerous serial killer'.

'I've been working on something,' he said, taking out the yellow handkerchief. As he opened it, Firangee noticed a coin sewn in the middle of the cloth.

'What is that coin doing there?' Firangee asked.

'That is my weapon!' Behram revealed. 'When you put the rumaal around their necks, the coin presses down on the Adam's apple and makes it easier to block off the air. It kills them instantaneously.'

Behram became an expert at 'casting' the rumaal quickly and accurately so it landed on the Adam's apple and in a swift move, extinguished people's lives.

Today, the infamous rumaal can be seen online, preserved in the private museum of an unknown collector.

What the world knows as a 'coin' was in fact a medallion. The medallion was mistaken to be a coin as it had a figurehead on one side. But this was not of any royalty or emperor, but that of the Italian painter Antonio Canova. And on the other side was the image of his famous painting, *Three Graces*.

After Behram's arrest, the British would christen it as the 'Canova medallion'.

These thugs were not only operating on land, but on water as well. As the body count continued to rise, the British administration received a slew of complaints. But they just didn't know where to begin. Entire caravans would disappear, with bodies evaporating into thin air.

* * *

Nasir was one of the young boys who had just been initiated into the gang. His father was a member and he was slowly introduced to the gang over a few months, as per tradition. He had been allowed to watch the killings. First, from a distance, then up close. Today, Behram would be teaching him how to bury the victims. It was a messy affair and not for the faint-hearted.

They had just 'sacrificed' five people—a woman, two traders and two students. A three-foot-deep grave had been dug. Behram looked at the boy and said, 'You have to hold the *cathmi* [knife for cutting the dead body in Ramaseena, a code language that the phansigars used] like this.' He showed him how to grip the knife. Nasir nodded attentively.

Behram took the sharp cathmi and made deep gashes— from under the armpits to the sides of the stomach, stopping at the feet—on both sides of the corpse. They split open the abdomen and divided the tendon at the heels. Blood flowed out, slowly seeping into the soil. Nasir looked at the process frightfully as Behram casually continued. He had done this a hundred times before.

'We carve the body, so it does not bloat up in the graves and push the mud up. That will alert others and, of course, jackals will find them,' Behram continued.

The only creature that Nasir had ever sliced open, dead or alive, were goats before they were cooked. His abbu had taught him to hold the goat firmly and do *zaba* by slicing open the food tract, the windpipe and the two jugular veins in one swift motion.

'This grave is a shallow, small one. A body of this size will not fit into it. So we have to make it fit,' said Behram. He caught hold of the corpse by its knee and kicked the kneecap with all his might. There was a crunching sound that made Nasir gag. As he vomited, the elders laughed. Behram repeated this with the second leg of the corpse, breaking it as well. The body had been reduced in size and they lowered it, face down, into the grave.

Behram and his men buried the rest of the bodies and disappeared into the dark of the night.[9]

* * *

How could a handful of men overpower a huge caravan full of people? And how was it that the travellers did not recognize a dacoit? Initial investigations by Major General Sergeant Leger gives us an insight into how the thuggees operated. They were master infiltrators. To warn travellers, Leger issued orders detailing their modus operandi.

The thugs would somehow always find out about those carrying money or precious cargo. Then, pretending to be fellow travellers, they would meet the victims and travel along with them to gain their trust. Sometimes they kept up their pretence for up to twelve days! And then at the opportune moment they would offer the victims food, tobacco or paan laced with the extract of a plant that would make the travellers sleepy. Once they would fall asleep, the thuggees would strangle them.

> Deleterious substance, commonly known as the seed of a plant called *Duttors*, which they contrive to administer in tobacco, pawn, hookah, food or drink of the traveler. As soon as the poison begins to take effect, by inducing a stupor or languor, they strangle him to prevent him from crying out. After stripping and plundering the victim, they stab him in the belly. This is done on the brink of a well into which they plunge the body so instantaneously that no blood can stain the ground or the clothes of the assassin.

This was the report issued by Leger, in the book on the thuggees called *The Thugs or Phansigars of India* by W.H. Sleeman, first published in 1839. The report also warned soldiers not to accept sweetmeats, hookah and paan from strangers.

Despite all measures, the body count continued to rise as people went missing, turning up after months in wells or shallow graves.

The British government shipped five investigators from England to look into the matter more intricately. However, all of them were killed. But not before they were able to report back to Governor General Francis Rawdon-Hastings about

Thug Behram. They mentioned just his name, which led to one of the biggest manhunts the world has ever seen.

The British wanted Thug Behram at any cost. So they set up the Thug Police, an elite force with no red tape, permissions or mercy. However, there seemed to be no takers for this high-pressure job till it was thrust upon Captain William Henry Sleeman, who was appointed as the superintendent of Thug Police.

Sleeman was one of the most colourful personalities in the British administration. He was single-handedly responsible for putting an end to the thuggee cult. He wrote three books on his experiences in India and survived three assassination attempts. Along with this, a village near Jabalpur, Sleemanabad, was named after him. He also unearthed fragmentary dinosaur fossil specimens in Bara Shimla Hills, thus becoming the earliest discoverer of such fossils in Asia in 1828.

Sleeman had just finished a stint in the Bengal army and was looking forward to some downtime when he was tasked with hunting down Behram. Sleeman wasn't a young man. He was over fifty. However, his enthusiasm made up for what he lacked in age. He was probably the only right person for the job, as we will see.

Behram and Firangee had heard about the gora who had vowed to take them down. As long as Ma Bhavani showered her blessings on them, they knew no one could harm them.

Sleeman was a man on a mission. He hunted down the thugs using undercover agents who lived with the locals and dug out information.

One of the most astonishing things that Sleeman unearthed was that the thugs had their own language and code words. In the book, *The Thugs or Phansigars of India*, Sleeman gives us an insight into Ramaseena or 'Phanseri ki Baat' (the language of the Stranglers).

So a rich man was *nyamet* (delicacy), a poor man was *lakra* (stick) and an old man was dhol.

'*Kantna pantelao* [Bring firewood]' meant to take up your allotted posts.

'*Paan ka rumaal nikalo* [Take out the handkerchief with the betel nut]' meant take out the handkerchief and be ready to strangle.

'*Pan khao* [Eat the betel leaf]' meant kill the person.

'*Kebdi gidbi dekho* [Look after the straw]' meant look after the corpse and bury it properly.[10]

The travellers never suspected anything when their 'new friends' spoke to each other and said, 'Get the firewood,' or 'Take out the handkerchief with the betel nut'—the nut was a euphemism for the coin.

Modern-day Mumbai underworld lingo of '*khoka*' and '*peti*' has probably been inspired by these seventeenth- and eighteenth-century gangs.

Sleeman knew that he would not be relieved or transferred from this post till he had finished the job. So with steely determination, he went about hunting down the thugs. The British Army and the colonial government, who till now had been wetting their diapers at the mention of the thugs, found renewed vigor under Sleeman's leadership. He is said to have brought more than a hundred thugs to the gallows during this tenure. It was payback time for all the humiliation that the goras had faced at the hands of these merciless killers.

Meanwhile, Behram's army grew with his reputation. Thugs from across the country wanted to be a part of his 'A Team'. Behram and Firangee were now leading a gang of over 200 thugs and massacring people by the dozen.

Sleeman was running out of time to prove himself. He laid elaborate traps along the roads, but none could capture Behram and his men.

Under pressure to make the thuggees accountable to the law, Lord William Bentinck issued the Thuggee and Dacoity Suppression Act in 1836. It stated:

> It is hereby enacted, that whoever shall be proved, to have belonged, either before or after the passing of this Act, to any gang of Thugs, either within or without the Territories of the East India Company, shall be punished with imprisonment for life, with hard labor.[11]

This, however, was not enough to scare the thuggees.

* * *

Behram, Firangee and three others had been travelling with a group for four days, pretending to be farmers. They had befriended them near Jabalpur and the group was now heading towards Delhi. The travellers—a rich merchant, his wife, their ten-year-old daughter and their six-month-old son—were sleeping inside a tent, while their four servants were asleep under a tree. Three horses were tied to a post beside the tent. It would have made a picture-perfect postcard, except for the dark, burly men seated around a campfire. They were ready to strike.

'But what about the four servants? What if they attack?' asked Firangee. Behram thought for a moment and said, 'As soon as I give the jhirnee [signal], Abdul and Hassan, release the two horses and make them run. Scream and say the horses have broken free. The servants will get busy trying to catch them; Firangee, Ghubboo Khan and I will perform the sacred task.' Behram looked into the distance where the servants were sleeping.

'Hassan, don't kill the one-armed servant. As per our rules, we do not kill maimed people. Now get ready!' Behram said as he loosened his rumaal.

The jhirnee was given, Abdul and Hassan untied the horses and slapped them hard on their hinds. The alarmed horses neighed and galloped away in panic. The duo screamed to get the servants' attention, who were startled out of their stupor and got busy trying to rein the horses in.

Behram, Firangee and Ghubboo entered the tent and immediately began throttling the merchant, who flailed his arms, hitting a brass jar that fell on the floor with a loud sound, waking up his wife. She screamed, alarmed at the attack and surprised that they had harboured these goons for so long as friends. She instinctively grabbed her infant son and tried to run. Behram threw his rumaal like a lasso from a distance, which snared the woman and reined her in. As he throttled her, the infant gazed at him wide-eyed. Ghubboo grabbed the baby as his mother collapsed and throttled the daughter. A hush fell over the tent except for the cooing of the infant.

Outside, the servants had been killed by Abdul and Hassan.

'Why did you kill the one-armed servant?' Behram yelled. Spittle flew from his mouth on to Hassan's face, as he held him by the collar of his kurta.

'He tried to stab me. I had no choice,' Hassan mumbled.

'You have broken a rule. Ma Bhavani save us!' Behram beseeched, pushing him to the ground. He turned around and yelled at the others, 'What are you watching? Dig the grave!'

A five-foot-deep grave was dug using pickaxes. The joints of the bodies were all broken and then the disfigured corpses were packed unceremoniously inside the pit.

Ghubboo still held the infant. Behram looked at him and matter-of-factly said, 'Throw the baby in.' The infant turned to the source of the sound and gurgled. Ghubboo's grip on the baby tightened. Nobody said anything.

'I want to adopt him,' he said meekly.

Behram glared at Ghubboo and repeated his instruction, louder this time. 'Throw the baby into the grave!' Ghubboo took a last look at the infant and threw him in the grave, amongst the twisted corpses.

'Fill it up quickly and let's move,' Behram barked.

The gang filled up the grave, burying the corpses and the baby alive.

As they started to move, a cry pierced through the stillness of the night, sending a chill down their spines.

'Did you hear that?' Firangee asked. It came again and echoed through the jungle.

'It is the cry of a *duheeaa* [hare]—a bad omen!' Behram said as he stared straight at Hassan.

'Now, only Ma Bhavani can protect us if she wants.'

The goddess had spoken. The end was near.

* * *

It was a rule amongst the thuggees that they would never leave a survivor when they attacked. But on a rare occasion, their heart and loins overrode their code of conduct. In an interview to Sleeman given in 1836, Firangee recounted how he and his men had met a handmaiden of Peshwa Baji Rao who was on her way from Poona to Kanpur. They had intended to kill her and her party, as she was carrying jewels worth a lakh and a half. But on seeing her beauty, Firangee's loins loosened and they all took turns having her for three days. After which they let her and her party leave unharmed. 'We had talked to her and felt love towards her, for she was very beautiful.'[12]

The thuggees had a list of people they never killed. And if they ever made the mistake of killing them, they thought the goddess would curse them. The list included:

1. *Dhobi*s (washermen)
2. *Bhart*s (bards)
3. Sikhs in Bengal
4. *Madari*s and fakirs
5. Dancing men or boys
6. Musicians

7. *Bhungie*s (sweepers)
8. *Teylie*s (oil vendors)
9. *Lohar*s and *Burhey*s, blacksmiths and carpenters, if found together
10. Maimed and leprous people
11. A man with a cow
12. *Brahmachari*s
13. *Kawruttie*s or Ganges water-carriers, when they were carrying the holy water; however, if their pots were empty, then they were not exempted.[13]

* * *

Sleeman went on a rampage. He hunted down the thugs, one group at a time, across India. It took him eleven years to capture Behram. And it was Firangee who led Sleeman to Behram.

A sharp man, Sleeman was able to think like the thugs and outwit them at their own game. He realized that even these hardened criminals had a weak spot. Family.

Firangee was bathing in the river with forty of his men when he heard an uproar. He saw his horse bolt towards the village. Hiding in the riverbank, he watched as a group of soldiers captured members of his gang. Half naked, he ran towards his village, where a surprise awaited him. Sleeman had taken Firangee's mother, his two children and his wife hostage. Sleeman had Firangee by his heartstrings. Firangee surrendered.

Sleeman sat on a wooden chair while Firangee sat on his haunches near his feet.

'So, you are the one who's called Firangee?' Sleeman asked.

'Yes, sahib,' Firangee answered, a shadow of his former macho self. He was broken and battered. He had seen a full life. At seventy, he was tired.

'Where is your leader? The one who's called Behram?' Sleeman wanted his main man.

'I do not know where he is. We got separated four months ago near Jabalpur,' Firangee answered without looking at Sleeman.

Sleeman kicked Firangee on his face. Firangee toppled over, trying to maintain his facade of bravado.

'Do you know what will become of your family?' It was Sleeman who was now garroting Firangee through his words. 'They will hang at the gallows like thugs.'

'Sahib, my family did not know about all this. They are innocent! Please, let them go. My sons are too young to die,' Firangee pleaded. His hands were folded and tears streamed down his cheeks.

'How is it that you murder families and expect sympathy for your own?' Sleeman asked. He could sense the fear in Firangee and now went for the jugular.

'There's only one way we can save your family from the gallows. But for that you need to do something for me,' Sleeman said. He tactfully used the word 'we' to make Firangee feel that Sleeman himself was now on Firangee's side.

A glimmer of hope shone in Firangee's eyes. 'Anything . . . I'll do anything!'

And that is how Sleeman got Firangee to turn approver. First, he asked him to prove that he was one of Behram's men. Firangee took him to some of the mass graves that were made to conceal their victims, where Sleeman twisted his arm further. 'I want Behram Jemedar!'

* * *

There are many versions, urban myths and stories about the lives of famous people. And so it was with the story of Behram's capture. There are two versions that have been put forward by historians. One is staid and simple, the other is dramatic. One can be read for accuracy, the other for entertainment. The latter is obviously a befitting climax to this rogue's life.

Version 1

Firangee told Sleeman about a thug, Ramzan, who could help him track down Behram. Sleeman captured Ramzan, who agreed to turn approver and led Sleeman and his team to Behram.

It was a cold night. Ramzan led eight sepoys to the house where Behram lived and told them to hide. Then he went inside and woke up Behram.

'How did you fall asleep so soon? Age is surely catching up to you!' Ramzan teased Behram. 'Come, let's sit beside the fire and get warm. It has been a while since I met you,' Ramzan coaxed him.

Behram didn't suspect a thing. He went out with Ramzan and sat beside the fire. At that moment, a sepoy came out of the dark. Immediately, Ramzan pointed to Behram and identified him. Behram didn't fight or resist. Maybe he knew that time had run out on him. He confessed immediately, identifying himself as Thug Behram Jemedar. The sepoys took him in.

Version 2

Firangee had informed Sleeman about Behram's regular haunt, the whorehouse. Behram, now seventy-five years old, still had a fire burning in his loins. He had taken a fancy to a whore called Mumtaz. He showered her with gifts and money.

Once when Behram gifted her a gold ring encrusted with a precious stone, she grew suspicious.

'You don't look like a rich merchant or zamindar, yet you've given me this expensive ring. Where did you get it?' she asked as she tried it on. Behram's instincts told him to whip out his rumaal and kill her. But his loins thought differently.

'How does it matter where I got it from? What matters is whom I got it for,' Behram said. He pulled Mumtaz towards him and buried his face in the nape of her neck.

Suddenly Behram heard a hullabaloo in the kotha's ground floor. He knew something was wrong. This didn't sound like an inebriated customer refusing to pay for his sins. Rushing out, he saw a posse of sepoys searching every room of the whorehouse. Behram knew he had mere seconds to flee. He ran towards the rear staircase as fast as his aging legs could carry him. His hard-on had withered and retreated like a tortoise hiding inside its shell.

He reached the rear staircase. This would lead him straight to the stables where he had tied up his horse. He was untying his horse when he heard a man say, 'Behram, where are you running off to?'

Behram turned around slowly. He was surrounded by ten or twelve sepoys whose rifles were pointed at him. Their leader was a white man.

The dreaded Behram Jemedar, king of thugs, was in the net.

'They call *you* the king of thugs?' Sleeman asked, highly relieved. The two ageing warriors—one, the protector of law; the other, the harbinger of death—faced each other. Both of them now stood at a monumental point in their lives, where their paths had converged. Destiny had brought them together finally. And both of them were tired.

'My name is Behram, that's all I know,' Behram said slowly. He felt old and a sense of desolation washed over him. He had always known that he would get caught someday, but had preferred to stay in denial.

'Where is the loot?' Sleeman asked.

Silence. Behram had been sworn to the cult and he wasn't going to say anything. He was flogged, tortured, beaten. But this Persian[14] man was made of solid steel.

'You white-skinned people have robbed this country. Looting, pillaging. Why should I tell you?' Behram said defiantly. He had a black eye and blood dribbled out from the side of his mouth.

'This bastard can surely take a solid flogging but he is not letting any information out,' one of the officers complained to Sleeman, who knew he had to bend the rules, and think rogue to get Behram to talk.

'I know what will make him open his mouth.' Sleeman smiled.

* * *

Behram thought he was dreaming. He could hear his son's voice calling out to him. It had been months since he had held his eldest son, Ali, against his chest.

'Abbu!'

Behram sat up in his cell, rubbing sleep out of his eyes. He looked in front of him and knew he wasn't dreaming.

Just outside his cell stood Ali, crying. Behram's rage erupted.

'*Haraam ka pilla!* [Son of a bitch!]' Behram screamed and rushed at the bars that held him captive and shook them violently.

'*Abbu, mujhe bacha lijiye!* [Father, please save me!]' Ali cried.

Sleeman held Ali by his hair and stepped back from the reach of Behram's outstretched hands. '*Kyun*, Behram? *Ab kya tum sab kuch bataoge ya phir Ali ka bali karna padega?* [Why, Behram? Now will you open your mouth or do we have to sacrifice Ali?]' Sleeman was at his best.

Behram was caught between his oath of loyalty to his cult and the responsibility of a father. He knew that the goras were ruthless and could hurt Ali. Behram decided to turn approver.

'*Main sab kuch bataunga. Lekin Ali ko chodhna padhega* [I will reveal everything, but you must let Ali go],' Behram pleaded, trying to strike a deal.

Behram confessed to have throttled 931 people and witnessed the murder of 956. But James Paton, an East India Company officer working for the Suppression of the Thuggee and Dacoity Office, issued a statement that said: 'Behram confessed to being merely present at 931 cases of murder; and had himself killed 120–50 people.'

Behram's plan worked and Ali was not mistreated, though the threat remained. But the magistrate prevented any sort of movement for Behram, and so Ali became the guide for the English officers. Behram would reveal the locations of the loot and Ali would lead the officers to the swamps and jungles and unearth the treasures.

There is an adage in Hindi, which goes: '*Kutte ki doom kabhi seedhi nahi hoti,*' or a dog's tail can never be straightened. So was the case with the English officers. They remained faithful to their thieving predecessors who had colonized India. The seizures of the loot never arrived at Jabalpur as evidence nor were they ever seen in court as evidence. They disappeared into thin air.

The East India Company officials pocketed the loot.

Behram had been taken for a ride. On the one hand, he had turned approver, on the other, the proof of his loot could not be provided to the court.

Behram got depressed and took an oath of silence. This put the ball back in the court of the EIC officers. How could they hang a King's approver? This was never heard of. But Behram was convicted without a trial and was hung in a private ceremony. His corpse was put on display for the public as an example to dissuade others from joining the thuggee cult.

Historians point out that this could have been a strategy for the British to demystify and deflate the legend around

Behram. But to this day, Behram is officially recognized as the serial killer with the most victims: 931.[15]

Firangee's family was released and he died in prison of old age.

It is estimated that the thuggee cult killed roughly 2 million people. Not all the thugs were caught and, therefore, not all the graves were exhumed. So, the estimated number of victims is just an approximation.

Sleeman was awarded the Order of the Bath for his work and chivalry in 1856. His book about the six true stories of feral children raised by wolves would become the inspiration behind Rudyard Kipling's Mowgli. His books about the thugs and the phansigars of India would become definitive historical testaments to one of the bloodiest cults ever.

Sleeman died on a ship near Ceylon on his way home to Britain. He was buried at sea.

Behram and Sleeman were like two faces of a coin. One killed monstrously and the other brought one of the bloodiest periods of Indian history to an end.

As promised to Behram, the EIC officers did not free Ali. They allowed him to run an Indigo factory at the Vellore cantonment. And every now and then, officers would come and ask him to reveal the whereabouts of more loot, as they were certain that Behram may have told his son about more locations.

According to author Naintara Deshpande, Ali managed to escape from the Vellore cantonment to Hyderabad. He later travelled to Awadh and was reunited with his mother. Ali knew that their lives would always be in danger. And so, he brought his mother and other family members to Nizamabad in Hyderabad, where it is said that Behram's descendants live incognito even today.

During the years 1831–37, 3266 thugs were disposed of one way or another, of whom 412 were hanged and 483 were admitted as approvers.[16]

If you want to see how the thuggees lived, you can do so even in modern India. According to an interview given by Firangee to Sleeman, the former mentioned that in the caves of Ellora, one can see carvings that depict the various operations of the thuggees.

> Every one of the operations is to be seen there: in one place you see men strangling: in another carrying them off to the graves . . . all is done just as if we had ourselves done it; nothing could be more exact.[17]

When Sleeman asked him if the thuggees had done it, Firangee said, 'It could not have been done by the thugs, because they would never have exposed the secrets of their trade; and no other human being could have done it. It must be the work of the gods: human hands could never have performed it.'[18]

* * *

We often wonder what would have happened had we taken a different decision at a certain stage of our lives or if something else had happened. How, then, would our lives have branched out?

On that day in 1765, what if Behram's mother had miscarried or Behram had been a stillborn? Over a thousand people would have lived their lives. Instead, their last sight was that of a big, burly man smiling devilishly while throttling them with a handkerchief.

We have no explanation as to why things happen in life. We are mere spectators—flying rocks in the midst of galaxies.

STONEMAN

INDIA'S MOST ELUSIVE SERIAL KILLER

'We haven't a clue.'[1]

—Rachpal Singh, deputy commissioner,
Calcutta Police

Shonjib tottered and fell on the pavement near Paltan Bazaar in Guwahati, Assam, having drunk copious amounts of cheap country liquor at a den nearby. The bazaar, which was a sea of cacophony and chaos during the day, was now silent and empty like his bottle of liquor.

Whatever he earned as a daily wage labourer seemed to magically evaporate into alcohol fumes every night. But Shonjib was a happy man. There was warmth in his belly and a song on his lips. He lay down on his makeshift bed—a cardboard box split at its ends and taken apart—on the pavement.

'*Junakee poruwa, puhoray puhoray . . . Protibhaa Boruai, okole aaqguwai* [The fireflies shine their light in the dark . . . emboldened by its abilities, and proceeding onwards, all alone],' Shonjib sang as he slowly drifted off to sleep. Little did he know that he was singing his swan song and that these were going to be his final breaths.

Shonjib's body was found in the morning with his head smashed. The weapon, a blood-smeared stone, was lying beside the body.

This was 2009.

The killer struck eleven times in Guwahati.

The corpses and the bloodied stones were enough to fuel nervous rumours across the city. It had been twenty-one years since a similar streak of murders had rung alarm bells in two other cities—Bombay and Calcutta. The fear had been passed on through generations. Each retelling of the heinous murders that had held the two cities captive only grew in prominence and was embedded into the subconscious minds of Indians. There was no escaping the realization that the Stoneman of the '80s was back.

But how was that even possible?

Was it that the serial killer who had tormented the two cities had now chosen Guwahati as his new hunting ground?

Usually, a serial killer hunts within a grid—a designated area in which he/she feels comfortable and is confident enough to find preys. Stoneman seemed to disregard this as he hunted down forty-five people in four different cities over twenty-eight years.

The killer first appeared in Bombay between 1985 and 1987, during which time he murdered twelve people.

There was a hiatus of two years before the killings resumed in 1989 in Calcutta, 2050 km away from Bombay. Here, twelve victims became light-headed (pun intended), and then the killings stopped just as abruptly as they had begun.

In 2010, Guwahati woke up to a series of eleven murders, and just when one thought the killer would now be too old to pick up heavy stones, he struck again. This time, he resurfaced in Kolhapur in 2013, after a gap of three years and over 3000 km away from his previous hunting ground. He killed ten pavement-dwellers before an arrest was made. However, the assailant was deduced to be a young man. He wouldn't even have been born in 1985, let alone kill people.

So where is the original Stoneman? Is he in hiding? Or is he dead? Were there different people in different cities following the same ritualistic sacrificial ceremony? Or were the killers part of a cult that propagated human sacrifice?

How did the killings begin?

* * *

Bombay, 1985

Amitabh Bachchan was ruling the box office with his latest blockbuster, *Sharaabi*, a movie about an alcoholic son who hated his rich father. The film would celebrate its platinum jubilee in a few weeks' time. Reflected against the glamour and sheen of Bollywood were the stark images of the migrants, the homeless and those who thronged the city to realize their dreams.

Soon, Bombay was about to face its worst nightmare.

Around 4 a.m., the shriek of a woman from a pavement near Gandhi Market at King's Circle pierced through the silence of dawn. Pavement-dwellers woke up and rushed towards the source of the sound. A woman was crying hysterically and gasping for breath, as she struggled to control her panic attack. She had woken up to find, just a few feet away from her, a bloody mess—a man's head had been smashed in by a boulder. There were bits of brain splattered on the pavement, while the bloody stone lay nearby. The left foot of the dead man twitched several times before finally coming to a stop.

This was the beginning of an epic run by India's most elusive serial killer. This first incident would be written off as a murder by an unknown assailant; probably a thief who had alerted the sleeping victim and then killed him to escape. After all, it was just a homeless pavement-dweller who was killed. There were too many of them and one death did not matter.

However, another pavement-dweller was found with his head smashed in by a boulder.

And another.

And another!

Till there were five deaths.

The modus operandi was simple. The killer chose his victims from among the pavement-dwellers, especially those who slept alone, far away from a group. The killer would crush the victim's head with a single boulder, weighing as much as 30 kg. In most cases, the victims did not have relatives or associates who could identify them.

It was only after the sixth murder that Bombay Police finally began to see a pattern in the crimes. A common modus operandi and murder weapon tied all the murders together. It was time for the police to suit up and find the killer.

The investigations revealed that the killer was operating within a radius of 5 km, between Sion and King's Circle. The postmortems and the discoveries of the corpses led to the conclusion that the killer hunted between 11 p.m. and 4 a.m. There were no eyewitnesses.

As soon as the cops entered the picture, the newspapers did too. Mumbaikars grew terrorized and panicky, especially those living between Sion and King's Circle. The masala-movie-obsessed Mumbaikars gave the killer its moniker 'Paththar-Maar' or Stone-Killer.

Residents—who usually stepped out in the morning for a brisk walk, taking advantage of the empty, traffic-free streets— were now terrified of going anywhere during that time. In the night, the streets became deserted by ten. Meanwhile, the homeless and the pavement-dwellers, fearing for their lives, formed vigilante groups to keep watch. Despite these measures, the killings still continued.

It wasn't like finding a needle in a haystack. A radius of 5 km is not a difficult area to cover and patrol. The police knew the killer's hunting ground. Teams were positioned through the night in the area in the hope of catching the killer, and yet, he outsmarted the police, picking off one homeless person after another, as if he were watching them from the dark alleys and waiting for them to fall asleep.

Panic among citizens and frustration among law-keepers reached their zenith. The cops were amazed by the size and weight of the boulders. To make things worse, no fingerprints were found on them.

With panic came the rumours. Many theories were suggested, as each killing pumped adrenaline into the veins of Bombay. One theory was that the killer was being guided by a tantric to attain spiritual goals and that each killing was an act of human sacrifice to please the goddess Kali. This theory was also fuelled by the realization that the killings took place on Tuesdays and Saturdays, the two days of the week ruled by the gods Mangal and Shani (or Mars and Saturn)—two astrological signs that are associated with evil, doom and black magic. What else explained the inability of the sniffer dogs to trace any smell at each murder scene?

'Sir, we have found a witness! He's currently admitted in a hospital in Sion,' Constable Chitale rushed into Sion police station and informed the investigating officer.

'Let's go, go, go!' The investigating officer rushed out and shepherded his team into the jeeps idling outside, probably fearing that the lone witness might get bumped off by the serial killer before they reached him. The jeeps wailed through the streets of the city, rushing at breakneck speed.

'Who is he?' the inspector asked.

'Sir, a waiter who works in a small Udupi restaurant. But he lives on the pavements.' Chitale was excited. He had been feeling under the weather, seeing his boss come under such tremendous pressure. The dead-end case coupled with endless hours of work had prevented Chitale from applying for leave.

He had promised to take his wife back to her village for a vacation. He said a silent prayer and the index finger of his right hand oscillated between his forehead and the centre of his chest in a shortcut version of pranam.

'How serious is it?' the inspector asked.

'He missed being bludgeoned to death by a few centimetres. But he has a big wound in his head,' Chitale said, as he stopped the jeep in the parking lot of the hospital.

The inspector rushed through the crowded general ward. He was hoping for a breakthrough.

The man was in a semi-conscious state and had a large white bandage around his head. His head had been stitched up to stem the flow of blood. The ward suddenly quieted down to a murmur as the inspector drew a rickety old wooden chair close to the victim's bed.

'*Kya hua tha?* [What happened?]' he asked. The murmur turned to silence as all heads turned to listen to the sole witness of Paththar-Maar.

Sushil, the waiter, groaned, as he began to speak. His voice was slow and laboured. The inspector had to lean forward to catch Sushil's words.

'I heard a noise near me and felt someone's feet on my shoulders, as I was lying on the pavement. I opened my eyes and saw . . .' Sushil groaned again, 'a man standing above me with a stone in his hand. As he threw the stone on me, I moved as fast as I could but it struck the side of my head and my scream awoke the others.'

'Did you see him properly? What did he look like? How tall was he? What was he wearing?' The inspector's questions rained down on Sushil. He wanted answers. As many and as quickly as possible.

'Sir, the street lamps were not working in the area. It was dark. I could not see the man or his face clearly,' Sushil muttered.

The inspector held his head in his hands, almost in a reverential gesture to the killer who had outsmarted the department, yet again.

The breakthrough came to naught. Who was this serial killer who was tormenting the people?

The police jeep silently cruised along the streets of King's Circle. Dawn was breaking. The inspector looked out. A sea of homeless people was still asleep on the pavements. There were individuals amongst them who were sitting upright, watching every movement, their eyes bloodshot from lack of sleep.

'Talk to every informer we have on ground. I want answers. I have a feeling that the killer is amongst them,' the inspector instructed Chitale.

Luck seemed to be on their side. An informant mentioned Mohammed, a taxi driver who drove only at night and of whom the pavement-dwellers were wary. He was described as dangerous, evil and lurking in the shadows.

It made sense. A killer could not possibly walk around the streets with a heavy boulder. It seemed plausible that he would carry it in his taxi. A manhunt ensued. It turned out that the taxi driver in question was actually a police informant, who had been told to keep his eyes open at night. Because of his constant patrolling of the streets, the pavement-dwellers had begun to view him suspiciously. Again, all hope was lost.

The police kept picking up known criminals in the city and interrogating them but to no avail. Two years passed by; and as suddenly as the killings had started in the middle of 1985, they stopped in 1987.

The Stoneman Murders (2009),[2] a critically acclaimed movie directed by Manish Gupta, advocated a very controversial theory. It had been heard of, often whispered in office corridors and dingy bars, but had never been confirmed officially. In the movie, Paththar-Maar was revealed as a Bombay Police constable who believed in black magic and killed the homeless as part of a ritual. This theory had been talked about for years and was one of the reasons cited for Paththar-Maar to have never been caught, as he had all the information required to keep him at an arm's length from the law—his own colleagues!

The movie concluded by pointing a finger at Bombay Police for covering up the constable's involvement and having him executed so the secret would go to the grave with him.

If this were true, it would mean that Paththar-Maar was dead.

This left unexplained the fact that just over a year after the killings stopped in Bombay, the first Stoneman murder was reported in Calcutta in June 1989.

This confirmed three things:

1. The theory of the Bombay Paththar-Maar being a constable was just an urban legend.
2. The killer was never apprehended and had, in fact, escaped the clutches of law, and travelled over 2000 km to a new hunting ground.
3. There was a possibility that the Calcutta murders were the works of a copycat killer, meaning that there was a new Paththar-Maar in town.

To date, there has been no proof that the Bombay killings were connected to the Calcutta ones. But the uncanny similarity in the weapon, the choice of victims, the style of execution and the time at which the killer struck suggested that the murderer was the same person.

Like Bombay, Calcutta was not prepared for what happened on its streets over the next few months.

* * *

Calcutta, 1989

On 3 June 1989, the world witnessed the brutal killing of hundreds of pro-democracy demonstrators at Tiananmen Square as the Chinese army opened fire and slaughtered them. Calcutta, then under a communist government, watched and prayed for no trickle-down effect. There would be a killing, the next day, but not in connection to the massacre in China. Nonetheless, it was something quite devious.

The first victim in Calcutta was claimed on 4 June 1989. She was a woman who made her living selling moonshine/hooch on the streets. She had returned to her spot on the pavement beside the road leading up to the iconic Howrah Bridge and had fallen asleep. She never woke up. Postmortem reports mentioned the time of the killing between midnight and three in the morning.

There was immediate panic as people connected the murder to the Paththar-Maar of Bombay due to the similar modus operandi. The killer sure knew how to make a grand appearance and grab the spotlight. He waited exactly a month after that. It was almost as if he was playing a game with the people of the city. Just when Calcuttans were beginning to think that the first murder was a one-off affair, he struck again, showing the city that a serial killer was now on the loose.

The second murder took place on 4 July 1989.

Social reformer Gopal Krishna Gokhale had once said, 'What Bengal thinks today, India thinks tomorrow.' And someone at a progressive English newspaper perhaps understood the fact that in years to come it would not sound cool to talk about a 'Paththar-Maar' killer! And, hence, decided to add some swag to the vernacular moniker that the killer had acquired in Bombay. A serial killer just wasn't cool if he didn't have a cool name. The very staid and boring Paththar-Maar became 'Stoneman'. Now Calcutta had everyone's attention.

Like the Bombay killer, the Stoneman of Calcutta too worked within a specific territory. His chosen hunting ground was central Calcutta and the areas adjoining the iconic Howrah Bridge. The only difference was that the killer fluctuated between using a boulder and a concrete slab.

Sanjoy Basak, a journalist for *Telegraph*, recalled in an interview: 'Apart from the pavement-dwellers themselves, no one was bothered much about it.'[3]

'For the first three or four murders, we did not have an idea that it might be methodical or the work of a single person,' Rachpal Singh, the then deputy commissioner of Calcutta Police, said. He also admitted, 'Initially, yes, I do admit some lack of concern because these victims were, after all, just pavement-dwellers.'[4]

On 7 September 1989, Stoneman claimed his seventh victim, who was described in the official police records as 'male, approximately thirty-five years old, beggar-lunatic type'. Due to the ensuing public outcry and panic, the police were forced to take notice. And what was audacious was that the killer had chosen to kill his victim just a block from the police headquarters in blatant defiance.

The City of Joy transformed into the City of Panic. The only conclusion Calcutta Police made was that the killer had to be a tall, muscular man, as it was quite evident that a lot of physical strength was required to lift the heavy stones and slabs.

While the police ran around in a frenetic game of 'we have no clue where to find him', the killings continued at regular intervals. Stoneman became a household name. Just like in Bombay, in Calcutta too streets got deserted early and pavement-dwellers sat up at night to avoid meeting the killer.

Singh thumped his desk in anger and disgust: 'We are going back to the Stone Age! Killing each other with stones shows what kind of progress we have made here!'[5]

The barbarity of the crime and the frustration of not making a breakthrough in the investigation were clearly getting to Singh. Journalists hounded Calcutta Police every day with the hope that someone would have an answer.

'We haven't a clue' was all that Singh could tell them.[6]

Policemen swarmed the central part of the city. Believing that Stoneman must be mentally ill, Calcutta Police zeroed in only on suspects who seemed lunatic or mad. This led to three false confessions.

When the dragnet failed to pick up anything, policemen began disguising themselves as pavement-dwellers, pretending to be asleep on the roads, wrapped tightly in thin blankets that hid their guns.

One eyewitness materialized in the form of a lunatic named Mohammad Akram who claimed to have been attacked by Stoneman. He later admitted that he had not been attacked and the police declared that his head injury was the result of a rat bite.

But Stoneman was on a roll. Rudyard Kipling had once called Calcutta 'the city of dreadful night'.[7] The city was living up to that description.

The confidence that he was invincible and could not be caught made Stoneman braver and more defiant and he began choosing public places to claim his victims. One of his victims was killed in the busy Sealdah railway station, another on a major street, and one even at the entrance of an underground metro station.

And just like in Bombay, people began to construct images of the killer inside their heads. A rumour spread that the cops could not catch him as they were looking for a man while the killer was a woman. The killings stopped after the murder of the twelfth victim. The city of Calcutta breathed a sigh of relief.

To date, it is unknown whether the murders were the work of a single man or a woman or a large group of people. The years between 1985 and 1989 are officially considered to be the years of Stoneman's action.

But the saga did not end there.

* * *

Berhampur, 1999

Exactly ten years after the killings in Calcutta stopped, Berhampur in Orissa was shaken awake.

The officer in charge at Badabazar police station was just nodding off to sleep, when the shrill sound of a telephone call woke him up.

There was heavy breathing on the other side.

'I am calling from Diamond Tank Road. There has been a murder near the Satyasai temple. Please hurry.'

Before the cop could react, the anonymous caller hung up.

Berhampur was rocked by six Stoneman murders before the police managed to arrest Maheshwar Padhi, a paan-shop owner, as he was about to commit his seventh murder.[8]

It appeared that Padhi was a fan of Stoneman and wanted to emulate the killings. Even though four eyewitnesses identified him, Padhi claimed to be innocent. He underwent a lie-detection test, which he predictably failed. He was then taken to Hyderabad where five attempts were made to hypnotize him. Just when the Orissa cops were thinking that they had their man in the net, Padhi managed to jump out of the moving train in which he was being escorted back to Orissa. The Falaknuma Express had slowed down near Palasa in Andhra Pradesh. Seeing the sleeping constables, Padhi sensed an opportunity and jumped. It would take the cops three months of tracking and surveillance before he was re-arrested.

And just when one thought it was finally over . . . it wasn't.

* * *

Exactly nine years later in 2008, Calcuttans awoke to the sight of a man's head crushed by a stone . . . again! The rumour mill buzzed with panic: was Stoneman back to haunt Kolkata again? It turned out to be a one-off incident, thankfully.

Till 2009, Stoneman's story usually covered Bombay and Calcutta . . . until copycat versions appeared in Guwahati in 2010.

So were members of a tantric cult carrying out these killings? Or was the killer a psychopathic fan of the original Stoneman and wanted to instill fear, create panic and gain fame?

Unlike in Calcutta and Bombay, the Guwahati police arrested a suspect. Twenty-two-year-old Krishna Timung, who was described as a psychopath and a drug addict, was employed to remove bodies from the railway tracks. He admitted committing the Stoneman murders using stones and sharp weapon. Guwahati breathed a sigh of relief![9]

Just when Guwahati settled down, the Stoneman murders surfaced once again in Kolhapur, Maharashtra, in 2013 when there were ten killings within a span of three months. A thirty-five-year-old man was arrested and he confessed to the crimes.

In 2013, four people were killed by a similar method in Pune. In 2016, in Howrah, a man was found with his head smashed by a stone. In 2016, Rajkot was rocked by three murders executed with the same modus operandi. The Rajkot police fortunately arrested the culprit. He was an auto driver named Hitesh Dalpat Ramavat.[10]

Barring solitary incidents of people being killed in a similar manner, it seems that the serial threat of Stoneman was finally over.

The Stoneman murders of Bombay and Calcutta rank amongst the most elusive unsolved serial-killer cases in the world.

Stoneman could still be lurking amongst us, old, senile but waiting to strike again!

KOLI AND PANDHER

THE NITHARI-*KAAND* KILLERS

'*Kitchen mai aakar chaakoo le ke gaya, aur usi time isko
turant kat kar ke aur iska maine baju aur ye seene ka ek
piece bhi khaya tha* [. . .] *jo maine ghar main hi, matlab
kitchen main banaya tha.* [I went to the kitchen and took a
knife and cut her into pieces and ate a piece of her shoulder
and her chest [. . .] that I had cooked in the same house, in
the kitchen.]'[1]

—Surinder Koli

March 2005

'*Behnchod! Ball deewar ke peeche chali gayi!* [Sister-fucker!
The ball went behind the wall!]' Prakash shouted at Munna,
who was at the striker's crease. Munna was, of course,
gloating after executing a good shot. Ramesh was wearing a
hand-me-down T-shirt, with a picture of the Taj Mahal and
a caption that read 'Via Agra: Man's Greatest Erection for
Love'. He laughed and said: '*Abbe, Prakash, chal na chutiye,
ball utha kar la!* [Stop complaining, you dickhead, just get
the ball!]'

The wall that the players were referring to was that of
D-5, a two-storey bungalow in Sector 31, Noida, and the ball
had fallen in between the compound wall and the bungalow.

Nobody was interested in climbing the wall of D-5 and
retrieving the ball.

Abuses and arguments ensued. Before a fight could break out, Manoj Kumar, another team member, stepped in and said, '*Main ball lekar aata hoon* [I'll retrieve the ball].'

Manoj scaled the compound wall of D-5 and jumped down to the other side.

'*Ball laaney gaya hai ki hilaaney?* [Have you gone to retrieve the ball or jack off?]' Manoj heard Mahendra yell.

He started looking for the ball. There was a lot of garbage in that strip of land. Finally, he spotted the red rubber ball and bent down to pick it up. As he was picking up the ball, he almost fell back in fear. Right in front of him was a plastic bag containing what looked like a severed human hand! It cannot be, his inner voice screamed. But it is, his logical voice insisted. Manoj picked up the ball, scaled the wall and joined his friends.[2]

He looked visibly shaken.

'*Kya hua tujhe? Itna paseena kyun chhut raha hai?* [What happened to you? Why are you sweating so profusely?]'

'*Kuch nahi. Main ghar ja raha hoon* [Nothing! I am going home].' Manoj ran back home, the severed hand haunting him.

It had grown dark when Surendra Singh came back home from work. He was surprised to see Ram Kishan and his nephew, Manoj, standing outside his house.

'We have something to tell you,' Kishan said, 'and you better sit down.'

Everyone respected Surendra Singh in Nithari. He was one of the elders of the village. Kishan had been dumbfounded when Manoj had told him about the hand earlier that evening. Kishan had made up his mind to speak to Surendra Singh right away. He might know what to do.

Surendra Singh listened to Kishan and Manoj patiently and unflinchingly. There was a brief pause as he thought about something.

'*Tunay kata hua haath dekha tha? Aisa?* [Are you sure you saw a severed human hand? Like this?]' he asked Manoj, holding up his own hand. Manoj nodded. He was certain.

'*Tu ghar ja. Hum dono kuch karte hai* [You go home. We will do something],' he told them.

Surendra Singh and Kishan headed to the police outpost in Sector 26 and apprised the cops there.

Four policemen arrived at D-5, scaled the wall and inspected the area. The cops found the plastic bag and said it didn't resemble human flesh, but could be an animal's body part. As per court papers, the policemen covered up the 'flesh' with mud in the same area behind D-5.[3]

The residents of Nithari and Sector 31 did not know what was in store for them. In exactly twenty-one months, two serial killers would be arrested from among them, right from the very house in which the police were now standing.

* * *

Two crime cases in recent times have really intrigued Indians: the Aarushi Talwar–Hemraj murder case (2008) and the Nithari killings (2006). Both cases have been hotly debated, discussed and clouded by controversies and conspiracy theories.

There are two sides to the Nithari killings story. The first is the official narrative, which we all know, and the other is the flip side that is rife with conspiracy theories. I have included both of these narratives. It is up to you, the reader, to believe what you want to and dismiss what you don't. After all, what is an investigative crime story if it doesn't have conspiracy theories attached to it? In no way am I questioning the judicial system of the country. I am simply bringing to light and quoting the conspiracy theorists who have voiced their thoughts on various public platforms.

Nithari, a small urban village in Noida, stands in stark contrast with its neighbouring sectors, 30 and 31. Over the years, with real-estate boom, the village gave way to multistorey apartments and high-rises and Nithari turned into an urban slum, filled with migrants and manual labourers. The village now houses servants, maids and drivers who work in the houses of sectors 30 and 31.

Nithari had always had a dark side. Even Noida Police had noted that there was an abnormally high number of women and children missing from the village. The fear was so high that parents always warned their children not to venture towards the huge water tank in that area.[4] From an aerial view, the water tank stood like a huge spaceship parked amidst the slums. From the ground, it looked like a gigantic octopus with its long tentacle-like pillars menacingly towering over the area, waiting to swallow its next prey.

Vinod Pandey, an investigative officer of the Nithari case, recalled in his interview for the Netflix documentary *The Karma Killings*,[5] how strange it was that so many children had gone missing from the area and that there were no leads whatsoever.

'Every fifteen to twenty days, a child would vanish. The significant thing is that this happened in one specific location. Rumours were that the children went to the water tower and disappeared. No one knew what happened to them. All these children were from lower-class families,' said Alok Diwedi, a TV news reporter in his interview for *The Karma Killings*.[6]

The families of the victims filed numerous missing-person reports but apparently, no action was taken. Noida Police posted security in and around the area for a few months and that seemed to stop the disappearances.

It was 8 February 2005 when fourteen-year-old Rimpa Haldar went missing. Her parents went to the police station to lodge a complaint but, predictably, nothing happened.

Anil Haldar had moved to Nithari from Nadia, West Bengal, in 2001. He had two sons and a daughter. He used to ply a cycle rickshaw and his wife, Dolly, worked as a maid to eke out a living. In January 2005, Dolly fell ill and started taking Rimpa along with her for assistance in the houses where she worked, for a fortnight. Thereafter, Rimpa replaced her mother and began working alone. On 8 February, she went missing.[7]

'Sir, *meri beti nahi mil raha hai* [My daughter can't be found],' Haldar pleaded with the officer in charge at the police station. The cop on duty looked up to see a disheveled man with a salt-and-pepper stubble standing in front of him with folded hands.

'*Beti ka naam kya hai?* [What's your daughter's name?]' he asked.

'Rimpa Haldar,' the father answered.

'*Nithari mein rehta hai?* [Do you stay in Nithari?]' the cop questioned.

Haldar nodded.

'*Arre . . . Nithari se bachche toh har saal gayab hote hai. Iss me chaunknewali kya baat hai?* [Nithari is a village from where kids regularly disappear. Why are you surprised?]' the cop replied.

'Sir, *beti hai, sirf chauda saal ki hai. Sir, please, madat kijiye!* [She is my daughter, only fourteen years old. Sir, please help me!]' Tears ran down Haldar's cheeks.

The cop asked Bina Haldar, whose daughter had also gone missing, why immigrants like them came to big cities with grown-up daughters. '*Jinhe jaldi hee shahar kee havaa lag jaati hai aur ghar se bhag jaati hai* [Who get affected by the fast life of the big city and elope with their lovers].'[8]

That was the end of the matter. At least for then.

This was exactly a month before Manoj discovered the severed hand wrapped in the plastic bag behind D-5.

It would be six months before the police would register Haldar's complaint, as per the high court judgment.[9]

A year went by and more girls vanished from the lanes of Nithari. But it was Payal's disappearance that finally unleashed the avalanche of what we know today as 'Nithari-kaand'.

On 7 May 2006, Payal informed her father, Nand Lal, that she was going to Moninder Singh Pandher's bungalow to help with the domestic chores. That was the last time Nand Lal saw his daughter. When she did not return home, Nand Lal went to D-5 and rang the bell.

Koli lied and told him that Payal had not come there.

'*Tumhare maalik, Pandher saab, se baat karne do* [Let me speak to Pandher saab, your employer],' Nand Lal, now desperate, tried to bypass the servant and meet the master.

'*Pandher saab Chandigarh gaye hai.*' Saying this, Koli banged the door in Nand Lal's face.

A distraught Nand Lal went to the police to lodge a missing-person complaint.

'*Nithari mein khud ka ghar hai ya kiraye pe rehte ho?* [Do you own a house or are you living on rent in the village?]' the cop asked Nand Lal.

According to a report written by Pushkar Raj on the People's Union for Civil Liberties and Democratic Rights (PUCLDR) website, the main reason for the police asking this strange question was to gauge 'the economic condition of the complainant and potential for possible community pressure that might follow if a formal complaint is not lodged by the police'.[10] This is true because when the cops refused to register the complaint of Ashok Kumar, who owned a house in the village and whose son went missing in 2004, the villagers jammed the road for a day and forced the police to lodge an FIR. In the case of the rest, there were no FIRs and, therefore, no action.

In a similar incident, Sonia, who had lost her nine-year-old son, Sheikh, in December 2004, recounted her experience at the police station:

I immediately went to the *chowki* [local police check post].
They told me to go and search for him in orphanages. When
I went again, they said the child is not in our pocket, he will
come on his own. When I asked them to register a report they
told me to get out of the police station [. . .] Having got sick of
abuses, I stopped going to the police station. I could not take
the insult of policemen along with the pain of losing my child.[11]

Nand Lal's case was no different. In an interview/testimony
given to Pushkar Raj, this is what Nand Lal recounted:

Next day, I went to the police station. I told them that she
had gone to meet Koli at D-5. They paid no attention to me.
I kept going to the police station. On the fourth day, they
told me that my daughter was a characterless woman and
mocked at me. They told me to run away from the police
station and never come back to bother them.[12]

Nand Lal had no other recourse but to return to D-5, the last
place his daughter supposedly visited. For a month, he kept
going there, pleading for answers. Pandher finally met Nand
Lal after returning from Chandigarh.

Pandher assured him that Payal did not turn up that day,
but Nand Lal suspected that something was amiss. He felt that
Pandher was lying.

Nand Lal recounts the day when his life changed forever.

When she did not turn up till 6 p.m. on 7 May, I started
calling Moninder Singh's mobile number and it was
constantly engaged. I tried till 11 p.m. and when I got him
on the line the next day, Moninder Singh told me that he
was in Chandigarh and was not aware of the developments.
He said what his servant had done was not known to him,
and he asked me to call him in the evening. I tried again

in the evening, but he had switched off his personal mobile number.[13]

It was only when the chief judicial magistrate (CJM) issued an order on 6 October 2006 that the first FIR was registered.[14]

That is when the dice began to roll.

The cops checked Payal's phone records. To their surprise, they found that Payal had called up Pandher a few days before she had gone missing. Then why hadn't Pandher revealed this bit of information to Nand Lal?

The cops called him for questioning. Pandher seemed calm and relaxed, as he told the police that at the time of Payal's disappearance, he was in Chandigarh. Pandey sent his officers to check Pandher's alibi. It turned out that he was indeed in Chandigarh to perform the final rites of his departed father. This was a spoke in the wheel. But Pandey was not one to give up easily, as his gut told him that there was more to it than met the eye.

He decided to take it up a notch and questioned Pandher aggressively. Pandher revealed, to the cops' shock, that he knew Payal as a prostitute who frequented his house in Noida. He apparently paid her Rs 2500 for having sex. He also claimed that Nand Lal had pimped out his daughter. He was not arrested, but a cloud of suspicion now hung over him.

The case was becoming sordid by the minute. The cops confronted Nand Lal, who admitted that he was his daughter's pimp but insisted that they find his daughter nonetheless. Suddenly, his desperation appeared to be the result of greed and money rather than paternal and emotional ties. It seemed Payal was on her way to becoming just another addition to the list of missing children in the area.

However, a few days later, an email arrived in Pandey's inbox from the cybercrime department. Payal's phone had finally been tracked.

Arun Kumar, CBI joint director, claimed that Koli had used Payal's mobile phone after killing her. 'Surendra Koli, after killing Payal with her *chunni* [scarf], took away her mobile phone and used a new SIM card for his personal use,' Kumar told Press Trust of India. The IMEI (international mobile equipment number) details of the phone were taken from the mobile company.[15]

According to a report in *The Hindu*, CBI investigations revealed that Koli first obtained a SIM card using an identification document of one of Pandher's friends. He then bought two more SIM cards in his own name and continued to use Payal's cell phone. He then lost the phone to a rickshaw puller, after which it changed several hands and was finally sold to one Arun Bajriwala.[16]

It was late evening when the cavalcade of police cars rushed towards D-5. Koli received the police team and calmly told them that the next-door driver had given the phone to him. The police confronted the neighbour's driver. Seeing the police, the man immediately blurted out that Koli had asked him to lie.

'*Saab, main jab Almora se nikal raha tha, tab Surinder ka call aaya. Woh mujhe kaha ki agar police mujhe poochega ki yeh phone kiska hai, toh bolunga ki tunay mujhe diya hai. Tu sirf haan bol dena* [Sir, when I was driving down from Almora, I received a call from Surinder. He said if the cops ask me about the phone, I will say that you gave it to me. You just say yes if they ask you].'

The police picked up Koli for further questioning. He was a skinny, diminutive man, with a thin, drooping moustache. He was interrogated by six officers who rained down questions on him relentlessly. But Koli wasn't going to break so soon. He was a cunning man, who shrewdly swatted away each question like flies. The policemen were getting frustrated and decided to push the envelope.

Their persistent and dogged questioning finally broke Koli's silence and he admitted that he had killed Payal.

'*Chal, maan liya ki tunay Payal ka murder kiya hai! Lekin saboot kaha hai . . . yakeen kaise karein?* [OK, let's say you've killed Payal, but where is the proof?]' Pandey asked.[17]

Koli said after killing Payal, he chopped her body into pieces and threw them along with her slippers, clothes and handbag in the enclosed gallery and nullah behind D-5. As per the court papers, Koli at this point also confessed to having slain several women and children and disposing of them in a similar manner.[18]

According to the disclosure statement as deposed by prosecution witness no. 35, Dinesh Yadav, Koli said, '*Payal alias Deepika ko maine maar diya hai; uska purse, chappal tatha ala katla chaku maine chhipa rakhe hain, main baramad kara sakta hoon* [I killed Payal alias Deepika; I hid her purse, slipper and the knife, I can retrieve those items].' He further confessed that: '*Nithari ke anya bachhon ki bhi hatyayein ki hain, jinke sar pichhe ki gallery main tatha dhadh nale me phaink diye hain* [I have killed other children of Nithari and thrown their heads in the gallery behind the house and bodies in the drain].'[19]

Sub-inspector Chhotey Singh of Sector 20 remembers rushing to D-5 along with Dinesh Yadav, the investigating officer, as well as other policemen. There, Koli pointed out the place where he had buried Payal's body, her slippers and her purse.

The digging began. This was on 29 December 2006. The New Year was not going to be a happy one for Koli and Pandher.

Bandana Sarkar, whose daughter, Pinky, was one of the missing girls, remembered being told about the discovery of the remains and rushing there. 'Reaching the spot, we saw the bright yellow clothes that she had been wearing that day.'[20] On seeing the clothes and realizing what had happened with her daughter, Bandana fainted.

As per the court papers, the cops recovered fifteen skulls and bones, a handbag, slippers and clothes. Nand Lal confirmed the purse, slippers and clothes to be Payal's.

When asked why he had killed her, Koli apparently said that seeing his master entertaining prostitutes at D-5 disgusted him. He requested Pandher to not bring them home; however, he dismissed him. Later, Koli too got excited and wanted the women for himself.[21, 22]

So on that fateful day, Koli called up Payal.

'There is a new client who is looking for a good time. Would you be interested or should I call someone else?' he asked her, using the classic push–pull technique.

'Who is it?' Payal asked.

'How does that matter? He has promised to give you Rs 2500 for two hours,' he tempted her.

'Only two hours?' Payal fell for it.

Koli slowly reeled her in.

'He is coming to my house in an hour and he will meet you here.' He hung up.

Payal arrived, eager to please the client.

'He hasn't arrived yet?' she asked, as she settled down on the sofa.

'He is on his way.' Koli's hands were trembling; he was excited. He wanted to have her desperately.

'While we wait for the client, why don't you . . . err . . . have sex with me?'

Payal was taken by surprise: 'You?'

'Why? Can't I have sex with you or what?' He pretended to get offended.

'How much will you pay me?' Like a seasoned lady of business, Payal was willing to trade for the right price.

Koli, who was just a servant and caretaker with meagre means, said: 'Rs 500.'

Payal burst out laughing, surprising Koli.

'*Saala, bhikari kahin ka! Paanchso rupaye me Payal ke saath aish karna chahta hai? Phut yahan se!* [Bloody beggar! You want to have Payal for just Rs 500? Bugger off!]'

Koli recalled that he did not know what came over him. He picked up her chunni and throttled her. When she died, he tried to have sex with her, but was unsuccessful.[23]

He carried her to the upstairs bathroom and chopped her into bits, wrapped the pieces in a plastic bag and dumped them behind D-5.

Pandey showed Koli the pictures of the missing children and he identified one of the girls from the photos: Jhumpa.[24]

'How did you kill her?' Pandey asked.

Koli recalled that that day the house was empty as Pandher was out of town. He stood by the entry gate, adjoining the main road, waiting to reel in a prey. He saw a teenage girl passing by the house. He invited her in, promising her a job. When she entered the house, Koli told her that his '*malkin*' (mistress) was on her way to discuss the wages. As soon as the girl's gaze wandered around the room, Koli strangled her with her scarf till she fell unconscious. He then tried to have sex with her but couldn't go through with it. He strangled her, dragged the body to the upstairs bathroom and chopped her up. He retained a breast and a piece of her shoulder, which he cooked and ate.

Never before in the history of Indian crime had there been a case of a serial cannibal. The police were flabbergasted. This was the beginning of the unravelling of the most gruesome serial killings of modern-day India.

Meanwhile, Nand Lal returned to Nithari and told everybody that Koli had confessed to the murder of the missing children. The parents of the missing children now crowded around D-5, screaming for answers, baying for blood.

According to the police narrative, Koli and Pandher both signed confessional statements, in which Pandher supposedly confessed that he used to first rape the children and then pass them on to Koli to do whatever he pleased with them.

This is what Bandana Sarkar (Payal Sarkar's mother) claimed in court. She stated that Koli had told her that Pandher wanted him to get girls as 'I cannot sleep without them', and 'after raping them, hand them over to Koli, asking him to do what he liked with them'.[25]

Remember this confession, as it will resurface at a crucial point in the story.

* * *

World news headlines on 29 December 2006 were about footballer Steven Gerrard being knighted by the Queen of England; Saddam Hussain's impending hanging and Arnold Schwarzenegger getting injured in a freak skiing accident. Back home, Indians were still reeling from the *Tehelka* exposé on a defence deal; the staff of Indian Airlines was threatening to go on strike; and a priest was demanding an apology from a Bollywood actress, as her bodyguard had entered the premises of a temple in an inebriated state.

However, everything took a back seat as the media went to town with this sensational case. And as always, no facts were verified and the truth was a good concoction of hearsay and whatever increased the TRPs. The number of skeletons recovered differed in press reports, ranging between fifteen and nineteen. At the end of the excavation, nineteen skulls were recovered, sixteen of which were found whole and three were recovered damaged. News anchors were already labelling Pandher as a rapist-murderer; and this non-stop reportage further incensed the villagers of Nithari as they realized that their last vestiges of hope in finding their children alive had been quashed. The reality, which all the parents had believed in (but had avoided so far), had just been uncovered: their children were dead.

The crowd went berserk as hundreds of people trashed D-5, breaking the car in the driveway, smashing air conditioners and windows and whatever else they could lay their hands on.

The anger of the parents who had just found out that their children had been raped and then butchered was justifiable. But the bigger damage was that the crime scene had now been contaminated.

The question arises: if only Koli had confessed to the crimes, then why was Pandher arrested? At this point in the investigation, there was no proof to tie Pandher to the crimes. Koli's confession did not mention Pandher of being an accomplice. Was this a case of a man being at the wrong place at the wrong time? Or was it media overkill for a juicy story that pushed the police to arrest Pandher? As Pandher's son says in *The Karma Killings* that the arrest of a rich man makes a better story than the arrest of a poor man, perhaps that's why his father was framed.

On the one hand, if you love conspiracy theories, you will question everything.

On the other hand, it could just be two very guilty but very smart criminals messing with our heads.

Or, neither of them could be guilty. Or one was, the other wasn't.

In the end, it is the law of the land that will decide the fate of the criminals and we are no one to contradict it.

As per the Nithari High Court Judgement at Allahabad, incriminating evidence was retrieved from D-5 in the days that followed.[26]

The twenty-ninth of December 2006 was an eventful day. The Sector 20 police went to D-2. A witness was needed for what was about to unfold. Pappu Lal was a servant who lived in D-2, along with his wife and children. He was scared at first but the cops assured him that all he needed to do was see what was happening and then appear in court. On hearing the word 'court', Pappu Lal shrank back in fear. No one in India likes to get involved in any legal case or court proceedings. There seems to be an allergy due to the reputation of courts being slow to dole out justice and labyrinthine in its proceedings.

'*Teri bachchi bhi toh khoyi hui hai* [Even your daughter is missing],' one of the constables egged on Pappu Lal.

Pappu Lal's eight-year-old daughter had gone missing since 10 April 2006. He had lost any hope of finding her. Watching the chaos unfold around him, Pappu Lal realized that the people of D-5 were in all probability responsible for his daughter's disappearance. He nodded and accompanied the cops.

Meanwhile, Koli took the police to the water tank on the roof of D-5 and said, 'You will find a knife there.' Sure enough, a knife was recovered. A memo was prepared and Pappu Lal affixed his signature on it, as witness. The knife was marked as Exhibit Ka 24.[27]

All the material that had been recovered from behind D-5 was packed and sealed. Parents who had earlier lodged police complaints about their missing children now trooped into the police station to identify clothes, bags, slippers and bangles.

A lot of questions have been raised on why the Nithari investigation was slow to take off. One of the reasons, according to late investigative journalist Arpit Parashar, was sub-inspector Simarjeet Kaur, who was the officer in charge of the Nithari police chowki from 18 September–30 December 2006. Apparently, she caused serious damage to the investigations as she tried to derail it. As per Parashar's report, she threatened the victims' families to withdraw their cases and even visited Nand Lal's house to keep him quiet.[28] Unknown to her, justice would prevail within a week.

On 3 January, Dolly Haldar reached the Sector 20 police station. Her employer, Lieutenant Colonel Shailesh (prosecution witness no. 26),[29] accompanied her. A sealed parcel containing clothes and chappals was opened in front of them. Sub-inspector Satpal Singh kept showing one article after another to Dolly till she suddenly screamed and grabbed a black bra and a white chunni from among the bundle of clothes in front of her. Rimpa was wearing these the day she had gone missing.

Slowly but surely, the noose was tightening around the Nithari killers. Dolly lodged an FIR, which was registered as case crime no. 3 against Koli and Pandher, and Rimpa's clothes were marked as Exhibit Ka 47.[30]

The Noida Police and the supposed written confessions by Koli and Pandher were driving the entire case at this point. The police was being forced to share all the information with the hungry media who kept pressuring them for answers. The media was on crack cocaine, fuelling frenzied reactions across the country. Suddenly, the politicians woke up and turned it into a political issue, trying to gain advantage against the ruling government.

Under pressure to deliver results, on 3 January 2007, the then UP government suspended Piyush Mordia, the senior superintendent of police (SSP), Soumitra Yadav, the additional superintendent of Noida, Sewak Ram Yadav, former circle officer, and six other sub-inspectors.[31]

On 9 January 2007, the Central Bureau of Investigation (CBI) was called in to take over the case from the local police. This was done to pacify the public and the victims' families.

With an alarming amount of bones and evidence turning up like New Year gifts, the forensics team got into action. Dr Manish Kamath, senior demonstrator at the department of forensic, All India Institute of Medical Sciences (AIIMS), reached D-5 on 12 January, along with CBI officials. They started sieving the mud behind the bungalow and recovered fifty-eight pieces of bone, forty-seven pieces of clothes, which were smeared and torn, seventeen chappals of varying sizes, hair clips, pieces of rope and bangles of different sizes. As many as forty-nine packets were prepared, which contained bones and soft tissues of the children.[32]

The enormity of the heinous crime was now sinking in.

However, conspiracy theorists were already talking. They pointed out to the strange fact that the torsos were missing in all the skeletons that were recovered. What the police dug up were skulls and limbs; no spines or ribcages were recovered. This brought a new angle into the investigation. Could these be the remains of human-organ-trafficking victims, where the torsos were harvested and the limbs thrown away?[33]

The CBI started digging deep to get to the root of this rumour. They zeroed in on Ramesh Prasad Sharma, a cook at D-6 whose boundary wall was adjacent to D-5's. Sharma revealed that his master was a doctor who had been earlier picked up in 1997 in a kidney-transplant racket. He was later released.[34] He also testified in the court that he had seen Koli cutting small trees with a small axe between September and October 2006. He stated that during the summer months, a foul stench would waft in from behind D-5.[35] Surprisingly, he was the only person amongst all the prosecution witnesses who mentioned the stench.

Six questions were raised at this point by conspiracy theorists:

1. If it wasn't organ trafficking, then why weren't the torsos found with the rest of the bodies?
2. If Koli had eaten the body parts, then what did he do with the torsos, the ribcages and the spine? Why didn't he get rid of them like he had done with the limbs and the skulls?
3. Thirdly, how could the torsos disappear magically or were they disposed of elsewhere?
4. If Pandher was guilty and knew about the murders, then would he be so stupid as to dispose of the bodies behind his house or allow Koli to do it, which could easily tie them to the crimes?

5. And why was the cook of D-6, Ramesh Sharma, the only one to get a whiff of the foul odour?[36] Had he been tutored to fill in the gaps in the narrative that was being constructed?

6. How come the other servants of D-5 did not know about the gruesome goings-on of Koli and Pandher, in spite of working under the same roof?

Nithari suddenly saw an influx of cars as all major political-party representatives visited the village and expressed shock at the incident and demanded a thorough probe into the case. But the parents of the missing children were unimpressed. They knew that the politicians were only there to milk the situation for their own benefits.

Meanwhile, CBI investigations revealed that Kaur and the officers under her had all along been hand in glove with Pandher. The CBI also established that Pandher had asked Kaur to shield Koli by fabricating eyewitness statements showing Koli to be in Chandigarh from 5 May 2006 till the case broke.[37]

Kaur was dismissed. The wheels of justice were finally turning.

On 18 January 2007, Virendra Dagar, who worked with the Food Corporation of India as a '*daftari*', was suddenly called to the office of the deputy general manager, who instructed him to head to the CBI office.

Neutral eyewitnesses are required during raids conducted by the police or the CBI. These people become prosecution witnesses in the court during the trial. Unfortunately, not many ordinary citizens volunteer to be witnesses as they are deterred by the facts that they have to appear frequently in court and might be threatened by the guilty party. So, government officials are often used as witnesses. They, of course, have no other choice but to agree. Dagar found himself reporting to the CBI office at Lodhi Road.

On reaching there, he met with officer Ajay Singh and others. He recognized the thin man sitting in the chair in front of him from newspaper photographs and news channels' reportage. Koli was in mid-conversation when he volunteered to get the axe with which he used to chop the bodies. The CBI officers bundled him and Dagar into a car and escorted them to D-5.

Koli slowly walked to the right side of the house and stopped in front of some bushes and pointed. The officers rummaged around in the bushes and pulled out an axe. It was sealed and labelled as Exhibit Ka 20.[38]

The conspiracy theorists were not having any of these charades. Their arguments were:

1. The public had already contaminated the scene of the crime. Any person could have placed the axe there and the authorities were just trying to stitch together the narrative. Koli being escorted to retrieve it in front of a witness was just extended play-acting.
2. The police had been searching the house and its surroundings for the past twenty days. How is it that none of them discovered this axe?

When Koli and Pandher's lawyers mentioned the above points during the court proceedings, Virendra Dagar denied the suggestion that he was a set-up witness deposing under the pressure of the CBI.[39]

The Uttar Pradesh Police took Koli and Pandher to Gandhinagar for a narco-analysis test. Koli allegedly confessed to the murders and gave his employer a clean chit, saying that Pandher was unaware of the crimes committed by him. He is further alleged to have confessed to strangulating, raping and chopping up the bodies of the victims in his bathroom.

Dr S.L. Vaya from the Directorate of Forensic Science examined and spoke to Koli in detail. She came to the conclusion that Koli had an erectile dysfunction or an ejaculation problem. Koli told her about his fantasies, which he started having when Pandher got prostitutes home. Koli told Dr Vaya about a silver-haired woman in a white sari who would stand near him and laugh, taunting him. This state of trance would last till he disposed of the body.

Meanwhile, the media continued sensationalizing the case. There were reports about the investigating team seizing pornographic, erotic magazines and photographs of Pandher with nude children and foreigners, along with a computer connected with a webcam from D-5. This immediately made people assume that the police had busted an international child-pornography racket.

Needless to say, *all* of the above turned out to be false.

The nation was like a dormant volcano, waiting to explode. And it did on 25 January, a day before Republic Day.

Koli and Pandher were brought to the CBI special magistrate's court in Ghaziabad at 10.30 a.m. Unknown to the duo, a group of lawyers, along with the residents of the area, had gathered outside the court. The mob could not tolerate the presence of such cold-blooded killers on the court premises. Sunder Singh, a Nithari resident, screamed: 'These two should not be killed. They should be kept alive and tortured every day.'[40] The police were on edge. A few lawyers even tried to break into the court, which led to a disruption in the proceedings.

The special CBI court sent the duo to CBI custody for fourteen days.

As soon as Koli and Pandher were brought out of the court, a hundred bloodthirsty screams were heard and the crowd surged towards the killers, blocking their exit. The mob pounced on them, shoving, punching and beating. The police were outnumbered.

Koli sustained injuries, while Pandher lost consciousness. The police took control of the situation and shipped the men out of the premises. Arvinder Singh, an advocate at the Ghaziabad court, was quoted saying: 'We wanted to punish both. Had the police cooperated with us and not saved them, we would have ended the case today.'[41]

The UP government ordered an inquiry into the attack.

The country as well the legal fraternity was shaken up by the incident.

Dr Sanjeev Lalwani was an assistant professor at AIIMS, New Delhi. On 3 February, he received a letter from the CBI, requesting him that all the skeletons and bones that had been recovered from D-5 be shown to Koli in the absence of police officers and CBI officers. Also, Dr Lalwani was requested that Koli be given a cadaver so it could be ascertained as to how he would cut the body into pieces.

Dr Lalwani arranged all the bones as per their measurement. There were nineteen sets of them. On 4 February 2007, Koli was brought to AIIMS. The proceedings were recorded on video. To warm things up, a lock of black-brown hair was shown to Koli. He said it belonged to Payal. He also recognized the button of a grey sweater that had belonged to Rimpa.

When the reports were made public, conspiracy theorists raised the question: how could Koli have recognized the victim from just one lock of hair or even recognize such a detail of a button and who it belonged to?

When he was shown the separate pieces of skull and asked about the cut marks, Koli told them that he used to sever the skull with the help of a kitchen knife. He was shown a cadaver and asked to cut it like he would hack the bodies of the children. Koli was handed a piece of chalk to use as a marker. Like a well-trained professional, Koli drew on separate parts of the body.

'*Kitna time lagta tha tumhe yeh sab karne ke liye?* [How long did it take you to cut the body?]' one of the doctors present asked.

'*Teen ghanta* [Three hours],' replied Koli.[42]

Fast forward to 11 September 2009: At the trial in the Allahabad High Court, two women took to the stands to testify against Koli. They were the ones who had supposedly got away. They both claimed that Koli had spoken to them just a few months before the Nithari slayings were discovered.

Flashback to early 2006: Pratibha used to go to work in Rail Vihar, Sector 30. This meant that she took the route via Sector 30 and passed by D-5 every day. It was 2 p.m. and Pratibha was tired as she trudged back home, when she suddenly heard a man call out to her. She looked up to see a dark, thin man standing at the gate of D-5. Koli asked her if she was a maid and was looking for a job. Pratibha nodded but said she would like to speak to the mistress of the house.

Koli stood there for a moment and went back inside, only to emerge a minute later, saying that the mistress cannot come outside as she is old and weak and that she had called Pratibha inside.

Pratibha suspected that all was not right.

She promptly turned and walked away. Her instinct saved her that day.

The second person who got away was Poornima, a Class V student, who used to pass D-5 on her way to school every day. She noticed beautiful flowers hanging from the branches of a tree in D-5. Koli tried to tempt her into the house by offering her the flowers. However, Poornima ran away. Koli grew desperate. On another occasion, when Poornima was passing by D-5 with her two sisters, Koli called out to her, saying there was a prayer meet (satsang) happening in the house. But as Poornima neared the gate of D-5, she couldn't hear any sound. The house looked empty. She felt uneasy and started retreating. Koli realized that his prey was getting away. He lunged at her but Poornima was more agile than him. She dodged Koli and ran away. Poornima too testified against him.

Back to February 2007: The CBI applied to the magistrate informing him about Koli wanting to record his confession on video.

For sixty days, the CBI investigated but found only circumstantial evidence, which they knitted to the initial confession made by Koli when the police arrested him.

Finally, on 1 March 2007, Koli recorded the infamous video confession in front of the chief metropolitan magistrate, which would be the basis on which Koli would eventually be convicted and sentenced to death. This would become the cornerstone for convicting Koli and Pandher.

Included here is an excerpt from the confessional statement of Koli, which I am quoting from the Nithari High Court Judgement at the Judicature at Allahabad (11 September 2009). All the text in italics are exact quotes from the judgment.[43]

Koli: *Mai* [sic] *ghar ke aage se Nithari gaon ke liye raasta jaata hai.* [The road leading to Nithari village is in the front of my house.]

Magistrate: *Achha.* [OK.]

Koli: *Aur vahi pe matlab raste mai hamara ghar hai, D-5, Sector 31 hai, main vaha par naukri 2000* [sic] *July 2004 se naukri kar raha hoon vaha pai* [. . .] *lekin 2005 shuru shuru ki baat hai, to January ya February ki baat hai* [. . .] *to aik ladki Sector 30 ke taraf se Nithari ki taraf aa rahi thi, jo jiska naam dikhane par aur baad mai pata chala ki iska naam rimpa hai, fir isko kaam ki liye maine bula liya andar*[. . .] *han aur jaise hi wo andar ko dekh rahi thi, maine peeche se isi ki chunni se iska gala daba kar aur isko behosh kar diya, aur uske bad iske saath sex karne ka koshish kiya* [. . .] *jab sex nahi ho paya mere se, maine gala daba kar isko bhi mar diya usi ki chunni se.*[44]

[My house, D-5, in Sector 31 lies on the road to Nithari. I have been employed there since 2000 (sic) July 2004. (*Probably this is a clerical typo. It could be 20 July*) (. . .) I can't recall clearly but it could be in January or February 2005 (. . .) I saw a girl coming from Sector 30 and going towards Nithari. I was told later that her name was Rimpa. I offered her employment and took her inside the house (. . .) As she was looking inside the house, I went from behind her and strangled her with her scarf and she fell unconscious. I tried to have sex with her (. . .) When I was unsuccessful in having sex, I throttled her using her own scarf.]

Magistrate: *Achha; kyon mar diya?* [OK; but why did you kill her?]

Koli: *Bilkul, man main isi tarah ka pressure bana tha ki isko kaat kar khoon karke, achha; to uske baad turant baad isko upar bathroom mai le kar gaya* [. . .] *upar bathroom me le jar kar, neeche aya, fir kitchen mai aakar chaakoo le ke gaya, aur usi time isko turant kat kar ke aur iska maine baju aur ye seene ka aik piece bhi khaya tha, achha; hanji, jo maine ghar mai hi matlab kitchen mai banaya tha.*[45]

[I felt an immense urge to dismember her after I had killed her. I took her to the upstairs bathroom (. . .) After I had taken her to the bathroom upstairs, I came down again and took a knife from the kitchen. Immediately I dismembered her. I cut off a piece of her shoulder and chest and ate it. Yes, I cooked it in the kitchen.]

Magistrate: *Kitchen mai banaya tha?* [You cooked it in the kitchen?]

Koli: *Hanji aur jab matlab matlab sham ko kitna khaya ye mere ko puri tarah se dhyan nahi hai* [. . .] *jab pure tarah se man shant hua, uske baad maine dekha ki matlab ki drawing room me hee iske sare chappal wagarah sab drawing room mai hi padi hui thi tab tak, matlab, tab koi wo nahi tha, matlab achha; jaise nasha type ka, mai kuchh nahi karta jaise main daroo, paan bedi cigarettee gutka kuch bhi nahi khata, achaa; to is tarah ka mera, mere ko man mai feeling hoti thi, kisi ko katoon khaoon kar ke [. . .] aur uske bad main uppar bathroom me gaya upar dekha, to bathroom me usko kat ke sab faili hi thi vo, jo mere ko us time katne ke time kuch pata hi nahi tha ki maine isko kya kiya hai karke, achha; aur uske baad fir maine usko dar ke maare fata fat panniyon mai bhar karke usko bathroom me rakh diya aur dho ke raat ko baki usko matlab ghar ke peeche ek gallery hai, jaha matlab ko aa ja nahi sakta hai, waha gallery mai faik diya tha usko.*[46]

[I have no idea how much I ate. I cannot recall. I ate till my mind was at peace. I saw that her slippers and belongings were still lying in the sitting room. No one had come to the house by then. It was as if I was in a stupor. I don't smoke, chew betel-leaf, or drink alcohol. But I always felt intoxicated with this urge to cut, kill, cut and eat people (. . .) I went to the bathroom upstairs and saw that the dismembered pieces of her body were scattered around. At the time when I was cutting her up, I had no idea what I was doing and what I had done. OK. After this, I panicked and put the pieces into a plastic bag and kept it in the bathroom and washed it. After which, I threw the bags into the gallery, which is behind the house, where no one comes and goes.]

Conspiracy theorists who have studied the case thoroughly call the video confession a well-tutored performance by Koli. What makes it even more bone-chilling is the fact that Koli has himself gone on record to say that he was tortured, repeatedly shown pictures of the girls and even told by the police how he supposedly killed them.[47] That is what emerged in the confession. When Koli was given access to a legal aid in the open court, he once again reiterated that his confession had come under duress.

Koli also stated that he was tortured by the police and that he had refused to identify the same photographs before the CBI.[48]

Section 24 of the Indian Evidence Act bars a confession if it appears to have been caused by threat, inducement or promise. It also states that the legal requirement for the admissibility of a confession is that it has to be a voluntary admission of guilt. But in this case the confession itself stated that Koli was tortured and tutored.[49]

Koli repeatedly described his mental condition as being in a trance and that of a man possessed. Hearing this, the magistrate asked him how, then, was he able to recognize the women whose photographs he was shown.

In an interview published by Scroll, Koli was quoted saying:

When the Uttar Pradesh Police arrested me, they made me see these photos again and again and told me the names of these people [. . .] For each photograph, they told me the name, the time, the manner, etc. But I don't know about the time even now. They had told me all this but I have forgotten.[50]

This would imply that Koli was completely innocent and hadn't even killed one person and was in fact tutored by the police completely, or he was super smart and toying with everyone. He also said:

At that time I used to be in a complete intoxicated-type state, so I did not know anything [. . .] I used to try and have sex with them [. . .] I used to try, as far as I can guess, but I definitely used to kill. [. . .] I was tortured a lot and only then, I mean, they made me confess. OK. I was made to suffer a lot of torture. OK. Because of these two–three photos [. . .] After coming to CBI, I denied, that you may do whatever you wish, but these I have not done.[51]

The question, then, is: was Koli innocent or was he a criminal mastermind who was playing the predictable sympathy card?

Ram Devineni, who directed the much-acclaimed *The Karma Killings*, recounted in an interview to *Mumbai Mirror* (published on 15 January 2017) that when he met Koli at Ghaziabad court, he always 'used subversion'. When Devineni asked him if he had indeed killed the children, 'he never denied it, but always blamed someone else. He threw me in different directions. He is without a doubt, the smartest and most cunning person I have ever met.'[52]

The CBI indicted Koli as a cannibal and found him guilty on the counts of murder and rape of Payal; they gave a clean chit to Pandher, stating that he was never present during the time of the crime and, therefore, had no knowledge of what was going on upstairs. The CBI court charged Pandher for immoral trafficking, harbouring a criminal, and corruption. The public and the media were stunned. They were not happy with the judgment. They wanted both of them to be convicted. The media now began suspecting the CBI and wanted to know if the influential Pandher had managed to bribe the agency and buy his freedom.

Meanwhile, on 13 March 2007, the blood samples taken earlier from the parents of the missing children came back as positive matches with the remains discovered. There were eight matches as per the court papers.

Remember the signed confessions by Koli and Pandher, which Noida Police had procured? Those resurfaced again. *Tehelka* challenged the CBI's exclusion of Pandher's statement in which he had supposedly said that Payal, whom he used to pay Rs 2500 per night, had started blackmailing him and, therefore, he decided to get rid of her. He supposedly confessed that he had asked Koli to kill her.

So the question was: why did the CBI not include this crucial piece of evidence—Pandher's supposed confession—that would have implicated him in Payal's murder? Had they overlooked this major evidence in a hurry to close the case?

It seems Pandher had told his son, Karan Deep, the day after his arrest, that he had been forced to sign on two blank pages; and that he knew he would be framed.[53] This could have been dismissed as a crock full of shit, if it wasn't for . . .

Arun Kumar's statement to Devineni: 'We spoke to the cops and they told us that he [Pandher] hadn't confessed. This confession has no evidentiary value. The officers presumed he was guilty and wrote the confession. No officer has said that he confessed in front of him.'[54]

That is why the CBI did not take the confessions into cognizance as they assumed these were crafted post facto by the police to fit the narrative.

What was really happening? It is for you to decide. There are two possibilities:

1. The confession was written by the cops and, therefore, the CBI was right.
2. The confession was indeed written by Pandher and he had bribed the CBI.

It is almost impossible and ridiculous to believe that a small businessman could bribe a premier investigative agency. Or had the cops been in a hurry to close the case under pressure and created their own narrative?

Devineni believes that the conspiracy theory about the CBI being bribed is completely bogus.

Pandher was definitely wealthy, but no CBI officer would take a bribe in such a sensational case. All of India's media was watching them, so I think the CBI did a thorough job, and the conclusion they came up with was not what everyone wanted to hear: Pandher was not involved.[55]

The families of the victims were up in arms. They could not believe that the 'womanizer' Pandher got away with blood on his hands.

According to Devineni, perception played a crucial role. 'I think Pandher looked like the "perfect" villain. His issues included everything from depression to drinking to his fondness for call girls—all this cumulatively portrayed him as a monster. For many, it was not a big leap to picture him as a killer. Class surely played a part and the poor saw this as an opportunity to go after someone privileged,' he told journalist Sowmya Rajaram in an interview.[56]

Therefore, Devineni remembers meeting Jhabbu Lal, the father of one of the victims, who 'immediately started talking about how his "destiny" was to go after Pandher. Koli was inconsequential to him'.[57]

Unhappy with the decision of the court, six of the parents—Anil Haldar, Jatin and Bandana Sarkar, Sunil Biswas, Karambir, Nand Lal and Jhabbu Lal—approached lawyer Khalid Khan to represent them.

Khalid had been a criminal lawyer before he moved to the Gulf. He worked as a chartered accountant there and had now returned to India and his first love, law. For Khan, who was looking for a big case to establish his name, this was a boon. He was a warrior who wanted to fight till the end. He made the parents sign copies of their statements and warned them that he would sue them if they backtracked or changed their statements in court midway. The parents had found their lawyer.

On 10 April 2007, the CBI filed a second charge sheet in the murder of twenty-year-old Pinki Sarkar. Koli was charged with abduction, rape and murder. Pandher was spared again.

The questions on everybody's minds were: how did Pandher not know? How was it that every time a murder took place, he was not in Noida? Was it an alibi?

Khan believed it was a well-crafted alibi.

Devineni points out that Pandher's fault 'was that he trusted Koli completely. Koli would often conceal the fact that Pandher would have call girls over, and so I think Pandher became fond of Koli for looking after him'.

The main evidence was the call record that clearly showed that every time a child went missing, Pandher was away. 'This proved that Koli was intentionally waiting and planning his killings based on Pandher's schedule. Since Pandher was the only other person living there, Koli only needed to worry about him,' Devineni observes.

Now dip your head in the murky waters of this case. There are two possibilities:

1. Pandher knew about Koli and the murders and, therefore, vanished on the day of the abduction to create the alibi. Khan argued that the date of abduction was clear and Pandher went away to create an alibi. But the day of murder wasn't clear and so, Pandher could have been in the house on the day of the murder.
2. During Pandher's absence Koli would abduct and kill the victims. When the master was away, Koli was at play.

Such was the concern and interest in the case that the Ministry of Women and Child Development (WCD) set up an expert committee in 2007 to investigate the Nithari case independently. Their report was a scathing criticism of Noida Police and the way the CBI had handled the investigation.

Dr Vinod Kumar (chief medical superintendent, Noida) informed the committee that he was surprised at the surgical precision with which the bodies had been cut and that it reeked of illegal organ trade.

The WCD report also mentioned that the drain behind and in front of D-5 wasn't too deep and always had stagnant water. Therefore, the disposed bodies would have stayed there, creating a foul smell due to decomposition, which wasn't the case. There was only one person in the witness stand who mentioned the stench: Ramesh Prasad Sharma. And remember, Sharma's employer was a doctor, who had been arrested and released in connection to a kidney-transplant scam a few years earlier. And to imagine there were nineteen carcasses that lay buried there. Was the smell being blocked as the body parts had been packed and wrapped inside plastic bags?

Another unique observation made in the WCD report was that it takes three years for a corpse to decompose. Yet, only bones and skulls were found, even though the murders had been committed only in 2006. Were the bodies chemically decomposed down to the bone before being discarded? If so, why hadn't the forensic team found chemical traces? Or was it again the ghost of illegal medical organ trading?[58]

The WCD committee made a few suggestions:

They wanted the CBI to look into the angle of organ trade. They also recommended that the CBI needed to study records of organ transplant of all the hospitals of Noida to trace the donor and the recipient; and to investigate further about the involvement of more people other than just the accused.[59]

Predictably, nothing came of it. No organ-trade racket was discovered.

It was time now for the judgments.

On 13 February 2009, Pandher and Koli were found guilty of the murder of Rimpa by a special sessions court in Ghaziabad. This was the opposite of what the CBI had said earlier, as it had given a clean chit to Pandher. The next day, the court gave both Pandher and Koli death sentences and classified the case as 'rarest of rare'.

The Allahabad High Court judgment on Koli was:

> There cannot be any doubt that the case of accused A-2 falls within the category of the rarest of rare cases. The depraved and brutish acts of Surendra Koli call for only one sentence and that is death sentence. We agree with the reasoning of the Sessions Judge awarding death sentence and affirm the sentence of death awarded by the trial court to Surendra Koli.

For Pandher, it was: 'The appellant Moninder Singh Pandher has been sentenced to death. Under section 368 Cr.P.C, it is envisaged the High Court may order retrial on the same and an amended charge.'

Rimpa's parents were overjoyed but it was short-lived.

Devraj Singh, Pandher's lawyer, presented two crucial pieces of evidence in his defence: Pandher's passport and his call records.

Rimpa went missing on 8 February 2005. Pandher had left for Australia on 22 January and returned to India only on 27 February 2005. So, as per the judgment by the Allahabad High Court, there was no way that Pandher could have knowledge of the crime or could have been a part of it, as his mobile records clearly showed that he was in Australia and his passport had the entry and exit immigration stamps. Koli's death sentence was confirmed but Pandher was acquitted.

If one were to believe Khalid Khan's theory, it is unlikely but probable that Rimpa may have been kept captive and alive by Koli till his master returned. Pandher could have raped her and killed her after coming back. However, given that Koli usually lured and killed the victims on the same day, this theory does not hold much water.

What had appeared to be a simple open-and-shut case had suddenly turned inconclusive.

An avalanche of convictions followed. Koli was finally paying the price for the heinous murders of the innocent little children.

7 January 2010: the Supreme Court stayed Koli's death sentence.

4 May 2010: Koli was found guilty of the 25 October 2006 murder of Arti Prasad (seven) and given a second death sentence eight days later.

27 September 2010: Koli was found guilty of the 10 April 2006 murder of Rachna Lal (nine) and given a third death sentence the following day.

22 December 2010: Koli was found guilty of the June 2006 murder of Deepali Sarkar (twelve) and given a fourth death sentence.

24 December 2012: Koli was found guilty of the 4 June 2005 murder of Chhoti Kavita (five) and given a fifth death sentence.

To describe Koli as a monster is an understatement. Here was a man who killed and raped innocent children as young as five to satisfy his sexual frustrations and chopped up their bodies. He even claimed to have cooked and eaten parts of his victims. This was Hannibal Lecter in flesh and blood. India had never seen such a monster before.

Pandey had a theory: if Koli could attack and kill Payal, who was a teenager, the five- and seven-year-olds must have been a cakewalk for him, as the little ones would not have managed to even put up a fight.[60]

With no recourse in the court, Koli applied for a mercy petition, which was rejected by then president Pranab Mukherjee on 20 July 2014.

On 3 September 2014, the court issued a black warrant[61] against him.

The CBI was determined to send him to the gallows. On the evening of the next day, Koli was transferred to Meerut Jail, as hanging facilities were unavailable at Dasna Jail in Ghaziabad, where he was housed.

Koli could not get a wink of sleep at Meerut Jail as he kept hearing about the executioner visiting the jail and checking the equipment for the hanging. He withdrew into a shell. He knew that time was running out. Meanwhile, the Nithari villagers waited with bated breath to hear about the exact date of the execution.

Koli was scheduled to hang at 5.30 a.m. on 8 September. His lawyers, Yug Chaudhry, Siddhartha Sharma, S. Prabhu Ramasubramanian, Paarivendhan, S. Gowthaman and Ragini Ahuja, moved like lightning. Their aim was to get a stay on the death warrant.

It was Sunday. The apex court registrar (vacations) wanted a confirmation but the bureaucrats they reached out to either had their phones switched off or couldn't confirm or deny the death warrant.

By midnight, they were camping outside the home of Justice H.L. Dattu, the second senior-most judge in the country and designated to take over as the next chief justice.

At around 1 a.m., the team sent in the application to stay Koli's execution.

Between 1 and 2 a.m., they kept running around and managed to get a stay order at 2.30 a.m., three hours before Koli was supposed to be hanged.

* * *

Never before had a serial killer grabbed India by its jugular like Koli. There was enough masala, plot twists and turns and voyeurism to write a movie. And the story is not finished yet.

Over the next few years, the killers have faced trial and their fate has been more or less sealed. If Pandher thought that the conspiracy theories would help his case, then he was wrong. He was arrested by the police again and more trials followed.

On 22 July 2017, the CBI court convicted both Koli and Pandher for kidnapping, raping and killing twenty-year-old Pinki Sarkar and sentenced them to death.

Pawan Tiwari, CBI special judge (anti-corruption), held prime accused Koli guilty of murder, abduction, attempted rape and destruction of evidence in the eighth case related to the murder of Pinki Sarkar; and 'Pandher was held guilty of murder, destruction of evidence and attempted rape'.[62]

On 9 December 2017, Pawan Kumar Tiwari, CBI special judge, called the killings the 'rarest of rare' and convicted both Pandher and Koli to the gallows to be hanged till death in the case of the rape and murder of a maid, Anjali.

At the end, I would like to point out the various questions that are still on the minds of the people.

No Witness?

Apart from Pandher and Koli, there were other people in the house. There was Maya Sarkar, a domestic help; a gardener; and two drivers. As per his conviction, Koli committed the murders in the living room between 9 a.m. and 4 p.m. He would carry the corpses upstairs to the bathroom attached to his room, strip the victims of their clothes and chop them up into pieces. Koli would leave the bathroom in that bloody condition while he cooked and ate some of the body parts. He would come out of his trance-like state only after three–four hours and clean the living room and the bathroom. The throttling of the victim was done in the living room while they were dismembered in the bathroom upstairs. It is too much to believe that not once during any of the nineteen murders did the other four employees notice anything. And why were they not tried as witnesses at the trial?

The Confession under Duress

Human rights activists point out that the only clinching evidence against Koli is his confession to the magistrate. Koli has repeatedly mentioned that he had been tortured to give the confession and had been threatened to not deviate from the police narrative. In his letter to the apex court, Koli mentioned that the magistrate failed to notice the telltale signs of torture—his fingernails and toenails were missing. Koli claims he was not medically examined before or after the confessional statement to determine his physical condition.

More importantly, the statement was taken down in English—a language Koli does not understand—and the stenographer was not examined in court.

The Missing Torsos

In the WCD report, Dr Vinod Kumar had mentioned that the bodies were cut with surgical precision and that the torsos of all the bodies were missing; and that the CBI should further investigate the motive of organ trafficking.

Extra Bodies

There were nineteen skulls recovered—sixteen complete and three broken. Koli confessed to killing sixteen kids. Then who killed the other three victims whose body parts were recovered? Whose bodies are they?

Devineni observes, 'India is a very emotional country and the rush for judgment was obvious to me. I think the media got caught up in the sensational nature of the crime and never questioned if Pandher could have been innocent. There was no reflection.'[63]

So is Pandher really innocent? Or is a loyal servant covering and protecting his master by taking the fall? Or are they both guilty of committing such dastardly murders? Or is Koli the only one guilty of the gruesome crimes?

On 7 April 2019, a CBI court awarded the eleventh death sentence to Koli.

This was in the case where a ten-year-old girl went missing after she had gone to deliver 'ironed' clothes at D-5. The court of special judge Amit Vir Singh held Koli guilty.[64]

The court acquitted Pandher due to lack of evidence.[65]

The saga continues.

RAMAN RAGHAV

A.K.A. INDIA'S JACK THE RIPPER

'*Ek marenge toh kabhi uthega hi nahin* [If I hit once, then
he will never rise again].'[1]

—Raman Raghav

It was 1968. Bombay was muggy, eerily still and depressed.
It was only 10 p.m. but the city's nightclubs had long
regurgitated its occupants, the drum sets had been packed. The
cigarette butts and dusty footprints on the dance floor were the
only reminders of revelry from a few hours ago. The nightclubs
should have been alive and full. There should have been music
wafting out of the restaurants. But the city lay silent, a blanket
of fear wrapped around it. A serial killer was on the loose and
nobody wanted to be his next victim.

Raman Raghav saw a light flickering inside one of the
houses in a slum alongside the Ahmedabad highway near
Malad. Stealthily, he peeped inside and saw a woman playing
with and nursing her infant son. Raghav's eyes quickly scanned
the interior of the house and came to a stop on what seemed to
be a gold chain around the woman's neck; it looked expensive.
His eyes glistened with greed.

He squatted in the bushes, waiting for the woman to fall
asleep so he could strike. But the woman had no intention
of falling sleep, maybe her intuition told her to stay awake.
Raghav gave up at about 3 a.m. and walked away. The woman
lived to see another day. And four more, till Raghav, who had

been relentlessly visiting her every night, finally found her asleep on the fifth night.

He slunk into the house. The woman and the child were fast asleep on one bed and her husband on the adjacent one. Raghav took out the iron rod he was carrying—his friend, the *akada*—and swiftly dealt a fatal blow on the man's head. A crunch was heard as the impact smashed the man's skull. The side of his face caved in. He convulsed and a stream of blood flowed out of his mouth. Raghav repeatedly hit him with the rod till the man's head was a messy pulp of blood, skull and brain.

The woman woke up due to the commotion and as she opened her mouth to scream, Raghav sneered and smashed her head with the rod, splitting it down the middle. It didn't take that much effort to kill the child, only three blows were enough. Raghav was on an adrenaline high. He snatched the chain from around the neck of the woman and wiped off the blood on it with the end of her sari. Something stirred in his loins at the sight of the dead woman. He tore open her blouse, unbuttoned his shorts and mounted her. With every thrust, her head bobbed and blood and brain dripped on to the floor. Once he was done, he buttoned up his shorts, picked up a can of paint that he found on the floor and was about to step out, when a woman outside spotted him and screamed. Raghav ran away into the night.

Three victims for a can of paint and a necklace that turned out to be made of glass beads and imitation gold.

This is the story of Raman Raghav, India's most depraved serial killer, who killed because the urge was too strong, motive be damned.

* * *

Cursed be the day in 1950 when a young, swarthy lad named Sindhi Dalwai arrived in Bombay from Tirunelveli, Tamil

Nadu, and was immediately absorbed by the city. Little did Bombay know that in a few years' time, Dalwai would be terrorizing it under a new name: Raman Raghav.

Dalwai worked as a millhand for a short while, thereafter doing odd jobs to fill his stomach. When that became challenging, he resorted to petty theft, for which he was picked up by the police and sent to jail. He was a regular at Byculla jail. He was short-tempered and easily upset by anything and everything. Once at a tea shack, when he ordered a strong milk 'cutting chai' and found the seller diluting the concoction by adding water, he lost his cool. He decided to kill the tea seller. He tracked him down to his house at night and was about to attack, when he was caught and charges of theft were slapped against him. He was sent off to jail for a year and a half. These short spells in the jail, however, had no effect on him whatsoever. Any other person would probably have hung up his thieving boots and tried to eke out an honourable way of living. But to Dalwai these punishments meant nothing.

Around 1966, the eastern suburbs of Bombay suddenly threw up a series of corpses, all of whose heads were smashed with a hard and blunt object. As many as nineteen people were attacked while they were asleep—nine succumbed to their injuries while the others had no clue what or who had hit them. Most of the victims were squatters, who lived in shanties along the municipality water pipeline, also known as the 'duct-line'. And so, Bombay police geared up and 24x7 patrolling became the norm. During one such patrolling session, the cops noticed a man prowling around suspiciously. He was picked up for questioning.

Detective inspector Vinayakrao Vakatkar, head of the homicide squad at Crime Branch, sat opposite the man.

'*Naam kya hai tera?* [What's your name?]' Vakatkar asked.

'Raman Raghav,' the man answered calmly.

'*Tera fingerprints humare record main hai . . . aur tera asli naam hai Sindhi Dalwai* [Your fingerprints are there with the police and your real name is Sindhi Dalwai].' Vakatkar had obviously done his homework.

When Raghav had been arrested by the cops, they had been stunned to find his prints in the police records, not once, but nine times. He had been convicted nine times for petty theft and had already spent five years in prison.

'*Tu toh purana chawal nikla!* [You seem to be quite a veteran!]' Vakatkar prodded. '*Har baar arrest hua hai, aur woh bhi naye naam ke saath?* [Every time you have been arrested, you have given a new name to the cops?]'

Raghav just sat there looking balefully at Vakatkar.

'Sindhi Dalwai, Tambi, Veluswami, Anna, Talwai, *YEH SAB TERE NAAM HAI?* [ALL THESE NAMES ARE YOURS?]' Vakatkar yelled.

Raghav did not bat an eyelid. '*Haan, saab. Yeh mere naam hai* [Yes, these are my names].'

While searching his belongings, the police had recovered a pocket diary. Vakatkar picked up the diary and opened it to a page on which two words were scribbled: '*Khatam*' and '*Kilas*', which means finished, or alludes to death. Beside these two words, Raghav had scribbled something in an unknown alphabet, followed by some numbers.

'*Ye sab kya hai?* [What is all this?]' Vakatkar demanded. He knew he was on to something. Could this be the killer who had attacked nineteen people on the streets? His gut told him 'yes'. But there was no concrete proof that tied him to the murders.

Raghav did not say a word. The police formally arrested and charged him with multiple murders. However, there was no substantial proof to nail him. The court had no other option but to dismiss the charges.

'He was a hard nut to crack,' recalled Vakatkar in an interview with Ramakant Kulkarni, the then deputy commissioner of police, crime investigation department (crime).[2]

The police, having failed to nail the suspected killer, did what they could do best. Raghav was externed[3] from Bombay city for a period of two years.

The Bombay police had the killer in their grasp but had to loosen their fists and watch him leave.

The killings stopped.

And then, exactly two years later, they started again. Slum-dwellers spent countless sleepless nights, fearing the worst.

Streets in the western suburbs got deserted by twilight and no one turned up for night shows any more. Alex Fialho, who was then a police sub-inspector, distinctly remembers the chaos unleashed by the man who admitted to have murdered forty-two people over a period of six years. 'Even the local trains were practically empty beyond Andheri till the end of the western line, since most of the murders were committed in the western suburbs.'[4]

Soon, an absurd rumour spread: the killer was a sadhu who had the ability to transform himself into a parrot or a cat to disappear into the night undetected. Panic led to pandemonium. Vigilante groups kept watch at night and even beat up and lynched sadhus when they saw them.

In an interview to *Indian Express*, film director Sriram Raghavan—who directed a short telefilm in 1987 called *Raman Raghav, a City, a Killer*, starring Raghuvir Yadav as the eponymous character—recalled:

Public imagination ran wild. At some places, he was spotted rushing into a bush, with a bird flying off from the swamp. In another instance, a dog was seen coming out of a hut where a murder had taken place. Soon, a rumour spread that he could change his form. He could become a parrot, a dog, or a cat. Some insisted that he had an alien presence about him, that he had supernatural powers.[5]

One of the reasons for this rumour to have reached epidemic proportions was the fact that English newspapers were on strike. 'There was a fortnight-long English-newspaper strike during the killings that made matters worse. In the absence of factual news, rumours spread faster,' recalled police historian Deepak Rao in an interview to *Indian Express* in 2016.[6]

Kulkarni was tasked with solving the case and catching the killer. He was at his wits' end. How could he search for a killer across the entire city? Where was he to begin?

In the meantime, Raghav continued his killings.

While the police searched slums and hutments, Raghav hid in the jungles near Jogeshwari and Aarey Colony. He lived in the thickets, cooked his own food on a stove and hid the loot from his murderous expeditions in the bushes.

* * *

During the attack on the woman with the imitation-gold necklace, Raghav had lost his akada as he had to run off when the neighbour started screaming. He needed a new weapon now. He approached an old friend, Michael.

Michael called Raghav 'Tambi' affectionately, meaning elder brother in Tamil. He had befriended Raghav at the mill where both of them used to work. They had become good friends and Raghav would often visit his house and play with his daughter, Violet.

'Where have you been for the last two years?' Michael asked, happy to see his old friend again.

'I was in the village. I returned recently and have no place to stay,' Raghav lied.

Michael grew nervous. Was Tambi expecting to be put up at his house? How would he explain this to his wife and pacify her?

As if he read his mind, Raghav hastily added, 'Don't worry, I am planning to build a hut for myself. I need to borrow a crowbar. Do you have one?'

Michael was relieved. He handed Raman an octagonal crowbar. 'This is the only one I have, so please return it to me once you are done with it.'

He returned after three days while Michael and Violet were having tea. Raghav told Violet, 'I have something special for you.'

Violet rushed towards him. 'What is it? What is it?' she asked excitedly.

Raghav pulled out two fountain pens and a magnifying glass from his pockets and gave them to Violet. Strangely, Michael failed to suspect anything fishy and instead, being the good host that he was, offered him tea.

'I do not drink tea made by Christians,' Raghav said. Michael was taken aback by this bigoted comment. After all, they had known each other for years and never before had Raghav said something so offensive.

Michael grew angry. He demanded rudely, 'When will you return my crowbar?' which made Raghav fly into a rage and he left.

* * *

Back in 1968, only a fistful of huts and shanties were sprinkled across Malad; there were no high-rises then. For Raghav, this was the ideal hunting ground. One day, he saw an old Muslim man sleeping outside his hut on a charpoy. Raghav crept up to him. In his hand was his akada, which was fashioned out of a motorcycle handle that he had found a few days earlier.

He smashed the old man's skull open and took the wristwatch that he was wearing. He also took the *jhaba* that belonged to the victim, along with some money that he found in its pocket. He also stole some groundnuts that were in a bottle next to the cot, an umbrella and a torch. He hit the jackpot that night. In the pocket of the jhaba, he found a hundred-rupee note, sixteen notes of Rs 10 and some loose change.[7] He lived lavishly for a few days before the money ran out and he had to go on a hunt again.

Raghav was a hunter and a scavenger. He killed because he had to. He was always short of money. In such a circumstance, any other person would have resorted to petty theft or burglary. But Raghav had an abundance of sinister urges. As Shakespeare wrote in *King Lear*, 'As flies to wanton boys are we to th' gods. They kill us for their sport.'

Meanwhile, Mumbaikars grew paranoid. Many people beat up hapless beggars, suspecting them to be the killer. The hunt was on but there were no leads.

Kulkarni prayed every night that no fresh corpses should appear in the morning. But the body count only swelled up. And although the murders were spread over two months, Raghav killed seven people within a week in August—a body every day!

The press dubbed him 'India's Jack the Ripper', but Raghav had no clue of this. He was lost in his own insanity.

Emmanuel Sumitra Modak, a soft-spoken Jewish gentleman, was at that time Mumbai's police commissioner. He had to face the music from politicians and the press. Fialho, who was eighty-six when he was interviewed by *Mumbai Mirror*, recalled: 'He [Modak] would sit down for breakfast each morning in his chambers and receive a call from some police station or another, with the same message, "Sir, murder."'[8]

Sami Iyer, deputy commissioner and singer Usha Uthup's father, was eager to nab the murderer. 'Before the ink even dries on the pad, there's another murder. We need to get this guy early and stop him.'[9]

For the first time, Crime Branch used a full-size map of the city to pin the murder sites. The ominous red dots denoting the murder sites grew in number every day, spreading across Oshiwara, Goregaon, Malad, Kandivali, Borivali and Dahisar.

One night, around 2 a.m., Raghav found a man sleeping inside a shack at Hanuman Nagar, Kandivali. The door was locked from inside. If he broke open the door, the man would get alerted. So with his akada, he started digging under the door and then crawled inside. As he was giggling at the ingenuity of his idea, the man woke up, groggy. Before his eyes could focus on Raghav, the akada smashed into his skull. The disoriented man lay writhing on the bed. Raghav kept hitting him on the head and the shoulder till he stopped moving; the pillows and bed sheet had turned scarlet with blood.

Raghav removed the wristwatch from the dead man's hand and pulled out five one-rupee notes from his pocket. He ransacked the room, looking for more stuff to loot. He broke open a box that contained books; he found a utensil that had dalda (hydrogenated vegetable oil), and a tin of wheat flour. He stole everything, along with a stove that he spotted in the room.

Did the man deserve to die such a horrible death? Was murder justified for a tin of wheat flour, dalda and five rupees?

Kulkarni writes aptly in his book, *Footprints on the Sands of Crime*: 'The murders were motiveless . . . if any petty gain had been achieved in the process, the violence inflicted on the victims was totally disproportionate to any such gain.'[10]

* * *

At Rawalpada, a milkman named Laxman Jetha and his relative, Devram Bharwad, usually kept guard at night. It was Bharwad's turn that night and he fell asleep on his charpoy while keeping watch, a plate of unfinished food lying beside him. Raghav had been eagerly waiting for this moment. He emerged from the shadows.

He smashed Bharwad's skull. It took five blows to kill him.[11] He looked around. There was no one. He sat on his haunches next to the body and ate the leftover dinner of rice, vegetable curry and buttermilk. He then frisked the body and extracted a matchbox and a few bidis from the breast pocket of Bharwad's kurta.

On his way out of the locality, Raghav spotted a woman sleeping with two infants. Shantabai was fast asleep, unaware that a predator was watching her and her children. Raghav struck her, swiftly, silently. Three blows and the woman never woke up. He lifted the thin blanket that she had used to cover herself and saw that she was naked.

'She had covered her body with a sheet of cloth, on removing which I found she was nude. I sucked her breasts and found the milk so sweet that I drank as much as I could,' he would later confess to R.M. Devre, presidency magistrate, on 11 November 1968. 'Then I had sexual intercourse with her [corpse].'[12]

Meanwhile, Kulkarni reduced the radius of the search from being wide and unmanageable to a concentrated area, according to the 'Geometry of Crime'.

'It was considered kind of nutty when it was first proposed,' says Marcus Felson of Rutgers University in New Jersey, who had propounded it.[13] The Geometry of Crime suggests that a killer commits murders in an area far away from his residence to avoid being recognized, and yet, not far enough away that he is unfamiliar with the area. Raghav always killed along the duct-line because it was far away from where he lived, and yet, he knew the area well.

In the second round of killings, he had chosen the suburbs around Malad, Jogeshwari and Kandivali as his hunting ground, which meant the police did not need to patrol the entire city, but just the areas around these sites. Unknown to Raghav, the police were closing in slowly.

Kulkarni knew that criminals behaved like ordinary people. They visited their hunting ground for reconnaissance to become familiar with the area and to avoid being caught in the act.

Kulkarni recalled the arrest of one Raman Raghav from two years ago. His instincts told him that there had been a slip between the cup and the lip and the killer had escaped from their clutches. It was too much of a coincidence that the killings had resumed just when his two-year externment period got over. Kulkarni got hold of the dossier on Raghav, which contained his photographs and fingerprints. He then compiled a list of people who had known him, even if it were casually. A lookout notice was issued and police teams fanned out in search of Raghav and his acquaintances.

There were a thousand policemen on patrolling duty at night looking for suspicious people and those who matched Raghav's description. Five days later, the dice finally rolled in their favour.

'"Anna" . . . that was what we called him,' Manjulabai Dalvi, who lived in Poisar village and worked as a maid, recalled, when she was shown Raghav's photograph.

'Sahib, I don't want any trouble,' she said haltingly. Manjulabai had been taken by surprise when two strange men had accosted her in the street and showed her the photograph. She had no clue that the men were police officers in plain clothes.

'Nothing will happen to you. We are just doing a routine check on him,' the policeman assured her.

'Has he done anything wrong, sahib?' she asked, adjusting and pulling the *pallu* of her sari to cover herself more.

When he didn't say anything, she continued: 'He used to stay alone in the locality and nobody knew what he did for a living.' The policemen let her go.

'This *madarchod* [mother-fucker] has made our lives miserable,' one of the cops muttered under his breath.

Just then, Manjulabai turned and walked back to them. 'I just remembered. I had seen him this morning.' She had their attention now.

'*Tula kaye disale?* [What did you see?]' the cop asked Manjulabai.

'I was on my way to fetch water from the well when I bumped into him. I asked him what he was doing here. He said he had some work to complete and then headed that way, towards Mochi Chawl,' she pointed into the distance.

'*Tane kapade kaya ghatale hote?* [What was he wearing?]' the cops could barely hide their excitement.

'Khaki shorts, blue shirt, brown canvas shoes . . . and, oh! he was carrying an umbrella.' The cops immediately jumped into their jeep and roared away.

A wireless message from the Crime Branch was radioed out. It seemed that the dragnet was finally tightening.

In the meantime, the forensics team came back with more good news. They had matched Raghav's prints from the dossier with the ones found at two of the murder sites and they were a perfect fit.

Police now had the proof required to formally arrest Raghav. But where was he? Had he given them the slip again?

Another blessing was on its way. On the night of 26 August 1968, two corpses were found at a cattle shed at Chincholi, Malad. Lalchand Jagannath Yadav and Dular Jaggi Yadav were daily wage labourers who worked there. Their place of work had become their place of death. What differentiated this incident from the others was a statement given by a thirteen-year-old eyewitness. He had seen the killer fleeing and then 'wading through a dirty nullah, clutching something under his armpit'.

The police remembered recovering the broken axle of a truck in one of the victims' houses (remember the akada that

Raghav had to leave behind after he was spotted by a neighbour during one of his kills?). In this case, too, the killer was seen carrying a rod.

There was a buzz in the Crime Branch like never before. The gloom and despair that had clouded the office over the past two months slowly seemed to be lifting off.

* * *

Fialho will always remember 27 August 1968. He was posted at Dongri police station and lived in the police quarters at Bhendi Bazar. It was morning and he was on his way to work. The bus to Dongri was due to arrive at the bus stop at any moment. He impatiently checked his watch.

'Those days I used to carry photographs of the serial killer, Raman Raghav, in my shirt pocket. As I was waiting for a bus, I saw this well-built man in khaki shorts and a long blue bush shirt walking in my direction,' Fialho recalled in an interview to *DNA* in 2007.[14]

His stomach was knotted in excitement as adrenaline coursed through his veins. Fialho replayed the wireless message in his head—the description of the person, the clothes he was wearing and the umbrella he was carrying—and found that everything matched. But he was cautious. He didn't want to lose the suspect. He casually waited for Raghav to pass him by first, so he could observe his reaction to a man in uniform.

'I didn't want to intercept him right away unless I was absolutely certain. Also, I wanted to see his reaction to a man in uniform. He gave me a sarcastic look and walked past.'[15]

As Raghav did not panic on seeing a cop, Fialho fell into a swamp of doubt. A regular criminal would have shown signs of panic or tried to run. But here, the fellow just walked past him calmly. For a moment, Fialho thought that this wasn't Raghav. But on second thoughts, he fished out Raghav's photo from his pocket. And he knew he had his man. The striking cold eyes that had stared into his just a few seconds ago now stared coldly back at him from the police mug shot.[16]

Fialho started following him and it was then that he noticed that Raghav's clothes were bloodstained.

That morning, roads were crowded with office-goers hurrying to their workplaces. Fialho wanted to nab Raghav before he crossed the Bhendi Bazaar junction to SV Patel Road, where the crowd would swallow him up. The junction was a few feet away, when Fialho finally caught up with Raghav. He tapped on his shoulder and said: 'Come with me, I have some work for you.'

It was a gamble. He was ready to chase in case Raghav tried to run. But he didn't have to. Raghav started following Fialho like a lost puppy who had found his master.

Fialho noticed that the umbrella Raghav was carrying was still wet. He looked up at the skies just to be sure. It hadn't rained in the area for the past two days.

'Where are you coming from?' he asked Raghav.

'Chincholi, Malad,' he replied matter-of-factly.

Fialho remembered that it had been raining in Malad the night of the double murders at the cattle shed.

'And that is when my doubts were confirmed; we had information that he was last seen ten days ago by a woman who resided in Malad. Also, her description of his clothes—a blue shirt, blue khakhi shorts and brown canvas shoes—matched.'[17]

Fialho called up the Dongri police station and asked for a jeep. Once the jeep arrived, Raghav sat unsuspectingly in it and Fialho drove to the police station.

'*Tera naam kya hai?* [What's your name?]' Fialho asked Raghav.

'Sindhi Dalwai, saab,' Raghav answered without batting an eyelid.

Fialho wasn't interested in trailers, he went straight for the movie. He gave Raghav a resounding slap across his face.[18]

'*Tera naam Raman Raghav hai* [Your name is Raman Raghav].' Fialho was impatient. He pushed the file photograph towards him and asked: '*Yeh tu hi hai na?* [This is you, isn't it?]'

Raghav took his time pulling out a pair of spectacles from his pocket and wearing them. He stared at the black-and-white photograph in front of him for some time before replying, '*Saab, mere jaisa hi dikhta hain, par main nahin hain. Yeh koi aur hain* [Sir, this person looks like me, but it's not me. It's somebody else].'[19]

While the fingerprint experts were on their way from the police head office, Fialho asked Raghav to empty his pockets.

A pair of spectacles, two combs, a pair of scissors, a thimble, a stand for burning incense, soap, garlic, tea dust and two pieces of paper with some mathematical figures on them came out. It was later established that the half-rimmed spectacles that Raghav was wearing had belonged to a school principal he had murdered a few days ago and the thimble had belonged to a tailor he had killed as well.

The fingerprints matched and Fialho handcuffed Raghav and formally arrested him under Section 302 of the IPC, charging him for the murder of two persons, Lalchand Jagannath Yadav and Dular Jaggi Yadav.

Fialho knew that if the public got a whiff of Raghav's arrest, there would be a riot and the mob would kill him. As he waited to hand him over to the Crime Branch, Fialho instructed the policemen to lock up the police station, called in reinforcements and waited for the commissioner to arrive. A crowd began gathering outside the Crime Branch head office at Crawford Market. The evening dailies had gone to town with the news of his arrest and the crowd wanted to take a look at the man who could supposedly transform himself.

The situation was getting hairy. Just then, commissioner Modak and inspector Vakatkar arrived and took custody of Raghav.

Fialho was rewarded Rs 1000 for nabbing Raghav.

If the Crime Branch thought their job was done, they were wrong. For two days, Raghav didn't utter anything. No amount of 'fireworks' (the term for thrashing criminals in lockup) produced even a squeak out of him. Veteran interrogators tried to break him but failed.[20]

As Kulkarni recounts, 'Two days passed. The suspect continued to maintain a studied silence . . . even the robust enthusiasm of some of our seasoned officers like Basil Kane, Vakatkar, Pendse and Dalvi started showing signs of flagging. In desperation I sent up a fervent prayer and the Lord answered it readily.'[21]

Out of the blue, one of the officers present in the interrogation room asked Raghav if he wanted something. His eyes lit up immediately and he answered, '*Murgi* [Chicken].'

Promptly, Kulkarni sent off a junior constable to a nearby restaurant. He returned with a large plate of chicken biryani. Raghav polished it off without taking a breath and then licked his fingers in relish. He burped. Suddenly, he seemed happy. The officer asked him if he wanted anything else, to which he replied 'murgi' again. He wolfed down the second plate of biryani as well. Soon, his body language changed from uptight and reserved to relaxed.

Next, he wanted perfumed hair oil, a comb and a mirror.

'I would also like a prostitute, but I guess the law does not permit that while one is in custody,'[22] he cackled like a madman.

'My father really believed in understanding the psychology of both the victims and the accused in all his cases. So, for him, sympathy was very important. Raghav liked perfumed hair oil and chicken biryani, so when his wishes were fulfilled, he talked. My father was successful in getting him to confess by softening him up,' recalled Anita Bhogle, Kulkarni's daughter.[23]

Kulkarni mentions in *Footprints on the Sand of Crime* that he came across an interesting book called *Criminal Investigation* by Arthur S. Aubry and Rudolph R. Caputo. In it, the authors had pointed out that 'one of the mental mechanisms involved is an unconscious desire on the part of the individual to repay the interrogator for the kindness and sympathy that he has offered to the individual'. When Kulkarni gave in to Raghav's wishes for chicken biryani and other demands, Raghav felt in debt for Kulkarni's generosity and decided to pay it back the only way he could: a confession.

That day, the constable again ran out to a nearby kirana shop and bought a bottle of perfumed coconut oil. Raghav poured some into his palms and inhaled deeply. He smiled.

'This smells really good,' he said, as he rubbed the oil over his dark, swarthy body. Sitting on a stool, flanked by six policemen, he took his time rubbing some of the oil on his scalp as well. He was the king of the moment. He combed his hair and looked in the mirror for a long time. Then, according to Kulkarni, he suddenly sat upright. He turned to the police officers and asked, 'Now tell me, what do you want to know?'

The show, it seemed, was about to begin.

'We want to know about the murders,' an officer told him.

'Get a vehicle, an armed guard and two witnesses. The law requires that,' he replied.[24]

The policemen were stunned at this sudden volte-face, but nonetheless overjoyed that they had finally managed to break through.

'We would like to know where you have hidden your weapon?' an officer asked.

Kulkarni recalls in his book that Raghav immediately replied, 'Yes, yes. I shall tell you that too . . . I will show you the iron akada that I used for doing khatam, and a jimmy, knives and other things that I have concealed in the bushes at Aarey Colony.'[25]

Had it occurred to Raghav that he had been arrested? That he had murdered over forty people and that there were serious consequences he had to face?

A motley gang of policemen, the DCP, Raghav and the witnesses boarded a police vehicle and, as per instructions from Raghav, headed towards Jogeshwari. The hunter was now showing off his hunting grounds. Near Aarey road, he asked the driver to stop the vehicle. Everyone alighted and Raghav crawled like a snake through a gap in the barbed-wire fence across the road and led the party to an overgrown field.

'You wanted to see my weapon?' he asked with a twinkle in his eyes. He put his hand in a bush and pulled out an iron fulcrum jimmy.

'This is my friend, akada,' he said, beaming.

Kulkarni looked at the weapon that had silenced over three dozen people. It was an octagonal rod bent at one end and tapering at the other. It looked like a car-cranking handle. There were bloodstains on it.[26]

'How did you use this?' Kulkarni asked.

Raghav proceeded to demonstrate with glee. 'I hold the long end of the rod and strike with the bent end.' He slashed in the air and giggled.

'I always hit on the head. *Ek marenge toh kabhi uthega hi nahin* [If I hit once, then he will never rise again].'[27]

One of the constables took the rod from his hand with a handkerchief to avoid contamination of fingerprints.

Out of the bush, Raghav also pulled out a bloodstained cloth bundle, which contained a screwdriver, an iron jimmy, a torch and a towel—his meagre loot after the heinous murders.

Raghav was produced before the presidency magistrate where he confessed to having killed forty people. When asked why he wanted to confess, he replied that he had been instructed to do so by the Almighty.[28]

When the case went to trial, the defence counsel said that Raghav was of unsound mind. Dr C.A. Franklin, the police surgeon, kept him under observation for three weeks and concluded that he was not certifiably insane and, therefore, could stand trial. The court was determined to hang Raghav, while the defence team cited one argument after another to prove that he had no clue about what he had done. They said that he had not resisted arrest; was seen wearing the same blood-soaked clothes in broad daylight and showed no fear or remorse, and, hence, did not understand the gravity of the crimes he had committed. They also mentioned that he suffered from auditory hallucinations.

Dr Patkar, who had examined Raghav earlier, was called in. He interviewed him for nearly two hours and concluded that he suffered from 'chronic paranoid schizophrenia' or a split personality.

Eminent journalist and author, Khushwant Singh, was covering the trial for the *Illustrated Weekly of India*. He wrote that Raghav wore a 'contemptuous disdain' throughout the trial and 'hatred of women is a dominant aspect of Raman Raghav's character'. He also wrote, 'He had his own notions of right and wrong,' and 'he is finicky as a middle-class spinster when it comes to hygiene.'[29]

Raghav repeatedly requested the police and his jailor for two prostitutes—the first for sex, and the other to take care of the first. Raghav, it seemed hated women, and yet, craved sex.

In his essay 'Portrait of a Serial Killer' (1969),[30] Singh throws light on why Raghav craved women's company despite being a misogynist. Apparently, as is customary with certain castes in Tamil Nadu, a marriage was arranged for him with his sister's daughter, Guruamma. Before he could consummate the marriage, he was arrested for theft and packed off to jail.

Meanwhile, his wife slept with another man, got impregnated and died while giving birth to a stillborn child. This was the first strike of betrayal.

When he returned to the village, the elders found him another woman. Raghav discovered that this woman had been rejected by another man and had had children by him. He was livid that he was being given another man's reject. This was the second strike.

When he came to Bombay, he befriended a millworker who worked night shifts, while he did day shifts. It seems, one rainy night, this friend's wife invited Raghav to share her bed. He refused. The next morning, the woman complained to her husband that Raghav had tried to seduce her. They all lived in the same chawl and due to the complaint, Raghav was thrown out of there. This was the third strike.

Singh writes: 'Thus was Raman Raghav betrayed, abandoned, abused. To his way of thinking, there was always a woman behind every episode. He became a confirmed misogynist and a lone wolf. If no one had any use for him, he in turn had no use for anyone.'[31]

The court directed a special medical board to interview Raghav—which it did across five sessions of two hours each. The board concluded that Raghav showed ideas of reference and fixed and systematized delusions of persecution and grandeur.

A different universe existed between his ears!

He believed that there were two distinct worlds: one, of 'kanoon' or the legal, righteous world, and two, the world in which he lived.

He also had an unshakable belief that people were trying to turn him into a woman and change his sexual orientation. He believed that people were trying to tempt him into becoming effeminate, and that the only reason they had been unsuccessful in their attempts was because he represented the world of kanoon.

In his conversation with Dr Patkar, Raghav said that he always killed after receiving the command to do so from a '*duniya* wireless' inside his head. He believed that it was Lord Shiva who was talking to him. These wireless messages in his head, which he referred to as kanoon, came as buzzing commands.[32]

Raghav believed that he was a power or Shakti and kept repeating to everybody that he was '101 per cent man'.

He believed that there were three governments in the country: the Akbar government (referring to Mughal Emperor Akbar who had ruled India from 1556–1605 CE), the British government and the Congress government, and that these three governments had brought him to Bombay to commit the murders.

The Bombay High Court in its order on 4 August 1987 observed:

> The accused has thought, or has suffered from a delusion, that he was acting under the command of a law which was higher than the law of the land. He also regarded that it was obligatory upon him to follow the kanoon which told him to kill persons.[33]

In their final interview when the doctors said goodbye to Raghav and attempted to shake hands with him, he shrank back, saying that as he was a representative of the world of kanoon, he could not touch people belonging to a lower, wicked world.

In his head, he belonged to a much higher and grander world than the one he was living in.

In an interview with *Indian Express*, Sachin Patkar, son of Dr Patkar, recalled reading and studying his father's notes about Raghav's command hallucinations closely. As per his father's conclusions, his biggest fear was becoming impotent and the voice asked him to kill all those who wanted to turn him into a woman. It was as if Raghav was protecting himself and his manhood through the murders and rapes.[34]

In *Portrait of A Serial Killer*, Singh writes that Raghav was so paranoid about losing his manhood that when a barber accidentally shaved off his moustache, he flew into a fit of rage, screaming that he didn't want to look like a woman or a hijra.[35]

The court and the public were shocked at the revelations and confessions made by Raghav. Calling the case 'unparalleled and unsurpassed in the history of crime', and declaring that he deserved the highest degree of punishment, the court sentenced him to death on 13 August 1969.[36]

Raghav was taken to Yerawada Central Jail in Pune. The prisoners, having heard about him, were terrified to be housed in the same premises as him.

While his case went to the higher courts, he kept writing letters asking for his trial to be expedited. Doctors re-examined him and concluded that his insanity was incurable. After nineteen years of him being sentenced to death, the Bombay High Court reduced the sentence to life imprisonment in 1987.

The most dreaded serial killer of India, a man who was lost in a haze inside his head, died at Sassoon Hospital due to kidney failure on 7 April 1995.

His story has inspired movies in various languages and Anurag Kashyap's film *Raman Raghav 2.0* (2016), starring Nawazuddin Siddiqui, was inspired by the real Raman Raghav. In an interview with *Hindustan Times*, Kashyap describes Raghav as someone who 'had no moral compass, there was no planning. He killed because some voice in his head told him to do so'.[37]

DARBARA SINGH

A.K.A. BABY KILLER

'I celebrated almost every killing with liquor and
good food.'[1]

—Darbara Singh

*Let me suggest at the outset that if you are reading this in
bed, or after a good, full meal, you should stop right away.
This is not for the faint-hearted. This is real, painful and gut-
wrenching.*

*If you are a parent, hug your little ones tight and say a
prayer of gratitude for they are beside you, safe.*

1975

There was a loud bang, followed by a siren at the air force base
in Pathankot. A few pilots ran out of the recreation room. A
dark plume of smoke was rising out of one of the houses on the
premises. A couple of fire engines zipped past them.

'What happened? Are we being attacked?' one of the pilots
screamed above the noise of the siren and the clanging of the
fire brigade truck.

'There has been an attack on the base,' a squadron leader
yelled back as he rushed towards the house.

There was tension in the air.

Junior Warrant Officer Praveen Sharma had just joined the
base a few months ago and he looked up at the skies to see if

he could spot any enemy aircraft, even though he knew that if there had been an air attack they would have heard the buzzing sound of the approaching aircraft long before the bombs would have hit the ground. He too ran towards the house. A thought raced through his mind. *Had the enemy managed to infiltrate the base? It just wasn't possible! This was an airtight fortress.*

Unfortunately, little did Praveen know in 1975 that his thoughts would turn into a nightmarish reality, forty years later, when terrorists would infiltrate the base on 1 January 2016.

He reached the site of the attack. It was Major V.K. Sharma's house. A posse of Indian Armed Forces soldiers with drawn weapons as well as curious onlookers stood in front of the house, the front of which was completely smashed. Praveen could see the living room through the gaping hole. Two medics rushed out of the house carrying a woman on a stretcher and loaded her into an ambulance and drove off. Two other medics carried out a teenage boy on a stretcher and loaded him into another ambulance, before speeding off towards the base hospital.

Someone yelled: 'Call Major Sharma. He is in the mess.'

By the time Major Sharma arrived, the fire brigade trucks had managed to extinguish the flames that had engulfed the front portion of the house.

This did not look like a terrorist attack, Praveen wondered. And if it were an attack by an enemy of the state, why would they target just one residential house? The logical approach would be to attack areas with 'high-value assets': the hangars with fighter jets or the ammunition depot. He shook his head. He couldn't make sense of what was going on.

It was only a day later that the special investigation committee managed to unravel the mystery behind the attack.

It wasn't terrorists or any enemy of the state that had bombed Major Sharma's house with a hand grenade. It was one Darbara Singh, a soldier with the Indian Armed Forces who was stationed on the base.[2] A few days prior to the attack, Singh had got into an altercation with Major Sharma. He was let off with a warning and a threat from the senior officer. Little did the Major know that he had managed to stir a hornet's nest. Singh, who was seething in anger, stole a hand grenade from the ammunition depot on the base and lobbed it at the Major's house. The Major's wife and teenage son were seriously injured in the attack. Singh was immediately dismissed from the armed forces, arrested and tried. However, he was acquitted for lack of watertight evidence. The base was a happier place without a loose cannon on its premises.

From serving in the Indian Armed Forces to being a serial killer of babies, Singh's journey is fraught with psychotic delusions, misplaced anger, racist, bigoted and prejudiced agendas. But all that mattered to him was slaughtering children.

He had already been married and had three children while he was in the army. Singh loved three things: liquor, beating up his wife and forcing her to have sex. He would cajole her in his drunken, libido-fuelled stupor. When she would resist, he would first thrash her and mount her forcefully. His personal life was a blur to him. After being dismissed from the army, he became more incorrigible.

'They are at it again!' Rukmini said to her husband, Sushil. There seemed to be a screaming match in progress at their neighbours' house.

'Darbara has to stop drinking. Only then will there be some semblance of peace in his household,' Sushil remarked.

The next morning, a noisy fight broke out again in Singh's house. Rukmini and Sushil ran outside their house and joined a crowd that had gathered to watch the tamasha unfolding outside Singh's house.

Singh was standing in a pair of white pyjamas and a singlet, while his wife was screaming at him as their children watched them silently. A tin trunk with its contents spilt, as if it had been disemboweled, lay on the road.

'Is she really throwing him out of the house?' Sushil whispered to his wife.

'Finally!' Rukmini replied, 'I never liked the man. He is an odd fellow.'

Singh did not even turn to look back at his wife and children. He walked out of the house, out of their lives and took his first steps towards hell.

He began doing odd jobs here and there. However, with no sex, Singh's libido began bottling up like a volcano, which was about to erupt. And erupt it did.

Metropolitan cities always attract migrant labourers. They arrive with hope in their hearts, and a dream in their eyes, but mostly they come to fill their empty stomachs. When they get a job, they bring their families, even though they cannot afford to keep them there. So their children often end up working at a brick kiln or a building under construction or left to loiter around the entire day.

Singh was desperate and sexually frustrated. He *had* to have sex. He knew that if he targeted any of the labourers' wives, they would thrash him. So he started looking around for softer targets. And there they were, right in front of him: the young migrant girls.

Kapurthala, 1996

Anger and frustration was writ large on the faces of the labourers. In the last two weeks, two of their little girls had been raped. The girls were aged between eight and ten and found in a semi-conscious state with blood on their frocks. Medical examination had confirmed rape. The builder had threatened the workers with dismissal without any compensation, if they complained to the police.

'*Behnchod, mujhe police nahi chahiye idhar!* [Sister-fuckers, I don't want any cops on my premises!]' he yelled at them.

The workers had no option but to stay quiet. They knew the perpetrator was known to the children and that he had been stalking them to abduct them when their parents were busy at the construction site. But Singh was clever. He did not remain at the construction site once his deed was done. He kept moving from one site to another, thus evading capture. But not for long.

A week later, a little girl's scream was heard from behind one of the makeshift tin sheds at a construction site. The workers rushed towards the source of the sound. There they found Singh with another girl child in flagrante delicto.[3] The labourers rained blows on him and had it not been for the intervention of the supervisor, Singh would have met his maker that day. The supervisor screamed at the labourers, saying that if they killed him, they would all go to jail. He said they should hand him over to the police.

Singh was arrested. He was convicted in three cases of rape and attempted murder and sentenced to thirty years of rigorous imprisonment. But it seems the devil was already at work here. In 2003, his mercy petition was accepted on the basis of his good conduct and he was released. He stepped out of the red-brick Ludhiana Central Jail. He was physically free; but his mind had already become captive to hatred towards migrants. In his head, he had done nothing wrong. He was going to seek revenge on them for sending him to prison in the prime of his life for seven years. He knew he could not get back those years; but he knew how to make them pay.

* * *

Jalandhar, 2004

Singh wanted a new start, so instead of going back to Kapurthala, he headed to Jalandhar. He found a job at a factory in the leather complex area of the city.

'I'll take the room,' Singh said to his prospective landlord, Joginder, who narrowed his eyes at him.

'Where did you say you're from?'

'Amritsar,' Singh said, without batting an eyelid. He knew that his past could get him into trouble. To start a new life, he needed a new history.

Joginder handed the keys over to Singh: 'Timely rent on the third day of every month or you can say goodbye to this room.'

Singh ran his fingers over the cold surface of the keys. He was now a tenant in his new home, in his new life. It was time to plan payback!

Singh's perverse hunger made him blind so much so that he now hunted in the same locality in which he lived: Model Town.

On 18 April 2004, Singh struck not once, but five times in a day.

To execute his plan, Singh went to a provision store and asked for candy.

'Give me fifty of the hard orange ones,' he told the shopkeeper.

'*Aapke kitne bachche hai?* [How many kids do you have?]' the shopkeeper asked curiously.

Singh smiled and answered, '*Teen. Unko yeh orange goli bahut pasand hai* [Three. They love these orange candies].'

The shopkeeper packed the sweets in a paper bag. Singh paid him and left.

He scouted the galis of Model Town looking for his first victim. It was afternoon. Most of the men were at work and the women were either busy with household chores or taking a siesta. The lanes were quiet except for the occasional street dog chasing a cat or a few kids playing hopscotch.

Ten-year-old Gudia threw a broken piece of tile on to a square, in which five was chalked, on the street. She began hopping towards that square. But before she could pick up the tile, a man picked it up. She got irritated. She was competing with her six-year-old brother, Satish. Now the game was spoilt.

'*Tuhada naam ki hai?* [What is your name?]' Singh asked.

Gudia could not understand what Singh said. Would she become his first victim?

'*Punjabi samajh mein nahi aata hai?* [You don't understand Punjabi?]'

'*Hum Bihar se hai. Main Punjabi nahi samajhti hu* [We are from Bihar. I don't understand Punjabi],' Gudia replied.

Singh looked around to ensure there were no adults nearby.

'*Naam kya hai tumhara?* [What is your name?]' he started, priming his victim.

'Gudia,' and lest her brother feel offended for being left out, she added, '*aur yeh mera chota bhai, Satish, hai.*'

Singh pulled out a few sweets from his pocket and offered it to the kids, who couldn't believe their luck. Just two days ago when Satish had demanded a new wooden top from his father, the reply had been simple. His father had yelled at him, reminding him how hard he worked to save money. Hence, such a demand was outrageous and to drive home his point, he followed his cruel words with a resounding slap. The children grabbed the sweets. The smiles on their faces were testimony of the orange goodness spreading inside their mouths.

'Do you want more?' Singh tempted them. He didn't know which way the water would flow.

Satish nodded excitedly. 'Follow me,' he said as he led the two siblings to their doom just like the Pied Piper had led the rats to their death.

En route, the trio met Shankar, an eight-year-old boy.

'*Kahaan ja rahe ho?* [Where are you going?]' Shankar had asked inquisitively.

'*Toffees khanay!* [To eat toffees!]' Satish answered.

'*Tumhe bhi toffees chahiye?* [Would you also like have toffees?]' Singh asked in a loving and paternal manner.

The three kids followed him to a deserted paddy field.

'Why have you got us here?' Gudia asked. 'Where are the sweets that you promised?'

Singh smiled and slit open Satish's throat. As blood spurted out of his tiny throat, both Gudia and Shankar ran for their lives. Singh chased Gudia. His long legs had a bigger reach than her tiny ones. He got hold of her and raped her. Gudia screamed for help. He clamped a hand on her mouth to stifle her screams as he continued to violate her. When he was finished, he finished her. He looked around for Shankar. He was nowhere to be found. Singh cursed his luck and spat into the ground in anger.[4]

Adrenaline was coursing through his veins as he snuffed out two innocent lives. He wanted more. He left the bodies in the field and went on a hunt again.

An hour after killing Gudia and Satish, he strolled into an area called Rasta Mohalla. Diksha (eight) and her sister, Asha (six), along with their two cousins, were playing badminton using makeshift wooden paddles and something that once resembled a shuttlecock. The girls who were lost in their game giggled and laughed, unaware that a man wearing a white shirt and coffee-coloured trousers was watching them; and that one of them would not live to see another day.

'Isn't it difficult to play badminton like that?' Singh was on his haunches to match the eye-line of the little girls. 'I'll buy you a nice racquet and a brand new shuttlecock if you come with me,' he promised. Diksha and Asha followed him, while their cousins stayed back.

Singh took them to the bank of a canal in Bahadurpur Uppal.

'I don't see any shops here,' Diksha asked innocently.

'Asha, you sit here. Before we go shopping, Diksha needs to have a bath,' Singh said matter-of-factly.

'But I had a bath this morning!' Diksha insisted.

'If you want the new shuttlecock, you must bathe. The shopkeeper does not like dirty children.' Singh's impatient libido was peaking. He wanted to have her.

Diksha was unsure. Something did not seem right. Yet, she got into the waters of the canal and started bathing. Singh followed her in. He had a large stone in his hand, which Diksha could not see. Asha had seen it and she screamed for Diksha to swim away. Diksha, who was under the surface, could not hear her sister's screams. When she came up to gulp in air, she saw Singh's silhouette against the sun. His hand was raised and he swiftly hit her. She screamed in pain as she felt the air rush out of her. She fainted. Seeing this, Asha ran away as fast as her little legs could carry her.

Singh watched Asha run away and cursed his luck that he would only be able to kill one child, when he had hoped to kill two.

He carried Diksha's limp body behind some bushes and laid it down. She was still breathing. Shallow, but still alive. He then raped her.[5, 6]

Suddenly, Diksha started spasming. Her eyes rolled back, but Singh continued to rape her undeterred. After he had finished, he slapped her to see if she was awake. When she didn't respond, he put his finger under her nose to see if she was breathing. She was not. Diksha was dead. He walked away leaving her naked body lying on a stone.

Unknown to Singh, the family of the two girls would lodge a missing-person report.

Asha ran as fast as the wind could carry her. When she finally stopped running, she looked around to see where she was. In her panic, she had kept running, taking every alleyway and turn that would increase the distance between her and the killer, carving out her own maze in the process. She couldn't recognize anything that she saw. She found herself in an unknown village. She panicked and started crying. Then she ran some more.

Malkiat Singh was on his way back from work when he spotted Asha crying on the banks of Badshahpur Jheel. He asked her where she was from and her name. Between sobs, Asha told him her name and where she lived. Malkiat Singh took her to a dispensary to bandage her bruised, bleeding knees. She had fallen many times while running. He gave her biscuits and took her to the local police station. Soon, Asha was reunited with her family.

On the one hand was Singh who hated migrants so much that he killed their children ruthlessly, and on the other hand was Malkiat Singh who didn't think twice before helping Asha.

Asha took the police to the spot near the canal where they found Diksha's naked body. A postmortem done by Dr Shamsher Singh revealed that Diksha had died due to neurogenic shock as a result of the injuries that she had suffered during the sexual assault.[7]

With five kidnappings and three murders, Darbara Singh a.k.a. the Baby Killer had made his debut.

What Singh did not expect was the heat that the killings generated in the area. He had assumed that the poor migrant labourers wouldn't report to the police and that even if they did, the police wouldn't take their complaints seriously. But that didn't happen. And so, he had to wait for exactly two months for things to cool off before striking again.

On 17 June 2004, Singh lured Jatinder, a nine-year-old boy, with the same modus operandi. This time he swapped the sweets for samosa. Jatinder was sodomized and killed. He was victim no. 4.

Singh celebrated every murder by drinking copious amounts of alcohol. Any ordinary criminal would probably take refuge in alcohol to boost their courage and dull their senses. But not Singh. He was completely sober when he killed. He was, after all, not an ordinary human being. He was a beast.

On 29 June, he struck again and abducted two children: Ravina and Patal Kumari, both around six years old. When he tried to rape them, they cried loudly and Singh had to escape as people nearby were alerted. However, as the children were very young, they failed to describe their assailant properly. Singh lived to hunt again.

He was highly frustrated now. Of the eight kids he had lured, four had managed to escape. As he chugged down the remaining whisky from a stainless steel glass, an idea struck him.

On 6 August 2004, he managed to lure seven-year-old Poonam with the promise of buying her a new frock. He slit open her throat so she would not be able to scream when he raped her. She was victim no. 5. He smiled at his own brilliance after he had finished the dastardly act.

'I did this so there would be no screams,' he confessed to the police when he was arrested in October 2004.[8]

His appetite was satiated just for nine days. It was 15 August and Basti Sheikh, a slum area, was all decked up to celebrate Independence Day.

Before Independence, Basti Sheikh was a Muslim locality. When Partition riots broke out, many of the Muslim families living in the area migrated to Pakistan, while some stayed behind. And as is the case with most Muslim areas in India today, the community is forced to wear its patriotism on its sleeves, lest they be suspected of being 'anti-national' and 'pro-Pakistan'. It is assumed that all Hindus love India and Muslims' patriotism is always suspect. That is why every time there is a terrorist attack or a bombing in our country, news channels always have a token Muslim who ensures that he spouts antiterrorist speech wearing his patriotism on his sleeve. This has been the case since the Partition; 2004 was nothing different.

Singh cycled through the lanes of Basti Sheikh scouting for his next target to quench his thirst and to ruin another migrant family. Lakshmi was playing in the street. Darbara Singh cycled up to her and asked her if she wanted to go for a ride on his bicycle. Like any other five-year-old, Lakshmi's eyes lit up and she hopped on to the cycle. She was never seen again till her mutilated corpse was discovered two months later in the Raiya canal.[9] Her father, Ripudaman, who had been searching for his daughter high and low, along with the police, for two months, collapsed when he saw the body. She was victim no. 6.

Singh was a man on a heinous mission and he did not waste any time. He wanted to kill as many migrants' children as quickly as possible. The very next day, he struck thrice.

Six-year-old Laloo Prasad was victim no. 7.[10] His next two targets, three-year-old Nitika and five-year-old Rajesh Kumar, managed to escape his clutches when Singh had to let go of them when people suddenly walked into the deserted alley where he was assaulting them.

Singh preferred to hunt between 10 a.m. and 12.30 p.m., when most parents were working at factories.

'*Mithai khaogay?* [You want to eat some sweets?]' he asked Tazbin (ten) who was playing with her sister, Mumtaz, in Avtar Nagar. Both the girls took the sweets, which the man on the cycle had offered them. He asked them their names and when their names indicated that they were not local people, Singh felt satisfied. He only had one rule: never kill a Punjabi as they were the children of his soil. Singh took out a blue glass bottle. The girls' eyes grew large in wonder.

'*Dekh, Mumtaz, dekh! Kitni achchi hai!* [Look, Mumtaz, look! It's so beautiful!]' Tazbin whistled in awe.

'This will fetch you a high price if you sell it,' Singh told the girls.

'How much?' Tazbin asked.

'Well, you will have to come with me to the shop to find out. Hop on to my cycle.' The die was cast and Tazbin immediately climbed up on the crossbar of the cycle. Mumtaz was hesitant.

'*Kya hua? Nahi aana hai?* [What happened? Don't you want to come with us?]' Singh asked her sweetly.

Mumtaz said no and ran off. She ran straight to her aunt who was at home. By the time both of them came back, Tazbin was gone.[11]

A week later, the Kapurthala police found a mutilated body of a ten-year-old girl under some bushes at Chaheru on the Jalandhar–Phagwara Road. Unknown to the police, this was the body of Tazbin. Postmortem reports revealed that the girl had been sexually assaulted. The police could not find any link to her family or her identity and Tazbin's body remained unclaimed for a while. The police had no choice but to cremate it at Phagwara.

But Singh did not stop there.

Sanju Kumar (five) would be abducted, killed and raped on 24 August 2004. Four days later, Singh would abduct Rajesh Kumar (seven) and his sister, Geeta (five).[12]

And then, for reasons only known to Singh, he took a break.

When he was arrested a month later, Tazbin's case was shifted to Jalandhar police and registered under sections 376 (rape) and 302. Unfortunately, as no direct involvement or proof could be found linking Singh to the crime, the court of B.S. Sandhu, the additional sessions judge, acquitted him.[13]

Panic was rife in the localities. Kids had gone missing and the ones who came back spoke of a man on a cycle who offered them goodies.

Two things happened almost simultaneously.

A child's arm was found near Wariana and a partly decomposed body of a ten-year-old girl (Gudia) was discovered in Chaheru. The police finally took notice and started joining the dots.

A special investigative team (SIT) to study the killer's modus operandi and prepare his sketch was appointed. According to the reports received, the police kept a sharp lookout for a middle-aged suspect, who used a cycle to pick up kids, lure them with goodies and was probably mentally challenged.

'How can one man do all this single-handedly? This has to be the handiwork of a gang of child abductors. Human trafficking has always been an issue,' the officer in charge of the case remarked.

'But, sir, all the children who gave testimony described a similar man: on a bicycle, offered sweets, middle-aged,' the junior officer reasoned.

'We have to catch this lunatic before it's too late!' The senior officer thumped the table in frustration.

And then Singh woke up from his siesta and struck again.

On 18 October, he spied on a group of children playing in the Urban Estate Phase II locality in Jalandhar. Seven-year-old Nishu was busy playing with other children when a cycle-borne man scooped her up and disappeared.

Her family searched for her but couldn't find her. The next day, they lodged a missing-person complaint.

On the same day, Bhana Ram and Gurdev Singh were working in a sugar cane field when they heard a girl screaming from somewhere inside the dense thickets. They rushed towards the sound. What they reached the source, the scene chilled them to the bone. A girl was lying on the ground, bleeding profusely. Her windpipe had been severed and she could not talk. Frantic calls went out to the police who admitted the girl to a hospital. She was Nishu. What had happened was that Singh in his lust-filled haste had tried to violate the child. However, Nishu screamed and the farmers were alerted, who in turn made their presence known. Hearing them, Singh quickly slit Nishu's throat and fled, leaving her for dead.

The police knew they were not dealing with some ordinary criminal, but a pervert and a psychopath.

Singh did not want to stop now. He had had enough of a breather.

On 25 October, Khursheed's mother rushed to meet her husband when he returned from work.

The couple had arrived in Jalandhar with dreams of making it big in a city that offered a lot of chances. They had raised Khursheed to be an obedient and well-mannered boy. That afternoon, Khursheed was last seen playing with his cousin sister, Roku, outside their house.

'I can't find them. I have searched everywhere,' she wailed.

The parents searched for two days. Khursheed's mother stopped eating and drinking. Finally, they filed a missing-person report.

Next, Singh abducted, murdered and raped eight-year-old siblings, Puja and Deepak, followed by the abduction and murder of another brother–sister duo, Amrit and Karu.[14]

But something happened that shook Singh to his core.

He had lured Puja with the promise of fresh sugar cane juice. She had innocently followed him. He had carried her in his arms. On reaching the sugar cane field, he threw her on the ground and drew out a knife from under his kurta. Puja started crying with her hands folded. She then uttered a sentence that made Singh stagger.

'*Menu na maaro. Menu baksh do!* [Please don't kill me. Please spare me!]' Puja said in fluent Punjabi.

Singh realized to his horror that Puja was not a migrant labourer's child but a Punjabi girl. His knees buckled under him as he asked her her full name and she replied: 'Puja Kaur.'

He had sworn to never harm or kill Punjabi children. If he killed her now, then the blood of a Punjabi would be on his hands. His own moral code would get broken and his cause would be lost. But if he let her go, then she would squeal to the police about him.

He sat on the ground. His hands were shaking. His throat was parched. He reached into his satchel and took out a bottle of rum. Puja, who was trembling in fear, watched her attacker gulp it down. Singh usually celebrated with liquor and good food after every kill. But that day, for the first time, he drank to steady his nerves.

He hesitated for a moment before slicing open Puja's throat with one swish of his knife. Puja did not know what had happened. She found it difficult to breath at first. Everything was going dark. She started choking on her own blood as it poured back into her lungs. The last thing she saw before she died was the back of the man who had promised her sugar cane juice walking away. Everything went black. Everything fell silent.

'Sir, someone has spotted a bicyclist. He resembles the sketch of the man we are looking for. And he has a big bag of toffees.' The constable was out of breath as he narrated the report to sub-inspector Nirmal Singh.

'Where was he spotted?' Nirmal Singh asked.

'Near Bastian,' the constable said, checking his notes.

Nirmal Singh dialled a number on his mobile phone. On the other end, Pritam Singh picked up the call.

'Pritam, the kidnapper has been spotted near Bastian. He is on a cycle. Where are you?'

'Sir, I am near Bastian. I will head there right away.' Pritam Singh drove his jeep at breakneck speed towards Adda Bastian.

Singh had just purchased a big bag of toffees. He was in the mood for another kill. He was now bicycling from the leather complex towards Kapurthala Chowk.

While Pritam Singh and his team were scanning the roads, they spotted a man on a bicycle with a big bag of toffees tied to the carrier. His face matched the police sketch. They gave chase. Singh pedalled as fast as he could but his cycle was no match for the jeep. When he realized that all was lost, he made a last-ditch attempt and dumped his cycle on the road and ran into the sugar cane fields. The jeep screeched to a halt and the officers chased him on foot. They finally caught up with him and handcuffed him, thus bringing to an end his killing spree.

He did not need to be slapped or tortured for his confession. As soon as he was caught, he rattled off the truth. In fact, he requested the police to not beat him up. In his head, after all, he was not a criminal, but a man on a noble mission, ridding Punjab of migrants.

Singh claimed he had targeted approximately twenty-three children and killed seventeen of them.[15] Gurpreet Singh Bhullar, SSP, was in charge of the case. The SIT had assumed that Singh would be just another psychopath. Only when he revealed his motive of targeting migrant children did they join the dots. They had not thought of that angle at all. In fact, the police had examined the case as that of just another child abductor going nuts. They were also astounded that Singh had single-handedly done all this. They were looking for a gang or just a man who trafficked children.

It was now time to tighten the noose and plug all the holes in the case. It was time to unearth the bodies.

Singh was cooperative. The very next day he led Bhullar's team, along with the executive magistrate, to a sugar cane field along the Jalandhar–Kalasanghia Road where he had buried Khursheed and Ruku.

The group of policemen led by Bhullar waded through the dense sugar cane field. The long leaves kept slapping them on their faces as they walked deeper.

'*Darbara, humhe chutiya toh nahi bana raha hai?* [Hope you are not taking us on a wild-goose chase?]' the constable leading Singh asked him.

'*Nahi, saab, idhar hi kahin hoga* [No, sir, it's somewhere here],' Singh replied sincerely.

If you ever ask a cop what is the sight that he has most been shocked by, even after years of service, he will say, the sight of murdered children. There is something evil and unsettling about it that immediately triggers a sense of hopelessness, almost channelling the last few moments of the dying child.

Near the burial ground, they were greeted by the strong stench of rotting flesh, followed by the buzzing sound of a thousand flies. Some of the policemen fought to keep their bile down, while some drew out their handkerchiefs to cover their noses.

SSP Bhullar had seen enough action in his days and couldn't be bothered about the smell. He just cared about getting his proof to nail Singh. He stepped forward and parted the leaves.

Khursheed's clothed body was lying on its back. His head was twisted to the left at a strange angle. His body had not decomposed. Ruku's naked body, on the other hand, was highly decomposed as she had been beheaded. Only a piece of flesh held the head to the torso. There were severe ruptures on their private parts.

Bhullar felt an inexplicable rage build up inside. He just wanted to pull out his gun and shoot Singh between his eyes. He closed his eyes and gritted his teeth, waiting for his anger to subside. As per the proceedings, the bodies were exhumed in the presence of the executive magistrate.

They say good news travels fast but bad news travels at the speed of lightning. News spread about the dreaded killer being in the dragnet of the police and that bodies were being recovered from the fields. A large number of people assembled at the field out of voyeuristic curiosity to see the bodies and, of course, to take a look at the killer who had wreaked havoc in the past few months. Some people on spotting Singh attacked him. The police had to intervene and take him to safety.

A bottle of rum and a glass were recovered from the field as well. Singh said he had consumed the booze before committing the crime. This was in stark contrast to the cool and collected Darbara Singh who only drank to celebrate each killing and not during or before the crime. The fact was that he had been completely shaken when he had killed the Punjabi girl.

The police took the bottle and glass into custody for matching fingerprints.

The Baby Killer then led the team to a location near Changi village where he had dumped Laloo's body. Laloo's naked body was highly decomposed and when Bhullar looked at Singh to gauge his reaction, he saw no sign of remorse, just a matter-of-fact expression on the killer's face.

Mohammed Vakil had heard about children going missing from the locality. But never in his worst nightmares did he imagine that someday his five-year-old son, Khursheed, would vanish. He had told his son to be careful when the first reports about the missing children had filtered into his mohalla.

'*Ghar ke saamne khelna aur koi bhi aapse baat karna chahe toh aap phauren ghar wapas aa jaiyega!* [Always play in front of the house; and if any stranger tries to talk to you, then immediately run back into the house!]' Vakil had instructed Khursheed, who was sitting on his lap one night after dinner.

'*Ji, Abbu*! [Yes, Abbu!]' Khursheed had replied earnestly.

When Mohammed Vakil walked in to identify the body, his knees buckled under him as the white sheet was pulled back to reveal his son's mutilated body.

'*Hai, Allah*!' he cried before collapsing on the floor.

When US president Dwight Eisenhower had lost his three-year-old son, Doud, to scarlet fever, he had said: 'There's no tragedy in life than the death of a child. Things never get back to the way they were.'[16] Vakil too died that day—a father who had breathed life into his son was now transformed in an instant into a shell of a human being.

He identified Khursheed and Ruku, the daughter of his younger brother.

Bhullar could not understand how someone could be so cruel and perverse as to kill three- and five-year-old children and then sodomize and rape them.

In an interview to the *Tribune*, when asked if he had any remorse in killing the children, Singh had grinned and answered: 'I have no remorse for having killed the children of migrant labourers as they were instrumental in sending me to jail.'[17]

'It [the crimes] never shook me from inside. I still think whatever I did was right and it was the demand of the time,' he summarized.[18]

He continued as he described his modus operandi, 'I abducted the children of the migrants, and if any of these girls or boys resisted my attempts, I would slit their throats and simply dump or drown them . . . I killed all the children to eliminate any possibility of leaving behind a proof.'[19]

'I don't dread anything. I think they [migrants] did wrong to me,' he added.[20]

Meanwhile, Nishu was still recovering in the hospital. The police reached out to her as she was one of the many children who had had a good look at the killer. She could not appear in court but she correctly identified Singh from his pictures in the newspapers from her hospital bed.

Singh was charged with eighteen cases of abduction, rape and murder. Bhullar and the SIT had thought that he would hang easily. However, due to lack of sufficient evidence, he was acquitted in three cases.

On 7 January 2008, Judge Iqbal Singh Bajwa awarded Singh the death sentence for the murders of Khursheed and Ruku.[21] He was shifted to Patiala Central Jail for his hanging.

In April 2008, he was tried for raping and killing Diksha. Her sister, Asha, who had run away from his clutches on that fateful day, identified him in the court. But Singh's legal team claimed that their client had been wrongly implicated and that the defence team had based the entire case on the testimony given by tutored witnesses. Just like Singh had been let off in the grenade-lobbing case in Pathankot for lack of evidence, here, too, in the case of Diksha, he was given life imprisonment on 25 April 2008 by Judge B.K. Mehta.

To make matters worse, the police messed up the evidence they had collected, which played a crucial role in the court proceedings. On 30 July 2009, Justice Mehtab Singh Gill and Justice Jitendra Chauhan of the Punjab and Haryana High Court reversed the death sentence that had been awarded to Singh for the murders of Ruku and Khursheed. The court pointed out that there was no mention of the liquor bottle and glass that had been recovered from the field near the bodies in the inquest reports. Additionally, these objects were recovered on 30 October but sent to the forensic science lab only on 11 November. Therefore, the court dismissed this piece of evidence, citing a 1997 Supreme Court judgment, which had ruled that the accused is entitled to acquittal if the fingerprints are kept in the police station for more than five days.

Also, the judges questioned why the police had not taken DNA or blood samples, and why they were investigating using archaic methods rather than scientific ones?

Singh was eventually acquitted in the murders of Khursheed and Ruku.

On 10 December 2010, Judge B.S. Sandhu acquitted him in the Tazbin rape and murder case because of insufficient evidence.

It seemed luck was on Singh's side. For the victims' families, this was painful. They just couldn't believe that this was happening. However, the Punjab government came to their help and moved the Supreme Court in February 2010, calling the high court's decision flawed.

Nishu, who still couldn't speak because of her throat injury, gesticulated to identify Singh as her kidnapper and attacker.

However, Singh escaped the gallows by some incredible luck and stayed in prison for the rest of his life.

He died at the age of seventy-five due to natural causes on 10 June 2018 at the government-owned Rajindra Hospital in Patiala. His family refused to claim the body.

To kill innocent children, sodomize and rape them can only be the brainwork of a perverted person. Singh was a madman, a psychopath and a man who didn't deserve to die a natural death. He should have faced death in a fit of fear like all his victims did.

JAKKAL, SUTAR, JAGTAP AND SHAH

THE JOSHI–ABHYANKAR MASSACRE

'When your time comes, not even god can save you!'[1]

—Sundar Hegde, father of victim

Pune has always been an ideal and quiet city for retirees to settle down in. Located approximately 90 km from its larger, louder, pacier, cosmopolitan big brother, Mumbai, Pune functions at a more relaxed pace; it has managed to retain its quaint charm and is asleep by 10 p.m. Or, at least, it used to back in 1976, when Pune was still known as Poona.

The Poona of 1976 did not boast of any major, horrific crimes. A murder here, a handful of burglaries there, nothing to get too alarmed about. Life seemed perfect in this almost sleepy and laid-back city.

Serial killers are considered lonely in nature, preferring to operate solo—like Manson, Bundy, Raghav—listening to some obscure radio channel playing inside their heads, dispensing twisted instructions to kill or not to kill. There have been very few instances across the world where a gang of people executed serial killings—Auto Shankar and his motley crew from India, the Ripper Crew from Chicago, the Skin Hunters of Poland, to name a few.

But four young men would soon carve their names in the ignominious roster of a gang of serial killers. And Poona, the quiet city, would be grabbed by its jugular as things would go south.

181

Rajendra Jakkal, Dilip Sutar, Shantaram Jagtap and Munawar Harun Shah were commercial-art students at Abhinav Kala Mahavidyalaya, Tilak Road, Poona. They would graduate in the school of murder in just over a year, after claiming ten innocent lives.

It was September 1975. Rashmi was walking towards the college entry gates. Her head was bowed to avoid any kind of eye contact. She passed by the cycle stand outside the college. Someone whistled loudly. Her pace hastened.

'Oho! Check her out!' Jagtap leered in his wide collared, polka-dotted shirt, the first two buttons undone.

'She is not even looking at us,' Jakkal said, as he leapt in front of Rashmi and blocked her way.

'Oye, first year! When we call you, you better stop. Or else . . .' Jakkal was multitasking. He was threatening her verbally, while ogling her breasts.

Rashmi's palms became sweaty with fear.

'Boss, the way you are staring at her, it looks like you will devour her,' Sutar cackled and slapped his thigh.

'What's going on here?' a deep voice interrupted them.

A professor had appeared and was glaring at the gang.

'Were these boys harassing you?' he asked Rashmi.

Rashmi darted a glance at Jakkal. Her fear doubled. She shook her head vigorously.

'Go to your class,' the professor told her and Rashmi bolted.

'Rajendra, Dilip, Shantaram and Munawar,' the professor spat out each name in disgust, 'there have been enough complaints about your drinking, misbehaviour and bullying. One more mistake and you can say goodbye to your future!' Saying so, he left.

* * *

'What is our future?' Jagtap banged down a stainless steel glass on the floor after downing his drink in one long gulp.

The inherent nature of liquor makes us do three things: (a) we become introspective, wherein we complain about how we have fucked up in our respective lives (b) it makes us boisterous, wherein we point out how others have fucked up in their respective lives (c) it just makes us dance! But Jagtap wanted to peer into his future.

The gang was sitting inside a small tin shed that Jakkal owned on Karve Road, which was 5 km from their college. This was their hang-out spot; they would while away time there, drinking and cooking 'khayali pulav' inside their twisted heads.

All of them had a lower-middle-class background. They robbed bikes to fuel their alcoholism. For entertainment, they eve-teased girls and got into scraps. Their reputation as 'good-for-nothing' bad boys preceded them everywhere. With their parents having given up on them, they were left to their own shenanigans.

'Boss? Boss?' Shah called out to Jakkal, who was staring blankly at the wall. Shah was stone-cold sober. As a Muslim, he didn't touch alcohol. The group had accepted Jakkal as their alpha male and called him Boss.

Jakkal awoke from his reverie. 'Future? I see our future! We will have money, fame and spit on the world,' he spoke like a seer who had just had a vision.

There was silence in the room and then the other three started laughing. Jakkal was taken aback at their reaction.

'*Abbey, chutiye, paisa chahiye ki nahi?* [You, cunts! Do you want money or not?]'

The trio warmed up. They knew Boss had a plan in his head!

* * *

14 January 1976

The men entered a small restaurant called Hotel Vishwa. As it was located right behind Abhinav Kala Mahavidyalaya, it was always full. Sundar Hegde, the owner, looked at the men as they sat down. He recognized them as students of the college. Prakash, his son, studied with them. The men ordered tea and samosas.

'See the crowd? Do the maths. It's in thousands, daily!' Jakkal whispered to the others.

'Do you want us to rob the restaurant?' Shah asked.

'No, no, you idiot! I don't want us to rob it. I have a bigger plan,' Jakkal replied.

'Who owns this place?' he asked loudly.

'Me,' Hegde replied, 'like you didn't know!'

Jakkal rolled his eyes, 'And he is the father of—'

'Prakash Hegde, who studies in our college,' Shah completed.

'But what's the plan?' Jagtap was getting impatient; he was also a little slow and everybody in the gang made fun of him.

'We are going to kidnap Prakash Hegde and ask his father for ransom!' Jakkal declared with an evil glint in his eyes.

Shah, who was sipping his tea, choked and coughed. 'Stealing bikes is one thing, but kidnapping?'

The other three, however, did not find anything wrong with the plan. They lured in Suhas Chandak, another classmate, to join in their diabolical plan with the promise of earning a quick buck. Prakash was kidnapped on 15 January 1976.

'Where are we going?' Prakash asked nervously.

'We want to copy your notes,' Jagtap answered nonchalantly.

'Just take my books. Give it back once you are done.' Prakash sensed something was amiss.

'Come with us. It won't take us long to copy everything,' Jakkal said.

They took him to Jakkal's tin shed. Once they reached there, they shoved Prakash inside. When Prakash protested, Jakkal slapped him so hard that his lips started bleeding.

'Why are you doing this to me? What have I done to you? I always salute you guys every time I pass you by!' Poor Prakash thought that he was being ragged.

They all took turns to hit him, till Prakash started begging them for mercy. Jakkal handed him a sheet of paper and a pen.

'Write a letter to your father saying . . .'

* * *

Prakash's father slowly opened the letter with trembling hands and handed it to the police inspector sitting in front of him. He had found it early in the morning, wrapped around a stone, in the portico of their house.

'It says that he has left the house willingly and wants Rs 1 lakh,' Hegde said. 'Something is not right. I feel he is in trouble!'

'Why do you think your son is in trouble and that he did not write this letter?' the inspector asked.

'Look, he has signed off as Prakash. But we never call him Prakash. He should've written Devdas, which is his nickname. Whoever wrote this letter for him did not know this. Or maybe, it is indeed Prakash who is sending us a coded message, telling us that he is in danger,' Hegde explained.

The police immediately filed a missing-person report. But little did Hegde or the police know that Prakash was already dead. He had been killed the previous night as soon as he had finished writing the letter. The gang had no intention of keeping him alive or even handing him over once the ransom was received. There were two reasons behind their gruesome decision. Firstly, Prakash knew them and there was a possibility that he would rat them out once he was set free. And, secondly, the men only wanted the ransom.

The men had gagged Prakash and taken him to Peshwe Park, a few metres from his father's restaurant.

There, Jagtap took out a blue nylon rope. He had learnt a few things while he had been with the National Cadet Corps and decided to make use of them. He tied a noose and strangled Prakash. Chandak watched petrified as his friends revelled in snuffing the life out of Prakash.

'*Kyun be, phat gaya?* [What happened? Shitting bricks?]' Jakkal asked Chandak.

Chandak's throat had gone dry and he could hear his heart thumping loudly in his chest.

The killers put the body in a barrel, filled it with stones and dumped it in the lake in the park. It was only the next morning that they sent the letter to Prakash's father.

The park has long erased the memories of the corpse at the bottom of its lake. It has now been transformed into an energy park, with beautiful bridges for kids to learn about renewable energy.

'Jakkal! We are not murderers! What have you done?' Chandak demanded, his voice trembling

'Suhas, we are all in it together. Your hands are dirty as well,' Jagtap yelled.

'I . . . I did not kill him. I did not even touch him,' Chandak argued.

'But you didn't stop us from killing him, did you?' Jakkal slowly measured out his words. 'You don't want to be a part of this, and that is okay. But if you open your fat mouth, you will join Prakash at the bottom of the lake. Do you understand?'

'Yes . . . yes, Boss!'

At best, it was an amateur plan destined to flop. They had not mentioned where the money had to be delivered or who would collect it. They did not even follow up with Hegde about it. They realized they were not meant to be kidnappers. Still, a crime had been committed, so the gang ran away to Kolhapur till matters cooled down in Poona.

Meanwhile, the cops searched high and low for Prakash but nothing came of it. All their leads led to dead ends. The case remained unsolved.

* * *

Kolhapur

In Kolhapur, the gang loitered around, stealing parked scooters. Jakkal had a nose for scouting out victims. He always kept his eyes open and his ears close to the ground. His hawk eyes would read a person—analyse their body language, clothes—shrewdly and decide if it was worth tailing the person.

That is how Jakkal found businessman Agarwal in Gujari Bazaar. Agarwal was a well-dressed man, who always carried a suitcase and regularly visited jewellery stores. He wore a thick gold chain and drove a brand-new Fiat car. Jakkal tailed him every day for a week, and one night in August that year, the gang decided to break into Agarwal's house.

They waited in the shadows, watching the house. Agarwal, who lived alone, was in his bedroom on the first floor. He switched off the lights and went to sleep. The gang waited for an hour and then broke into the house by smashing a window on the ground floor. Agarwal was a heavy sleeper and, therefore, did not hear the noise and wake up. The men stealthily made their way upstairs to the bedroom and switched on the light. When attempts to rouse Agarwal from his sleep failed, one of them kicked him. Agarwal woke up with a start, shocked upon seeing four hooded men in his bedroom. One had a knife, the other a blue nylon rope and the other two demanded that he open his safe and hand over the money.

Thankfully, Agarwal kept a revolver under his pillow for safety. He whipped it out and fired. The bullet didn't hit any of the men but they scampered away for dear life. Agarwal chased them but they somehow managed to escape.

When the police came to investigate, they seized the blue nylon rope as evidence.

After the failed robbery attempt, the gang moved to Bombay for some time before heading back to Poona. They didn't have enough money, which made them short-tempered and frustrated. Without money, they couldn't enjoy the life they had envisioned for themselves.

'What happened to us becoming rich, famous and spitting at the world?' Jagtap asked Jakkal. They were mulling over the recent incident in Jakkal's tin shed. Jakkal didn't say anything. He just looked up at the ceiling. There was silence. No one ever questioned the Boss! And then, Jakkal disappeared from their lives for a week.

The next time they met at the shed, Jakkal was smiling and brimming with news.

'I have found a new target. They are an old couple. No guns or servants. It will be easy to scare them and they are bound to have some jewellery in the house!'

'When do we strike?'

'Tonight.'

* * *

31 October 1976

Back in 1976, Vijaynagar Colony, Poona, was a quiet suburb with a handful of houses. Jakkal, Jagtap, Sutar and Shah slunk into the Joshis' single-storey structure. This time they didn't break into the house but, rather, rang the doorbell and quickly wore their hoods. As soon as the door opened, they barged inside and rounded up the occupants, Achyut Joshi and his wife, Usha, taking them hostage. The couple was pushed on to the sofa at knifepoint.

'Where is the jewellery?' Jagtap asked the quaking couple.

'In the bank . . . in the bank,' Usha replied, 'in the locker.'

Jakkal screamed in frustration.

'Where is your money?' he demanded brusquely.

Joshi handed over his wallet, which contained a few hundred-rupee notes.

Sutar snatched the *mangal sutra* from Usha's neck. 'You won't have any use for this where you are going,' he said with a cold laugh.

The Joshis were petrified. The gang immediately got to work. They tied the hands and legs of the couple and put a gag in their mouths. Jagtap tied his special knot on his trusted blue nylon rope and the gang took turns to strangulate the couple.

Just then the bell rang.

The four of them froze in their tracks.

'Now what?' Shah asked; he was always the one to panic first.

'Go see who it is,' Jakkal whispered.

Sutar went and peered through the peephole.

'Boss, *ladka hai! Sattra–athra saal ka lag raha hai* [Boss, there's a young boy outside. Probably seventeen–eighteen years old],' Sutar reported back.

'Open the door. Let him come in,' Jakkal instructed.

The door was opened and as soon as the boy entered, Sutar and Shah jumped on him and pinned him down. The boy was Anand Joshi, Achyut and Usha's teenage son. Seeing his parents dead, Anand began flailing and screaming. Jakkal swiftly stuffed his mouth with a wad of cloth. He then instructed the boy to strip naked. Anand was stunned. He cowered in fear and pleaded for his life. But Jakkal threatened him with the knife. After he took off his clothes, Jakkal strangled him with the nylon rope.

The gang surveyed the scene for a while. They took off their hoods and set to work, going from room to room, looking for more loot, while spraying perfume everywhere.

'*Police ka kutta bhi humhe soong ke dhund nahi payega* [Even the police dogs will not be able to sniff us out],' Jakkal had told his gang members while explaining the need to spray perfume in the houses that they attacked.

They finally left the Joshis' house with a few thousand rupees, Usha's mangal sutra and Achyut's wristwatch.

The next morning, as assistant commissioner of police Madhusudan Hulyalkar stood at the scene of the crime, he wondered who could've committed the murders so cold-bloodedly. He hadn't encountered anything like this before, in fact, neither had the city of Poona. As he was cautiously walking around the crime scene, looking for clues, a forensics team member approached him.

'Sir, we have lifted some fingerprints from the handles of the drawers and the almirahs.'

'Get them identified as soon as possible,' Hulyalkar ordered.

As predicted by Jakkal, the sniffer dogs failed to pick up any scents in the house, thanks to the perfume.

Hulyalkar realized that this was no ordinary burglary, when the forensics team failed to figure out anything. The killers had probably worn gloves or removed all their traces; the fingerprints were of Joshi's family's and not the murderers'.

The assumptions Hulyalkar drew from the crime scene were:

1. It was planned and done by experts—no fingerprints and the use of perfume.
2. At least two or more people were involved—it is physically difficult to overpower three people single-handedly.
3. Why was the young boy stripped naked? It looked like he had taken off his clothes himself—they were found in a neat pile next to the body.

4. The method of killing involved gagging the person and strangling him or her.

But to Hulyalkar, this was an isolated incident. He didn't know about Prakash Hegde or the attack on Agarwal, as these cases were lodged in different police stations.

* * *

'The police have no clue who the killers are,' Sutar said, as he closed the newspaper. The murders had made it to the city pages' headlines. 'Boss, we are famous, just like you had predicted. Poona is shitting bricks!'

Jakkal smiled. He was happy. At last there was some loot to enjoy after their previous failed attempts.

'Did you see how her eyes bulged out when I tightened the noose around her throat?' Jagtap proudly looked for some accolades to come his way as he finished off his beer.

'But, Boss, why did you strip the boy?' Shah asked.

'So that if he survived, it would give us time to flee. *Nanga thodi bhagega humare peechay?* [He won't run behind us naked, will he?]' Jakkal said, as all of them rolled on the floor, laughing.

More than the looting, the gang had enjoyed the killing.

'I love it when I can see life slowly fading away from them . . . their eyes become glassy and still,' said Jakkal, the most psychotic in the gang.

Poona was now abuzz with the news of the brutal murder of the middle-class family in a quiet, safe neighbourhood. Before the city could come to terms with the horrific crime, the gang struck again.

* * *

22 November 1976

Jakkal had been trailing Yashomati Bafna to her bungalow on Shankar Sheth Road for a couple of days, keeping an eye on her.

'She is alone; lives in a bungalow; no husband; no children. Easy target,' Jakkal summarized for the others.

However, the gang broke into her house only to find out that she lived with two servants. The trio fought back bravely.

'BOSS, LET'S GET OUT OF HERE!' Shah screamed as one of the servants kicked him in the stomach. They ran for the door. They somehow scaled the barbed-wire fence and escaped. They'd had a close shave again. Just when they were convinced that they were invincible, a good whacking at the hands of Bafna and her servants rudely burst their bubble. They were angry and wanted to make up for the humiliation.

Bafna reported the attempted break-in to the police. Poona was on edge. From a sleepy city, it suddenly woke up to find itself the hotbed of crime. The police were on tenterhooks.

* * *

1 December 1976

The Abhyankars were a closely knit family and lived in a bungalow on Bhandarkar Road. The head of the family was octogenarian Kashinath Shastri Abhyankar, a noted Sanskrit scholar. He was a well-respected man in the city.

He lived with his wife, Indirabai, son, Gajanan, his wife, Hirabai, grandson, Dhananjay, and granddaughter, Jai. Sakubai Wagh, their stay-at-home maid, had been with them for years.

The four had been staking out the house for three days. Why they chose this particular house or this family can only be conjectured. Firstly, the family was well known, therefore, it can be assumed that they were well-to-do. Secondly, there was only one person in the house who was big and strong enough to offer resistance (if it came to pass), Gajanan. Thirdly, the bungalow was big enough for them to assume that the family would be *maaldaar* (rich).

They waited for the right opportunity to strike and it came on 1 December 1976. Bhandarkar Road was empty that night. Gajanan and Hirabai had gone out for dinner.

The doorbell broke the stillness of the winter night. Kashinath looked at his watch. It was 8 p.m.

'Gajanan and Hirabai back already?' Kashinath wondered.

Jai ran to the door and opened it, expecting to see her parents. Instead, there were four men, holding a knife. They pushed her inside. They tied her hands, stuffed her mouth with a piece of cloth and told her to lead them into the house. Inside, the moment everyone saw the four men, chaos unfolded.

Kashinath begged them to take whatever they wanted and leave them.

'Please let my granddaughter go, take us hostage,' Indirabai pleaded.

However, the four killers had no such intention.

They gagged Kashinath, Indirabai, Sakubai and Dhananjay and strangled them. Jai, the sole witness to this slaughter, was kept alive.

'Take your clothes off,' Jakkal told her calmly.

'Please let me go. I don't want to die,' cried Jai.

'I said, take off your clothes!' Jakkal barked, holding her at knifepoint.

Jai shred one layer of cloth after another till she stood stark naked, humiliated and scared in front of the killers.

'Now show us where the money is kept,' Jakkal thundered.

They rampaged through the house, opening cupboards and drawers, throwing stuff out, looting whatever they thought was valuable. When they were convinced that they had gathered sufficient loot, they turned to Jai.

'Get on your knees,' Jakkal instructed coldly.

Jai was weeping inconsolably. 'I have given you everything we had in the house. I have followed all your instructions. Please let me go.'

Sutar laughed and leered at Jai's naked body: 'Well, there is something else you can give us.' Saying this, he stepped forward with the intention of raping her. Jakkal blocked him and screamed: 'NO!'

He took the blue nylon rope from Jagtap and tied it around Jai's neck, pulling it with all his might. Jai fought for air, thrashed her hands and legs and spasmed. Life had been snuffed out of her; unshed tears still gleaming in bulging, glassy eyes. Jakkal let go of the rope and the body fell on the floor with a thud.

The men sprayed perfume everywhere in the house, laughing raucously, before melting into the darkness.

When Gajanan and Hirabai returned home after dinner, they were surprised to see the front door open. They rushed inside and collapsed when they saw the five bodies.

Hulyalkar arrived with the other cops. He realized that whoever had killed the Joshis had also killed the Abhyankars. The modus operandi seemed to be the same.

Poona came to a standstill. Panic was rife and rumours aplenty. Hulyalkar knew that a merciless bunch of serial killers were on the loose. Eight brutal murders within a span of thirty-one days were enough to shake a city to its foundations. Markets started emptying by 6 p.m. No one ventured out and no stranger was allowed to enter homes. Many people kept weapons within grabbing distance at home, fearing an attack while they were in bed at night. It was rumoured that people were carrying knives in their office briefcases! Everyone eyed everyone suspiciously.

The police formed teams to patrol the streets at night. Check posts mushroomed to scan every passing vehicle. Nothing came of any of these measures. It seemed that the killers had disappeared into thin air.

Meanwhile, inspector Manikrao Damame joined Hulyalkar in the investigation. Damame was a no-nonsense cop with an eye for detail and it was he who found the biggest clue that everyone else had failed to notice.

However, not before the killers struck again.

With the loot from the Abhyankar household fast depleting, the gang had to strike again if they were to keep up their drinking binges. So Jakkal came up with another target.

It had been three months since the Abhyankars.

* * *

23 March 1977

This time, Jakkal went back to their alma mater: Abhinav Kala Mahavidyalaya. The gang's target was Anil Gokhale, younger brother of Jayant Gokhale, both of whom were students there.

So far, their motive had solely been monetary. However, with Anil, it seemed they had crossed into a darker, psychotic realm of killing for fun. Perhaps, they had become addicted to lapping up the moment when life slowly ebbed out of their victims, or maybe it was a disagreement that they had had with Jayant.

On 23 March 1977, Anil was supposed to meet his brother Jayant at Alka Talkies in the evening. When he could not find Jayant, Anil started walking back home. Jakkal rode up beside him on a motorcycle.

'*Arre*, Anil! Where are you headed?' he asked innocently.

'*Ghari* [Home],' Anil replied.

'I'll drop you home. Come,' Jakkal offered a ride.

Without suspecting anything, Anil boarded the bike and they rode off.

'Rajendra, this is not the right route,' Anil protested when he realized that they were not on the right track.

'Of course, I know where your house is. I just need to stop at my shed to pick up some stuff,' Jakkal lied.

At the shed, the other three were waiting to drag Anil inside. They beat him up, took his money and strangled him with a blue nylon rope. Then they tied an iron ladder to the corpse, weighed it down with boulders and dumped the body into the Mula-Mutha river near Bund Garden.

Unknown to the four killers, three things happened.

1. They didn't know that Anil was supposed to meet Jayant, who when his brother didn't turn up, went home expecting him to be there. When he didn't come home for a long time, the Gokhales lodged a missing-person report.
2. The killers got rid of the body but forgot to remove Anil's college ID from his pocket.
3. They assumed no one would ever find the body.

The next evening, the police control room received a call. A body had surfaced near Yerawada. A police team led by Damame rushed to the spot.

They found that the corpse was tied to a ladder. Damame knew he wasn't dealing with an ordinary killer but a perverse and very clever one.

A constable came forward and showed him a wet scrap of paper, which looked like an identity card. Thankfully, 'Anil Gokhale' and 'Abhinav Kala Mahavidyalaya' were still legible.

Every criminal makes a mistake. The four killers had made theirs and the police had their first lead. Damame sat down on his haunches to get a closer look and found a blue nylon rope tied around the neck of the corpse, similar to the ones found at the Joshi and Abhyankar residences. This was the job of the same killers.

Damame immediately reported the discovery to Hulyalkar, who pulled out the file photographs of the Joshi triple murders and the Abhyankar family slaughter and laid them all out on the table. The rope was the clue, a part of a pattern, which had been there all along and they had failed to see it.

Postmortem examination of Anil's body revealed that he had been killed the previous day.

According to Hulyalkar, 'The similarity of the knots in all the cases, made us link the serial killings together. This is when I realized that the gang was from Pune and not from outside.'[2]

They knew they had to act fast before the trail went cold again.

Hulyalkar and his team reached Abhinav Kala Mahavidyalaya immediately and started talking to the students. The police hoped that the people last seen with Anil would probably be able to shed more light.

Mostly, nobody had a lead till one student recalled seeing Anil riding pillion on Jakkal's bike.

* * *

Sutar rushed up to Jakkal, who was on his way to the canteen.

'Boss! The police are here and they are asking about Anil!' he was breathless.

'How did they find out about him?' Jakkal was furious.

Just then Shah and Jagtap approached them.

Shah's face was ashen. 'Boss, the body floated up.'

'*Behenchod!*'

Unfortunately for the gang, the boulders had come loose. The Mula-Mutha river, unlike the Peshwe Lake, has currents, which loosened the boulders and the body surfaced. If only they had studied their dumping ground a little!

'Okay, we will go our separate ways. Don't run away or they will suspect us. Act normal. I'll see you in the evening at the shed.' Saying this, Jakkal left. Just as he was about to exit the college, a hand rested on his shoulder. Jakkal turned to face Damame.

'*Tumhara naam Rajendra Jakkal hai?* [Is your name Rajendra Jakkal?]'

Jakkal nodded.

'*Chala!* Come to the police station with us. We need to ask you a few questions,' Damame said in the calmest voice possible. He did not want to spook the only lead he had in his hands.

At the police station, Jakkal claimed that he had been with his friends—Sutar, Shah and Jagtap—the previous evening. Hulyalkar rounded up the other three and interrogated all four separately. And that is when cracks began to appear in their story. All four of them gave contradictory statements about their whereabouts the previous week. Damame and Hulyalkar knew they were on to something.

Hulyalkar was an ace interrogator. He was known to have the tenacity to get under the skin of the criminal. He was smooth; he played the role of the 'good cop' very well. And that is what he did. He offered a cigarette to Jakkal, who accepted it hesitatingly. Hulyalkar lit a match. The sudden flare of the flame threw an amber glow on Jakkal's face. Jakkal didn't blink. He lit his cigarette and took a long drag. It had been quite a few hours since he had smoked. The nicotine slowly took over his bloodstream and calmed him down. He had been primed.

Hulyalkar leant forward with his hands clasped together. His body language exuded friendship, camaraderie. It seemed Hulyalkar was about to share some secret with Jakkal.

'See, Rajendra [*he deliberately used his first name to establish familiarity*], these murders are really making

Punekars uneasy [*sharing a problem as if he could help as a friend*]. We are also clueless [*putting the police in a helpless position and making Jakkal appear to be in a superior position; gaining empathy*]. If you know anything about the murders, please tell me. It would be of immense help [*asking for help, a personal favour, as if they were long-lost friends*].

Jakkal let his guard down. His overconfidence and the fact that Hulyalkar had made him comfortable enough to drop all defences made Jakkal commit a fatal mistake.

'I think there might be a connection between the Prakash Hegde and the Anil Gokhale murders,' Jakkal said, not realizing what he had unleashed.

'*Achha*? That's interesting,' Hulyalkar's mind was racing but he pretended to be unperturbed, 'why do you say that?'

'They both studied in the same college . . .' Jakkal said nonchalantly, thinking he was smarter than the cops.

After coming out of the interrogation room, Hulyalkar shouted, 'Find out everything about Prakash Hegde!'

Once Prakash's file had been procured from another police station, Hulyalkar punched the air. 'Hegde went missing a year ago. There were no leads, until today . . . when Jakkal said that he had been "murdered"! Either he is the one who killed him or he knows the people who did. Keep a watch on him and the other three.'

When Lady Providence decides to play her cards, there is no stopping the domino effect. Things started falling into place, without much effort. The police knew that they had no tangible proof to tie the four men to the nine murders. So they were released. What the men didn't know was that two plain-clothes policemen were following them around and keeping a close watch on Sutar and Jagtap.

One day, Sutar and Jagtap were standing near the gate of their college, deep in conversation. 'Will the police find out now?' Jagtap asked, furrowing his eyebrows. Sutar smiled: 'Don't worry, Boss will take care of the police.'

The mufti cops reported back to HQ and repeated the conversation. Hulyalkar recalled something and sprang up from his chair. 'Get me the file on the attempted robberies at the Bafna residence.' He hit jackpot. There on the sheet was clearly mentioned that the burglars had used the word 'boss' liberally during the course of the attack.

Hulyalkar declared triumphantly: 'We nearly have them. These four are the same people who had broken in at Bafna's house and the ones who massacred the Joshis and the Abhyankars! We just need an eyewitness to seal the case.'

The teams went back to the college, asking about the four men. Thanks to their reputation, most students had horrible things to say about them—they were drunkards, lechers. But one student, Satish Gore, seemed jumpy when the cops questioned him. Damame knew there was something wrong. Gore was called to the police station.

A few threats of breaking his hands and teeth yielded quick-fire answers from Gore. The newspapers had reported about the gruesome killings, but there had been no information about the killers. The four of them obviously wanted to be famous and bask in the blood-soaked limelight. The fatal mistake they had made was to open their mouth and tell Gore all about the killings to impress him. And Gore gave a detailed confessional about the killings as narrated to him by Sutar, Jagtap, Jakkal and Shah.

'Sir, Suhas Chandak knows them as well. He even used to hang out with them,' Gore said, trying to leverage his innocence by providing a lead.

Chandak was promptly picked up and questioned and he immediately spilt the beans. After witnessing Hegde's murder, he had stopped associating himself with the four, despite their dire threats.

The four men were formally arrested on 30 March 1977. They confessed to everything and led the police to Peshwe Lake, from where the barrel containing Hegde's body was fished out. The police raided Jakkal's tin shed on Karve Road and recovered a lot of incriminating evidence, along with many of the items that had been stolen from the Joshi and Abhyankar households.

Headlines screamed that the killers had been caught. The city breathed a sigh of relief. The citizens wanted to take a look at these depraved killers. Hulyalkar and Damame wanted to nail these bastards and make them face the maximum penalty possible. They did not want any untoward incident to mar the trial. So they were transported from their cells to the court under heavy security.

Shamrao G. Samant, a senior criminal lawyer, was appointed as the special public prosecutor for the trial. The case began on 15 May 1978 and lasted more than four months. Meanwhile, Maharashtra claimed back one of its own. Poona was renamed Pune. And then, the day that Hulyalkar, Damame and the entire city of Pune were awaiting arrived. On 28 September 1978, Pune sessions court judge Waman Narayan Bapat sentenced the four to death. The city erupted in joy. Chandak was let off as he had turned approver for the police.

But the men weren't going to give up easily. They sent a review petition to the Supreme Court and a mercy petition to then President of India, Neelam Sanjiva Reddy.

Punekars were outraged and wanted no mercy for these cold-blooded murderers. A thousand prominent citizens of Pune signed a joint note addressed to the Supreme Court to argue the case on behalf of the state.

Meanwhile, the criminals were trying all the tricks in the book to delay the execution or to garner sympathy. Shah wrote an autobiography in jail, *Yes I Am Guilty*, in Marathi, in which he claimed that he was an innocent bystander who did not take part in the killings. In the book, he described the gang members as young and ordinary. And then went on to question himself: how could he be so blind as to not foresee the repercussions of their deeds? He claimed he should have had the courage to tell them that he could not work with them, but he didn't.

The criminals talked about how they wanted to donate their vital organs and, therefore, should not be hanged and executed.

Jagtap pointed out that since his incarceration, he too had written a book *Kalyan Marg* in Marathi and translated into Marathi an English book written by Dhirendra Brahmchari, *Yogic Sukshama Vyayam*. To gain further sympathy and to show that he had left his wayward ways behind, Jagtap told the court that he was studying Buddhism and translating the *Dhammapada* into Marathi.

Shah tried another trick. He said he was studying homeopathy, learning Arabic and translating the Quran into Marathi and needed time to finish these projects.

'Good education [. . .] can prevent more criminal minds from taking shape,' said Hulyalkar.[3]

When everything seemed to be failing, Jakkal came up with the master stroke. Their lawyer appealed to the court stating that 'hanging by the noose' was a painful form of death and, therefore, they should die in the electric chair.

The men by now had tested the patience of the Punekars and the bereaved families, who wanted justice. The victims' families took written opinions of ten doctors from across the country, who unanimously agreed that execution by the noose was, in fact, the least painful of all execution procedures.

The signed petition and this statement from the doctors highlighted the severe anger and frustration that the people were now experiencing due to delayed justice. These helped the case from dragging on further.

The Supreme Court turned down their appeals and their last hope too came crashing down when the president did not pardon them.

So six and a half years after the trial began, the four were hanged to death in Yerawada Jail on 25 October 1983, bringing to an end one of the bloodiest and most heinous serial killings that the country had ever witnessed.

Hegde has since made peace with the loss of his son. In an interview conducted by Rahul Chandawarkar for *Sunday Mid-Day*, he said: 'When your time comes, not even God can save you. Prakash's time had come and he went away. We could not do anything.'[4]

Hulyalkar was also interviewed for the same news story. Then seventy-eight years old, Hulyalkar had long retired from the force and completed a PhD thesis.[5]

When the same interviewer approached Chandak in 1998 for his reaction on the twentieth anniversary of the massacre, Chandak—who was then a commercial artist in Pune—said: 'I would not like to discuss the case any more. I am trying hard to forget all about it. It has affected me a lot.'[6]

The murders inspired movies such as *Maaficha Sakshidar* (1986)—a Marathi film starring Nana Patekar, who portrayed the role of Jakkal—and *Paanch* (2003), an Anurag Kashyap movie.

Today, the murders are almost forgotten and its victims relegated to old news items and police records. The four did become infamous. However, instead of spitting at the world, the world spits on them for their inhuman and heinous crimes.

AMARDEEP SADA

THE WORLD'S YOUNGEST SERIAL KILLER

'*Khapda se mar mar ke suta deliyay* [I repeatedly hit her
with a brick and killed her].'[1]

—Amardeep Sada

He has the lowest number of victims in this book—three.
When compared to the other serial killers of India who
have notorious body counts of five, twenty and even 931, this
career statistic seems almost like an apology.

Most of the killers in this book reigned terror for years,
honing their skills, kill after kill. But Amardeep's reign barely
lasted for a few months. And his reign was not of terror. In fact,
it was of silence.

What makes him the epitome of evil is that Amardeep
became a killer when most children are still learning maths.

He was just seven years old when he first discovered the
pleasures of killing. This makes Amardeep the world's youngest
serial killer! This is his story.

* * *

2007

Inspector Shatrughan Kumar, officer in charge of Bhagwalpur
police station, sat opposite a dark, thin, small boy in a white,
yellowed singlet. The boy looked calm. Kumar had always been

teased as his namesake was Bollywood-actor-turned-politician Shatrughan Sinha. After every arrest, his juniors would say, '*Sir, aap toh Shatruji ke jaise famous ho rahe ho* [You are becoming as famous as your film-star namesake is]!' However, nothing in his career had prepared him for whom he was facing.

An eight-year-old boy had been arrested for the murder of three infants. Kumar's head was wrapped in a fog of disbelief.

He cleared his throat and pulled his rickety wooden chair closer to Amardeep's. The boy's legs were dangling a few inches above the ground. He was too tiny, thought Kumar.

Kumar asked the boy, '*Kaey maar dilayee bachwa ke?* [Why did you kill the kids?]'

Amardeep looked at the inspector and smiled. '*Bhookh lagal chahiyee . . . biskoot daho!* [I'm hungry. I want biscuits!]'

A shiver ran down Kumar's spine. He was facing a boy who wanted biscuits for recounting his story of killing three infants![2]

Amardeep continued to smile mischievously at Kumar, while dangling his feet, as if he was playing a game with him.

'*Hamra la biskoot labho ki naa?* [Are you getting me those biscuits or not?]'

If the criminal would have been above eighteen years of age, Kumar would have swung his right hand and given him a slap that would have made his ears ring, but it was an eight-year-old he was dealing with.

* * *

Amardeep's parents were impoverished and had been overjoyed when he was born. They named him 'Amardeep' or eternal light. Little did they know that their son will extinguish the lives of others in seven years' time.

Amardeep was a quiet child, given to bouts of tantrums and sulking, temper and mischief like any other kid. One day, when he was five, he came home after playing in the village—dirty, with a stained vest and a cut on his knee. His mother, Parul, who was making rotis, immediately started fussing over him. The next day, she went to the local Hanuman mandir and asked the priest to make a *taweez*—a holy amulet—that she could make her son wear to protect him from evil.

When Amardeep refused to wear it, Parul convinced him that it was a piece of jewellery and a gift from Bajrangbali himself. He smiled. She tied it around his neck with black thread and prayed to God to keep him away from harm.

The older he got, the quieter he became. He hoarded things and hid them, including his broken toys and bits and pieces of knick-knacks. His father, Balaram, barely made ends meet and, therefore, Amardeep had to repurpose or reimagine everything he laid his hands on to be a toy or a thing of interest and entertainment.

He was seven when his cousin brother came to visit. Amardeep's aunt had turned up one day out of the blue and told Parul that she would be leaving her six-month-old son with them for a month, as she had got a job in Patna as a domestic help. Parul was tense. They could barely feed three mouths and now there would be four. Her sister probably sensed the apprehension.

'I'll send you money as soon as I get my first payment!' she assured her.

On the day of her departure, his aunt spent ten minutes with her son. She hugged him close to her chest, tears rolling down her cheeks. She then put a black tika with the kohl from her eyes on the side of his forehead to ward off evil. The little boy had no clue what was going on. That was the last time his mother saw him alive.

A few weeks into the infant's stay, Parul went to the local market to buy vegetables. She was pregnant. She instructed Amardeep to look after his cousin. Amardeep watched his mother walking slowly towards the bazaar. He walked over to where his brother had been laid down. The little boy was fast asleep. Something stirred inside Amardeep. He laughed at some private joke of his own.

He pinched his cousin's ear. The infant immediately woke up and started bawling. Amardeep quite enjoyed the fact that he had managed to upset the baby. He cried helplessly while Amardeep teased and prodded him—sometimes pinching him on his stomach, sometimes pulling his nose, sometimes slapping him. Every time, the baby cried louder and Amardeep's laughter became more raucous. Then he put his hands on the infant's throat and applied pressure. The baby's voice was muted, his arms and legs started flailing. The pressure increased on the throat. The baby's eyes grew wider. And then, he lay still. During this whole time, Amardeep's smile never faded. He picked up the dead infant in his arms, awkwardly balancing him. He walked towards the paddy fields behind his house. The air was stiflingly hot. He picked up a brick, using both his hands, lying nearby and brought it down on the infant's head. The soft skull immediately turned into a disfigured mess. He then dug a hole in the mud with a stick, dumped the boy in it, covered it up with mud and walked back home.

When Parul came home, Amardeep was busy playing with a broken plastic toy car. She saw the empty mat on which she had placed her sister's son.

'Where is Babua?' she asked in panic. Amardeep smiled at her.

'*Arre*, where is the baby? Stop smiling!'

What he said next chilled her to the bone.

'I have killed him!' Amardeep said matter-of-factly.

The bag of vegetables dropped from her hand as Parul collapsed to the ground. She didn't know what to make of it. She waited for the information to sink in.

'Stop fooling around. Are you playing a prank? Have you hidden him somewhere?' She was now trying to cajole him to speak the truth. He was. She just didn't know.

He nodded. There was a look of relief on Parul's face. Her face broke into a smile.

'You gave me such a fright. Don't play such scary pranks . . . *chal*, take me where you have hidden him,' Parul said, holding Amardeep's hand. He took her to the paddy fields.

'Why did you hide him here? Don't you know there are snakes here? You could have hidden him in the house if you wanted to play this game!' She felt tense again. 'How much farther do we have to go?'

Amardeep stopped walking. Parul asked, 'Where is he? I can't see him!'

He tugged her hand and pointed to a mound of fresh mud and said, 'I have hidden him here.'

Parul's knees buckled under her. She pushed her son away and started digging frantically. The smashed skull confirmed that it was too late. She threw up.

That night when Balaram returned and heard the story, he gave Amardeep the thrashing of his life. However, his parents did not report the incident to the police. The next month when Parul's sister arrived to collect her son, Balaram collapsed at her feet. Meena was shocked—'What are you doing?' she asked. It was a simple question, but its answer blew Meena's world to smithereens. She watched Amardeep smile at her. She couldn't believe that this seven-year-old had killed her only son.

'It was an accident,' Parul said, 'and we had to bury him, lest the villagers find out and complain.'

'We should keep this information within these walls,' Balaram pleaded with his hands folded, 'it is a family matter. Please don't let it become public or else his life will be ruined.'

What reasons made Meena agree to their appeals, we do not know. Perhaps, it was because Parul was her elder sister and, therefore, Meena couldn't afford to shame and destroy her life. Alas, if only Parul could look into the future, then she herself would've taken her son to the police station.

Parul gave birth to a beautiful daughter in the next few days. Balaram and Parul were overjoyed. They could not have asked for a better gift from the Gods—a son and a daughter. Now their family felt complete. The 'accident' was soon pushed away to the back of their minds.

'This is your little sister!' Parul tried to make Amardeep understand the relationship. 'You are now a big brother. You have to protect and look after her from now on.'

Amardeep kept looking at his little sister—not quite fathoming the relationship or the fact that here was a stranger who had suddenly appeared in his life.

Parul noticed that there were days when Amardeep sat for hours just staring at his little sister and smiling. She was happy that her son was normal and was taking to his sister like any loving brother would. On some nights, the horrible sight of her sister's dead infant lying in the shallow grave with his smashed head would make her shudder, but she would force the memory to recede into some obscure corner of her mind. She would also think that it was a good decision on the family's part to not report the matter. After all, it was just an 'accident'.

It had been eight months since Amardeep had strangled his cousin. It was a winter afternoon and his parents were taking a siesta. His sister was lying in her cot, lost in her infant thoughts, when Amardeep approached her. The little girl cooed seeing her brother, a familiar figure to her. She was smiling. Amardeep smiled back. He then snuffed out her life by strangling her. For no reason.

When Amardeep's mental state would be evaluated after his arrest, Shamshad Hussain, a psychoanalyst, would reveal to reporters that Amardeep was likely a sadist who found injuring others pleasurable.[3]

When Parul woke up and tried to rouse her daughter from what she assumed was slumber, it turned out to be futile. Her body was cold. She looked at Amardeep playing nonchalantly nearby and shrieked, 'WHAT HAVE YOU DONE? DID YOU KILL YOUR SISTER?'

Amardeep just nodded and smiled. Parul and Balaram broke down.

Karma had come to pay Parul back, punishing her for condoning her son's earlier crime.

Balaram slapped Amardeep again and again and asked him, 'Why did you do it?'

Amardeep, now in tears, answered, 'Just like that!'

Their wailing and crying alerted the neighbours, who crowded into their house and put two and two together.

'Balaram, you must report it to the police. Put a stone on your heart and do it,' Mir chacha, a neighbour, advised.

'*Is manhoos ko to main hi maar dunga!*' [I will kill this unlucky fellow myself!] Balaram lunged to attack his son. But Amardeep couldn't understand what the fuss was about.

'So what if I have killed her?'

There was silence in the room. No one could believe what they had just heard.

Two days later, Balaram requested some of the neighbours to not let the news out, as it was a family matter, and put it to rest.[4]

This was sheer negligence and obstruction of the law on the part of Amardeep's parents. But for a second, try and think—how would you react if you found out that your eight-year-old child is a cold-blooded murderer? The need for Parul and Balaram to protect their child was real, though wrong.

And so another murder was hushed up. But it seemed the tiger had now tasted blood.

* * *

2007

Chunchun Devi had a lot of work on her hands. She had to go to the market to buy vegetables, then to the ration shop to get her monthly quota of oil, rice and pulses. She left her eight-year-old daughter at the village primary school to sleep— where she would be safe—and left. But when she came back, her daughter was gone. She panicked and started screaming and crying. Some of the people who knew about Amardeep's killing past immediately caught on and went to his house. They interrogated him, 'What have you done to Khushboo? Have you killed her?'

Amardeep smiled and said yes. It seemed he was very proud of what he had done, so much so that he even led the villagers to the freshly dug grave, which was covered with stones and fresh grass to conceal it.

The villagers could not tolerate this psychotic killer amidst them. In spite of protests and pleadings by his parents, Amardeep was handed over to the police.

Khushboo's mother screamed at Balaram saying, 'I have lost my daughter only because of you and your wife! If you had reported him last time, my daughter would've still been alive.'

All Balaram could do was join his hands in apology and cry.

* * *

Amardeep dunked the glucose biscuit into a glass of tea. The moist biscuit almost broke off but Amardeep managed to transfer it inside his mouth in the nick of time. With his stomach full, he began describing the killings.

'She was sleeping in the school. I took her away and killed her with a stone and buried her,' he said.[5]

Kumar could not believe what he was hearing.

'I made her lie down in the grass and smashed her head with a stone. *Khapda se mar mar ke suta deliyay* [I repeatedly hit her with a brick and killed her].'

The police recovered Khushboo's body from the shallow grave. Amardeep took the police to the other two burial sites.

Nobody could believe that an eight-year-old could be capable of doing something so brutal.

The police concluded that the reason why Amardeep had targeted the babies was because they were smaller than him and, of course, could not retaliate.

Psychiatrists evaluated Amardeep and concluded that he was suffering from a conduct disorder, where he felt gratified after inflicting injuries on others.

According to a former professor at Patna University, Amardeep did not have a sense of right or wrong.

In an interview to *Telegraph* in June 2007, Nand Kumar, a psychotherapist who works at AIIMS, said that Amardeep's actions were symptomatic of a chemical imbalance in his brain and that he was dangerous.

'Such aggression may be hereditary and may be caused because of great chemical upheavals in the brain.'[6]

Amardeep was charged with murder. Under Indian law, a juvenile cannot be sentenced to death or sent to prison, but can be detained at a children's home till they turn eighteen. The maximum sentence he received was three years in a juvenile facility. There was no publicly released information regarding his sentencing, trial or conviction. The case may have shocked the nation and the legal department so much that they decided to play it quiet.

The case even made world headlines and Amardeep was billed as the 'World's Youngest Serial Killer'. And just as quickly as his story had stormed its way to the front pages, it disappeared.

There was no news of Amardeep for a while. Then the police confirmed that Amardeep had been placed in a remand home in the nearby town of Munger.

Time would fly by. There would be rumours that he had contacted a female journalist in 2015 and told her that he was to remain in the remand home till 2018. There were also rumours that he had changed his name to Samarjeet.[7]

Amardeep was eight years old in 2007 when he was arrested, which would make him twenty years old now in 2019. He was tried as a juvenile and is probably roaming the streets as a free adult while you read this.

Hopefully, he has reformed himself and got rid of his demons during psychiatric and counselling sessions. And, hopefully, we will never hear of him again.

CYANIDE MOHAN

THE TEACHER-TURNED-SERIAL-KILLER

'Every time a woman died, I felt very bad but it only lasted
for fifteen to twenty days. Then another woman would
come along and I would forget all about the past.'[1]

—Cyanide Mohan

Kamala was waiting at Majestic Bus Station to take a bus back to her native place. Back then, Majestic was located opposite Bangalore City railway station, and is known today as Kempegowda Bus Station. KBS is the hub of all buses plying intra-city and out of station.

Kamala had a lot of things on her mind. Her parents wanted to marry her off, but were unable to find a suitor, as she was already thirty-two. The prospective matches were all older men who wanted a huge dowry that her family couldn't afford.

To add to her misery, a strange man was staring at her from across the road. His gaze was burning down her back. She met his gaze and he smiled. He was stocky and had a moustache. He had an air of confidence about him. His jet black hair was short and wavy, combed neatly. The most arresting thing about him was his piercing gaze. And there was something kind about him. It had been a long time since a man had looked at her like that. It felt nice.

Bhaskara a.k.a. Mohan a.k.a. Anand was watching Kamala from a distance. He made sure that she was unmarried, having scanned her neck and the parting of her hair for clues. This was a ritual he always followed. Then, he gauged her demeanour. She seemed passive, the kind who would want to get married and settle down. She did not meet his gaze and her head was bowed down. She looked past the marriageable age. Given the simple sari that she was wearing, he could tell that she was not from a wealthy family.

It was now time to put on his charm and find out whether she would take the bait.

Was he walking towards her? Kamala looked from the corner of her eye. Before she could think, he was beside her, greeting her softly.

He asked her her name. She shyly told him. He laughed a gentle laugh and said, 'What a coincidence! I am of the same caste.' She smiled. For a moment, their eyes met. She thought he looked smart and his voice was kind. He enquired about her bus. When she told him, he checked his watch and said, 'Oh! We have some time on our hands. You look thirsty. Would you like to have a juice? I am thirsty as well and could use some company.'

Before she could decide, her lips formed the words: 'Okay.'

Mohan chose a nearby restaurant, where they sat opposite each other and drank sweet mosambi juice. He soon extracted all the information he needed from Kamala.

'Is it my fault that everybody wants dowry and that we cannot afford it?' she said, as her eyes welled up a little. Mohan reached across the table and held her hand. Gently squeezing it, he said: 'Well, not all men are like that. I do not support dowry at all.'

She looked up to meet his comforting eyes. Her heart skipped a beat. She didn't pull her hand away. Could this conversation be heading towards where she was hoping it would? Why was a stranger's presence so reassuring?

'I work for Malnad Area Development Board. I have a stable government job and I am past the marriageable age too. I had also given up hope of finding someone special,' he said, pausing a bit for effect, and continued: 'till I saw you!'

This was the modus operandi of Cyanide Mohan or Professor Mohan Kumar. He always targeted naive women; always waited for the women to disclose their names so he could make up an alias that would have a surname of the same caste as theirs. He would always say that he was a government employee with a stable job. To impress his targets, he would pass himself off as an executive of Kudremukh Iron Ore Company, Malnad Area Development Board or some such government department.[2]

In an interview to *Bangalore Mirror*, Mohan said:

> I mostly found these women at bus stands. I would strike up a conversation with them and exchange phone numbers. If they agreed to come with me for a glass of juice, then I would gauge whether they were likely to succumb and surrender to me. We would go to a park and I would see how they responded to my physical overtures. I was attracted to women who were very simple looking. I always targeted women who would put their head down and walk. Though such women pretend to mind their business, they are easy to strike a conversation with.[3]

A month later, Kamala was found dead in one of the toilet cubicles of the same bus stand, wearing a wedding sari.

What had followed was a whirlwind romance for a month. Mohan called her up all the time and they spoke on the phone endlessly. He warned her that her parents might not like the idea of her romancing a much older man. She understood. And then, one day he popped the question that she had longed to hear: 'Will you marry me?'

Tears streamed down her cheeks in happiness. She was sure that her life would be happier now. She said yes.

'So listen to my plan . . .' he said.

As per their plan, on the decided day, Kamala secretly packed her bags, stole her mother's jewellery and money and boarded a bus to meet Mohan. She had thought for a moment if it were too good to be true and whether he would really be there, as promised. But he was there all right, waiting for her, wearing that kind smile of his.

Mohan and Kamala checked into a lodge near the bus station. As she sat on the bed, Mohan slowly lifted up her face and kissed her lips. She blushed and buried her face in his chest.

'Should we tell my parents now?' Kamala enquired.

'First, I want you to meet my parents and seek their blessings,' Mohan replied. He told her that he would take her to his village the next day. But first, more important things were on hand. At a temple, in the presence of a priest, Mohan 'married' Kamala.

That night Mohan and Kamala consummated their marriage by making passionate love. Kamala had never felt that way before. The next morning, Mohan asked her to dress up in her wedding sari.

'Nīvu sundaravāgiddīri [You look beautiful],' he said and Kamala blushed like the newlywed bride that she was.

On the way to the bus stand, Mohan asked, 'Can I ask you something personal?'

Kamala replied, 'Yes, of course, you're my husband.'

'When are your periods due?'

Kamala was taken aback by the question and blushed. She was not used to such frankness about her menstrual cycle.

'Chee! Those are womanly things. Why do you need to know?'

'Because we had unprotected sex last night and you might get pregnant. I don't want our parents to think that we are of loose morals,' he said, looking worried. 'I suggest you take this contraceptive pill.'

Saying this, Mohan handed over a capsule to Kamala. She took it hesitantly.

'Trust me,' Mohan assured her. 'Go into a toilet cubicle at the bus stand. You might feel sick and vomit. But don't worry. I'll be waiting for you here with the luggage.'

Kamala walked towards the restroom. She turned to look at her husband. He smiled and waved at her. Kamala walked into the toilet, locked herself in a cubicle and swallowed the capsule.

The effect was immediate. She began frothing at the mouth and collapsed, as the world grew dark around her.

Meanwhile, Mohan waited for ten minutes and then walked away with her suitcase containing the money and jewellery.

Later, the cubicle door was broken down and Kamala was brought dead to the hospital. Her body remained unclaimed. The police closed the case thinking it was a destitute girl who had committed suicide after being abandoned by her lover.

This exact scenario played out again and again for five years while Mohan took the lives of twenty girls through a cold-blooded and meticulously calculated modus operandi.

The victims were all in their mid-twenties or early-thirties; eighteen of the twenty bodies were found inside toilet cubicles of bus stands, which had to be broken into because they were locked from inside; and all of them were dressed in what appeared to be wedding sarees with not a single piece of jewellery on them. Of the twenty victims, eight were recovered from Mysore city's Lashkar Mohalla bus stand alone and another five from Bangalore's busy Kempegowda Bus Station.

Strangely, their families had no clue that the girls were having an affair or planning to elope; and the investigation was immature. For example, when a twenty-year-old woman named Sunanda was found at the Mysore bus stand on 11 February 2008, her cause of death was recorded as epileptic seizure. The postmortem report that was received after twenty months, however, stated that her death was caused due to cyanide consumption. By that time, Mohan had already claimed more victims.

All twenty cases were labelled as 'unnatural deaths' and 'suspected suicides' and no attempt was made to identify the victims and trace their families. As the girls were far away from their homes, there was no one to claim their bodies. So the police disposed of the unclaimed victims' bodies as per civic norms. The police concluded that they had been dumped at the altar or their elopement had gone wrong and, therefore, had consumed poison and committed suicide.

This left Mohan free to pawn the victims' gold with a gold-loan company, and spend the cash in pursuit of other potential victims.

Surprisingly, no red flags were raised even after the forensic tests revealed that it was cyanide poisoning—a chemical not easily available and certainly not commonly used in suicides. It seemed the police had not bargained to find such a cold-blooded serial killer.

In an interview with *Telegraph*, Nanjunde Gowda, the head of Sampigehalli police station, Bengaluru, said, 'He observed unmarried working women from middle-income and lower-income backgrounds at bus stops and became friendly with them. He then proposed marriage. He wanted no dowry, he said, and urged the women to elope with him to faraway towns after swearing them to secrecy.'[4]

'Not being asked for dowry is a big thing in these parts and he took advantage of that vulnerability. Many women left their homes with their best clothes and jewellery,' said Chandra Gupta, superintendent of police, Bellary, who as then assistant superintendent of police, Puttur, had led the investigations.[5]

But who was Mohan Kumar and how did he become Cyanide Mohan?

Mohan taught science, English and mathematics at Shiradi Primary School in rural Mangalore. Nobody knows how he transformed into a serial killer.

He was a quiet, polite teacher; he was married thrice. He first fell in love with Mary, who was only a Class VII student at Shiradi Primary School at the time. Mohan waited for her to turn eighteen and married her. But the marriage did not last long and Mary divorced him. Mohan's second wife, Manjula, lives with his two sons in rural Mangalore. He has a daughter and a son with Sridevi, his third wife, who lives in Deralakatte. Though Mohan was separated from Manjula, he still visited her in Uppala every two days to spend time with her and his two sons.

Nobody noticed the devil inside Mohan when he lured a young woman and pushed her off a bridge in 2005. This was the first time he had shown his true colours. According to the police, Mohan tried to kill his first victim by pushing her off a bridge into the Netravathi river in the temple town of Dharmasthala. The woman was rescued and a case of attempted murder registered, but the case fell through in a local court. Mohan was, however, sacked from his job.

When he was asked why he stopped teaching, he said, 'There was a woman who wanted to marry me but when I refused, she started arguing with me and fell in Nethravathi. But some fishermen nearby thought I had pushed her and registered a complaint against me.'[6]

While the case was underway, he was jailed for a month, before being acquitted. In prison, he met a goldsmith who was doing time for killing eight cows and a few goats. The cause? The goldsmith had carelessly discarded the waste after cleaning the gold ornaments with cyanide and the animals had come into contact with the poisonous waste.

The goldsmith told Mohan how cyanide can kill instantaneously and about its easy availability in the market. In 2003, one could buy it off the shelf in Karnataka for Rs 250 a kilogram.

When Mohan got out of jail, his evil mind started whirring with activity. He went to a chemical dealer's shop.

'You don't look like a jeweller!' Abdul Salam, the chemical dealer, said, raising his eyebrows at Mohan.

Mohan couldn't afford to panic.

'Does a doctor look like a doctor or an engineer like an engineer?' Mohan said, as he chuckled to look convincing.

'That is true. How much do you need?' Abdul Salam asked.

Mohan successfully managed to pose as a goldsmith and buy cyanide from the dealer, who was easily hoodwinked. When the case unfolded, Abdul Salam was arrested for selling cyanide without proper authorization.

Mohan was now on his way to execute his modus operandi.

One of his early victims was twenty-five-year-old Baby Nayak, a resident of Peraje near Sullia. He lured and wooed her, and then took her to a lodge near KSRTC bus stand in Madikeri on 3 January 2008. There, after satiating his sexual urge, he gave her an 'oral contraceptive' pill. She consumed it in the toilet of the bus stand and Mohan fled with the jewellery. By the time she was found, it was too late.

Thirty-two-year-old Shanta Kumari was an attendant at a Mangalore college. What her family did not know was that she was secretly head over heels in love a man. On 9 November 2006, she walked out of her home, dressed in special clothes after telling her family that she was going to attend a function in her college. Hidden in her bag were twenty *paun* gold[7] (or 160 gm) and some cash. When she did not return that night, her family called up her college. The watchman sounded incredulous and said: 'College function? Nothing of that sort took place today.' And to increase the family's misery, he added: 'Shanta madam had come, but she took half-day leave and went off somewhere.'

Her family waited for her to return for days but to no avail. Then one day, her elder brother, Raju, read a news report of a woman found dead. 'The newspaper report said the woman died after getting a fit and that the police claimed she was an AIDS victim,' said Raju to his parents. 'She was buried in the town cemetery.'

Raju and his relatives visited Kollur and identified Shanta's earrings, blouse and wristwatch. They were devastated. They demanded that the administration exhume the body but the gravediggers refused to cooperate as she had been declared an AIDS victim.

The family was adamant and managed to exhume the body and a second postmortem was conducted. They went around the town's lodges with Shanta's photo, begging and pleading for any lead, and finally got one.

When asked in an interview after Mohan's arrest, Raju recalled: 'An auto driver said he had dropped my sister and a middle-aged man at a lodge. The people at the lodge refused to confirm that they stayed there and the police did not enquire any further.'

Sujatha (twenty-eight) disappeared from Bajpe near Mangalore airport after she borrowed jewellery from her neighbour for a special occasion.[8]

Sunanda (twenty) disappeared from Vaipala near Bellare in Sullia, with gold ornaments and Rs 65,000 in cash.[9]

Kaveri (thirty), from Sullia, had left home with a gold chain that she had borrowed from her neighbours, gold rings from her brothers and Rs 40,000 in cash.[10]

It seemed Mohan's charm managed to entrap every woman he encountered. But that was not the case. What irritated him were the women who refused to succumb to his charm. Post his arrest, the police found a diary where he had maintained a list of all the women he had approached. He had struck off the names of those he'd had no success with, by marking their names in red. Of every ten women he met, he apparently succeeded only with two.

Nelyadi Vanitha was a twenty-two-year-old member of a women's self-help group in Uppinangady. Everybody thought that she was too 'modern' in her outlook.

'Nobody will want to get married to you, if you keep inciting the womenfolk to stand on their own feet and be more independent. No man likes to be told off by his wife,' her neighbour once told her.

Nelyadi smiled and said, 'Times are changing. We can no longer be doormats.' The woman harrumphed and shut her door in Nelyadi's face.

When Mohan met Nelyadi, he immediately assessed her, and wrote a script inside his head. He pretended to be a champion of women's rights and gave her a passionate speech on how times had changed and that society needed to change too. Nelyadi was bowled over. She laughed aloud. Mohan was surprised.

'Did I say something funny?' Mohan asked.

Nelyadi shook her head. 'A neighbour had said that I would never find a man who supported women's rights. I wish she could meet you. I want to see her face!'

Mohan's charm was so well planned and administered in the correct dosage that even Nelyadi fell for it. She left home on 27 May 2004, never to return. Though her family lodged a complaint, the police could not trace her. When her body was found at Hassan bus stand a few days later, the local police assumed her to be a destitute woman and buried her without an investigation.

On 23 January 2008, Sharada Gowda (twenty-eight) left home as usual to take a bus to Udupi, where she worked at a private firm. 'Please come back on time,' her mother told her, as Sharada rushed out of the house. She looked over her shoulder and said: 'I will come on time.' She held her look just a little bit longer than usual. It was as if she wanted to see her mother a little longer—perhaps it was a premonition that this was going to be the last time she looked into her mother's eyes. She was found dead at Mysore bus stand a few days later. The local police concluded that this 'unknown' person had committed suicide.

The police's lackadaisical approach suited Mohan just fine. In his article for *Open*, Anil Budur Lulla writes:

> Police lethargy and lack of communication gave Kumar plenty of leeway. The women remained 'missing' in their records though many were found dead in the toilets of bus stands in other towns and cities within days of the missing complaints being lodged. Local cops passed these off as destitute deaths. Even if froth was found on the deceased's mouth, a sign of poisoning, they put it down as suicide by an impoverished depressive. They made no effort to match the details of those reported missing with those found dead. This suited Kumar well.[11]

Mohan's next victim was left activist Leelavathy, a thirty-year-old resident of Vamanapadavu in Bantwal. The local police did not bother to probe her disappearance when her family lodged a complaint. Instead, they insisted she had run away to join the Naxalites, whose presence in the region had been noted for some time. She was found dead at the Mysore bus stand a few days after she went missing.

Sunanda Poojary, who rolled bidis for a living, would also be found dead at the same bus stand a few days later. But such was the apathy and shortsightedness in the investigation that nobody joined the dots. The police saw nothing odd about two women being found dead in the same place within a fortnight of each other.

Shashikala of Balepuni was found dead at a Bangalore bus stand. A member of a self-help group, she had taken a loan of Rs 90,000 right before she went missing. Filing their complaint, her family members said she was wearing a 50-gm gold chain (which was never found).

Exactly a year after Shashikala, Kamala was found dead at KBS. On 25 September 2009, Yashoda was discovered lifeless at Hassan bus stand, but on a bench, not in the washroom.

Meenakshi (twenty-five) of Alike is still missing. Arathi (twenty-two) went missing in January 2006, so did Baby Nayak. These women are yet to be traced, but since Kumar has confessed to poisoning them, they are presumed dead.

Mohan's victims were:[12]

1. Baby Nayak (twenty-five) from Peraje near Sullia
2. Sharada (twenty-four) from Kedila in Puttur
3. Kaveri (thirty) from Sampaje in Sullia
4. Pushpa (twenty-six) from Mulleria in Kasaragod
5. Vinutha (twenty-four) from Puttur
6. Hema (twenty-four) of Mittur in Bantwal
7. Anitha (twenty-two) from Barimar
8. Yashoda (twenty-six) from Madanthyar in Belthangady
9. Vijayalakshmi (twenty-six) from Kasaragod
10. Sarojini (twenty-seven) from Uppala
11. Shashikala (twenty-eight) from Kariangala in Bantwal
12. Sunanda (twenty-five) from Peruvaje near Sullia
13. Leelavathy (thirty-two) from Vamada Padav
14. Shantha (thirty-five) from Kankanady
15. Vanitha (twenty-two) from Nelyady
16. Sujatha (twenty-eight) from Mucchur near Bajpe

Mohan was such a devious killer that neither his third wife Sridevi nor his mother-in-law or his own mother had any clue about his actions. When he was arrested, his family members and neighbours reacted with incredulity.

Sridevi said in an interview that Mohan was a loving husband.

> I have never seen any cyanide in his possession. I used to check his handbag, which contains a small mirror and some papers. He had a small plastic bottle filled with talcum powder. Whenever it was empty, he filled it from the actual container [. . .] I gave him money several times after borrowing from my Swasahaya account.[13] If he was connected to those killings, he would have earned a lot of money.'[14]

Manjula said he kept accounts of every rupee spent and noted even daily expenses. She claimed he was a simple man and worried about unnecessary expenses. She said she was not aware of the killings. 'He was in my house every two days and spent the rest of the time with his third wife,' she said.[15]

So how was this cold-blooded serial killer who had the perfect modus operandi caught?

Because even a perfect criminal leaves behind traces. And four key people were responsible for nabbing Cyanide Mohan.

1. A victim
2. A priest
3. A survivor
4. A nephew

Mohan would let his guard down for inexplicable reasons and commit two errors, both of which would leave eyewitnesses who would help nail him in court.

The first error would involve the priest. The second error would be on account of him altering his modus operandi for the first time.

And a gobsmacked police team would unravel and chase one lead after another in a breathtaking chase to the finale.

The Victim

It was June 2009. There was no one at home. Anitha Moolya wore an off-white sari with an intricate zari border. She looked at herself in the mirror. Something was missing, and then she realized. She quickly tucked fresh flowers into her hair, wore gold earrings, slipped her beautiful feet into a new pair of sandals and put the new, expensive cell phone that her brother, Madhav, had gifted her, into her handbag. She felt complete.

Why not? Her life was taking a turn for the better. She had always been told that a woman's life is only complete when she gets married. And here she was, all excited, going to get married in a temple to her boyfriend in a few hours' time.

'Is this happening for real?' Anitha asked, as she kept her head on his bare chest and looked into his eyes.

'You tell me,' Mohan asked teasingly.

Anitha had arrived in an interstate bus a few minutes ago. Mohan, or in this case Anand Kulal, had promptly picked her up from the bus stand and they had checked into a lodge nearby.

Anand told her that they would get married the next day. She couldn't wait. They made passionate love. She was making love to her future husband. He was fucking his next victim.

The next morning, Anitha showered and wore her wedding sari. She was about to wear her gold jewellery when Anand asked her to come for a walk with him.

'A walk? Now? We will get late for our own wedding!' she exclaimed.

Anand seemed serious and asked her not to wear her jewellery. They would return after the walk and get ready for the wedding.

He then enacted the same script that he had written inside his head, like a well-performed play. He reminded her that they had had unprotected sex and that she could get pregnant and he couldn't take the risk. She was excited at the thought of becoming a mother. Anand raised his voice.

'I am not yet ready to become a father!' he said, a little sternly. 'You have to take this contraceptive pill.'

Anitha looked at Anand. She didn't like the scowl on his face. She was surprised at the sudden change in the tone of his voice. He had always been polite and soft-spoken. Something was off but she could not put her finger on it. She pleaded, 'Anand, please don't get angry. I will take the pill if it makes you happy.' She took the pill from Anand's hands and hurried into a women's toilet at Hassan town's intercity bus stand. Anand kept watching till he heard a woman scream. He knew that Anitha was dead. A crowd started gathering around the toilet. The police were called to the scene. Anand walked away and was soon swallowed up by the crowd in the bus stand. He returned to the lodge and entered the room. The crumpled bed sheets were a reminder of the passionate encounter the previous night. He scoffed, picked up their belongings and her jewellery, and vanished.

When Anitha was discovered missing, local right-wing organizations in her village alleged that she was the latest victim of 'love jihad'—a name given to the alleged phenomenon of Muslim youths luring Hindu women away and converting them to Islam. When her parents filed a missing-person complaint with the police in the Dakshina Kannada district of Karnataka, the cops on duty too dismissed it as a case of love jihad. But nobody had a clue if she'd vanished with a lover of another faith.

In an interview to *Open* in 2014, Anitha's father, Duggappa Mulya, said: 'The police asked us to keep our mouths shut. They were not willing to listen, despite no one having seen Anitha talking to any person of [another] community.'[16]

After waiting for three months for the police to respond, communal riots broke out. A posse of 150 protesters from her community, the Bangeras, took out a morcha and threatened to burn the police station down if the police did not make efforts to track down Anitha. The petrified cops assured them that within a month the case would be closed. Little did they know that Anitha was already dead and that her unclaimed body had been disposed of by the police team that had discovered her three months ago, as they could not identify her.

The case was handed over to the Corps of Detectives (COD), a premier investigating agency, which operates under the Crime Investigation Department (CID) of Karnataka police. And these investigators started joining the dots and a pattern began to emerge.

It began with the call records of Anita's landline, which revealed that she used to have long conversations late into the night with a particular person . . . the trail had been discovered.

Could it be the lover who had lured her away?

The cops in charge were not expecting what unfolded next. It was the mother of all chases, not in any way inferior to the best action movie ever made.

The eager cops, who thought they were going to capture the 'lover', discovered that the phone number belonged to one Kaveri Manku in Madikeri, who, to the policemen's shock, was missing too.

A study of Kaveri's call dump records revealed a very high number of calls from a number that nobody in her family could identify. This number led the COD team to Pushpa Vasukoda in Kasargod. And (hold your breath!) she too had been reported missing a year ago. The case was getting murkier.

The team was now in a tizzy. Their adrenaline was pumping as they started picking up the crumbs.

The COD team studied Pushpa's call records and to no surprise, another number popped up, leading the police to another missing woman, Vinutha from Puttur.

The COD team was breathless with anticipation and excitement. With every crumb they picked up, they thought they were getting closer to finding the criminal. But at the back of their minds, the fear grew.

'When will this trail end?' asked one of the team members. 'How many missing girls will it take for us to find out the truth?'

They waited patiently for Vinutha's call records to be analysed. And as they feared, her call records led them to yet another missing woman . . . and her records to another . . .

The COD team were baffled. Either they had a case of trafficking on their hands on a large scale or it was a cold-blooded serial killer. But the latter seemed an unlikely option, as they could not imagine how someone could murder so many women.

Nonetheless, the COD succeeded where the police had failed. They came to the conclusion that the killer/trafficker used one victim's cell phone to call another.

While the investigation was going on, unknown to the COD team, Mohan was back on the streets, hunting down innocent and unsuspecting preys and then killing them. Finally, the investigators picked up the correct scent, like bloodhounds on a hunt. But were they moving fast enough to stop the devil in his tracks?

The COD team now spread their net wider.

The detectives scanned and pored over the files of every missing person, examined the details of bodies found in bus stand toilets and put all the clues together to crack the cases of twenty missing women. They now knew that it wasn't a case of human trafficking, but a serial killer on the loose.

Unknown to Mohan, the COD was closing in on him. Mohan, who had become overconfident, continued scanning bus stands and public places for his next victim—or what would be his last—the twentieth, before finally getting caught.

The Priest

So far, Mohan had succeeded in maintaining his good-man image. But for some strange reason, something clicked in his head after he killed Anitha. Had he truly fallen in love with her?

He experienced a pang of guilt. He had never felt like that before. Anitha was his sixteenth victim. If guilt had to strike him, it should have logically hit him in the early days of his killings. Why so late? We don't know. His conscience was racked by the unforgivable deeds he had done.

A night after he killed Anitha, Mohan could not sleep in his house in Deralakatte. He tossed and turned in his bed. His wife asked him what was wrong. 'I have a headache,' he lied, before heading out of the house where he sat in silence, staring blankly at the blanket of stars. He felt nauseated, uneasy and miserable. He did not know why.

The next morning, he let his guard down. He took bus no. 51 from Deralakatte and headed towards Mangalore. There, he went directly to Annapoorneshwari Temple. The priest, Ishwar Bhat, remembers seeing a stocky man who was scowling approaching the sanctum sanctorum and waiting for him to finish his pujas and chores. As soon as he came out, Mohan rushed to him and asked: 'Is there a special puja that you can do that will relieve me of my sins of killing a woman?'

Bhat was stunned. He recalled: 'I was shocked, but thought that he was a bit off and told him to offer kumkuma archana, which he did.'[17]

Bhat was one of the key witnesses in the trial of Cyanide Mohan.

* * *

Whatever guilt and remorse Mohan may have felt after Anitha's murder was temporary, as he went back to hunting for his next target.

To date, Mohan cannot explain why he made the mistake of changing his modus operandi of isolating his victims from their families. He had always insisted that the women keep the news of their relationship a secret, for obvious reasons. The family would have no clue about Mohan and, subsequently, would not know how their wards disappeared.

But maybe it was sheer fatigue or overconfidence or the fact that his greed got the better of him that in the case of his twentieth victim, he agreed to meet the family of the girl.

Poornima (thirty-five) was a resident of Manjeshwar in Kerala. She was from a well-off family and insisted that her parents would like him and that she would marry him only if he met them. So Mohan dressed up for the occasion, wore a smart blue shirt and dark blue trousers and headed to meet Poornima's parents. They too were taken in by Mohan's well-spoken and polite demeanour. Mohan sought their permission to marry Poornima. Her parents insisted that they required some time to think things over.

Mohan coaxed Poornima to elope and they travelled to Bangalore. They checked into a lodge in the Majestic area, where he killed her, and vanished with her jewellery and money. But Poornima's parents knew what Mohan looked like.

The Survivor

Meanwhile, the COD had unravelled another facet of the murders: the cause of death. While the police had termed the deaths as either suicide or unnatural, the COD received the postmortem reports of one of the victims, which clearly stated the cause of death to be 'cyanide poisoning'.

While continuing to examine the trail of call records leading them from one missing woman to another, they were utterly shocked one day to hear a woman on the other end of the phone say: 'I have met him.'

She was given the codename the 'Woman of Bantwal',[18] as she did not want her identity to be revealed. She is the only survivor who managed to see the next day, after Mohan had handed over the pill to her. She offered clinching evidence that would strike yet another nail in the coffin of conviction for Mohan.

She narrated her story to the police. Mohan had lured her to a Madikeri lodge and when he had handed her the capsule, she had become suspicious. Something inside her head had told her not to eat it. She had only licked the capsule and not swallowed it. She had collapsed immediately in the washroom of Madikeri bus stand. Commotion ensued and Mohan made a quick exit, assuming she'd been found dead by onlookers.[19] What Mohan did not know was that the woman had recovered after five days in the hospital and had returned home with the help of some money that the nurses gave her. She did not tell anyone about Kumar and her ordeal and got married within months. The police were the first people she told about Mohan.

'She had to be gently persuaded to become a witness,' says a policeman. 'We promised her that her husband's family would not know anything. She agreed to an in-camera hearing and was our star witness.'[20]

The Nephew

While Mohan (unknown to the police at that time) was wooing Poornima, the police unravelled a major clue. They found that all the phones that they had been tracking were at some point active in a village called Deralakatte in Mangalore. How could so many different phones, previously owned by so many different people be active in that one village? The police knew they had something big in their dragnet. Could their chase be finally coming to an end?

The police came in droves to Deralakatte and began raiding small hotels and lodges, looking for any clue or lead, and it seemed fate and luck were both in cahoots to finally abandon Mohan.

The police were suddenly informed that Anitha's phone had been switched on for three minutes in Deralakatte. The call was traced to a young boy named Dhanush, who told the police that his uncle, Mohan Kumar, had given him the cell phone.

Mohan had murdered Kaveri just before Anitha. After Anitha's death, as per his modus operandi, Mohan threw away Kaveri's phone and gave Anitha's handset to his nephew, Dhanush. The sixteen-year-old started using Anitha's phone after a month with his own SIM card. That is when the police zeroed in on him. This was Providence.

The police went into a huddle. They knew it was just a few more days before they could zero in on Mohan who was now the prime suspect in the case.

At the time, Mohan was making long calls to another woman, Sumithra Shekhara Pujari of Bantwal. The cops laid the trap. Sumithra was nervous. The police assured her that no harm would come to her.

'All you have to do is invite him to meet you. Once he is with you, we will arrest him,' they assured a shivering Sumithra. The blood had drained from her face. She asked for water as she sat down on a chair. She could not believe that the police were chasing her boyfriend.

'There has to be some mistake. He doesn't look like the type who can kill people. He is polite and has a government job,' she pleaded.

'Madam, trust us. He is dangerous. We don't know if he is the murderer yet but we are sure that he is connected to the missing women.' The policeman continued, 'If he is armed and tries to attack you, then we will shoot him. So, please, do not panic.'

On D-Day, policemen in plain clothes positioned themselves in and around the temple to which Sumithra had called Mohan. And as soon as he arrived, Sumithra nodded and coughed into her closed fist—a predetermined signal to confirm that this man was Mohan. The policemen swarmed in and caught Mohan, who was taken completely by surprise. But what struck the arresting officer as odd was that after the initial surprise, Mohan had a smile on his face, almost as if he was cocking a snook at the policemen.

The police raided Sridevi's house and recovered vials of cyanide, fake identity and visiting cards, fake government seals and rubber stamps, gold jewellery (belonging to Anitha) and a diary in which Mohan had written the names of all the girls he had approached.

Mohan was arrested and interrogations followed for days, with sordid details emerging: his modus operandi; his inability to give the exact number of murders (the official count is twenty; some suspect it could be as high as thirty-two); and the usage of cyanide to get rid of the women.

As his picture and news splashed across the country and the world, he no longer was Mohan Kumar, the teacher, but Cyanide Mohan, a moniker that the public gave him.

The police gathered enough evidence and eyewitnesses—the survivor, the priest, the chemical dealer and Poornima's parents—for the trial. Mohan was calm as he fought his own case in the court. Just like serial killer Ted Bundy had done.

When journalist Iram Siddiqui asked Mohan why he had killed so many women, he apparently twirled his moustache and replied: 'I did not say that I killed them. I did not kill anybody.'[21]

Then how did they all end up dead in the toilets? 'I created that situation,' he answered carefully.[22]

And why would you do that? 'They would threaten me, saying that they would reveal our love story to their families or file a complaint of sexual harassment against me. It would get problematic.'[23]

Mohan's version was that the women killed themselves when he told them he could not marry them. They committed suicide and he had nothing to do with their deaths.

He managed to charm twenty girls in spite of not being employed or good-looking; and astounding is the gullibility and naiveté of the women who agreed to rob their own families of money and jewellery!

Even the police found it astounding how Mohan managed to hoodwink the women. In an interview to *Open*, one of the policemen said:

> How these women fell for him, don't ask me [. . .] But, they always seemed to fall for his idea that they should be dressed in bridal finery to meet his parents, who he said would accept very little dowry. Without confiding in any family member, these women would walk away with the gold and cash their parents kept aside for their marriage, travel with him to other cities to visit temples, and have an illicit relationship [with him].[24]

Did he ever feel any remorse or guilt for killing so many women? 'Every time a woman died, I felt very bad but it only lasted for fifteen to twenty days. Then another woman would come along and I would forget all about the past.'[25]

Why wouldn't he marry these women? 'I was already managing two wives. I was juggling between two wives and would spend alternate days at their houses.'[26]

Mohan claimed that he had murdered at least thirty-two women, but beyond twenty, there was no evidence for the rest. He was tried for the murders of Anitha Barimar, Leelavathy Mistry and Sunanda Pujari. On 21 December 2013, Cyanide Mohan was sentenced to death.

On 15 November 2017, the Karnataka High Court, calling it a 'rarest of rare' case, confirmed the death penalty imposed on Mohan for murdering Sunanda of Sullia.

On 24 February 2018, sixth additional district and sessions judge D.T. Puttarangaswamy sentenced Mohan to life imprisonment. This was his fifth conviction.[27]

On 27 March 2019, Cyanide Mohan was convicted for life in two rape and murder cases by two courts in Dakshina Kannada and Kodagu districts.

The number of rape and murder cases in which Cyanide Mohan has been convicted for life has reached nine.[28] Mohan Kumar alias Shashidhara alias Bhaskara lies in wait to be hanged at the gallows. He is bound to appeal to the Supreme Court. But as the judge at the high court called it a 'rarest of rare' case, Mohan might not get respite from the gallows. Or he will just live the rest of his life behind prison bars.

ANJANABAI, SEEMA GAVIT AND RENUKA SHINDE

CHILD KILLERS OF INDIA

'In one of their particularly gruesome murders, they hung a two-year-old upside down, bashed his head against the wall and chopped him into pieces. They then went for a movie at a local theatre in Kolhapur, eating bhel puri. All the while, the bag, with the chopped remains remained under their feet.'[1]

—Aseem Sarode, human rights lawyer and activist

June, 1990

Twenty-one-year-old Renuka excitedly burst into the rented room at Gondhalinagar, Pune, where she lived with her second husband, Kiran Shinde, her son from her first marriage, her mother, Anjanabai, and her younger stepsister, Seema Gavit. She had just been struck by an idea that she desperately wanted to share with her mother—an idea so sinister that it would shake the country with the brutal murder of nine children and earn Renuka, Seema and Anjana the title 'India's Child Killers'.

Anjana's first husband deserted her soon after Renuka was born. She then met Mohan Gavit, a retired Indian Army soldier, and Seema was born. To make extra money, Anjana started picking pockets. This led to her being questioned by the cops and being locked up many times. Mohan asked her to stop, but when she didn't, he got fed up and left her. He

238

married Pratibha, moved to Nashik and had two daughters, Kranti and Devli.

With no source of income, greed for money and a total disregard for the law, Anjana continued chain snatching and pickpocketing on temple premises. She roped in her daughters as well. Renuka was a natural and Seema was told it was a game. By her third time, Seema had begun to enjoy it. Their tiny hands could dip into pockets and open bags quite effortlessly, pulling out their contents.

The trio often came under the scanner of the police. They were picked up several times. But the shrewd matriarch would grease the palms of the cops and they would be let off.

What you are about to read will make you break into a cold sweat. This story would not have played out in real life had the cops arrested the trio and nipped their crime spree in the bud. They probably never imagined that one day these petty pickpockets would turn into ruthless serial killers.

By 1990, Anjana had been arrested for sixteen cases of theft; Renuka, five or six times; and Seema, thrice.

That day Renuka and her infant son, Aashish, had gone to visit Chaturshringi temple on Senapati Bapat Marg in Pune. A cunning thief like her wasn't visiting the temple to pay her respects but to target vulnerable temple-goers. But it seems Goddess Ambareshwari tempted Renuka by showing her a path to riches and to test her rectitude.

She had just pulled out a wallet from a man's pocket and was about to walk away when the man screamed, '*Pakdo, pakdo, chor, chor!*'

A crowd gathered around Renuka. Aashish began to bawl in fright. Some of the women in the crowd threatened Renuka to cough up the stolen goods. Others tried to pacify the shrieking child. Suddenly, Renuka had an idea. Breaking into tears, she said to the mob, 'How can a woman with a child commit a crime?' And that was it.

The mob was instantly pacified. They shook their heads, berating the man for thinking 'bad' about a mother and walked away. Renuka realized she was on to something. She rushed back home and said, 'Aai, you won't believe what happened at the temple today.'

The three women decided that from thereon they would always carry a child with them. The children would serve as a foil to gain sympathy or to simply create a distraction. Their modus operandi was to first kidnap little children or infants as they would be too young to understand what was happening and, hence, not able to raise an alarm, from crowded public places, use them as long as they were useful and then kill them or abandon them somewhere.

This idea would lead to the kidnapping of forty children and the horrific deaths of nine, over a period of six years.[2] The unlucky ones had their heads smashed in; some were throttled and their bodies disposed of in the most horrific ways. If you think you can stomach this, you may proceed to read about Anjana, Renuka and Seema.

A month after this idea was conceived, the trio arrived at the Kolhapur State Transport Bus Stand. They scanned the area for their first victim, and there he was: an infant in the arms of a beggarwoman. Renuka walked up to the woman and struck up a conversation. 'How old is your beautiful child?' she asked, cooing admiringly. The infant looked up at Renuka and gurgled.

'He likes you,' the mother replied. 'He is eighteen months old.'

'What is his name?' Renuka asked.

'Santosh,' the woman answered.

'It must be difficult for you to make ends meet?'

'What's new? Every day is a struggle for a poor woman like me,' the woman replied.

'I could give you a job. But it's in Karad.' Renuka's mind was ticking fast. On hearing this, the woman's eyes lit up. Renuka now moved in for the kill. 'But I guess it's far for you,' she said, pretending to walk away. The woman ran after Renuka. 'I can go to Karad with you. It's only an hour and a half from here,' she reasoned.

Renuka boarded the bus with the woman and her child. Anjana and Seema were sitting behind them, posing as travellers, and watching the charade play out. On reaching Karad, Renuka gave some money to the woman and said, 'You must be hungry. Here's some money. Why don't you get some misal pav for both of us? Let me hold Santosh for you.'

The unsuspecting woman walked towards the food stall. By the time she returned with the food, the trio had vanished with Santosh. The first part of their plan had been a success. Now it was time to put the second part to test.

Mahalakshmi temple in Kolhapur is one of the holiest temples in India and is listed as one of the 108 Shakti Peethas mentioned in the Puranas. The trio knew it would be crowded. But things did not go according to plan.

Seema was caught trying to steal a wallet. Amidst shouts of 'thief, thief!', the crowd began beating her up. Anjana tried to rescue her daughter but failed. To create a distraction, she flung the infant on to the hard stone floor. Santosh wailed; his head was bleeding.

'Look, what has happened. Because of your jostling and pushing, the child fell out of my hands!' Anjana screamed and wept.

The crowd grew instantly sympathetic towards them. They let the trio go, voicing their concern for the child.

The relieved women headed back to the bus stand. They bought some vada pav, while Santosh continued bawling. His tiny head was clotted with blood. The incessant crying got to the women. Seema warned her mother that the infant's crying could attract attention. Anjana calmly pressed the infant's mouth and smashed his tiny head repeatedly against the iron rod of the bus stand till Santosh became silent. Seema and Renuka were sitting ten feet away, eating their vada pav and silently watching the spectacle; they were not even in the least bit perturbed.

They carried Santosh's body and dumped it near an old, scrapped autorickshaw. The first murder had been committed; it wasn't going to be their last.

1991

Their next victim was nine-month-old Naresh. The same modus operandi was used. Renuka befriended the mother, then kidnapped the child. They used Naresh as a foil for the next few months. Renuka nursed the infant, breastfeeding him. In the process, she probably got attached to him. When Naresh fell ill and was useless to the trio, Renuka stood up to her mother when she decided to kill him. This saved Naresh's life. He wasn't killed but abandoned near the Ramkund temple in Nashik. Naresh was one of the lucky kids who got away. He grew up in an orphanage and was adopted by a childless couple. Today, he lives in Nashik and should be around twenty-seven years old. However, the others were not so fortunate.

The mother and the daughters lay low for a while. It wasn't conscience for sure. As soon as money ran out, the hunters went on the prowl again.

1993

The sisters and their mother decided to change their hunting ground from Pune and Nashik to Bombay. They abducted one-year-old Bunty from Kalyan station and headed to Bombay, looking for targets in the extremely busy Victoria Terminus.

Within a few days, the trio abducted three-year-old Swati and two-and-a-half-year-old Guddu. The three kids were trained to act as foils as the trio continued pickpocketing. Of the three children, fate was kind to one of them: Swati. Was it because she was a girl that the women took pity on her? Whatever the reason, Swati did not meet the gruesome end that was in store for Bunty and Guddu.

The trio shifted back to Pune when they had their temporary fill of Bombay and took up residence in Matwad chawl. Unfortunately, the crying children attracted attention from the neighbours. So the women decided to shift to Labade chawl. While shifting, Swati was left behind and later rescued by the police.

Once, during a theft, Seema threw Bunty on the road like her mother had done with Santosh earlier. Bunty got injured and his wound became septic. Soon, Guddu fell ill and the boys kept crying.

In May 1993, just a month after their abduction, the two children were bundled into a vehicle at night. Anjana had a devious plan. The vehicle was heading from Pune to Khopoli. As it entered Khandala Ghat, the car slowed down. It was 11.30 p.m. There weren't many cars on the highway. The chirping of crickets and the honking of trucks were the only sounds that broke the stillness of the night. The car stopped and Kiran deboarded to keep an eye out for any possible interruption. Bunty and Guddu were fast asleep. On cue, Renuka strangled Bunty and Seema throttled Guddu. Within minutes, the helpless kids had met their maker. Anjana took hold of Bunty's tiny body and flung it into the dark valley. Seema was about to dispose of the second body when Anjana intervened.

'Tu murkha aahes ka? [Are you stupid?]' she said, explaining that disposing both the bodies at the same place would make it easier for people to find them. So they drove on into the night, with Guddu's body hidden under a blanket in the back seat. When their vehicle reached Shil Phata, 5 km from Mumbra in Thane, Anjana stopped the vehicle and left Guddu's body beside the road.

What was astounding was that after the police discovered the bodies, no one joined the dots. Maybe the parents tried to lodge a missing-person report but were turned away as they were poor and uneducated.

Every child killed meant the beginning of a search for another victim. This time it was Anjali.

It was October and there was a nip in the air. Sujata Diwan walked towards Kalika Mandir in Nashik. She wanted to perform a small puja. Behind her, her husband was carrying their two-year-old daughter, Anjali, in his arms. Little did they know that three pairs of eyes had seen them entering the temple premises.

Anjana nudged Seema and pointed towards the family.

'Keep an eye on them. I think we have to move fast,' she said.

It was a moment of carelessness on the father's part that led to Anjali's abduction. He put her down on the floor and went to hand over the items needed for the puja to his wife.

'You don't go anywhere, okay? You stay right here. Baba will be back in just a minute,' he told his daughter.

'Where are you going?' Anjali asked with a lisp.

'To help your aai,' he answered, tousling Anjali's hair and smiling. That was the last time he saw his daughter. As he walked away, the vultures moved in and swooped down on their prey. When the parents returned, they could not find Anjali. They searched for her everywhere before lodging a complaint with the police.

Like the other children, Anjali was given a new name, Pinky. And like the other children, when she cried and outlived her utility, she too was disposed of. It happened one day when Anjana found the girl's crying unbearable. She kicked her down the stairs. Injured, Pinky began crying even louder.

'Shut up!' Anjana screamed. 'I can't take this any more.'

She clamped down her hand over Pinky's mouth and nose. As Pinky thrashed her arms and legs, Renuka rushed to hold them down. Soon, the crying stopped.

'Wait till it gets dark, we can't get rid of the body now,' Renuka instructed her mother.

They stuffed the body into a bag and sat down for dinner. They ate their food like they did every night, except that five feet away lay the cold body of a two-year-old. At about 1.30 a.m., they headed along Saswad Road up to a canal. Pinky's body was ditched in some shrubs in the area.

Raja lived only for seven months before his life was snuffed out as well and Shraddha for a year and nine months.

Till 1995, Anjana's motive for killing the children was money. But now she wanted revenge. It was time to get personal.

Anjana had never really forgiven Mohan Gavit for deserting her and her daughters. She had bottled up her rage and was now ready to pour it out. Her plan was to kidnap Mohan and Pratibha's youngest daughter, Kranti.

Seema turned up to meet her father and told him that Anjana wanted to meet Kranti. Mohan refused, saying Kranti had her school exams.

'Isn't Kranti my sister? Isn't she a daughter to my mother?' Seema wailed, emotionally blackmailing her father.

Mohan let his guard down. If he had remembered why he had left Anjana in the first place, then perhaps Kranti's life would have been saved. He agreed to let Kranti go with Seema. At no time did Mohan feel that his nine-year-old daughter could be in any sort of danger. After all, how could an elder sister hurt her younger sibling?

When Seema did not bring Kranti back the next day, Pratibha let her husband have it.

'You *chutiya*! How dare you send my daughter to the house of those thieves? What were you even thinking? Were you drunk?' she cried. They lodged a police complaint. But the sisters and their mother had vanished along with Kranti.

It's a mystery why the trio waited for more than three months to kill Kranti. Had they got attached to her? Whatever the emotional bond was between Seema and Kranti, it was taken care of before it became too strong.

On 5 December 1995, Anjana said it was time.

'Do you want to visit the fair at Narsoba Wadi?' she asked Kranti.

'A fair with a Ferris wheel?' Kranti asked excitedly.

Seema patted Kranti on her head and said, 'And a merry-go-round and pav bhaji too.'

Kranti hugged Seema's legs, smiling from ear to ear.

Anjana, Seema, Renuka, Kiran and Kranti took a taxi from Kolhapur and headed towards Narsoba Wadi.

Kranti stuck her head out of the window, deeply inhaling the cool wind as it whipped her hair back from her face. She ducked back in and touched her nose. 'My nose has gone numb because of the cold breeze, I can't feel it,' she said, breaking into a peal of laughter. Seema was about to pinch her cheek affectionately when she noticed Anjana's stern expression.

The taxi was nearing Narsoba Wadi, speeding through sugar cane fields, when Anjana suddenly asked the driver to stop the taxi.

'*Kaye zhala?* [What happened]' the taxi driver asked.

'We want to eat sugar cane,' Anjana replied, signalling to Seema.

Renuka, Seema, Kiran and Kranti entered the field. Kranti was dwarfed by the enormous height of the sugar cane stalks. Anjana sat outside the taxi, saying she needed some fresh air. The taxi driver saw it as an opportunity to snooze and promptly fell asleep.

In the sugar cane field, the group walked along. A cool breeze was blowing, the leaves rubbed against each other, whispering and warning Kranti to run for her life.

'Why can't we just pick these ones?' Kranti asked, pointing to the nearest stalks. 'Why do we need to go deeper into the field?'

'Because the sweetest ones grow deep inside the field,' Renuka answered.

Kranti seemed to believe her story. They had been walking for ten minutes when Renuka asked Kranti to lie down in the field, amidst the tall canes.

'But I am not sleepy! And, Didi, this is an odd place to lie down, isn't it?' Kranti asked quizzically, looking at Seema.

The breeze grew stronger and the whisper from the leaves frantic. Nature was urgently telling Kranti to bolt, to run as fast as her tiny legs could carry her and disappear into the maze of the crop. It was as if the stalks were assuring her that they would hide her in their folds. Before Kranti could register what was happening, Renuka pushed her down on the ground. She lunged at her throat, squeezing it with her right hand as hard as she could. Her other hand covered Kranti's mouth, stifling her screams. Kranti's eyes widened as she fought for breath, her limbs spasmed as she tried to fight off Renuka.

'Grab her hands and feet!' Renuka hissed. Seema held Kranti's hands and feet till she stopped fighting. The wind died down.

Renuka pushed the body deeper into the soft ground and the trio walked back to the taxi.

It was only in the evening that the taxi driver noticed the missing girl.

'*Ti chhoti mulgi kuthe aahe?* [Where is the small girl?]'

'She met her mother at the fair and left with her,' Anjana replied.

Anjana had had her revenge at last. She smiled, knowing that she had destroyed the joy of Mohan's life. Now she could get back to business. She was at peace.

On the banks of the Godavari in Nashik is the Ganga ghat vegetable market. It is noisy, huge and crowded. And, therefore, the ideal hunting ground for the trio. Chhaya was holding the hand of her granddaughter, Bhavna. She reminded her, 'Don't lose your grip.'

One may question whether fate has a role to play in such incidents. Why were these kids destined to fall victim to these serial killers? Is it because someone had to? Or were these children paying for the misdeeds of a previous lifetime?

In the pushing and shoving of the people thronging the market, Bhavna got separated from her grandmother and Renuka picked her up. She was renamed Gauri. She served as a foil for four months. She would often fall ill and was cranky. In May 1996, Kiran, Anjana and Seema checked into Pallavi Lodge in Kolhapur. Dayanand, the manager, checked in one man, two women (Seema and Anjana) and five small children (one of whom was Gauri). Dayanand found this motley group a little strange. In an interview, he recalls going to the room when the occupants had rung the bell. Inside, he had found an elderly woman sitting with a small girl who was crying. Dayanand loved children. He took the little girl to the balcony and gave her two biscuits, quieting her temporarily. But she started crying again at around 8 p.m., sounding the death knell.

'Let's kill her. End this misery,' Seema said. On cue, Anjana throttled the child. No second thoughts; everything got over in a few seconds. It seemed Seema had taken over the mantle of the killer from her mother. 'Where will we dispose of the body?' Anjana asked.

'There is a cinema hall nearby. I think we should watch a movie and dispose of the body inside the cinema hall,' Seema said.

Anjana looked at her proudly.

Pallavi Lodge was near Usha Theatre, where they often ran Bollywood blockbusters.

Dayanand looked up to see the two women and the man walking out of the hotel at around 10 p.m.

'Where are you off to?' he asked, noticing the large Rexine bag Seema was carrying.

'To see a film at Usha Theatre,' Seema replied nonchalantly.

'So late at night? And what's in the bag?' asked Dayanand, probing.

'Clothes for laundry,' Seema replied.

'But the picture would—' Before Dayanand could complete his sentence, Renuka (who had checked in later), Kiran and Seema walked out of the hotel. Anjana had stayed behind in the room. Dayanand saw Seema shifting the bag from her right hand to the left. It looked heavy.

By the time they reached Usha Theatre, the movie had already begun.

'How can I let you in now? The movie started a while ago. We have stopped selling tickets for the show,' Appasaheb Avati, the watchman, said. He refused to slide the collapsible gates open.

A ripple of panic swept through the three members. They had a corpse in the bag and needed to get rid of it quickly.

Kiran, the only man in the group, decided to be aggressive. 'So what if the movie has started? Take us to the booking clerk. We have to get tickets for the show,' he ordered.

After fifteen minutes of wrangling, they managed to get tickets for the show.

They took their seats in the dark theatre to watch the latest blockbuster. On the screen, the hero was singing and gyrating to a hit song. Their view was getting blocked by the people in the front rows who would every now and then stand up and start dancing. Someone threw a handful of coins at the screen as a salute to their idol. The three murderers watched the movie silently with the Rexine bag at their feet.

During the interval, Renuka and Kiran came out to have a cup of tea. Renuka went to the bathroom. She returned with a smile, relieved.

'The bathroom has no lights, it is completely dark. We can keep the bag there,' she whispered to Kiran. Fifteen minutes into the second half of the film, Seema and Renuka carried the bag and left it inside the lavatory.

Renuka did not realize that while walking out of the lavatory, her sari had got stuck to a nail in the door. She had pulled hard to free it, leaving behind a piece of fabric, which would play an important role in nailing her and her family.

The trio now decided to leave the theatre. Once again, they bumped into Appasaheb.

'You came late, quarrelled for tickets and are now leaving early. What is going on with you three?' he asked, scrutinizing them.

There was silence.

Kiran came to the rescue: 'My wife's stomach is paining. I have to take her to the doctor.' To make the story sound more convincing, he added, 'You people are selling stale samosas, that's how she has fallen ill. Would you like it if she vomited here for everyone to see? Open the gate now.'

Appasaheb did not want any mishap to bring disrepute to the theatre. He quickly slid open the collapsible gates and let them out.

Once again, the serial killers escaped. It was three days before the body was discovered. And another case was registered and shut. Dead infants were turning up every few months but no one seemed to see the connection.

A note of caution to parents: in crowded areas do not let your child out of your sight. Firmly hold their hands and be attentive. Do not go off somewhere and allow somebody to take care of your child even if they offer to help. A criminal looks just like any one of us. Nowadays, our heads are always buried in our phones and it becomes very easy for criminals to prey on our children and us.

I write this as Pankaj's parents were not attentive. If they had been, then Pankaj would have been alive today. He would have been twenty-five today. Unfortunately, fate had other plans for the three-year-old in 1996.

July 1996, Mumbai

Vitthal Mandir. The trio had returned to the city to steal and hunt. While Anjana waited nearby, Seema and Renuka went about stealing purses from the crowded temple complex. Then they spotted two women with a boy. It may have been desperation that led the duo to kidnap an older boy rather than their usual target, infants. Pankaj was around three years old. The two women with Pankaj seemed to be lost in conversation. Pankaj loitered near them. Sensing an opportunity, Seema swooped down on him like a hawk, scooped him up in her arms and ran. The child began to cry loudly. Seema covered his mouth with her palm as she ran. She reached Anjana, who immediately slapped Pankaj, while Seema punched him. The stunned child buckled, coughed and then cried himself to sleep.

He was old enough to speak and said his name was Pankaj, and it was his talking that got him into trouble.

Pankaj lived for a month and a half with the serial killers. He was used as a foil for committing thefts in and around Pune. Every time they went out, Seema warned Pankaj to remain silent. But Pankaj was a child who had just discovered that he could communicate and connect with people through speech. Though he remained quiet during the thefts in fear of being beaten up, he could not control himself when he was at home. He wandered off to the neighbour's house and began speaking to them.

'Anjana tai, this boy says he is from a rich family in Mumbai and that his father has a big car?' the neighbour asked Anjana.

There was stunned silence in the room.

'I thought you said he was from Lahvit and he is your cousin sister's son?' the interrogation continued.

The wheels in Anjana's brain spun into action.

'Arre, Kusum, you know how children are. Their imagination runs wild. My sister's husband keeps telling his son that one day they will all shift to Mumbai and buy a big car,' Anjana tried to sound as convincing as possible. She could cook up a story faster than she could cook pav bhaji.

Kusum laughed and so did Anjana. But the latter's laughter had an edge to it.

When Kusum left, the two sisters and their mother got into a huddle.

'That was really close!' Seema complained.

'This boy might spill the beans on us, and that will be the end!' Renuka said.

'Let's get rid of him . . . tomorrow!' Anjana passed the verdict in a sinister whisper.

If you are squeamish, then I advise you to skip the next paragraph. If you want your blood to boil at the heinousness of these monsters, then read on.

The next evening, Renuka and Seema hung Pankaj up by his legs to the ceiling. He swung like a pendulum, screaming in pain and begging the sisters not to hurt him. On cue, they pushed and swung him hard. His head smashed against the wall. He cried out in pain. But that did not stop them. They repeatedly smashed his tiny, frail head against the wall till he was lifeless (twenty-five times, to be precise, according to their confession).

Renuka took the bloodied clothes off Pankaj and put fresh clothes on the body. With Kiran's help, she packed the body inside a jute sack. Kiran tied the neck of the sack with a string and stuffed it in a suitcase.

At 11 in the night, when the streets were quiet, the husband and wife carried the suitcase in an autorickshaw.

They disposed it near the Maharshi Karve Shikshan Sanstha temple in Karve Nagar.

11 September 1996

Francis Aadghav of Kothrud police station was taking down a complaint about two neighbours quarrelling over garbage disposal when the telephone on his desk rang. He ignored it. He had got a migraine from dealing with the two warring gentlemen. The jangling of the telephone only added to his misery. He picked up the receiver when he could no longer tolerate it.

'Kothrud police station,' he boomed.

'*Sir, mee Karve Nagar madhun Shivanand boltoye* [Sir, this is Shivanand speaking from Karve Nagar].'

'*Kaay traas aahe?* [What is the issue?]' Aadghav enquired.

'Sir, there is a strange bundle near the temple,' Shivanand panted into the public telephone.

It had been just over three years since the twelve serial blasts had shaken Mumbai, killing 257 people. Aadghav did not want to take a chance. He instructed a junior to take over the neighbours' case as he rushed to the site. On the wireless, he ordered the bomb squad to reach the spot. Police head constable Zunzarde was also asked to report there.

Zunzarde was enthusiastic and young. Maybe that's why he ignored protocol or the possibility that it could be a bomb, or maybe he realized that a bomb did not have a human shape, and opened the sack to discover Pankaj's bruised body. He also found a ladies' handkerchief stuck to the sack!

The handkerchief belonged to Seema and, unknown to her, was now one of the prime evidence that would be produced in court when they would be arrested, along with the torn bit of sari found in the lavatory of Usha Theatre.

Police reports state that as many as forty-two wounds were found on the body of the child.

Little did Anjana, Seema, Renuka and Kiran know that they would soon be running out of luck. That is why they defied one of the main rules of crime: never revisit a crime scene. It was overconfidence or pure foolishness that made them return to Nashik. This was a year after they had kidnapped and killed Kranti.

October 1996

Anjana seemed to have devised a new plan.

'I want to kill both his daughters. I want to ruin his life forever like he ruined mine!' Anjana looked at Renuka and Seema as she spoke. Her voice was slightly slurred from the liquor she had been drinking.

'We have killed Kranti already, isn't that enough?' Seema argued.

'That bitch, Pratibha, will learn the lesson of her life and regret that she ever laid her eyes on my husband,' Anjana continued. 'We will kidnap Devli as well. She will meet her younger sister in heaven!'

The thirst for revenge had consumed Anjana so much that taking lives was now just an emotionless action for her.

On 10 October 1996, Seema and Renuka headed to Rani Laxmibai Primary School at Nashik, where Devli studied. There, they met Sumanbhai Navale, the peon.

'We are Devli's stepsisters. Please understand it is an emergency. Devli's sister, Kranti, is not well and we have to take her to see her,' Renuka pleaded.

It is providence that the peon refused to allow the two to take Devli. That is why she is still alive. Seema even offered him a thousand rupees, but the peon stuck to his guns. Seema and Renuka returned empty-handed.

Navale was suspicious about the way the two sisters had tried to get hold of Devli. He ran to meet Mangala Parnerkar, a teacher in the school, and told her in detail what had happened. The teacher narrated the incident to Pratibha, who realized what the devious plan was. She registered a complaint at Panchavati police station that very evening.

This incident should have alerted the killers. They should have moved their base like they had always done, not staying in one place for more than six months. But they didn't, and exactly ten days after this incident, their luck finally ran out.

On 20 October 1996, Pratibha spotted Seema and Renuka at a nearby vegetable market. Pratibha accosted them, screaming, 'Where is Kranti? What have you done to my daughter?'

Renuka replied calmly, '*Chhinal!* [Whore!] You have ruined my mother's life and so you will not get back your daughter.'

Pratibha was stunned. She immediately went to her husband and both of them registered an FIR under Section 363 (kidnapping) of the IPC against Renuka and Anjana.

Even after this incident, the killers did not run away. It seemed that the gods, tired of watching them massacre little children, had now chained their feet to the ground. That very evening, at 5.40 p.m., Renuka, Seema and Kiran were arrested.

When Shashikant Bodhe of CID (crime) took over the case, he thought it was simply a case of kidnapping. But the police did not have to work too hard in extracting information. Seema was already in a state of panic and began to sing within two days of her arrest. Bodhe was flabbergasted by what now lay in front of him. During the interrogation, Seema broke down and confessed to kidnapping Kranti. She said it was done on the insistence of their mother, Anjana.

This confession led the police to Shiv-Shashi Apartments, where they found Anjana, who till then had been under the radar.

The police searched the flat and found a big bag with wheels, at the bottom of which was dried blood. This was the same bag they had used to carry Pankaj's body. The police also found the bloodied clothes belonging to Pankaj. Seema showed the police the exact portion of the wall against which Pankaj was smashed to death. Chemical analysis of the dried blood from the bag and the plaster on the wall tallied with Pankaj's blood group. Case no. 1 was in the bag!

What was suddenly baffling to Bodhe was the presence of discarded toddler clothes lying around in the apartment. To top it off, Bodhe discovered photographs of birthday celebrations of Renuka's children. In them, he saw kids and toddlers who were not locals. So who were these children?

One police investigator, Mandaleshwar Madhavrao Kale, remembers all three women as being tough witnesses, particularly Anjana.

'She would just sit there and look. Never once did that woman crack,' he said.[3]

Bodhe began investigating and discovered the old reports of dead infants and children, now piecing the puzzle together. Anjana, Renuka, Seema and Kiran denied having a role in the deaths of the other children. Seema and Renuka had seen what their mother had gone through when she was betrayed by her husband. And now Renuka would experience it herself. Her husband turned approver and spilt the beans to the police on every murder they had committed.

Eventually, the four of them were charged with the kidnapping of fourteen children and the murder of nine. Charges against Kiran were dropped as he had turned approver.

At each hearing, the gruesome nature of their crimes came to the fore. The nation was seething.

During their hearing, the two sisters blamed their mother for teaching them how to kill and for pushing them into the trade of pickpocketing. But this was probably an effort on their part to escape the inevitable judgment and place the blame squarely on Anjana. This was only partly true, as, notwithstanding Anjana's role in the murders, the sisters themselves had started enjoying killing little children.

While the trial was on, Anjana died in prison in 1998.

On 29 June 2001, a sessions court convicted the sisters of kidnapping thirteen children and killing six: Santosh, Anjali, Raja, Shraddha, Gauri and Pankaj. On 9 September 2004, the Bombay High Court upheld the conviction but acquitted them of the kidnapping and murder of Raja.[4] On 31 August 2006, the Supreme Court confirmed their death sentence. Asim Sarode, a human rights lawyer and activist, met Renuka in prison. He described her as being enveloped in an 'eerie calmness'[5] as she answered his questions about the killings, all the while petting a stray cat.

'While I'm professionally and personally against capital punishment, this is one of the rare cases where the perpetrators deserve the death sentence,'[6] Sarode told *The Hindu*.

Ujjwal Nikam, the special public prosecutor who sought death penalty for the duo, recalled a chilling fact. 'We limited the period of killing to six years. However, this had been going on for longer than that. The women could not remember how many children they had killed. It is estimated that the kidnappings might have been more than forty in number, but we had no evidence to back that claim,'[7] he said.

The final nail in the coffin came on 14 August 2004 when former president Pranab Mukherjee rejected the mercy petition filed by the sisters. India had not seen a woman being hanged since 1955, when Rattan Bai Jain was sent to the gallows for killing three children, making her the first woman to be hanged in independent India.

Sudeep Jaiswal, the sisters' lawyer, told news.com.au that the two women—known as the Gavit sisters—hoped to have their death penalty commuted to life in prison. Speaking from his chambers in Nagpur, Jaiswal described plans to execute the sisters as 'a barbaric act'.[8]

The sisters are currently on death row, lodged in Yerawada Central Jail.

The Chaturshringi temple is only 10 km from Yerawada prison and it was here that the story of Renuka Shinde, Anjanabai and Seema Mohan Gavit started in 1990.

Life and death have finally come full circle for the sisters.

ACKNOWLEDGEMENTS

My grandmother was fourteen when she got married in 1935. So, she could not complete her education. Over the years, however, she taught herself to read and write at a time when women were just supposed to play the roles of a dutiful wife and caring mother. She, thereby, ensured that all her children and grandchildren fell in love with reading and stories. She didn't want them to feel as helpless as she had once felt. I owe this to my Thammu, the late Kamala Devi Bhattacharyya, who taught me the beauty of words and stories. And I owe this to my grandfather, Sachindra Kumar Bhattacharyya, my first best friend in the whole wide world.

This book would not have been possible for the patience and understanding of the two people who allowed me to slink off into dark corners and write till 4 a.m. Thank you, Erum, my wife, and Kabir, my beautiful son, who gave up his room for me to live in for a year.

I'd like to thank my father, mother and brother for being there and supporting this journey.

I grew up in the '80s in a boarding school in Kalimpong called Dr Graham's Homes and was blessed to have had some incredible teachers and mentors who taught me to imagine and dream the extraordinary. This is for you: K.T. Bhutia, Carol Freese, Louis Xavier, Cheryl Xavier, Terence Monteiro, Shyamal Mukherjee, Noreen Mukherjee and Bernard. T. Brooks. And to my two professors of English at St Xavier's College, Kolkata, Rohinton Kapadia and Bertram Da Silva, who made us fall in love with Rosalind, Riders and rock and roll.

This labour of love would not have materialized if a chance meeting hadn't taken place. Thank you, Suhail Mathur and his fabulous literary agency, Book Bakers.

Finally, a huge thanks to my editors, Gurveen Chadha and Indrani Dasgupta, at Penguin Random House India for painstakingly editing the dozen tales of blood, lust, insanity and fears, and the legal team for going through the book with a fine-tooth comb.

NOTES

GOWRI SHANKAR: A.K.A. AUTO SHANKAR

1. Nirupama Subramanian, 'Ex-convict Auto Shankar's Autobiography Takes Madras by Storm', *India Today*, 30 November 1994, https://www.indiatoday.in/magazine/crime/story/19941130-ex-convict-auto-shankars-autobiography-takes-madras-by-storm-810324-1994-11-30.
2. S. Manikandan, '"Auto" Shankar: A Ride of Terror in the Madras of the 80s', *The Hindu*, 23 August 2013, http://www.thehindu.com/news/cities/chennai/auto-shankar-a-ride-of-terror-in-the-madras-of-the-80s/article5049710.ece.
3. Nirupama Subramanian, 'Ex-convict Auto Shankar's Autobiography Takes Madras by Storm', *India Today*, 30 November 1994, https://www.indiatoday.in/magazine/crime/story/19941130-ex-convict-auto-shankars-autobiography-takes-madras-by-storm-810324-1994-11-30.
4. Supreme Court of India Judgment, Shankar @ Gauri Shankar and Ors. vs State of Tamil Nadu, 4 April 1994, Indian Kanoon, https://indiankanoon.org/doc/63794871/.
5. Ibid.
6. S. Manikandan, '"Auto" Shankar: A Ride of Terror in the Madras of the 80s', *The Hindu*, 23 August 2013, http://www.thehindu.com/news/cities/chennai/auto-shankar-a-ride-of-terror-in-the-madras-of-the-80s/article5049710.ece.
7. Ibid.
8. Nirupama Subramanian, 'Ex-convict Auto Shankar's Autobiography Takes Madras by Storm', *India Today*, 30 November 1994, https://www.indiatoday.in/magazine/crime/story/19941130-ex-convict-auto-shankars-autobiography-takes-madras-by-storm-810324-1994-11-30.

9. Anand Vishwanathan, 'Legendary Tamil Criminal Auto Shankar Pulls off Daring Escape from Madras Central Jail', *India Today*, 15 September 1990, https://www.indiatoday.in/magazine/indiascope/story/19900915-legendary-tamil-criminal-auto-shankar-pulls-off-daring-escape-from-madras-central-jail-813002-1990-09-15.

10. Nirupama Subramanian, 'Ex-convict Auto Shankar's Autobiography Takes Madras by Storm', *India Today*, 30 November 1994, https://www.indiatoday.in/magazine/crime/story/19941130-ex-convict-auto-shankars-autobiography-takes-madras-by-storm-810324-1994-11-30.

11. Ibid.

BEER MAN: BEERLY A SERIAL KILLER

1. Gajanan Khergamker, 'The Stranger Murders', Fountain Ink, 4 December 2012, https://fountainink.in/reportage/the-stranger-murders.

2. 'India World Leader in Greasing Palms', *Times of India*, 5 October 2006, https://timesofindia.indiatimes.com/world/rest-of-world/India-world-leader-in-greasing-palms/articleshow/2091020.cms?

3. Ambarish Mishra, 'Shiv Sena to Break away from BJP', *Times of India*, 5 October 2006, https://timesofindia.indiatimes.com/india/Shiv-Sena-to-break-away-from-BJP/articleshow/2091057.cms?

4. 'India-Born Beauty Was on Hijacked Plane', *Times of India*, 5 October 2006, https://timesofindia.indiatimes.com/india/India-born-beauty-was-on-hijacked-plane/articleshow/2091099.cms?

5. Bharati Dubey, 'Madhuri to Make a Comeback in Bollywood', *Times of India*, 5 October 2006, https://timesofindia.indiatimes.com/entertainment/hindi/bollywood/news/Madhuri-to-make-a-comeback-in-Bollywood/articleshow/2093115.cms?

6. Rashmi Rajput, 'Welcome to the Clan . . .', *Mumbai Mirror*, 13 January 2007, https://mumbaimirror.indiatimes.com/mumbai/cover-story/welcome-to-the-clan-/articleshow/15672564.cms.

7. Ibid.

8. Ibid.
9. Ibid.
10. 'Police Map Beer Man's Next Strike', *Mumbai Mirror*, 14 January 2007, https://mumbaimirror.indiatimes.com/mumbai/cover-story/police-map-beer-mans-next-strike/articleshow/15672813.cms.
11. Ibid.
12. Gajanan Khergamker, 'The Stranger Murders', Fountain Ink, 4 December 2012, https://fountainink.in/reportage/the-stranger-murders.
13. Lhendup G. Bhutia, 'The Serial Killer Who Wasn't', *Open*, 28 July 2012, http://www.openthemagazine.com/article/india/the-serial-killer-who-wasn-t.
14. Gajanan Khergamker, 'The Stranger Murders', Fountain Ink, 4 December 2012, https://fountainink.in/reportage/the-stranger-murders.
15. Ibid.
16. Marc Lallanilla, 'What Is the Single-Bullet Theory?' Live Science, 20 November 2013, https://www.livescience.com/41369-single-bullet-theory-jfk-assassination.html.
17. 'Beer Killer Confesses to 15 Murders', *Times of India*, 16 February 2007, https://timesofindia.indiatimes.com/india/Beer-killer-confesses-to-15-murders/articleshow/1624942.cms.
18. Ibid.
19. Lhendup G. Bhutia, 'The Serial Killer Who Wasn't', *Open*, 28 July 2012, http://www.openthemagazine.com/article/india/the-serial-killer-who-wasn-t.
20. Ibid.
21. Gajanan Khergamker, 'The Stranger Murders', Fountain Ink, 4 December 2012, https://fountainink.in/reportage/the-stranger-murders.
22. Lhendup G. Bhutia, 'The Serial Killer Who Wasn't', *Open*, 28 July 2012, http://www.openthemagazine.com/article/india/the-serial-killer-who-wasn-t.
23. Ibid.
24. Gajanan Khergamker, 'The Stranger Murders', Fountain Ink, 4 December 2012, https://fountainink.in/reportage/the-stranger-murders.

25. Ibid.

26. Lhendup G. Bhutia, 'The Serial Killer Who Wasn't', *Open*, 28 July 2012, http://www.openthemagazine.com/article/india/the-serial-killer-who-wasn-t.

K.D. KEMPAMMA: CYANIDE MALLIKA

1. Rudyard Kipling, *Rudyard Kipling's Verse: Inclusive Edition 1885–1918* (London: Hodder & Stoughton, 1919).

2. The Siddaganga Mutt was established in the fourteenth century. It started off as 101 caves for disciples and students to study in. As per legend, to quench the thirst of one of his disciples, the head of the monastery, Sree Gosala Siddheshwara, hit a rock and miraculously, a stream of water gushed out of it. The holy water was called Siddaganga or the holy Ganga. And that is how the monastery got its name.

3. Anil Budur Lulla, 'Lady Killer with Cyanide Prasad Prayer Bait for Victims,' *Telegraph*, 1 January 2008, https://www.telegraphindia.com/india/lady-killer-with-cyanide-prasad-prayer-bait-for-victims/cid/627689.

4. D.V. Kumar Shylendra, B.V. Pinto, the Registrar General vs Mallika @ Lakshmi @ Shivamogga, 2 August 2012, Indian Kanoon, https://indiankanoon.org/doc/151419510/.

5. Choultry is a resting place, an inn for travellers, pilgrims or visitors to a site, typically linked to Buddhist, Jain and Hindu temples. It is also known as *chottry, choultree, choltry, chowry, chawadi*. This term is more common in south India, central India and west India. In north India, similar facilities are called dharmashalas.

6. Ashwaq Masoodi, 'Serial Killings: India's Untold Story,' *Mint*, 14 October 2016, https://www.livemint.com/Politics/tA3y9h6kitDz4K1eVVU7FN/Serial-killings-Indias-untold-story.html.

7. Ibid.

8. 'First Woman Serial Killer Nabbed,' *Times of India*, 1 January 2008, https://timesofindia.indiatimes.com/city/bengaluru/First-woman-serial-killer-nabbed/articleshow/2665976.cms.

9. Whoever commits murder shall be punished with death, or imprisonment for life, and shall also be liable to fine.

10. 'Cyanide Mallika Gets Death,' *Times of India*, 31 March 2012, https://timesofindia.indiatimes.com/city/bengaluru/Cyanide-Mallika-gets-death/articleshow/12476553.cms.

11. Ibid.

12. 'Serial killer Mallika's Death Sentence Reduced to Life', 2 August 2012, NDTV, https://www.ndtv.com/south/serial-killer-mallikas-death-sentence-reduced-to-life-495237.

13. 'With Sasikala in Bengaluru Jail, Serial Killer Cyanide Mallika Shifted Out', *Deccan Chronicle*, 22 February 2017, https://www.deccanchronicle.com/nation/current-affairs/220217/with-sasikala-locked-up-in-bluru-jail-jaya-fan-cyanide-mallika-shifted-out.html.

THUG BEHRAM: THE WORLD'S MOST DANGEROUS SERIAL KILLER

1. W.H. Sleeman, *The Thugs or Phansigars of India: Comprising a History of the Rise and Progress of That Extraordinary Fraternity of Assassins* (Carey and Hart, 1839).

2. Kos is a subcontinental Arthashastra standard unit of distance, about 3.07 km or 1.91 miles.

3. W.H. Sleeman, *Rambles and Recollections of an Indian Official* (Humphrey Milford Oxford University Press, 1915), https://www.gutenberg.org/files/15483/15483-h/15483-h.htm#App.

4. Ibid.

5. W.H. Sleeman, *The Thugs or Phansigars of India: Comprising a History of the Rise and Progress of That Extraordinary Fraternity of Assassins* (Carey and Hart, 1839).

6. This strange cult finds its origins in a very interesting story.

         Many millenniums ago, a demon attacked the earth and devoured mankind as soon as it was created. The world was thus left unpeopled till the goddess of the thugs—Devi or Kali—came to the rescue. She hunted down the demon and hacked him. But every drop of that demon's blood birthed a new demon. The goddess continued to hack down each new demon, but others sprung up rapidly. Devi became tired and disheartened. She was at her wits' end. That is when she decided to change her tactics.

She formed two men from her perspiration. To each one, she gave a handkerchief and commanded them to kill the demons by strangling them with the handkerchiefs so that no more blood was shed. The two men followed the instructions and soon all the demons were killed. Having strangled all the demons, the two men offered to return the handkerchiefs. However, the goddess said that they should keep them, not as a trophy for their heroic deed but as a tool of a new lucrative trade, which they and their future generations should use and thrive. They were, in fact, commanded to strangle men as they had strangled the demons. (W.H. Sleeman, *Rambles and Recollections of an Indian Official* [Humphrey Milford Oxford University Press, 1915], https://www.gutenberg.org/files/15483/15483-h/15483-h. htm#App.)

7.   W.H. Sleeman, *The Thugs or Phansigars of India: Comprising a History of the Rise and Progress of That Extraordinary Fraternity of Assassins* (Carey and Hart, 1839).

8.   Ibid.

9.   The tradition of burying the bodies of the victims was not prevalent during the early days of the thuggees. The story goes that as per the arrangement, the goddess would relieve them of the trouble of burying the bodies by devouring them herself. One day, after killing a traveller, the body was as usual left unburied. One of the rookie thugs looked back and saw the goddess feasting upon the corpse, half of the body hanging out of her mouth. From then onwards, the goddess declared that she would no longer devour the corpses. She presented the thuggees with one of her teeth for a pickaxe, a rib for a knife and the hem of her lower garment for a noose; and ordered them to cut and bury the bodies of those they killed in the future. (W.H. Sleeman, *The Thugs or Phansigars of India: Comprising a History of the Rise and Progress of*

That Extraordinary Fraternity of Assassins [Carey and Hart, 1839].)

10. Ibid.

11. Thuggee and Dacoity Suppression acts 1836–48, Wikipedia, https://en.wikipedia.org/wiki/Thuggee_and_Dacoity_ Suppression_Acts,_1836%E2%80%9348.

12. W.H. Sleeman, *The Thugs or Phansigars of India: Comprising a History of the Rise and Progress of That Extraordinary Fraternity of Assassins* (Carey and Hart, 1839).

13. Ibid.

14. Thug Behram was Persian by descent. It is said that his lineage dated back to a soldier from the invading army of Nadir Shah. Behram wore his Persian lineage proudly on his sleeve. It seemed he was always born to be a rebel. He was a Shia Muslim married to a Sunni woman. When he could fight against the strict diktats of his own community, he surely wasn't going to take shit from a bunch of pale-skinned idiots.

15. Rishabh Banerji, 'The World's Most Feared Serial Killer Was an Indian and He Killed over 900 People in Cold Blood,' India Times, 3 March 2016, https://www.indiatimes.com/culture/ who-we-are/the-world-s-most-feared-serial-killer-was-an-indian-and-he-killed-over-900-people-in-cold-blood-251454. html.

16. 'Thug Indian Bandit,' Britannica, 20 July 1998, https://www. britannica.com/topic/thug.

17. W.H. Sleeman, *The Thugs or Phansigars of India: Comprising a History of the Rise and Progress of That Extraordinary Fraternity of Assassins* (Carey and Hart, 1839).

18. Ibid.

STONEMAN: INDIA'S MOST ELUSIVE SERIAL KILLER

1. Mark Fineman, 'A Calcutta Murderer Slinks from Depths of Depravity,' *Los Angeles Times*, 9 October 1989, http:// articles.latimes.com/1989-10-09/news/vw-166_1_murder-weapon.

2. *The Stoneman Murders*, directed by Manish Gupta (Mumbai: Kaleidoscope Entertainment Pvt. Ltd, 2009).

3. Mark Fineman, 'A Calcutta Murderer Slinks from Depths of Depravity,' *Los Angeles Times*, 9 October 1989, http://articles.latimes.com/1989-10-09/news/vw-166_1_murder-weapon.

4. Ibid.

5. Ibid.

6. Ibid.

7. Rudyard Kipling, 'The City of Dreadful Night' (Alex Grosset & Co., 1899).

8. 'Gadget Helps Orissa Police Nab Stoneman', *Telegraph*, 4 January 2000, https://www.telegraphindia.com/india/gadget-helps-orissa-police-nab-stoneman/cid/906489.

9. 'Guwahati Stoneman Arrested,' Zee News, 19 March 2009, http://zeenews.india.com/home/guwahati-stoneman-arrested_516278.html.

10. 'Rajkot Stone Killer Held for 3 Murders, Labourer for Fourth,' *Indian Express*, 2 July 2016, https://indianexpress.com/article/india/india-news-india/rajkot-stone-killer-held-for-3-murders-labourer-for-fourth-2888585/.

KOLI AND PANDHER: THE NITHARI-*KAAND* KILLERS

1. The confessional statement of Surendra Singh Koli as quoted by the Nithari High Court Judgement by the High Court of Judicature at Allahabad, and as published by the website indialawyer.wordpress.com, https://indialawyers.wordpress.com/nithari-high-court-judgement-acquits-pandher/.

2. This is according to the deposition statement given by prosecution witness no. 23, Manoj Kumar, as mentioned in the Nithari High Court Judgement by the High Court Judicature at Allahabad, on 11 September 2009.

3. The Nithari High Court Judgement by the High Court of Judicature at Allahabad, and as published by the website indialawyer.wordpress.com, https://indialawyers.wordpress.com/nithari-high-court-judgement-acquits-pandher/.

4. *The Karma Killings*, directed by Ram Devineni (New York: Rattapallax Production, 2016), retrieved from https://www.netflix.com/in/title/80158549 (video file).

5. Ibid.

6. Ibid.

7. The Nithari High Court Judgement by the High Court of Judicature at Allahabad, and as published by the website indialawyer.wordpress.com, https://indialawyers.wordpress.com/nithari-high-court-judgement-acquits-pandher/.

8. Arpit Parashar, 'Nailing the Lies of Nithari', Fountain Ink, 4 March 2013, https://fountainink.in/reportage/nailing-the-lies-of-nithari

9. Ibid.

10. Pushkar Raj, 'The Story of the Poor Who Lost Their Children', Internet Archive, February 2007, https://web.archive.org/web/20170803050855/http://www.pucl.org/Topics/Child/2007/nithari.html.

11. Ibid.

12. Ibid.

13. 'Cops Harassed Me: Noida Victim's Father', Rediff, 3 January 2007, https://www.rediff.com/news/2007/jan/03noida5.htm.

14. Ibid.

15. 'Cell Phone Led to Koli's Confession', News18, 23 March 2007, https://www.news18.com/news/india/cell-phone-led-to-kolis-confession-261486.html.

16. 'First Charge Sheet Filed in Nithari Case', *The Hindu*, 23 March 2007, https://www.thehindu.com/todays-paper/First-charge-sheet-filed-in-Nithari-case/article14736898.ece.

17. *The Karma Killings*, directed by Ram Devineni (New York: Rattapallax Production, 2016), retrieved from https://www.netflix.com/in/title/80158549 (video file).

18. The Nithari High Court Judgement by the High Court of Judicature at Allahabad, and as published by the website indialawyer.wordpress.com, https://indialawyers.wordpress.com/nithari-high-court-judgement-acquits-pandher/.

19. Ibid.

20. Arpit Parashar, 'Nailing the Lies of Nithari', Fountain Ink, 4 March 2013, https://fountainfink.in/reportage/nailing-the-lies-of-nithari.

21. Ibid.

22. *The Karma Killings*, directed by Ram Devineni (New York: Rattapallax Production, 2016), retrieved from https://www.netflix.com/in/title/80158549 (video file).

23. Ibid.

24. Ibid.

25. 'Pandher Plays the Victim Card Horror House Still Gives Locals around the Creeps', *Times of India*, 25 July 2017, https://www.pressreader.com/india/the-times-of-india-new-delhi-edition/20170725/281788514124633.

26. The Nithari High Court Judgement by the High Court of Judicature at Allahabad, and as published by the website indialawyer.wordpress.com, https://indialawyers.wordpress.com/nithari-high-court-judgement-acquits-pandher/.

27. Ibid.

28. Arpit Parashar, 'Nailing the Lies of Nithari', Fountain Ink, 4 March 2013, https://fountainfink.in/reportage/nailing-the-lies-of-nithari.

29. The Nithari High Court Judgement by the High Court of Judicature at Allahabad, and as published by the website indialawyer.wordpress.com, https://indialawyers.wordpress.com/nithari-high-court-judgement-acquits-pandher/.

30. Ibid.

31. 'UP Suspends 2 SPs, Fires 6 Cops in Noida Case', Rediff, 3 January 2007, https://www.rediff.com/news/2007/jan/03noida9.htm

32. Usha Ramanathan, 'Organ Trade, Missing Piece in Nithari Puzzle?' *The Hindu*, 29 October 2014, https://www.thehindu.com/opinion/op-ed/comment-organ-trade-missing-piece-in-nithari-puzzle/article6542026.ece.

33. Ibid.

34. Ibid.

35. Ibid.

36. Ibid.
37. Arpit Parashar, 'Nailing the Lies of Nithari', Fountain Ink, 4 March 2013, https://fountainfink.in/reportage/nailing-the-lies-of-nithari.
38. Ibid.
39. The Nithari High Court Judgement by the High Court of Judicature at Allahabad, and as published by the website indialawyer.wordpress.com, https://indialawyers.wordpress.com/nithari-high-court-judgement-acquits-pandher/.
40. Gyan Varma, 'Mob Assaults Pandher, Koli outside Court', DNA, 25 January 2007, http://www.dnaindia.com/india/report-mob-assaults-pandher-koli-outside-court-1076296.
41. Ibid.
42. The Nithari High Court Judgement by the High Court of Judicature at Allahabad, and as published by the website indialawyer.wordpress.com, https://indialawyers.wordpress.com/nithari-high-court-judgement-acquits-pandher/.
43. Ibid.
44. Ibid.
45. Ibid.
46. Ibid.
47. Ibid.
48. The Nithari High Court Judgement by the High Court of Judicature at Allahabad, and as published by the website indialawyer.wordpress.com, https://indialawyers.wordpress.com/nithari-high-court-judgement-acquits-pandher/.
49. Ibid.
50. Shivam Vij, 'Nine Reasons Not to Hang Alleged Nithari Serial Killer Surendra Koli', Scroll, 17 September 2014, https://scroll.in/article/679297/nine-reasons-not-to-hang-alleged-nithari-serial-killer-surendra-koli.
51. Ibid.
52. Sowmya Rajaram, 'The Man Who Wasn't Around', Mumbai Mirror, 15 January 2017, https://mumbaimirror.indiatimes.com/others/sunday-read/the-man-who-wasnt-around/articleshow/56548400.cms.

53. *The Karma Killings*, directed by Ram Devineni (New York: Rattapallax Production, 2016), retrieved from https://www. netflix.com/in/title/80158549 (video file).

54. Ibid.

55. Ibid.

56. Sowmya Rajaram, 'The Man Who Wasn't Around', *Mumbai Mirror*, 15 January 2017, https://mumbaimirror.indiatimes. com/others/sunday-read/the-man-who-wasnt-around/ articleshow/56548400.cms.

57. Ibid.

58. Report of the Committee Investigating into Allegations of Large-Scale Sexual Abuse, Rape and Murder of Children in Nithari Village of Noida (UP), *The Hindu*, 17 January 2007, https:// www.thehindu.com/migration_catalog/article11115216.ece/ BINARY/nitharireport.

59. Ibid.

60. *The Karma Killings*, directed by Ram Devineni (Ratapallax Production, 2016), retrieved from https://www.netflix.com/ in/title/80158549 (video file).

61. A black warrant is the final piece of paper that sanctions a government to take away a man's life.

62. 'Nithari Serial Killings: Pandher, Koli Convicted of Murdering 20-Year-Old Woman', *Hindustan Times*, 22 July 2017, https://www.hindustantimes.com/noida/nithari-serial-killings-pandher-koli-convicted-of-murdering-20-year-old-woman/story-z6paYQH6kXcrItVZqMEG4N. html.

63. Sowmya Rajaram, 'The Man Who Wasn't Around', *Mumbai Mirror*, 15 January 2017, https://mumbaimirror.indiatimes. com/others/sunday-read/the-man-who-wasnt-around/ articleshow/56548400.cms.

64. 'Surendra Koli Gets 11th Death Sentence in Nithari Murder Case', IANS, 7 April 2019, https://www.ndtv.com/india-news/ nithari-murder-case-surender-koli-gets-11th-death-sentence-in-nithari-murder-case-2019188.

65. Ibid.

RAMAN RAGHAV: A.K.A. INDIA'S JACK THE RIPPER

1. Yogesh Naik and Kunal Guha, 'The Man Who Nabbed Raman Raghav', *Mumbai Mirror*, 26 June 2016, https://mumbaimirror.indiatimes.com/others/sunday-read/the-man-who-nabbed-raman-raghav/articleshow/52921404.cms.

2. Ramakant Kulkarni, *Footprints on the Sands of Crime: A Crime Watcher's Reflective Autobiography* (New Delhi: Macmillan, 2004).

3. Externment proceedings are initiated against criminals as preventive action. It is a convenient tool to ensure that such people are kept away so that they are dislodged from 'their area' and unable to create trouble.

4. Yogesh Naik and Kunal Guha, 'The Man Who Nabbed Raman Raghav', *Mumbai Mirror*, 26 June 2016, https://mumbaimirror.indiatimes.com/others/sunday-read/the-man-who-nabbed-raman-raghav/articleshow/52921404.cms.

5. Smita Nair, 'The Real Man behind Raman Raghav 2.0: Mumbai's First Big-Ticket Serial Killer', *Indian Express*, 26 June 2016, https://indianexpress.com/article/lifestyle/life-style/the-monsoon-murders/.

6. Ibid.

7. Ramakant Kulkarni, *Footprints on the Sands of Crime: A Crime Watcher's Reflective Autobiography* (New Delhi: Macmillan, 2004).

8. Yogesh Naik and Kunal Guha, 'The Man Who Nabbed Raman Raghav', *Mumbai Mirror*, 26 June 2016, https://mumbaimirror.indiatimes.com/others/sunday-read/the-man-who-nabbed-raman-raghav/articleshow/52921404.cms.

9. Ibid.

10. Ramakant Kulkarni, *Footprints on the Sands of Crime: A Crime Watcher's Reflective Autobiography* (New Delhi: Macmillan, 2004).

11. Smita Nair, 'The Real Man behind Raman Raghav 2.0: Mumbai's First Big-Ticket Serial Killer', *Indian Express*, 26

June 2016, https://indianexpress.com/article/lifestyle/life-style/
the-monsoon-murders/.

12. Ibid.

13. Mark Buchanan, 'Sin Cities: The Geometry of Crime', New
Scientist, 30 April 2008, https://www.newscientist.com/
article/mg19826541-000-sin-cities-the-geometry-of-crime/.

14. Nikhil S. Dixit, 'On Trail of City's Own Kill Bill', *DNA*, 16
January 2007, http://www.dnaindia.com/mumbai/report-on-
trail-of-city-s-own-kill-bill-1074803.

15. Yogesh Naik and Kunal Guha, 'The Man Who Nabbed
Raman Raghav', *Mumbai Mirror*, 26 June 2016, https://
mumbaimirror.indiatimes.com/others/sunday-read/the-man-
who-nabbed-raman-raghav/articleshow/52921404.cms.

16. Ibid.

17. Ibid.

18. Ibid.

19. Ibid.

20. Ramakant Kulkarni, *Footprints on the Sands of Crime: A
Crime Watcher's Reflective Autobiography* (New Delhi:
Macmillan, 2004).

21. Ibid.

22. Ibid.

23. Pallavi Prasad, 'Raman Raghav: The Serial Killer Who
Paralysed Bombay with Fear,' Quint, 23 June 2016, https://
www.thequint.com/voices/blogs/raman-raghav-the-serial-
killer-who-paralysed-bombay-with-fear.

24. Ramakant Kulkarni, *Footprints on the Sands of Crime: A
Crime Watcher's Reflective Autobiography* (New Delhi:
Macmillan, 2004).

25. Ibid.

26. Ibid.

27. Yogesh Naik and Kunal Guha, 'The Man Who Nabbed Raman
Raghav', Pune Mirror, 30 June 2016, https://punemirror.
indiatimes.com/others/special/the-man-who-nabbed-raman-
raghav/articleshow/52978270.cms.

28. Yash Kasotia, 'All You Need to Know about Raman Raghav,
the Serial Killer Who Inspired Anurag Kashyap's Next,'
ScoopWhoop, 11 May 2016, https://www.scoopwhoop.com/

The-Real-Raman-Raghav-Serial-Killer-Anurag-Kashyap/#.
uy22s04hf.

29. Khushwant Singh, 'Uncollected Khushwant: Portrait of a Serial
    Killer,' Scroll, 1 August 2015, https://scroll.in/article/745430/
    uncollected-khushwant-portrait-of-a-serial-killer; Mala Dayal,
    *Portrait of a Serial Killer: Uncollected Writings by Khushwant
    Singh* (New Delhi: Aleph Book Company, 2015).

30. Ibid.

31. Ibid.

32. Smita Nair, 'The Real Man behind Raman Raghav 2.0:
    Mumbai's First Big-Ticket Serial Killer', *Indian Express*, 26
    June 2016, https://indianexpress.com/article/lifestyle/life-
    style/the-monsoon-murders/.

33. Ibid.

34. Ibid.

35. Khushwant Singh, 'Uncollected Khushwant: Portrait of a Serial
    Killer,' Scroll, 1 August 2015, https://scroll.in/article/745430/
    uncollected-khushwant-portrait-of-a-serial-killer; Mala Dayal,
    *Portrait of a Serial Killer: Uncollected Writings by Khushwant
    Singh* (New Delhi: Aleph Book Company, 2015).

36. Pallavi Prasad, 'Raman Raghav: The Serial Killer Who
    Paralysed Bombay with Fear,' Quint, 23 June 2016, https://
    www.thequint.com/voices/blogs/raman-raghav-the-serial-
    killer-who-paralysed-bombay-with-fear.

37. Poonam Saxena, 'Inside the Mind of Raman Raghav,
    Mumbai's Serial Killer of the 60s,' *Hindustan Times*, 14 June
    2016, https://www.hindustantimes.com/bollywood/inside-
    the-mind-of-raman-raghav-mumbai-s-serial-killer-of-the-60s/
    story-LaA01MtT0wrAM0ZprCoLYJ.html

DARBARA SINGH: A.K.A. BABY KILLER

1. Varinder Singh, 'Devilish Darbara Remorseless Ex-armyman
    Slit Throats of 17 Children and Then Raped Them',
    Tribune, 5 November 2004, https://www.tribuneindia.
    com/2004/20041105/jplus.htm#1.

2. Manish Sirhindi, 'Child Serial Killer Dies at 75, Family
    Refuses to Claim Body', *Times of India*, 10 June 2018,

https://timesofindia.indiatimes.com/city/ludhiana/child-serial-killer-dies-at-75-family-refuses-to-claim-body/articleshow/64533207.cms.

3. Tribune News Service, 'Serial Baby Killer Held', *Tribune*, 29 October 2004, https://www.tribuneindia.com/2004/20041030/main3.htm.

4. Varinder Singh, 'Devilish Darbara Remorseless Ex-armyman Slit Throats of 17 Children and Then Raped Them', *Tribune*, 5 November 2004, https://www.tribuneindia.com/2004/20041105/jplus.htm#1.

5. Darbara Singh vs. State of Punjab, Indian Kanoon, 20 February 2013, https://indiankanoon.org/doc/143465181/.

6. 'Missing Girl's Body Found', *Tribune*, 20 April 2004, https://www.tribuneindia.com/2004/20040421/punjab1.htm#23.

7. Darbara Singh vs. State of Punjab, Indian Kanoon, 20 February 2013, https://indiankanoon.org/doc/143465181/.

8. Varinder Singh, 'Devilish Darbara Remorseless Ex-Armyman Slit Throats of 17 Children and Raped Them', *Tribune*, 5 November 2004, https://www.tribuneindia.com/2004/20041105/jplus.htm#1.

9. '"Baby killer" Acquitted in 2 Cases for Want of Evidence', Murderpedia, 12 July 2007.

10. 'Serial Killer Leads Cops to Bodies of 2 Victims', Murderpedia, 30 October 2004, http://murderpedia.org/male.S/s/singh-darbara.htm.

11. Varinder Singh, 'Who'll Bring Back Our Daughter?' *Tribune*, https://www.tribuneindia.com/2004/20041105/jplus.htm#3.

12. Varinder Singh, 'Devilish Darbara Remorseless Ex-armyman Slit Throats of 17 Children and Then Raped Them', *Tribune*, 5 November 2004, https://www.tribuneindia.com/2004/20041105/jplus.htm#1.

13. 'Serial Baby Killer Acquitted in Rape, Murder Case', *Tribune*, 10 December 2010, https://www.tribuneindia.com/2010/20101211/punjab.htm#16.

14. Varinder Singh, 'Devilish Darbara Remorseless Ex-armyman Slit Throats of 17 Children and Then Raped Them',

Tribune, 5 November 2004, https://www.tribuneindia.com/2004/20041105/jplus.htm#1.

15. 'Death Sentence to Child Serial Killer in Punjab,' One India, 8 January 2008, https://www.oneindia.com/2008/01/07/death-sentence-to-child-serial-killer-in-punjab-1199776446.html.

16. Dwight D. Eisenhower, *Forbes* quotes, https://www.forbes.com/quotes/11290/.

17. Varinder Singh, 'Devilish Darbara Remorseless Ex-armyman Slit Throats of 17 Children and Then Raped Them', *Tribune*, 5 November 2004, https://www.tribuneindia.com/2004/20041105/jplus.htm#1.

18. Ibid.

19. Ibid.

20. Ibid.

21. I.P. Singh, 'Girls' Testimony Nails Baby Killer', *Times of India*, 26 April 2008, https://timesofindia.indiatimes.com/city/chandigarh/Girls-testimony-nails-baby-killer/articleshow/2984280.cms.

JAKKAL, SUTAR, JAGTAP AND SHAH: THE JOSHI–ABHYANKAR MASSACRE

1. Rahul Chandawarkar, 'The Evil and the Dead,' *Sunday Mid-Day*, 6 September 1998, http://murderpedia.org/male.S/s/shah-munawar.html.

2. Ibid.

3. Ibid.

4. Ibid.

5. Ibid.

6. Ibid.

AMARDEEP SADA: THE WORLD'S YOUNGEST SERIAL KILLER

1. Santosh Singh, 'Serial Killer Taint on Eight-Year-Old', *Telegraph*, 1 June 2007, https://www.telegraphindia.

com/states/jharkhand/serial-killer-taint-on-eight-year-old/cid/701781.

2. Peter Foster, 'Serial Killer, 8, Charged with 3 Murders', *Telegraph*, 1 June 2007, https://www.telegraph.co.uk/news/worldnews/1553310/Serial-killer-8-charged-with-three-murders.html.

3. Rajeev Kumar, 'Eight-Year-Old Serial Killer Held after Third Murder', *Times of India*, 1 June 2007, https://timesofindia.indiatimes.com/india/Eight-year-old-serial-killer-held-after-third-murder/articleshow/2090290.cms.

4. Peter Foster, 'Serial Killer, 8, Charged with 3 Murders', *Telegraph*, 1 June 2007, https://www.telegraph.co.uk/news/worldnews/1553310/ Serial-killer-8-charged-with-three-murders.html.

5. Randeep Ramesh, 'Eight-Year-Old Boy Accused of Three Murders', *Guardian*, 1 June 2007, https://www.theguardian.com/world/2007/jun/01/india.randeepramesh.

6. Santosh Singh, 'Serial Killer Taint on Eight-Year-Old', *Telegraph*, 1 June 2007, https://www.telegraphindia.com/states/jharkhand/serial-killer-taint-on-eight-year-old/cid/701781.

7. Rachel Hadlock, 'Where Are They Now? Amardeep Sada, the World's Youngest Serial Killer', Postmortem Post, 4 May 2015, https://web.archive.org/web/20180223162752/http://www.thepostmortempost.com/2015/05/04/where-are-they-now-amardeep-sada-the-worlds-youngest-serial-killer/.

CYANIDE MOHAN: THE TEACHER-TURNED-SERIAL-KILLER

1. Iram Siddiqui, 'Prof Mohan Kumar, the Man Who Killed 20 Women with "Anti-Pregnancy" Pills', *Bangalore Mirror*, 9 October 2016, https://bangaloremirror.indiatimes.com/bangalore/cover-story/prof-mohan-kumar-the-man-who-killed-20-women-with-anti-pregnancy-pills/articleshow/54758093.cms.

2. Anil Budur Lulla, 'Cyanide Mohan', *Open*, 18 January 2014, http://www.openthemagazine.com/article/india/cyanide-mohan.

3. Iram Siddiqui, 'Prof Mohan Kumar, the Man Who Killed 20 Women with "Anti-Pregnancy" Pills', *Bangalore Mirror*, 9 October 2016, https://bangaloremirror.indiatimes.com/bangalore/cover-story/prof-mohan-kumar-the-man-who-killed-20-women-with-anti-pregnancy-pills/articleshow/54758093.cms.

4. 'Sex, Lies and Cyanide', *Telegraph*, 25 December 2011, https://www.telegraphindia.com/7-days/sex-lies-and-cyanide/cid/1667775.

5. Ibid.

6. Iram Siddiqui, 'Prof Mohan Kumar, the Man Who Killed 20 Women with "Anti-Pregnancy" Pills', *Bangalore Mirror*, 9 October 2016, https://bangaloremirror.indiatimes.com/bangalore/cover-story/prof-mohan-kumar-the-man-who-killed-20-women-with-anti-pregnancy-pills/articleshow/54758093.cms.

7. The pound sovereign, also spelt pawan or paun, is a unit of mass that is commonly encountered in India's gold industry. While it is technically equal to 7.98805 gm, it is usually rounded off to 8 gm.

8. Anil Budur Lulla, 'Cyanide Mohan', *Open*, 18 January 2014, http://www.openthemagazine.com/article/india/cyanide-mohan.

9. Ibid.

10. Ibid.

11. Ibid.

12. 'Mangalore: Serial Killer Who Accounted for 18 Girls Arrested', Daiji World, 21 October 2009, https://www.daijiworld.com/news/newsDisplay.aspx?newsID=67226.

13. Karnataka has many Swasahaya Sanghas or self-help NGOs and groups that help women with loans.

14. 'Mangalore: Neighbours, Family, Refuse to Accept Mohan as Serial Killer', Daiji World, 23 October 2009, https://www.daijiworld.com/news/newsDisplay.aspx?newsID=67282.

15. Ibid.

16. Anil Budur Lulla, 'Cyanide Mohan', *Open*, 18 January 2014, http://www.openthemagazine.com/article/india/cyanide-mohan.

17. 'Sex, Lies and Cyanide', *Telegraph*, 25 December 2011, https://www.telegraphindia.com/7-days/sex-lies-and-cyanide/cid/1667775.
18. Anil Budur Lulla, 'Cyanide Mohan', *Open*, 18 January 2014, http://www.openthemagazine.com/article/india/cyanide-mohan.
19. Ibid.
20. Ibid.
21. Iram Siddiqui, 'Prof Mohan Kumar, the Man Who Killed 20 Women with "Anti-Pregnancy" Pills', *Bangalore Mirror*, 9 October 2016, https://bangaloremirror.indiatimes.com/bangalore/cover-story/prof-mohan-kumar-the-man-who-killed-20-women-with-anti-pregnancy-pills/articleshow/54758093.cms.
22. Ibid.
23. Ibid.
24. Anil Budur Lulla, 'Cyanide Mohan', *Open*, 18 January 2014, http://www.openthemagazine.com/article/india/cyanide-mohan.
25. Iram Siddiqui, 'Prof Mohan Kumar, the Man Who Killed 20 Women with "Anti-Pregnancy" Pills', *Bangalore Mirror*, 9 October 2016, https://bangaloremirror.indiatimes.com/bangalore/cover-story/prof-mohan-kumar-the-man-who-killed-20-women-with-anti-pregnancy-pills/articleshow/54758093.cms.
26. Ibid.
27. 'Cyanide Mohan Kumar Gets Life Sentence in Fifth Murder Case', *The Hindu*, 26 February 2018, https://www.thehindu.com/news/cities/Mangalore/cyanide-mohan-kumar-gets-life-sentence-in-fifth-murder-case/article22853049.ece.
28. 'Cyanide Mohan convicted for life', *The Hindu*, 27 March 2019, https://www.thehindu.com/news/cities/bangalore/cyanide-mohan-convicted-for-life/article26656491.ece.

ANJANABAI, SEEMA GAVIT AND RENUKA SHINDE: CHILD KILLERS OF INDIA

1. Michael Higgins, 'Notorious Killer Sisters, Who Kidnapped and Murdered Babies, to Become First Women Executed in India', National Post, 19 August 2014, https://nationalpost.com/news/notorious-killer-sisters-who-kidnapped-and-murdered-babies-to-become-first-women-executed-in-india.
2. Nikita Doval, 'The Case of the Sisters on Death Row', Mint, 2 September 2014, https://www.livemint.com/Politics/Xqy5b3m9sluIV1044grKzL/The-case-of-the-sisters-on-death-row.html.
3. Ibid.
4. Michelle Soriano, 'Baby Killing Sisters to be First Women Executed in India', Rebel Circus, 18 July 2017, https://www.rebelcircus.com/blog/baby-killing-sisters-first-women-executed-india-2/full/.
5. Ibid.
6. Shoumojit Banerjee, 'Jail Officials Await Final Word on Kolhapur Sisters', The Hindu, 18 August 2014, https://www.thehindu.com/news/national/other-states/jail-officials-await-final-word-on-kolhapur-sisters/article6329091.ece.
7. Ibid.
8. Candace Sutton, 'Serial Killer Sisters Renuka Shinde and Seema Gavit Who Abducted and Murdered Children in Bid to Avoid Execution at the Gallows,' News.com, 22 April 2017, https://www.news.com.au/world/asia/serial-killer-sisters-renuke-shinde-and-seema-gavit-who-abducted-and-murdered-children-in-bid-to-avoid-execution-at-the-gallows/news-story/ef93b4b1ccc699db80223bbf0b4018ad.